DEATH
IN
PARADISE

Forge Books by Kate Flora

Chosen for Death
Death in a Funhouse Mirror
Death at the Wheel
An Educated Death
Death in Paradise

DEATH IN PARADISE

Kate Flora

A TOM DOHERTY ASSOCIATES BOOK □ NEW YORK

DEATH IN PARADISE

Copyright © 1998 by Kate Clark Flora

This book is printed on acid-free paper.

A Forge Book
Published by Tom Doherty Associates, Inc.
175 Fifth Avenue
New York, NY 10010

Forge® is a registered trademark of Tom Doherty Associates, Inc.

Library of Congress Cataloging-in-Publication Data

Flora, Kate Clark.
    Death in paradise / Kate Flora.—1st ed.
        p.   cm.
    "A Forge book"—T.p. verso.
    ISBN 0-312-86398-5
    I. Title.
  PS3556.L5838D43   1998
  813'.54—dc21   98-21184
                                          CIP

First Edition: October 1998

Printed in the United States of America

0 9 8 7 6 5 4 3 2 1

In memory of my beloved sister, Sara Lloyd
Sorrow is the price we pay for the joy of having known her.

ACKNOWLEDGMENTS

Thank you first and always to my husband, Ken Cohen, who said, "keep writing" instead of "get a job." Second to Tom Doherty and all the great people at Forge, for publishing my first Thea and keeping her going. I owe a lot to the generous people who have read my books, given advice, and answered my questions. They include: Robert Moll, Diane Englund, Jack Nevison, Nancy Mc-Jennet, Sgt. Tom Le Min, Reid Nakamura, Vicki Stiefel, Robert Matthews, and David Learnard. I am always grateful to Thea's role model, Margaret Milne Moulton, and, for this book especially, to the National Coalition of Girls' Schools, Professor Frances Miller, Mount Holyoke College, and the American Association of University Women for information on single-sex education.

CHAPTER 1

I WAS IN Hawaii. The double doors opening to a lanai, the swaying palm trees, the inviting blue water all confirmed it. So did the airy tropical decor. So had my ticket. I knew for certain that I had gotten on a plane in Boston, flown to Honolulu, and changed to a plane for Maui. So why the heck was I crawling around on my hands and knees searching for a dropped earring when it wasn't yet 6:00 A.M., already late for my first meeting of the day? Why was my skin still pasty white? And why was I gulping decongestants for the stuffy head I always get from too many hours in air-conditioned rooms, instead of walking on the beach? Because I was a grown-up, a working girl, and a slave of duty.

Where was that damned earring? If I didn't find it, the maid's vacuum surely would, and it was a favorite. The phone rang. I was certain it was Martina, she who never slept, calling to complain about my tardiness. Martina Pullman, conference director, head of the National Association of Girls' Schools. I had been on Maui for about thirty hours, many of them in her company, and there had already been four occasions when I had wanted to strangle her. I considered not answering it, but then again, I am that slave of duty.

I grabbed the receiver. As I pulled the phone to my ear, I shifted my weight, bringing my knee down hard on the lurking earring. The sharp post stabbed me like a bee sting. Instead of the brisk hello I'd been forming, I yelped an ouch into the receiver.

"It can't be that bad," Andre said, "you're in paradise, remember?" Detective Andre Lemieux, Maine State Police. The love of my life.

"Frankly, dahling, I'm finding that one hotel is much like another. For all the fun I'm having, for all the sea and sand and sun I'm getting, I might just as well be in Juneau or Poughkeepsie."

"I'm so glad you're miserable," he said, "because I'm miserable and . . ."

"Misery loves company, right?"

"It's a damned cold spring, that's all I can say."

"That's *all* you can say?"

"The bed is cold."

"And?"

"And if you were having a good time, I could start feeling awfully sorry for myself."

"Well, don't. It's not yet six A.M. here. I'm late for a meeting. And I just found my missing earring by having it stab me in the knee. . . ."

"You're just trying to make me feel better. I know . . . you're all done up in one of those teeny bikinis you packed . . . and on your way to the—"

"The ones that have a distinct effect on your anatomy?" I interrupted.

"Beach," he finished. "Yes. The ones that just thinking about, sitting here thousands of miles away, have a distinct effect on my anatomy. Can't you tell?"

"Sure. I can hear the strain in your vocal chords. I'm glad you miss me. I'd hate to go away and have you indifferent."

"The day I'm indifferent to you, Kozak, is the day they plant me. I've prayed for indifference, or at least more self-control, but—"

"Your prayers weren't answered," I finished.

"Or they were," he said. "So it's bad, huh? As bad as you expected? Martina, I mean?"

"Worse. She expects me to be governess, gofer, and CEO all at once. We've been visited by more plagues than God and Moses visited on Egypt and each time she turns to me with that tight, sullen look, raises those dumb plucked eyebrows, and says, 'Thea, can you handle this?' as though I was the one who organized this stupid conference instead of her. I'm not even supposed to be here."

"I'm sorry," he said. "Jealous as I am, I still wish you were having a good time. I thought I was going to get you back all brown and cheerful and relaxed."

"Bristling like a hedgehog and growling through clenched teeth is more like it. Another day like yesterday and I'm going to kill her. I swear."

"Everything is not your job," he reminded me. "You're just one of the people on the board. You're just a conference speaker, remember? So tell her that."

"Don't think I haven't tried. She said I was also a consultant paid to provide certain services to the association, and as an employee, I owed her . . . well, anyway . . . we damned near came to blows. Reasoning with her is like trying to talk to a cinder block. You ever have that experience?"

"There's this girl, uh, woman . . . I sleep with sometimes, and trying to talk with her, when she's tired, or has her mind made up, is a bit like that. . . ."

"Andre . . ." I didn't point out that he was occasionally less than perfect himself. He'd been a stone-hearted bastard when I first met him—the cop investigating my sister Carrie's murder. We've come a long way since then.

"Sorry. You've talked about Martina before. You were expecting this. But remember—"

"No one can make you do something if you don't let them," I finished.

"Right," he said, "so tell her to handle it herself and then you go out and sit in the sun. You've got to come home with tan lines."

"Why?"

"So I can trace them with my—"

Someone banged on the door and I missed the last word. "Hold on a sec. Someone at the door. It's probably her. The wicked witch . . ."

"Don't answer it."

"I wish." The banging increased. If I didn't answer it, the witch would wake my neighbors. Not that she cared. Spoiling paradise for as many people as possible was right up her alley. She was as self-centered as a two-year-old. "But she won't give up. She makes persistence into a four-letter word. You going to be home later?"

"I am home. It is later, remember? It's eleven here. Trying to do my damned homework but I can't seem to work up much enthusiasm." Andre was on temporary leave from the Maine State Police, doing a course in Boston. A gift from his boss, Jack Leonard, who for some reason had decided to help smooth out the bumps in our relationship. Bless Jack. We had just had four wonderful months together, in my condo, deliciously domestic. No one had fired a shot at either of us. Both of our lives had been blissfully free of death. We started the day jogging together and ended it in the same bed. I had never been so happy. It was an idyll that would end soon but I didn't want to think about that. For now, the compulsive consultant from Massachusetts and the zealous homicide detective from Maine were taking it one day at a time. One lovely day at a time. Only now, because my partner, Suzanne, had gotten sick, I was wasting five of them here at this conference.

"I'll call you," I said. "You can tell me more about tan lines."

"I'm going to start in the middle of your back, and . . . hey, do you know what day this is?"

"Later." I didn't want to let him go. I wanted to flirt and giggle. Tease and play. I could have spent an hour just listening to his voice, long-distance rates be damned. But the banging wouldn't let up.

"Later," he agreed. "Miss you. I don't care if you're knee-deep in bodies by noon, you call."

"I'll call. Come hell or high water." If the banging was Martina, hell was a likely prospect. I disconnected, limped to the door, and jerked it open, wondering what he'd meant by what day it was.

It wasn't Martina Pullman, the wicked witch, it was Rory Altschuler, her pallid acolyte, officially titled executive assistant. Black hair, dark eyes, black clothes, frog-belly skin, the only spot of color was her glistening red mouth, pursed in a fretful O as though the frog had been stabbed with a pen. "Thea! Thank goodness. I was afraid you were still asleep."

"After all the banging you did, I doubt if anyone on this floor is still asleep."

Unlike her boss, she had the grace to look abashed. "Sorry. I forgot. I've been up forever, getting those damned hand-outs typed and copied. It practically took an act of God. For a place that promotes itself as a conference hotel, they have a remarkably casual attitude toward business . . . but that's not why I came up. . . ." She pulled a lank strand of hair out of her eyes and jammed it behind her ear. "Something's wrong."

"What now?" I sighed. This was supposed to be a fun, upbeat conference of the principal women—and men—involved in promoting single-sex education for girls, sponsored by the National Association of Girls' Schools, which lent itself to the unfortunate acronym, NAGS. So far, the wrangling, backbiting, and political maneuvering behind the scenes, mostly orchestrated by Martina, had made the term seem fitting. Maybe we were all sisters but we came from a dysfunctional family, while the men at the conference had been remarkably self-effacing. What we needed were a few of those droning, self-centered, conversation-dominating guys—the ones who dominate most conferences—to take our minds off each other and give us back our focus. I looked around warily, expecting the wrath of the PC gods to fall upon me for even entertaining the thought.

"Something's wrong," Rory repeated. "I was supposed to have a premeeting meeting with Martina at five-thirty. She didn't show up." She made it sound dire and portentous, as though Martina's lateness was rare and unique instead of frequent. With Martina, though, lateness was a one-way street. She could keep people waiting with impunity but heaven forbid that anyone should keep her waiting. *Her* time was valuable.

"Maybe she overslept. She did have a lot to drink last night." I stepped back into the room. "Come on in. We'll call her."

"I already did that. Three times. She isn't answering." She followed me into the room, the stack of papers she carried held stiffly against her side, moving with the unsure hesitation of the young woman who hasn't spent much time in hotel rooms. I remembered the feeling, that odd, almost illicit sense of being somewhere I wasn't sure I belonged, where no one knew me, where the dominant piece of furniture was a bed. I'd gotten over it. As a consultant, I now spend enough time on the road to make me feel like a traveling saleswoman. Which, as a consultant, I suppose I am. Only what I sell is myself.

She followed me to the phone and hovered there, too close, her eyes darting from me to the phone. Standing beside her, I noticed that she was actually quite tall, maybe five feet seven or so, which surprised me. She had such a tentative way of moving, approaching life with the awkward gait of a wading waterbird, and such a hunch-shouldered, defensive posture, that I'd always assumed she was much smaller. I picked up the phone, dialed Martina's room, and let it ring while Rory watched anxiously.

"Maybe she's downstairs waiting for us," I suggested. "Let's go see." I slipped on my sandals, straightened the bent post and put on my second earring, and grabbed my briefcase. Briefcases in paradise. Increasingly, it seemed to be the story of my life.

We went out into the sunny atrium that formed the center of the hotel. Long corridors ran along the sides of this atrium, separated from the open center by waist-high walls. All the rooms opened off these corridors. Long cascades of hanging plants and a courtyard full of chirping birds, soothing fountains, and lush tropical gardens almost canceled out the "big house" effect. As we hurried through the lobby, I made a face at the sign that insisted bathing suit cover-ups must be worn in the public areas. I had yet to get into a bathing suit.

The conference room was ready for us, set up with coffee and muffins and cups on a tray. I would have poured myself a cup and discussed the situation—I was feeling a serious need for caffeine—but Rory dropped her papers onto the table and faded back against the wall, staring at the center chair as though Martina's ghost sat there glaring at us. "She's not here." Her voice had dropped to a whisper.

Her anxiety was irritating. We were all grown-ups here. The

world wouldn't end if Martina overslept. I couldn't help saying so. "Things will be fine," I said. "We really don't need to have a preliminary meeting before every session. That's just Martina's obsession with control."

Rory stared at me like I'd just uttered blasphemy. "How can you say that? Martina is just so fabulous! I've never worked for someone who is such a perfectionist. It's hard, sure, but jeez, Thea, she does such a wonderful job."

I wasn't sure I agreed. Yes, her conferences were supremely well planned and content rich, but both organization and content were achieved through the brutal application of harassment and bullying, with plenty of it aimed at Rory, as well as through the heroic last-minute efforts of the rest of the board. I bit back my comment, "At least she's done a wonderful job of brainwashing you," and bounded into action. Maybe poor Rory was a masochist. I poured a cup of coffee for myself and poised the pot over a second cup. "You want some?"

"We don't have time for coffee right now. We've got to find Martina. She's giving the breakfast speech this morning. In two and a half hours, a hundred and eighty women, uh, conference attendees . . . are going to be expecting her to perform."

"That's at eight-thirty. This is now." I added cream and sugar and took a sip. Ambrosia. I pulled the wrapper off a bran muffin and took a bite.

Again her look suggested impropriety, as if I'd unwrapped myself and not just the muffin. "I have a bad feeling about this," she said ominously. She stood with her hands clasped in front of her chest, like a diva about to sing something sad. "Maybe her phone isn't working. I'm going to go up and knock on her door." She dropped her hands and marched to the door of the conference room, where she hesitated. "Aren't you coming?"

I would have answered, but my mouth was full of crumbs and we all know what our mothers had to say about that. I made a gesture intended to say that I'd be along soon and sloshed coffee onto the table and the sleeve of my cream-colored blouse. And the coffee was supposed to have improved my mood. I grabbed a handful of napkins, did some damage control, took one last lingering drink, and reluctantly set the cup on the tray. "All right. We'll knock."

I followed her to the elevator, observing, since I was walking behind her, that her shapeless dress concealed quite a nice figure. I'm not into ostentation but I did wonder why an attractive woman in her early twenties insisted on dressing like an Italian grand-mother. It wasn't a group that was on the cutting edge of fashion but most of the women at the conference had a pretty good sense of their personal styles. Rory's dress resembled a plastic trash bag with holes cut for the head and arms. Shiny, loose, and boxy. Maybe it was the latest fashion. I wouldn't know. I don't shop.

We drew up outside Martina's door, I, at least, with a sense that we'd been galloping. Instead of knocking, Rory stared at her shoes. "Would you?" she murmured. So I, having the bigger fist and the more elevated title, pounded vigorously, waited, and pounded again. I considered the outrageous yet pleasing possibil-ity that the other board members had had her kidnapped so we could proceed with the conference in peace. The pleasure didn't last long. Rory's uneasy state was contagious. I was beginning to feel nervous myself.

"You see," she said in a voice that was close to tears. "You see. Something has happened."

"We'll go down to the desk, explain the situation, and get someone to let us in. I'm sure everything is fine. She's in the shower, or talking on the phone and doesn't want to be inter-rupted. . . ." I didn't add, "or deep in drunken sleep." Rory knew as well as I did that Martina had been drinking heavily last night.

She plucked at my arm with nervous fingers. "I don't think so. I don't think so. Something awful has happened. . . ." She looked almost pleased with the idea.

I rolled my eyes. "You've been watching too much television. Come on. We'll go get the key."

Now she was the one trailing behind. Andre says that I have two speeds—all and nothing. Right now, I'd switched into all. And when a woman my size, I'm five feet eleven, steps into high gear, the world had better watch out. I stopped at the elevator and punched the button, half expecting it to say ouch. Instead, the door opened instantly. We stepped in and were carried, with stomach-dropping speed, down to the lobby. Past the trickling fountains, past the chirping birds, past the omnipresent sweepers. We rushed up to the front desk and explained our dilemma.

They directed us to a banquette, where we were joined by an assistant manager, who needed the story repeated. He, in turn, summoned security, the story was told again, and the four of us marched back to the elevator and rose skyward to Martina's room.

Our little procession hurried out of the elevator and once again came to a halt outside her door. This time it was the assistant manager who raised his fist and knocked, announced himself, paused, and knocked again. Then there was a pause in the action. It seemed that he had fully expected Martina to appear at his official summons, as if our gentler or more meager female knocks hadn't been quite the thing. When the expected result didn't occur, he and the security man consulted briefly and then unlocked the door.

There was a short contretemps, while I waited for management and management waited for me. Then the assistant manager, a rounded, polished gentleman of Hawaiian descent with a broad, solemn face, stepped back and gestured for me to enter. "Perhaps, as you're her colleague, it would be best . . ." His words trailed off.

I stepped past him and into the room, calling, "Martina? It's Thea. We had a meeting this . . ." Martina, being the VIP, had a suite. A big, beautiful sitting room with the obligatory cellophane-wrapped basket of fruit. The management greeting card was still flying from the top, like a flag, unopened. A table set for two sat before the open doors. Champagne in a bucket. Glasses. A plate of soggy caviar and toast. A bowl of strawberries. I hesitated. Why had she ordered this feast and left it untouched? Although her papers were spread all over the desk, this looked like provisions for a romantic rendezvous, not a late-night business meeting.

Moving more slowly now, I stepped into the dressing room and peered into the opulent bathroom, hoping, as my anxiety grew, that I might find she'd fallen and hit her head. It looked like she'd taken a bath—the tub was dirty, there were towels on the floor and a terry-cloth robe thrown over the edge of the tub—but no Martina. I stepped backward and bumped into Rory. She retreated with a squeak, like a startled mouse.

I stepped around her and went into the bedroom, calling Martina's name again. I called, waited, and called again as I stepped around the corner and the bed came into sight. I stopped as suddenly as if I'd run into an invisible screen. Stopped, stared, and turned my head away. I stopped so suddenly that Rory, hesitantly dogging my steps, ran right into me, gasped, apologized, and stepped back.

"Don't look," I said. "Turn around and go out. Now! You don't want to see this."

I tried to block the way but she wriggled past me, gave a blood-curdling scream, and then, still screaming, turned and ran from the room.

Maybe it's because I'm an oldest child, but I'm a real take-charge type. I didn't scream or cry or faint. I turned to the assistant manager, who was staring bug-eyed at the woman on the bed and pointed in the direction Rory had gone. "Find her. Take her somewhere and shut her up before you have the whole hotel in an uproar. And you, security, call the police."

I took another step into the room, drawn reluctantly toward the figure on the bed. Martina Pullman, president of the National Association of Girls' Schools, was one of those tall, handsome, fashionably thin women who loved elegant clothes and wore them well. The outfit she had on would, under other circumstances, have been laughable. Under these circumstances, it was jarring. Embarrassing. Horrible.

She lay on her back across the bed in a scarlet lace bustier, red thong panties and lacy red garter belt. Her long, unnaturally dark hair, hair that was usually confined in a severe chignon, spread out around her head, as though she awaited a lover. The garter belt still held up one sheer black stocking, that foot still sported a scarlet spike-heeled shoe. The other shoe was on the floor beside the bed; the other stocking was knotted tightly around her neck. Her eyes were open, protuberant, and staring from a grotesquely purple face.

In my shock, the absurd, awful thought raced through my head that the advice our mothers gave us about clean underwear ought to be expanded to include not wearing anything we wouldn't want to be caught dead in.

The security man stepped past me, reached out a cautious hand, and touched the bare leg. "Cold," he said. "She's dead."

I shuddered, glad I hadn't had to touch her. I closed my eyes but the image was just as vivid, just as grotesque, and I saw it just as clearly. The lingerie ad from hell. I had not liked this woman. That was no secret. But I had admired her. I wanted to remember her good qualities, her talents, her strengths, not this. Not this wrinkled, bony, middle-aged woman got up like a young vixen, sprawled indecently across the bed, legs spread, exposing graying pubic hair, old silvery stretch marks, and most of one small breast, strangled with her own stocking, her gaping mouth still slick with scarlet lipstick, lipstick on her teeth, a bit of swollen tongue protruding.

Please, God, I thought. *Let me die in bed in my own flannel nightgown.* And then, because my nature is always to be moving on to the next task, the next chore, and because anything was better than thinking about this, I remembered the hundred and eighty people who were expecting Martina's speech at breakfast. "Oh, hell," I said aloud. "I guess it will have to be me."

The security guard was staring, his hand on the butt of his gun. Did he think I'd just confessed? "I'm sorry," I said quickly. "We're running a conference together. She is . . . was . . . supposed to give the breakfast speech . . . now I'll have to do it." His look said more plainly than words that he found my reaction almost as shocking as Martina's death. He clearly expected me to be more like Rory. To run and scream and fall apart. I can run, but screaming and falling apart aren't generally in my emotional vocabulary. I try to be open-minded, but I'm quite intolerant of people who fall apart. Still, I didn't want him to get the wrong impression. I was plenty shocked, I just wasn't given to hysterics. If he expected a fragile female, I would do my best to oblige. Just because I didn't scream and thrash didn't mean I wasn't shaken.

I closed my eyes, turned my head, and reached out a groping

hand for his sleeve. "I think I'd better sit down," I said. "In the other room . . ." I wanted to run downstairs, pack my stuff, and get the hell out of there. By the time he'd escorted me to a chair, my distress was genuine. I couldn't run on these shaky legs and I'd begun to feel sick and dizzy. I buried my head in my hands. I couldn't pack up and leave anyway. Someone had to run the conference now. Damn Suzanne. Suzanne, my partner. The one who was supposed to be here schmoozing and speechifying instead of me. Suzanne was at home with pneumonia. I would have taken pneumonia over this any day but when it comes to violent death and its violent consequences, we are rarely given any choice. I was going to be the Jill-on-the-spot for the National Association of Girls' Schools conference on death in paradise.

CHAPTER 2

EVENTUALLY THE ROOM filled up with people. First it was just a uniformed officer, there, as he told me, to "secure the scene." That evidently meant securing me, as well. He was followed by a crowd who didn't seem to want to have anything to do with me, but each time I tried to leave, a large, scowling man in a badly fitting jacket who hadn't bothered to introduce himself told me to sit down. I sat for a while, fretting about the passing time and longing for the coffee I'd left downstairs. Too bad the beverage of Martina's feast was Champagne. Had it been coffee, I would have drunk it hot or cold, evidence or not. These days I seemed to be having a lot of trouble keeping my eyes open—a strange and scary turn of events for a normally high-energy person. I entertained secret fears of some dread disease, but I was too busy, and the symptoms—exhaustion, nausea, and excessive thirst—too vague for a doctor's visit. Besides, I was afraid he'd diagnose mono and send me to bed for an extended rest. I never had time to rest.

I was sitting there, feeling a peculiar combination of numbness and high anxiety, when I remembered the speech. Breakfast would go a whole lot better if we had Martina's speech. Some quick study could read it. Probably me, since I'd written most of it. I went over to her desk and started pawing through her papers. Not on top, where it should have been. Not in the first stack, nor the second. My search grew frantic. There it was. I reached.

The hand that grabbed my arm was not gentle. "What in hell do you think you're doing?"

I shook off the hand and turned. He was a big block of a man, wide bodied, thick necked, with a big head. His round eyes had a steely, opaque sheen. "Step away from there, please," he said. It was not a request.

"I'm sorry," I said, "Detective . . ."

"Nihilani," he said.

"Martina is . . . was . . . Martina, the woman in there . . ." What was the matter with me? I was dithering like an idiot. "We're running this conference together. She's supposed to give the breakfast speech this morning . . . a speech about sexual harassment and teenage girls that we wrote together. And it looks like I'm going to have to give it instead. I was trying to find it so I could start preparing."

His face didn't change. There was no emotion as he said, "You can't touch her papers." A man of few words.

"Just the speech," I said. "Look, you can watch me. Or look for it yourself . . . or whatever you want. You can initial every page before I leave . . . anything . . . but I do need that speech."

"No." He folded his arms and stepped back. "You already screwed around with the papers."

"What harm can it do?" I argued. "We've got close to two hundred people at this conference. We want to keep things as normal as possible. It won't help to start off the day disorganized and chaotic when it isn't necessary."

"No," he repeated.

"Do you have a boss I could talk to? Someone who could authorize me to borrow the speech? That's all I want to do—to borrow it—you can have it back after breakfast."

"I am the boss," he said.

Good going, Kozak, I thought. *Now what do you do?* At that point, my body decided for me. The additional stress of having to beg for the speech on top of finding the body on top of the last two days. Jet lag, lack of food, too little sleep, too much work. Shock. "I think I'm going to be sick," I said. I headed for the bathroom but he blocked my path. "Now what?"

"Crime scene," he said.

My room was five floors down and my stomach suggested that it didn't want to wait five floors and two long corridors. "Can you at least get me a towel?"

Reluctantly, he went to get it and I yielded to a momentary criminal impulse. I had just time to grab the speech and shove it into a pocket before he returned and handed me the towel.

After seven years as a consultant, I've acquired a measure of poise in awkward situations, but there is no graceful way to be sick in front of strangers. Even alone and under the best of circumstances, it is not an aesthetic activity. The toughest among us can be reduced to a quivering mass with streaming eyes and heaving chest. Red faced, breathless, and depleted. I did my best. I was subtle, discreet, quiet, and wretched. A diner at the next table would hardly have been disturbed. And the steely-eyed bastard watched me the whole time as if it were an event being staged for his benefit. I wiped my face, wadded up the towel, and threw it in the trash. It was wasteful but I didn't care. I couldn't very well rinse it out in the sink, could I?

"Just a few questions," he said. They were not along the lines of "Was I feeling any better?" After he'd gotten my name, room number, and an account of how I came to be in Martina's room, he marched me back into the bedroom and asked me another bunch of questions. I have no idea what I said. The shock of seeing her a second time was worse than the first. I pride myself on being calm and maintaining my poise in tough situations, on being organized and articulate. I know I was neither. Seeing her there, surrounded by prying strangers, staring at her, photographing her, touching her, I wanted to protect her, to shelter her from all those eyes, all those men. I even—it's so stupid I can hardly believe I did it— asked if they could cover her up. That's when he told me I could go. "But don't leave the hotel," he cautioned. "I'll need to talk with you again."

Oh, lucky me, I thought. More time in his icy company. As if I *could* leave the hotel. I was here on a job, just like he was. I got up and walked out, feeling like I'd been subjected to a bizarre form of torture. Just because I'd found her body didn't mean I wanted to stand and stare at it for an extended period of time. By the time I left, I was stunned and dizzy and desperate to lie down. I wanted to take a long hot shower and then leave the hotel. Get outside. Get some air. Put some distance between me and what I'd seen. I wanted to call Andre and cry on his shoulder. I wanted to go home.

I settled for a soothing glass of seltzer from my minibar and a toothbrush followed by a shot of mouthwash. I was gathering things for a shower—I'm a big believer in hydrotherapy—when the phone rang. Shannon Dukes, another member of the board. "Thea . . ." Her loud voice boomed out of the phone. "I just heard . . . isn't it terrible? We're all meeting in my room in ten minutes to decide what to do. They're going to send up coffee. Have you seen Rory?"

"Not since she ran out screaming. You might call the desk and see if they know. I sent the assistant manager after her so she wouldn't disrupt the whole hotel."

She lowered her voice. "Was it awful?"

"Yes." She waited for me to say more and was disappointed.

"So, I'll see you in a few minutes. You're going to have to give the breakfast speech. You know that, don't you?"

"I'm already working on it."

"You don't sound great, Thea. Are you all right?"

"It was a shock, Shannon." She understood that I didn't want to discuss it.

Miserable, I dumped my robe back on top of my suitcase and sat down at the desk. Hydrotherapy would have to wait. It was the first full day of the conference. We'd had an afternoon of seminars, our cocktail party for VIP guests, and an opening dinner with the author of the current hot book about how we were losing our girls as keynote speaker. Off to a brilliant start, notwithstanding that for cocktails they'd booked us into a room for seventy-five when we were closer to two hundred and I'd had to yell and scream at the convention office staff, and then at dinner they had failed to set up enough tables so that twenty-five people were left standing, even though we'd furnished an accurate count. We were professional women. We were recovering nice girls. We dotted our i's and crossed our t's and did our homework twice. Our signatures were still legible and we were just beginning to learn how to make ourselves heard.

Despite these glitches, and despite the frustration among the organizers, the attendees all seemed to be in high spirits. There was a wonderful sense of shared mission, coupled with a sense of having done something almost illicit by getting away to a conference in such a nice place. Everyone I'd talked with was having good time. Everyone, that is, except our leader, Martina. Her attitude had had a decidedly negative effect on her fellow board members.

Martina was—had been—a complicated person. Had been? No. I wasn't ready to think of her in the past tense yet, despite the evidence of my own eyes. In a world where people were judged by whether they viewed the glass as half-full or half-empty, Martina was in a class by herself. She was prone to think her glass had been stolen, or poisoned, or was full of the wrong liquid. Martina was an equal-opportunity crab. She snapped at underlings and peers equally, had more meetings than a busy Hollywood agent, obsessively micromanaged nearly everything she touched, delegating grudgingly only at the last minute, and nothing was ever her fault. The rest of us had been conspiring to oust her, not a simple task since the association had been her idea, and beating our heads against the wall in frustration. If Rory broke down sometime in the next hour and confessed to killing her, I wouldn't be surprised. The only part that wouldn't make sense was the lingerie. What had Rory done with the gentleman caller?

It was all too unreal. I opened the doors and stepped outside, out of the air-conditioned chill and into the soft caress of warm, tropical air. Below me, palm leaves rustled in the breeze. I heard the distant sounds of splashing and children's voices from the pool. Out on the water, a little knot of jet skis was already circling, the engines roaring like water-borne motorcycles. I longed to go out and play, to put something pleasant and normal between me and what I'd just seen, but the clock was running. Tucking the little slip of paper with Shannon's room number into my pocket, I picked up my briefcase and went out, taking one last look over my shoulder at the beautiful world I was missing.

Shannon was a big, vibrant redhead with an infectious laugh and heavy southern accent. She took one look at my face, steered me into a chair, and shoved a cup of tea into my hand. "It must have been just terrible. I can see from your face, honey. You look like you just saw your grandma's ghost." I sipped tea and tried to avoid their staring faces. Waited for conversation to pick up again, but it didn't. They were all waiting for my story.

"I'm sorry," I said finally. "I know you want to know what happened but I can't . . ."

"Well, of course you can, honey," Shannon drawled. "Just take yourself a little old deep breath and plunge right in."

"I don't mean I can't bring myself to talk about it, I mean a policeman about the size of that ship out there"—I pointed to a large vessel passing outside the window—"told me in no uncertain terms to keep my mouth shut. And he wasn't particularly polite about it, either."

"Well, now, how would he ever know?" Shannon began, but Jolene Hershey, who was my candidate for Martina's successor and the levelest head in the room, interrupted.

"Shannon, don't you ever watch TV?" Shannon nodded, looking puzzled. "So you've seen what happens when a body is discovered, right? They question everybody. And since they're going to question everybody, they don't want us to know the details, because they're checking to see if maybe we know too much, isn't that right, Thea?"

I shrugged. "Sounds right to me . . . I didn't ask him why. I just got the hell out of there as soon as I could."

"Come on," Shannon snapped, not managing her disappointment in a calm and mature way, "don't be coy with us. We know you've got a cop for a boyfriend. And we know all about what happened out there at the Bucksport School. I know Dorrie Chapin thinks you walk on water. Why, you're practically a detective yourself, after that."

Not bloody likely. Dorrie probably wished I'd sunk to the bottom and never come up. But that was an old, sad story. The death of a student is always a terrible thing and the Bucksport School would be years recovering. Dorrie was lucky she still had a job. I rubbed my forehead wearily. "Whatever you do, any of you, don't you dare tell the police about that."

"Why not?" Jolene asked.

"Because cops have a habit of asking me to get involved, and I don't want to be any more involved in this business than I already am. I can't tell you what I saw, but I can tell you that I wish I hadn't, and that right now, I am not a happy camper. I am"—I realized the truth of it even as I said it—"the natural liaison between the group and the police, now that Martina's . . ." I hesitated. "For better or for worse, I've had some experience dealing the police, and those guys upstairs . . . they . . ." I fumbled for words, wanting to warn them about what they would face, yet not wanting to sound like a wimp. "They seemed particularly unfriendly."

Jolene put a comforting hand over mine. Her hand was warm. I resisted the urge to grab it. "Scary?"

"Scary and mean. Hard. Unreasonable." I felt vaguely sick just thinking about it, but whether it was fear of those impassive men with their cold eyes or just shock from what I'd seen, I didn't know. I looked at my watch. "We've got one hour until the breakfast meeting. How are we going to handle it?"

"I favor the truth," Jolene said. "We say there's been a tragic accident and Martina is, uh, no longer with us . . . but that she had a mission, in trying to bring the girls' schools together to share our strategies, to try and achieve our common goals, and we would dishonor her memory if we abandoned the conference now."

"Well, now," Shannon said. "That sounds very impressive to me."

Rob Greene, the only man on the board, and a guy I admired for his ability to stay comfortable and a team player in a room full of women, was frowning. "Rob doesn't agree," Jolene said. "Do you, Rob?"

He shrugged. "I don't disagree with the stuff about Martina's mission. That's absolutely right. I just think we're going to get off on a bad footing if we don't tell the truth. That she's been murdered. They're going to know it soon enough, anyway. These are educated, informed people. They read. They think. They listen. They're not on a beach vacation, shut off from the real world. I mean . . ." His laugh was a bit cynical. "Has any of us even set foot on the beach?"

"I've logged my three miles. Jogging," Shannon said. "I believe I was on the beach. Too dark to tell, really, but it felt like sand under my feet. And I think those things I kept dodging were boats."

There was laughter at that. Then others chimed in and a swirl of conversation rose around me. I was in it and yet I wasn't a part of it. I was tuned out, hunkered down inside my own head, trying to get my balance back. I was yanked abruptly into the conversation when someone said, "You saw them, didn't you, Thea?"

"I'm sorry. I missed what you were saying. Saw what?"

"Rory and Martina, screaming at each other like a couple of fishwives," Zannah Wu said. "Last night outside the bar."

I nodded. "Martina had had too much to drink. Rory was trying to get her to go to bed."

"Right," Zannah said. "And that's when you told Rory to go and then told Martina to stop acting like a spoiled princess who expected everyone else to pick up the pieces, and she slapped you and ran away."

That wasn't exactly what had happened, but it was close enough. And I didn't think anyone had seen us, which was why I'd dragged Martina down what seemed like a dim, deserted corridor to have our little tête-à-tête, which had nearly ended up in fisticuffs. Looking across the room at Zannah's placid face, I wondered what else she'd seen. Had she seen me comforting Rory? Heard Rory's bitter outburst? Had she seen Martina go back into the bar and later leave with Lewis Broder, the assistant head of the Fowler School, a slight, supercilious man with a voluptuous mustache and shifty eyes, his arm around Martina's waist, her head against his shoulder?

As a child, one of my favorite books was a Dr. Seuss called *Bartholomew and the Oobleck*. In the story, the king is bored with the weather and wishes for something new, so he gets oobleck, a thick, sticky green stuff that falls from the sky instead of rain and gums up the kingdom. Right now, it seemed like we were experiencing an onslaught of ooblick. The fallout from Martina's death was going to gum up everything. I already felt like I was about knee-deep in the stuff. Meanwhile, we had to get back to the other business at hand. And I, who pride myself on being calm and competent, was feeling awfully shaky, my thoughts scurrying around like frightened mice.

"All right. Jolene, you can deliver the bad news, eulogize a bit, and declare that the show must go on. To create a transition, maybe Shannon or Zannah should introduce me and explain that I'll be the speaker. Which means"—I heaved myself to my feet, feeling ancient and heavy—"that I'd better go upstairs and use my remaining twenty-five minutes getting ready to deliver something coherent in the way of a speech." Jolene looked so relieved I realized she must have been afraid she was going to have to give the speech. "What's after breakfast?" Suddenly I couldn't remember. If my brain didn't come alive soon, I was in for an embarrassing time.

"Bus tours with lunch stops, followed, in the late afternoon, by a choice of workshop topics on 'The Value of Single-Sex Education in the Middle-School Years,' " Jolene reminded me. "Are you sure you're up to this? The breakfast speech, I mean? I could muddle through something, you don't . . ." She bit her lip. "You don't look like you're feeling very well."

"Rotten," I agreed. "But I worked with Martina on the speech. I know the subject pretty well." Worked with was a euphemism. Typically, she had let it go to the last minute and then called on me to write it when she found she couldn't produce anything of quality on such short notice. "The show must go on."

It almost didn't. I found Rory leaning against the wall outside my room. When she spotted me, she ran at me and consumed me in the grip of a lost child recovering her missing mother. I practically had to pry her off before I could get the door open. She followed me inside and collapsed into a chair. "It's horrible. Wasn't it horrible? Wasn't it the worst thing you've ever seen in your life?"

It wasn't, but I didn't need to tell her that. Even if I was interested in telling horror stories, which I was not, this was neither the time nor the place. I had less than half an hour to compose Rory and myself before I had to give a speech. And she was more in need of composing. She huddled on the edge of the chair, bent low with her arms wrapped around her knees. Her eye makeup had smudged under her eyes and run down her face in little rivulets, so that she looked like an actor made up to play a chimney sweep.

"They're going to think I did it," she whispered. "Because of last night. I should just go jump off your balcony and be done with it. I can't take it, Thea. Those cops! You saw them. Big as houses and mean. They wanted me to talk, but I got so upset I told them to come back later."

"You haven't talked with them yet?"

She shook her head. "I've been hiding, since then, because, you know, they scare me." She clenched fistfuls of her dress in her hands. "I didn't do it, Thea."

"Why would they think you did it, Rory? You're her assistant. The two of you were very close. You admired Martina. Everyone knows that."

"And everyone in the hotel knows we had a fight last night, too. You know you can't keep a secret in this group. I don't think I can take it." She jumped up and started pacing in the small area between the foot of the bed and the windows. "I don't think I can take this . . . being questioned, everyone looking at me, prying into my private life, prying into hers. Of course it will be me they ask . . . who else knew her like I did? They'll make me sit there and keep asking me questions until I say things I didn't want to say and poor Martina won't have any privacy left at all and it will be horrible. I can't take it. You know. I just can't take it." She was working herself into a state of hysteria, with churning arms and bobbing head and her speech coming faster and faster.

I picked up the phone to call for help. "What are you doing? Put that phone down!" she wailed. "I'm not ready to talk to them yet. Please. Thea. Give me some space. I've got to think about what to do. . . ."

"Front desk," said a voice in my ear.

Before I could speak, Rory grabbed the phone out of my hand

and slammed it down. "You're not going to turn me in," she said. "I'm not going to let them get me!"

"Then calm down," I said. "Sit back down in that chair and take some deep breaths. I'll get you some water."

Obediently she sat in the chair. I went into the bathroom. As I came out with the water, she dashed to the door, opened it, and rushed out onto the lanai. I shoved the water glass onto the nearest surface and went after her. She climbed onto a chair and tried to get up onto the railing but I was there by then, with my arms wrapped around her waist, holding her back. She kicked and flailed and punched, and all I could do was hold on. If I freed a hand to do more, she might get away from me.

A gasp and cry made me look sideways. A plump, pleasant-faced woman, with big, brassy hair was standing on the next balcony, staring. "Get help!" I said. "Call security and get someone up here!" She continued to stare at us, unmoving, as though we were staging this. "Stop staring and do something." I was yelling now. "Please. This is an emergency! Get someone up here to help me before she jumps." Or before Rory successfully bruised me from head to toe. The woman retreated, still staring, bumped off the wall, and disappeared inside. I could only hope she was calling for help and not writing her exciting adventure down in her vacation diary.

I'd never had such a vivid understanding of the expression, "having your hands full." I sure did. Rory was slight but no weakling, and she squirmed in my grasp like an eel within the slippery fabric of her shapeless black sack. It was like wrestling with my brother, Michael, when we were kids. Like Michael, she didn't follow any of the rules of fair play, and I was taking quite a beating. I was trying to be calm and uncombative, but if she went for my nose, I'd let her jump. I knew from personal experience there was little more painful or unaesthetic than a broken nose.

Finally I got her pinned against the railing, freed one hand, and slapped her hard. "Snap out of it," I ordered. She swore at me. I slapped her again.

She went limp, cowering against the railing, her hand on her face. She raised stricken eyes. "You hit me," she said. "You hit me."

"What do you think you've been doing? Dancing a jig?"

At that moment help arrived in the form of a couple security men, two cops, including the big cop, Nihilani, and the goggling woman from next door. Better late than never. "I won't tell them anything," Rory whispered, cowering against my side. "No one needs to know."

I explained the situation as briefly as possible, happy to hand Rory—reduced now to a limp, sobbing lump—over to professionals. I recommended sedatives and a physician and collapsed in my chair, head in hands. Eyes closed. Ten minutes to prepare a speech, and I felt like I'd just been poured out of a cocktail shaker.

I heard the door open and shut. Heard someone still moving around the room. Looked up. The big cop was coming out of the bathroom with a glass in his hand. He held it out to me. I took it, sipped it, set it. My hands were still shaking. I closed my eyes again.

"Scary, huh?" he said. I heard the creak of springs as he sat on the bed. Looked over at him. He was pulling out a notebook. He definitely had that ready-to-talk look.

"Not now," I said. "I can't talk to you right now. We've got a breakfast meeting in ten minutes and I have to give the speech."

"We're investigating a murder," he said.

"And I'm not being uncooperative. I'm just trying to keep a hundred and eighty more people from getting hysterical. After breakfast, I'm all yours. I'm not going anywhere. I'm trying to keep this conference from falling completely apart. I'm trying to do my job. Just like you." It sounded more defensive than I'd meant it to, but I couldn't help it.

"I could keep you here," he said. His cool, unblinking stare was faintly reptilian.

"Of course you could. I'm hoping you won't." I tried to smile but my face, battered by Rory's fists, and my disposition, battered by the whole morning, wouldn't cooperate. The result, reflected in the mirror across the room, was tentative and pathetic.

He snapped his notebook shut and looked pointedly at his watch. "How long?"

"Hour. Hour and a half."

"Ten o'clock. Back here. You're mine."

Not in a million years am I yours, buddy, I thought. "Deal," I said. "Now, if you don't mind, I could use a few minutes by myself."

He stood up, turned toward the door. A crisp, military turn. Turned back, slightly less crisp. "You okay?" he asked.

I tend, with cops, to be stand-offish and stoic, but I know they like you better if you act like a proper victim, so I told the truth. "I'm not sure. I feel shaky . . . and . . . uh . . . battered."

"I'll bet she was a handful," he said. "Why you?"

I shrugged. My shoulder hurt. And time was rushing past so fast I could feel the seconds slip away. "I'm everyone's mother, I guess."

The heavy features lifted in something like a smile. "Some mother," he said. "Catch you later."

Five minutes to speech time. Oh, well. I could be a little late to breakfast. Nothing ever starts on time. I might just make it—if I didn't eat but spent the time reading. I didn't feel very hungry. And anyway, wasn't I the one who said life was no fun without challenges?

CHAPTER 3

BREAKFAST WENT WELL. We tiptoed adeptly through a minefield and emerged without getting blown up thanks to Jolene's calm grace, Shannon's hearty bonhomie, and Zannah's surprisingly moving eulogy. We compromised with Rob Greene and attributed Martina's demise to "mysterious circumstances under investigation." I tap-danced briskly through my part, internally thanking my demanding lawyer father and a brutal college speech teacher for giving me the tools to think on my feet. Good mentoring and seven years in the field were beginning to pay off. I might not have been the world's most eloquent speaker, but the subject was familiar enough so I didn't have to read it word for word, and people didn't fiddle and chat or get that bored, glassy-eyed look speakers recognize as the kiss of death.

Afterward, I was mobbed with people who had questions, or wanted copies of the speech, or wanted to get together for some follow-up. Shannon waded through the crowd to command my presence at a lunch meeting, claiming she and Jolene and Zannah needed to talk further about damage control. Several people handed me business cards with scribbled messages on the back. Others tried to get me to give them the inside scoop on what had happened. I was relieved that things had gone well and wished I could have stayed and talked, but I was late for my date with the detective, and getting nervous about keeping him waiting. He hadn't struck me as the understanding type.

I was making a beeline for the door when someone grabbed my arm. I don't like being grabbed under any circumstances and this was particularly unpleasant as the grabber managed to hit several spots already bruised in my wrestling match with Rory. I turned to find that the hand belonged to Lewis Broder. "Thea," he whispered, "we need to talk."

"Not now, Lewis. I'm late for a meeting."

"With the cops, right?" I nodded. "That's what I wanted to talk to you about. I know you saw me last night. With Martina?" I nodded again. "Don't tell them about it, okay?"

Obviously Lewis hadn't seen my inquisitor and didn't know what I was up against. "I won't volunteer it, but if they ask a direct question, I won't lie to them, Lewis."

The hand gripped tighter. "Thea . . . you've got to . . . you know how it is . . . I'm a married man. Besides, nothing happened. . . ."

I shook him off and took a step backward. "If nothing happened, you've got nothing to worry about. Look, I've got to go."

He must have missed my displeasure completely, because he gave me a professionally charming smile. "Remember," he called after me. "Mum's the word." I recalled no such agreement and was not charmed, but I restrained myself from making a rude gesture at his departing back.

Much of the group left for tours of the Napali coast or Mt. Haleakala. We had been told by those experienced in conference management that these things worked best when the conferees were given part of the day to go out and play, with substance in the morning or afternoon, with the other half of the day off, so that was the model we were using. I, being adventurous, or at least determined to get out of the hotel once while I was there, had signed myself up for the twenty-mile bike tour down the mountain on Sunday morning. Now, it was only Friday, and if I didn't get some sun and unconditioned air, I was going to go bonkers.

On the other hand, I had a hot date who would be waiting for me in my room. Hot to grill me, at least. I still felt faintly sick and, now that the speech was over, a kind of depleted weariness. Maybe eating would have helped but I didn't feel at all hungry. I'd settled for juice and water and half a piece of toast. A chaise in the sun would have been heavenly. Instead, I trundled upstairs to do my civic duty.

My mother used to have an expression, Let George do it, she used when she was tired of the endless tasks. Of course there never was a George, but increasingly, as my life seemed full to over-flowing, I wished there were. I would love to have sent George upstairs to deal with the waiting cop.

He was standing outside my door, arms folded across his chest, leaning against the railing. Stolid, placid, official. Something Andre had said popped into my head, a bit of loverly advice. "Don't drive like you do in Massachusetts, Thea. Those Hawaiian cops are tough." This guy certainly looked tough. He stood up straighter when he saw me and acknowledged my presence with a nod. Only a nod, no words, not even a grunt. It was disconcerting. Unsettling. He stared, he nodded, he didn't speak.

I opened the door and he followed me in, settling himself in a chair without asking my permission. His looming bulk made the room seem small. The still-unmade bed and my scattered papers made it seem cluttered. I felt claustrophobic. I opened the door to the lanai and warm air streamed in. I wanted to spread my arms and close my eyes and embrace it but not in front of this hulking policeman.

It was odd, the impression he gave of being big and bulky. Andre is a big guy. A shade over six feet and solid, with big shoulders and a wide chest and strong arms and legs. This guy wasn't much taller, but he would have made Andre look slight. He filled the chair and gave off a primitive aura of strength and power. He made me feel as tiny as Tinker Bell when I often feel big as an ox.

I sat down in the other chair, kicked off my shoes, curled my legs up underneath me, and waited. He opened his notebook, clicked his pen, and nodded. "Tell me about Martina Pullman," he said.

I said the name to myself and contemplated where to begin. Physical? Domestic? Official? What did I know about Martina, really, that he might need to know? That mattered to this case? He was watching me intently, a look that invaded my personal space the way some people do when they stand too close. I lowered my eyes. It's not easy to back away from a look. "I don't know what you want to know," I said. "We were sort of co-workers, I suppose. At least insofar as we were both working for the National Association of Girls' Schools. She is . . . was . . . the executive director. I'm a board member and I've done some consulting work for—"

"Tell me about this conference," he interrupted. "What's it all about?"

"Making the case for single-sex education for girls."

He looked surprised. "This conference is about sex education?"

I shook my head and tried not to smile. I didn't think he had much of a sense of humor. "Single-sex education. Girls' schools or all-girl classes. No boys. We're talking about the ways girls do better when they're in classes with other girls, the way their confidence grows, the way they discover their voices. We're talking about encouraging and mentoring girls so that they can take an equal place in science and engineering, in physics and math. Did you know that only about ten percent of physicists, and the same number of architects in AIA, are women? And this is after twenty years of struggle?" Another nod. *Get off your soapbox, Thea*, I reminded myself. *This isn't what he wants to hear.*

"We're talking about educational issues as they relate specifically to girls. Whether girls have different learning styles, different learning needs, how girls approach technology—"

"Okay. I got it. What was your relationship to the deceased?"

The deceased. That had an aura of finality, didn't it? Not even seeing her lying there, ugly as it was, had made her seem as dead as his dropping her name and using the generic "deceased" instead. The words seemed to hang in the air between us; he was here because of the "deceased." Because Martina was dead. Ungracefully, embarrassingly, grotesquely dead. I knew too much about dead. It was final. Irrevocable. And hard to comprehend.

I swallowed and forced myself to answer the question. "Professional," I said. "I'm a partner with the EDGE Consulting Group. We do a lot of work for independent, that is private, schools, on admissions issues, management issues, image and perception, crisis management. . . ." He was nodding but not writing anything down. "The National Association of Girls' Schools came to us as a client, looking for some basic research and marketing—"

"And Martina Pullman was director of the association?" he interrupted.

"Yes. Basically she started it. It was her baby."

"What was she like?"

"Smart. Very smart. She was a real quick study; had an amazing ability to master the necessary facts very quickly and speak about them articulately. She was superb at getting press, at attracting media attention to the group, to our issues. She had a vision, a sense of mission, that was inspiring to all of us."

He clapped his hands together twice in slow-mo imitation of applause and I felt my face getting hot. "What was she like as a person? What was she like to work with? Was she difficult? Beloved? Detested?"

I resented being made fun of. I didn't want to talk to him anymore and I wanted him to go away. I knew my reaction was childish. This was a murder investigation. Not an unexplained death, despite what we'd said at breakfast. Not a potential suicide. No one knots her own stocking around her throat and strangles herself. Of course, we've all heard about autoerotic strangling, but that's not what this was, I was sure. His job was to get the facts, not to be charming. But it was so new. I didn't feel like I'd even had time to catch my breath since I'd found the body, and here he was, expecting coherence. I inhaled, slowly. Let it out, slowly. We don't like to speak ill of the dead. It seems, after a person has already met an ugly end, that at least we should accord them some privacy and grace. But, as Andre told me when he was investigating my sister, Carrie's, death, the dead have no privacy rights. Protect their privacy and you may, unwittingly, protect the killer.

I stifled a yawn. The warm air was making me sleepy. "She was an impossible woman," I said. "She was great on her feet, she truly did have a wise vision for the organization, but beyond that, she was awful. Disorganized, controlling, irresponsible, self-aggrandizing—"

"What does that mean?"

"She wanted all the power and glory. She took credit for other people's work, other people's ideas. She couldn't bear to share the spotlight. Martina was like a piece of blotting paper. She wasn't that good at original thinking herself but she could sit down with anyone for twenty minutes and parrot their whole speech better than they could. She was bad at delegating. She'd micromanage to the point of obsession and then, when it was too late for anyone to do a good job, she'd delegate in desperation and then criticize the quality of the product. The organization had outgrown her, I think. She would have made a good figurehead but she wasn't capable of the day-to-day management anymore."

I swallowed. I sounded like such a shrew. But was I really trashing Martina if all I was saying was the truth? "She was a user. Assistants like Rory . . ." I paused to make sure he knew who I was talking about. "You know, little hysterical Rory from this morning?" He nodded. "She'd run them right into the ground, promising them bigger and better things that never materialized in return for massive amounts of drudge work." I stopped. "Is she okay? Rory, I mean?"

He grunted but I couldn't tell whether it was an affirmative or not. "This young woman, Rory Altschuler, how long has she worked for Ms. Pullman?"

"I don't know. A year and a half, maybe longer. You'd have to ask her."

"What kind of working relationship did they have?"

I considered. I didn't really have an answer to that, only an outsider's opinion. I told him that.

"Give me your opinion, then."

"As I said, Martina was a user. She abused Rory. Yelled at her, criticized her, pushed her unmercifully. Demanded unreasonable hours, unfair amounts of work. But Rory seemed to be able to see Martina's good side, her strengths. I think Rory imagined she wanted to be just like Martina. And despite the helplessness you've seen today, Rory is a very competent young woman." I wondered if the phrase "young woman" was condescending? Probably. Despite my sensitive job, I sometimes err on the side of political incorrectness. "And then, Martina could be very charming when she wanted to be. When she wasn't abusing Rory, she treated her like a favorite daughter. So I guess you'd say mixed." He seemed to be waiting for more but I had no more to offer.

"Ms. Pullman was married?" I nodded. "Any children?"

"None of her own. I believe her husband has a child from a former marriage who may live with them."

"You know her husband?"

"I've met him."

"What can you tell me about him?"

"Very little. He's a lobbyist. Good-looking. Midfifties. They've been married about eight years. I don't know whether he was married when they met or not. I've never heard anything about his first wife. Nor have I met her, though I understand she's involved with education in some way. Martina was also a lobbyist. For teachers. Then she got this idea for the association, and turned it into a full-time job for herself. She pays herself pretty well, too." It was a catty thing to say. I know only too well that women are chronically underpaid. But Martina's generosity extended only to herself, and put a strain on the association's finances when it tried to do other things. At first she'd been defensive about it, but the last time the board had brought it up, she'd flatly refused to discuss it.

"Her husband didn't come with her?"

"Not that she mentioned. And I haven't seen him. You haven't spoken with him? Surely he's been notified?" Even as I said it, I knew he wouldn't answer. My mind raced ahead, thinking about how it would be for Jeff. That heart-stopping moment when you realize how bad the news really is. I bit my lip against the surge of my own memories and forced them away, pressing them back into the secret place where feelings live, closing the door against the weight of them, like shutting out an unwelcome guest. My sorrows were my own business; I didn't like people to know things about me.

"Okay," he said, tapping his notebook with a pencil. "So she didn't get along very well with her board. Is that what you said?"

"Not exactly." I could hear my father's voice in my head, reminding me never to let anyone put words in my mouth. His advice had come in handy more times than I could count. "We all admired her. And it's hard when a person is an organization's

founder to . . . that is, because it was her vision, she thought she . . ."
Spit it out, Kozak. "She thought she ought to have lifetime tenure, as director, and we thought she ought to stay on the board in an honorary position and let someone else take over the reins."

"So there was a lot of backstabbing and squabbling?"

"We don't do things that way," I said, primly.

"You just said you didn't get along."

"I said we disagreed. The way mature professionals deal with disagreement is to talk about their differences."

He twisted in the chair, a sudden, violent movement that made me jump. "Oh, give me a break, Ms. Kozak. Somebody killed the woman."

"It wasn't one of us."

He leaned forward and stared. He had strange eyes that, when the light hit them, seemed to flash. "How do you know? You know who did it?"

"Of course not. But you saw how she was dressed. Obviously she was waiting for someone, and it doesn't look like it was a woman."

"Maybe. Maybe not." He leaned back in the chair. "Tell me about this morning. Everything that happened from the time that Ms. Altschuler came and knocked on your door."

There was a knock on my door. I looked at him, feeling stupid to be asking for permission to answer the door in my own room, but he had that kind of presence. Overpowering. He nodded. I went to the door and opened it. A smiling bellboy stepped in, carrying a vase of gorgeous pink roses. He set them on the table, I tipped him, and he left. I picked up the card and hesitated. Maybe I should open it later.

"Go ahead," he said.

I ripped it open and turned away from him to read it. It said, "Happy 31st Birthday to the one who makes life worth living. Andre." And now I knew what day it was. It wasn't a particularly happy birthday, so the roses made a big difference.

I sat back in my chair, clutching the card. More than ever, I wanted him to go away. I wanted privacy to bask in Andre's loving gesture. I didn't want to be thinking about Martina Pullman and who might have killed her. I wanted to think about how lucky I was to have met Andre and gotten a second chance at the happiness I thought I'd lost forever when my husband, David, died. If only I could have stood up, thrown my arm over my eyes in a dramatic, old-time movie gesture, and declared to that opaque, looming presence, "I vant to be alone." Reality is a bitch.

"Boyfriend?" he asked. I nodded. "Special occasion?"

"My birthday."

"Oh." He didn't wish me a happy one, or even many returns of the day. "Tell me about this morning."

I took him through it, step by step. The lost earring, the phone call. Rory pounding on the door. Going down to the conference room and then up to Martina's room. Back down to the desk to get security and a key. Back to the room, and what we'd found. "Who went in first?" he asked.

"I did. The manager asked me to. In case she wasn't dressed or something, I suppose."

"Tell me everything you did."

"I walked into the living room and I called her name. I said something like, 'Martina, it's Thea, are you okay?' I waited and she didn't answer. That was when I noticed the table and the food. . . ."

"Did you touch anything?"

"Of course not."

"Of course not? Didn't I find you going through the papers on her desk? That was touching something, wasn't it?"

"I meant I didn't touch anything important."

"You don't know what might be important. How long did you stay in the living room?"

"I don't know. Half a minute, perhaps. When she didn't answer, we went on."

"We?"

"Me, then Rory, then the assistant manager and then the man from security."

"And . . ."

There was another knock on the door. This time it was the maid. He sent her away. "And?"

"And we went on into the dressing room. By then, I was getting nervous. I thought maybe she'd had a fall in the tub or something, but when I looked into the bathroom. I could see she'd taken a bath, but there was no one in the room. And then I . . . then we . . ." He waited, eyelids lowered over the gleaming eyes like a reptile waiting for prey. "We went into the bedroom. . . ."

"Back up a minute," he said. "Tell me everything you noticed about the bathroom."

It seemed like an odd question. "You saw it. . . ." I began.

"Tell me," he repeated.

I closed my eyes and tried to remember. "The tub was dirty . . . you know, it had a ring . . . and there were some towels on the floor. And a terry-cloth bathrobe over the edge of the tub."

"Anything else?"

"Slippers. Those little useless backless slippers. Lined up neatly in front of the sink."

"Anything else?"

"Some clothes, I think. Underwear on the floor and some folded clothes on the counter. Makeup. Hair dryer. All that stuff. And a book on the floor beside the towels."

"Was the book open or shut?"

"Shut."

"Good. Now you can go on."

What was this, I wondered, a test of my memory? Couldn't we just stop here? The next part was going to be hard. I hesitated.

"Go on," he ordered.

"When we went into the bedroom, I saw her and I immediately tried to keep Rory from seeing, but I couldn't stop her. I told her to go back, not to look, but she hurried past me, saw Martina, and started screaming."

"She started screaming and then what did she do?"

"She ran out of the room and I sent the assistant manager after her so she wouldn't get the whole place in an uproar."

"She didn't touch anything?" I shook my head. "You're sure?"

"I'm sure."

"But you didn't scream?" I shook my head. "Then?"

"Then I told the security man to call the police."

"Did he use the phone in the room?"

I tried to remember. "He reached for it, but then he stopped himself and went out to the other room to use the phone."

"That's everything? No one touched the body to be sure she was dead?"

"Oh, yeah. He did that."

"Who? The assistant manager or the security guy?"

"The assistant manager went after Rory. I sent him after Rory. I don't know what he might have touched on his way out. The security guy reached out and touched her leg. He said she was cold so she must be dead. That's when I told him to call the police."

"He didn't touch anything else? Just turned and left the room?"

I closed my eyes and tried to remember, wondering why this was important. What difference did it make whether the guy might have touched her knee and her foot? "There was one of those room-service breakfast slips lying on the floor. He picked it up and put it back on the pillow."

"And then?"

"He went to the phone, reached for it, hesitated, and went into the other room. I don't know what he did after that."

He nodded. "Good."

"Why does it matter?" I burst out. "What difference does it—"

He put a finger to his lips. "I ask the questions," he said. "Now, what about you? Did you touch the body?" The body. At that point, she was still Martina. Had I touched her? All I'd done was pick up her shoe. "It helps me a lot if you answer out loud."

Bastard! He didn't have to be like this. He could just ask and I'd tell him what he wanted. I glared at him but somehow, in midglare, I began to imagine Andre in his place, trying to interview someone like me. Someone touchy and smart and impatient. Someone with her own agenda. Someone who might be involved. Or someone who knew the players and could be a useful resource if she'd only get off her high horse and cooperate.

I pushed back the hair that was straggling into my face. It felt like I'd been holding my breath for hours. I let it out with a sigh. "I'm sorry," I said. "I don't mean to be uncooperative. It's just such a shock."

"Of course," he said. "When you're not used to . . ."

Sometimes it seemed to me that I was getting much too used to bodies and death, though I wasn't about to tell him that. But I didn't want to listen to him, I wanted to talk. "It was so ugly. Grotesque. When I saw her, the first thing I thought was that she'd been . . . killed by a lover, because of the way she was dressed, but then it came to me that it was too artificial. She seemed . . ." I hesitated, searching for the right word, expecting him to say "Go on" in his impatient way, but this time he kept his mouth shut. "Posed. Arranged to sort of . . . maximize the indignity. The whole of it . . . the outfit, the position of the body, her having been strangled with her own stocking . . . it was all so . . . theatrical. So completely contrived to degrade her. Actually, I didn't think of that right away. I was too stunned, too embarrassed for her. I wanted to cover her up. . . ."

The phone rang. "Don't answer it," he said. "Go on."

"I have to answer it. It's Andre." I just knew. Under the wilting glare of his eyes, I picked it up. "Thea Kozak, the girl of your dreams."

"You betcha," Andre said. "Only I think you mean woman. You get the flowers?"

"You betcha," I echoed. "They're so gorgeous. Why aren't you here?"

"I'm not even going to be here for long," he said. "Gotta go back to work. They're shorthanded and they've got an especially gruesome murder on their hands. My bag is packed and the motor's running. I'll be at Jack's if you need me. You have that number. Hey, before I go, I've got a little song I want you to listen to. . . ."

"Andre . . ." I tried to interrupt, but he was fiddling with his tape. Across the static-filled lines I heard a snatch of Willie Nelson, "You Were Always on My Mind," Eric Clapton, "Beautiful Tonight," and then Meatloaf, "Paradise by the Dashboard Light." Any other time, I would have cracked up. I started to cry.

"So," he said, coming back on the line. "When I get back . . . when you get back, you know what I'm going to do? I'm going to wish a belated happy birthday to every inch of you."

"Don't," I said. "We're not alone." I took a deep breath and tried to explain, but it came out as a great big sob.

"What the hell does that mean?"

"Martina Pullman has been murdered."

"What the hell!"

I shoved the phone at my glowering companion. "Here. You explain it," and fled into the bathroom in search of tissues.

By the time I returned, red-faced and snuffling, the guys had bonded. It's a goddamned fraternity, with a few sorority sisters allowed in these days. They can spot each other across a crowded room the same way people on the make can. My inquisitor smiled—he actually smiled—as he handed me the phone. "So, darlin'," I crooned, "did you tell him not to be so mean?"

"Isn't that funny," Andre said. "You want him to be nice; he wants you to stop acting like he's going to bite you and just answer his questions. Maybe the two of you could work something out." Then he said, "Wait a minute. I'm not sure I mean that. What does he look like?"

"About twice as big as you and scary as hell."

"Good," he said. "Not your type."

"I only have one type," I interrupted. "You. I'd better go before he starts throwing me around the room. He doesn't look patient. Call me when you can—even just a message, your voice—and I'll keep you posted."

"Thea." His voice was dead serious now. "For heaven's sake, be careful. I know you're going to think you've got to fix this, but for once, please, let the police handle it."

"Happy to," I agreed. "You be careful, too. There are an awful lot of bad guys out there." I hung up the phone and returned to my chair, feeling much better and much worse. For four blissful months, I hadn't had to worry about him. Classwork made him grouchy, but at least no one tried to run him down with cars, or shoot him. I could stand a little bad temper. Sometimes he even let me help him with his homework.

I curled up in a ball and crossed my arms defensively. Now this guy knew too much about me. He knew I was in a seriously romantic relationship with another cop. I'm a private person. I don't like people knowing anything about my personal life. That's why it's called personal. "Where were we?"

He checked his notes. "You wanted to cover her up."

I closed my eyes and pictured myself standing beside the bed. The shoe on the floor. The shoe on her foot. "They weren't her shoes," I said.

"What?" He sat up and stared.

"You asked me if I touched the body. And I just remembered. When the security guard checked to see if she was dead, he touched her leg . . . and her shoe fell off. I don't know why . . . I guess I was stunned and not thinking clearly . . . but I picked it up and tried to put it back on. It wouldn't go."

"Her foot was stiff."

"It was the wrong size. Martina is tall. Look at the rest of the shoes she brought. She must wear at least a nine. That was no bigger than a seven."

He shook his head and wrote something in his book. "But the rest of the stuff fit."

"Not exactly. Tall women are hard to fit. Especially thin ones like Martina." Dr. Kozak was about to lecture on ladies' lingerie. "The other thing that makes me think it wasn't her stuff . . ." I didn't even know I had these thoughts, and now I was lecturing an experienced policeman. Perhaps the whole experience had unhinged me. "The exposed breast . . ." God, this was ugly stuff to be talking about, especially to such a sympathetic listener. I took a deep breath and let it out very slowly. "Things like that bustier, they're all stretch lace and elastic and internal boning to make them stay in place and stay up. No way it would have shifted around like that. Either it was too small, which would be my guess, or it was deliberately pulled down to look like that."

I choked on the ugliness of my own words, feeling sick again. "Are we almost through? I don't think I can do this much longer."

"I'll get you some water," he said.

"Water? I want a respite from remembering. I want to feel the sun on my back and hear the roar of the surf and feel gentle breezes."

He looked like I was spouting hogwash. "I think you need some rest."

According to my watch, I had about forty minutes before I had to meet the ladies for lunch. "I want to go outside."

Nihilani pushed himself out of the chair and waved his notebook toward the door. "Then go outside. We're finished for now. I'll probably have more questions for you. In the meantime, don't share our conversation with your buddies on the board. And . . ." He held out his hand. "I'd like to have that speech back now. You did a pretty good job, at least the part I heard."

I blushed so red I was probably glowing like a candle as I reached in my pocket, pulled it out, and handed it to him. "Andre says you can be quite willful. I wouldn't suggest trying my patience too far. People say I have a very bad temper." He turned on his heel and left.

CHAPTER 4

I GRABBED MY room key, put the notice for the maid to make up the room on the door handle, and rushed out. I was headed for sand and sun and nothing was going to stop me. Halfway through the lobby, Lewis Broder stepped out from behind a potted palm like someone in a B movie and reached for my arm. This time I was ready for him. I stepped backward, clasped my hands to my breast, and said, in my best Margaret Dumont voice, "Don't you know any better than to go around grabbing women, Lewis?"

"Sorry. Sorry." He tucked his hands behind his back like a chastened schoolboy. "I have to know. Did you tell them?"

I shrugged, tempted to keep him waiting for my answer, but I didn't have time for games. "They didn't ask. See you later." I put on a burst of speed and got myself out of the lobby and into the sunshine without a hat or sunglasses or sun screen or any of the practical amenities, paused at the top of the steps to gaze down through the artificial green grotto they'd constructed, and headed out across the lawn instead, nodding politely to Buddhas and dragons who lurked among the flowers. Fountains gurgled, the sun was hot on my shoulders, the brisk ocean breeze toyed with my hair. I was free, pasty white, and thirty-one.

"Theeaah! Theeaah!" I didn't recognize the woman coming toward me in the gigantic hat, a pareo wrapped around her ample midriff. "Why, honey, what a treat to see you here. Are you on vacation, too?"

Too late to hide from the wicked twist of fate that had dished up my mother's dear friend Alyce during the first free moments I'd had in two days. I shook her hand, pumping vigorously and watching with malicious pleasure as the hanging rolls of flesh on her upper arm danced and jiggled. It's not that I'm so mean, really, but when we were little, Alyce was the kind of person who was always spying on us and calling our mother. She got me and my brother, Michael, in so much trouble that to this day, I haven't forgiven her.

"Are you alone?" she asked, peering around as if I was hiding someone behind my back. "Or did you bring that nice policeman?" I was sure my mother had given her an earful about the "nice policeman," little of it favorable. My mother persists in a rigid prejudice against the police. She considers them lower-class brutes, and thus unsuitable for her daughter. Even though she has met Andre many times, and observed that he is handsome, educated, articulate, and good to me, she refuses to see him as he is. The minute he's out of sight, she's back to calling him Andy and scheming about how to introduce me to someone more suitable.

"I'm here on business, Mrs. Edgerton. I'm one of the organizers of the education conference. Are you staying at the hotel?"

She nodded, her piggy little eyes opening wide. "A dreadful place, Thea. It's a wonder I haven't asked for my money back. Last night in the middle of the night, there was the most dreadful commotion. . . ." She studied my face. "Didn't you hear it?"

My ears pricked up like an eager terrier. Did Alyce have information about Martina's murder? "I'm afraid not. What time was this?"

She waved a plump, beringed hand toward a bench. "Do you mind if we sit down? I've been walking along the beach for what seems like hours. After a while all this sand and sun becomes so boring, don't you think?"

I gritted my teeth as I followed her to the bench. "I'm afraid I've been rather busy. This is my first time out of the hotel."

"Well, I won't keep you, dear. You do look like you could use some sun. You're awfully pale. Anyway," she plunked herself down, rearranged her draperies, and began. "I think it must have been around two in the morning. I'd just gotten to sleep and suddenly there was all this screaming and crashing, like people having a fight. Of course I called security right away. Then I put on my robe and looked outside to see if I could see what was happening. I opened my door just in time to see a lamp go flying right over the railing. After the lamp there was a wastebasket, and then a chair, and finally an entire suitcase. Well, honestly, Thea, it was just like something out of a movie, the way things spilled out and drifted down and draped themselves all over the bushes in the lobby, and all the while the two of them were screaming and yelling and hitting each other."

She sniffed. "It seemed like security took their sweet time coming . . . I suppose it's Third World time or something. . . ." From where we were sitting, I could see the beach. I could almost smell the beach. I wanted to yell into her complacent face that Hawaii was hardly the Third World, but she'd tell my mother, and then my mother would call me up and complain. We hardly spoke these days, not since my mother had roped me into saving one of her protégés from a murder charge. We'd ended up having a huge fight at my brother's engagement party and I'd walked out. Since then we'd been at an impasse. She was still waiting for me to say I was sorry; I still wasn't sorry.

"Well, it turns out," Alyce Edgerton said, "that this isn't that uncommon. Hawaii is a very popular honeymoon destination, and from time to time, couples who think they know each other and are ready to start a life together get into a hotel room by themselves and find they're stuck with a stranger. Sometimes the guy gets drunk, or the wife does, or they both do, all those confused feelings come out, and bingo, they just lose control!" She'd been leaning forward eagerly. Now she settled back on the bench with a sigh. "I can't believe you didn't hear a thing."

"What floor are you on?"

"Sixteen. And you?"

"Twelve." And Martina had been on seventeen. Evidently Alyce hadn't heard about that, or she'd want to talk about it. Alyce loved to talk. Even my mother complained about that. And Alyce was going to have a lot to talk about when she got home. First a fight and then a murder. I hoped I didn't run into her after she heard about that. "Quite a story," I said, getting up. "I hope tonight is quieter." I headed for the beach. I didn't care if Godzilla stepped into my path, I was going to get my toes on that sand. I found a vacant lounge chair, lay down with my arms across my eyes, and fell asleep.

I've been known to claim that sleep is one of the things I'm good at, but that's only when I don't have something serious on my mind, which isn't very often. When something is bothering me, my mind likes to replay it as I sleep. I work out a lot of stuff that way. Sometimes I end up with terrible dreams. It's so far out of my control that I've come to imagine an evil entity I've titled the director of dreams who likes to play scary scenarios in my head while I'm trying to rest. So, even though I was basking in the sun on a beautiful Maui beach, the images inside my head were dark.

In my dream, I was lying by the pool in my bikini, lulled by the sun against a backdrop of murmured conversation and cavorting swimmers, when suddenly there was a shadow across the sun. I opened my eyes to complain, and found Martina standing there, clad in the absurd outfit she'd died in, her face bloated and purple and her eyes protruding, the silky stocking still dangling from her neck. She tried to speak but emitted only a rough croak. Raising her hands, she untied the stocking and let it drift casually to the ground. "That's better," she said.

People around me were staring. I picked up the bathing-suit cover-up I'd worn. "Don't you want to put this on?" I asked.

"What difference does it make now, Thea?" she snapped, her voice still a harsh whisper. "I'm dead."

"Then what are you—"

"Doing here? Unfinished business. Look at me. They've made a mockery of me . . . they've made me a laughing-stock! I want them to pay!"

"We'll go find the police," I said. "We'll tell them what happened and they can arrest the person who did this to you."

"Oh, sweetie . . ." She reached out a cold white hand and stroked my cheek. Her nail polish matched her outfit. "You're so naive for such a smart girl. Don't you understand? I don't know who did it. That's why I came to you. Everyone says you're good at solving mysteries. Besides, you're the only one who can see me." She bent down, scooped up the stocking, and disappeared. After that, the director let me sleep.

I woke only because someone was grabbing me again. I don't wake up easily, nor usually in a very civil frame of mind, and I was forming a juicy string of curses and considering the possibility of physical action when I opened my eyes and saw that my assailant was a pale red-haired girl about eleven. "I'm sorry, ma'am," she whispered, stepping away from my angry face. "My mother said I should wake you before you got a bad sunburn. That's my mom over there." She pointed to a woman carefully shaded by an umbrella, who was waving at us.

I checked my watch. I'd slept for forty minutes in the midday sun. Even though I tan easily, that was courting disaster. I turned my snarl into a smile. "Thank you very much. Your mom was right." I stuck out a hand. "I'm Thea Kozak."

She presented a small freckled hand with bitten fingernails. "Laura," she said. "Laura Mitchell. This is my first time in Hawaii."

"Pleased to meet you, Laura Mitchell. Are you staying at the hotel?" She nodded. "Well, maybe we'll see each other again. Thanks for rescuing me."

That brought a smile and revealed a mouthful of braces. "Well, 'bye," she said, and scampered back to her mother. Reluctantly, I turned my back on the bright blue waves and went inside, already late for lunch, my head stuffed with sawdust, wondering if I looked as groggy as I felt.

Zannah was arriving late, too. She stopped me outside the dining room and gave me a hug. "Was it awful?" she asked.

I thought she meant the dream. But how could she know? She took in my blank stare. "The police," she said.

"Yes."

"They won't tell us anything. I don't think most of the people in the hotel even know what happened."

"I think you're right. Too bad it won't stay that way."

Shannon, Jolene, and Rob were already at the table and though it was only lunch, they all had what looked like piña coladas in front of them. "Thea. Zannah," Rob said genially. "Welcome. How about some drinks? We've already started drowning our sorrow."

"Hey!" Shannon nudged him the ribs. "You don't want to be seen looking so cheerful or that nosy Hawaiian cop will put you on his suspect list."

"I expect we're already on his suspect list. What did you tell him about us, anyway, Thea?"

"I'm not supposed to talk about it. But nothing you guys need to worry about. He asked if we disagreed and I said we had differences which we discussed and dealt with like reasonable adults."

"Cripes, someone didn't!" Shannon said.

"Yeah," Rob said. "Let's go around the table and list our favorite suspects. Other than ourselves, I mean."

"You're being very coldhearted about this," Zannah said. "We might not have liked her, but without her, we wouldn't even be here today, and it's probably fair to say that the issues around single sex education would be much less well known and—"

"Relax," he said. "You're not on my suspect list."

"That's not why I—"

"Hey," Jolene said, "this is going to be hard enough without us squabbling among ourselves. We've still got two more days of this conference to sort out, and all of Martina's gaps to fill in. We don't have a lot of time to waste playing whodunit games. I left a message for Rory to join us but she didn't return my call and I haven't been able to find her. It's going to be hard to do much without her. She's in charge of the schedule and has all that stuff on her laptop, plus the lists of all the contacts in the hotel and out—"

"You want to know who's number one on my suspect list?" Rob interrupted. "Drusilla Aird."

"Drusilla Aird? You're kidding. Is she here?" Shannon said. She dropped her voice to a confidential whisper, though given her normal booming quality, Shannon's whisper was like anyone else's normal voice. "I would have thought, after she lost her lawsuit, that she'd be embarrassed to be seen by this group, but I guess some people have no shame."

"I don't see what's so shameful," Jolene said. "Drusilla had a contract to ghost-write a book for Martina. She delivered the book. Martina said it was a lousy book but paid her anyway."

"And then six months later Martina published her own book under her own name, which Drusilla claimed was the book she'd written, without giving Drusilla any credit."

"Well," Rob said, "too bad for Drusilla that she didn't have a lawyer read the contract before she signed it, or she would have known she was giving sole rights to Martina to do whatever she wanted with the finished work. She did the work. She got paid. Other than the complaint we all have, that Martina was a pit viper who didn't care who she bit and what harm she caused, I don't see where she had anything to complain about."

"Except that Martina bad-mouthed her work all over Washington, and then went and published a virtually identical work under her own name. If it wasn't good enough when it was submitted, why was it suddenly good enough later? I can see where Drusilla might have been angry," Zannah said. "It's reasonable for a person to take pride in her work. All she was trying to do was force Martina to admit the published work was the manuscript she, Drusilla, had written. The court said it didn't matter. But both her reputation and her income suffered. She has . . . had . . . good reason to be mad at Martina. But, Rob, did you say you'd seen her here at the conference?"

"That's right. Last night in the lobby, looking as cheerful as a cat that just had cream."

"I wouldn't want to be in that policeman's shoes," Shannon said. We all agreed that none of us would. "I mean, trying to figure out who might have had it in for Martina. We know how she's treated all of us. . . ."

"Are you suggesting that we're all suspects?" Jolene asked. There was a dangerous current in her voice that Shannon didn't miss.

"No more than the rest of the world. A lot less than some. Now, if I had to pick someone—"

"I thought we weren't going to do this," Zannah interrupted.

"If I had to pick someone," Shannon repeated, "my choice

would be his first wife, Linda. I've heard she was none too happy when Martina stole her handsome husband away."

"Martina didn't steal him from her," Rob said. "You can't attract a man who doesn't want to be attracted."

"At least you don't subscribe to the black-widow theory of attraction," I said.

"The what?" Shannon asked.

"The notion that men are helpless in the hands of poisonous, devious, scheming females."

"She's here, you know," Zannah said.

"May I take your order?"

The waitress had materialized behind me so quietly I hadn't even known she was there. I glanced at the menu, which I hadn't opened, and ordered a shrimp salad with fresh pineapple and iced tea. I still didn't feel hungry, which was unusual. The others teased me for not getting a drink. "It would put me right to sleep." I waited while the others ordered, then said, "Are we all set for this afternoon? Early evening seminars and then the luau? Martina wasn't leading anything today."

"Maybe the hula," Rob said.

I expected Zannah to say something. Of all of us, she had tolerated Martina the best and Martina had considered her a friend, but it was Jolene who spoke. "I really do think," she said in her careful, considered way, "that we need to be awfully circumspect about what we say from now on. This is no joke. Martina isn't going to come dashing through the door and cry 'April fool.' She's dead. Any time that human life is taken, the . . . deceased . . . the, uh, victim . . . should be spoken about with respect . . . and gravity . . . so there's that, but—"

"Come on, Jolene," Rob interrupted. "You didn't even like her. The two of you fought like cats and dogs over organizational decisions and board policy. I know you were pissed as hell when she stole that speech you were going to give at Radcliffe and presented it at a press conference as her own work. Isn't it hypocritical to—"

"Please let me finish," she said.

"—to pretend to be sorry that she's dead when you publicly threatened to kill her yourself?"

Jolene's face was an unflattering pink. "That's what I was about to say, Rob. That everyone one of us has had at least one occasion . . . oh, no!" She paused, glaring at his shaking head, and half rose from her chair, her voice dropping to a growl. "You included, don't you go shaking your head like that. You, perhaps, most of all. If the incident has slipped your mind, I could refresh your recollection." His gaze wavered and dropped to his lap as his face flushed red. I couldn't help wondering what the incident was. Maybe I could get Jolene to tell me.

"Everyone one of us," she repeated, "has had at least one occasion where we've had a confrontation with Martina we'd rather not have made public. Something we would rather not have the Hawaiian police asking us about. Right?" Even Zannah nodded.

"Well, now, all Ah can recall," Shannon said, dropping into the deep "southern speak" she sometimes affected, "is that time she promised to come and give a speech at mah school, and Ah invited every single important alumna and the whole board of trustees was there and all the girls and everybody was dressed to the nines and just shimmying with anticipation, waiting for the arrival of the great Martina Pullman, heroine of American girls' schools. The time comes for her arrival and she doesn't show up. We wait and we wait and the salads wilt and the dinners dry out and the desserts melt and finally someone comes in with a phone message. She's so sorry, she's been unavoidably detained in Washington. If she'd been nearby, then Ah would have killed her. But Ah like to think Ah got ovah it." She batted her eyes and shrugged.

"We got lucky that night, though. Thea's partner, Suzanne Begner, Suzanne Merritt now, was there, and she stepped right up to that podium and started speaking and after about twenty minutes, there wasn't a soul in that room who cared that Martina hadn't come."

I'd heard that story from Suzanne. Reported slightly differently. Not that Suzanne's speech hadn't gone well. Suzanne is as close to perfect as anyone I know. But Shannon had been ready to hop on a plane to Washington and personally dismember Martina. It had taken all of Suzanne's vast store of diplomacy to keep it from happening. I looked around the table. I knew Jolene's story, and Shannon's, but what about Zannah? It was hard to imagine Zannah mad at anyone. She had what my mother would have called "a pleasant disposition." That meant always pleasant, superficial, with never a mean word about anyone. Martina could have stolen Zannah's babies and boiled them, and it would hardly have shown.

"Here you go," the waitress said cheerfully, setting my iced tea in front of me. "Your food will be right out. Can I get anyone another drink?"

It was foolish and I didn't need anything to dim my wits, but I have a weakness for the soothing effects of alcohol, especially when everything else is being abrasive. And it was my birthday. "I'll have a piña colada," I said. Everyone smiled and nodded and the table ordered another round of drinks. Some responsible grown-ups we were turning out to be.

We concentrated on drinking, and then on eating, and kept the conversation casual, light, and impersonal. When enough time had elapsed and enough alcohol had been consumed, we returned to the matter of schedules. "Tonight," Jolene said, "all our workshop leaders are thoroughly professional. I think we can count on them not to let this get in their way. After that, everyone is going to be getting dressed for the luau and that should pretty much take care of itself. Unless, of course, we have a snafu like last night. You'd think the people here couldn't count. Maybe one of us had better—"

"Not me," I mumbled through a mouthful of shrimp. The drink had miraculously restored my appetite. "I did it last night."

"Well, it's Rory's job. She's turning out to be the original gutless wonder, isn't she," Shannon said. "All that time she spent lurking at Martina's heels, learning to be a baby Martina, you'd think she'd have gotten a few calluses, wouldn't you?"

"At least," said Zannah, "you'd think the girl would have a little gumption."

"Well," Jolene, our peacemaker, said, "she did find Martina—"

"Thea is the one who found Martina," Rob interrupted. "And she's the one who has had to deal with police, and she hasn't taken to her bed."

"Not yet, anyway," I said. "It could happen at any moment. Actually," I pushed my chair back, "I should go and see if I can find her. If she hasn't learned from last night and checked the numbers, someone has to do it." I scribbled my room number on the check, added a tip, and picked up my glass. I wasn't quite done, and wasn't willing to leave a slurp of that ambrosial liquid behind.

"You're so heroic, Thea," Rob said.

I drifted to the door and had just managed to disappear through it when my grim companion of the morning, the massive Hawaiian cop, Nihilani, arrived at the table and lowered himself into my empty chair. I wasn't heroic; I'd just developed eyes in the back of my head and a keen instinct for self-preservation.

CHAPTER 5

THE DRINK MADE me bold. I rang Rory's room from the lobby and when she didn't answer—and I hadn't expected that she would—I took the elevator to the seventeenth floor and banged on the door. Doing it reminded me of the banging on my own door that had begun this awful day. It didn't like half a day had gone by. It seemed like weeks and weeks had passed, weeks during which people's stories of animosity and conflict had begun piling up at my feet like blown leaves. Weeks during which I had grown older and tireder and more cynical. So much had happened since I responded to that knock.

I stood in the hall and looked around. The hotel's opulent decor, the bird-filled lobby, the sound of fountains, and the cascades of green vines that hung over the balconies, couldn't mask the utilitarian quality of the tiers of rooms that circled the atrium center or banish the dull anonymity of all those rows of blond doors. I could hear the raucous shriek of a parrot, a disgruntled woman complaining, a tired child whining. Down the hall a maid was singing as she worked. And Rory wasn't answering. I pounded again and this time, for good measure, I announced my presence.

"And I'm not going to go away, Rory, so you might as well answer the door. Tragedy or not, we've got a conference to run." I waited a gracious minute, timing it on my watch, and knocked again. "If you don't let me in, I'll call security, claim I'm afraid you're sick or injured, and get them to open the door. You can save us both a lot of trouble by answering."

I waited. I gave her another whole minute. "Okay," I said. "You've got thirty seconds and I'm calling security."

The door flew open so violently it slammed into the wall. She stood there, red eyed and pale, her arms folded across her chest. "You are such an aggressive bitch, Thea," she said. "I was trying to rest, you know. Why can't you people leave me alone? Don't you have any idea how upset I am? How traumatic this is for me?"

"A pretty good idea," I said, walking past her into the room. Unlike her boss, she didn't have a suite. The truth is that I'm not especially sympathetic to people who collapse and stop doing their jobs. I'm from the old school, despite my tender—or as of today, not quite so tender—age. I truly believe that when the going gets tough, the tough get going. That the measure of an adult and a professional is the ability to do what has to be done, even when things are hard. That if someone throws a curve ball, you catch it anyway and throw it back twice as hard. A lot of the people I know think the tough are supposed to go shopping. Rory obviously believed the tough got to go to bed.

She leaned against the wall, arms folded defensively across her chest. "I was almost asleep," she whined. "What is it that was so important you had to wake me?"

She was doing a good job of combining aggrieved with wan and weary. A more sympathetic person probably would have bought the act, apologized, and retreated, but I needed Rory to do some work, to be doing her job like the rest of us. And there were a few things about the scenario that didn't quite ring true. Rory was wearing a long sundress of off-white linen. Sleeveless, well cut, expensive. Not the sort of thing one naps in. Only Victorians, fools, or those with a wait staff, irons poised, nap in linen dresses. And the dress had nary a crease. Nor was the bed rumpled. Her hair was freshly washed. She was wearing perfume. And the air in her room was scented with something other than her perfume—something that smelled to me like a man's aftershave. Unless, of course, it was one of those newfangled unisex scents—part of the movement to render us all androgynous, in which case, why was she wearing two different scents? Maybe it was a trend I had missed?

I didn't think so. Plus, I'd known plenty of vain and peculiar people, but few who put on earrings and bracelets to take an afternoon nap. "I'm sorry to have to bother you like this, but I need to go over the arrangements for this afternoon and tonight," I said. "Particularly tonight. I don't want the same seating problems at the luau that we had at dinner last night. You have all that stuff on your laptop, right?"

"I don't know why I have to. . . ." she began.

At least I'd said I was sorry; she'd never uttered a word of apology for punching and kicking and generally thrashing me earlier. If she'd accepted my apology and gone to work, I would have let it go, but she was heavily into her aggrieved role. I know all about aggrieved. My mother does aggrieved better than anyone I know. "You think the world has come to an end because of what happened to Martina? You think the conference and all its attendees have suddenly vanished into space?" I said. "If not you, then who? Whom? I understood that you were very eager to be a key player in all this. Martina told me you wanted to be in charge of arrangements because you wanted the experience."

"Yes. But that was before . . ."

"The show goes on, Rory."

"You're horrible," she snapped. "You know what Martina used to call you? The pit bull. She said once you got your teeth into something, you wouldn't let go."

"I believe the polite term is tenacious," I suggested. "Can we look at the records now? You aren't the only one who's tired, you know. Nor the only one who would like to have a nap." I didn't add, "Nor the only one who saw the body." Instead I added, "This is hard on everybody."

I thought I heard someone cough in the bathroom. I was tempted to ask if I could use her facilities, just to see her reaction, but there was work to be done. I didn't need to push her into hysterics and this morning had shown me that she could be pushed.

"Oh, all right!" She flounced over to the window, opened the curtains, then sat down at the desk and switched on her computer. I pulled up a chair and sat down beside her, noticing that her computer was just like mine. A phone rang in the bathroom. At least, it sounded like the bathroom, and since it didn't also ring in the room, it wasn't the hotel phone. Maybe it was next door or someone with a cellular phone out on a balcony. Rory appeared not to have heard.

But thinking about phones reminded me of something I'd been worrying about. "How did Jeff take the news?" I asked.

"Jeff?" she said, as if unfamiliar with the name. Silly. As Martina's assistant, she'd dealt with him every day.

"You didn't call him?"

"Me? Why would I call Jeff? I assumed that the police did that."

"I thought you might have wanted to make the call yourself, since you are . . . were . . . so close to Martina, and to Jeff. I always think these calls are best coming from a friend. That's all."

"I wouldn't have been comfortable delivering such awful . . ." she muttered, leaning forward and concentrating on the screen.

"So the police did it. But you gave them his cell phone number."

"Why would I do that?" She turned around and glared at me, as though my suggestion that she ought to have informed Jeff Pullman about his wife's death so that he didn't get the news from an impersonal policeman was somehow bizarre and shocking and a terrible imposition on her and that it was even more outrageous that I'd expected her to provide an appropriate phone number. "I gave them the home phone."

Honestly, you'd think the woman had just come in off the farm instead of working at least eighteen months in Washington, where everyone carries a phone everywhere. They've become such a de rigueur accessory that sooner or later we're going to have fashion phones and designer phones. Sports phones, dress phones, formalwear phones. *Oh, Thea,* I told myself, *don't get started. Stick to business.*

"Because that's the only way they could reach him," I said. "Jeff is never at home during a business day, not even on Saturday. We both know that. But he's never more than an inch from his cell phone."

She shrugged. "I just didn't think of it, that's all. I gave them the first number that came to mind. I'm sure it worked just fine."

She pulled up the menu for the seminars. Most of that material was in the conference program but her screens also had details on room capacity, room arrangements, and comments on special needs. She also had a contact person listed at the hotel who was in charge of the arrangements. "Okay, there's the seminar stuff. Now are you happy?"

I wasn't sure why it was supposed to make me happy. "You've spoken with the hotel about each of these things since you arrived?"

"Of course."

I thought about the twenty-five people left standing without tables at dinner. "And the room capacities? We've got four seminars and one hundred eighty people . . . so you need rooms that can hold at least fifty people."

She rested wearily on her elbow and gave me a sideways look. "I assumed that the hotel would . . ."

"Right. But after the fiasco at dinner last night, you know you can't make that assumption. You can't make any assumptions. You have to call Mrs. . . . . uh"—I leaned forward to check the name— "Nahman . . . and be sure we're in big enough rooms. It's called learning from experience. It's called anticipating."

She raised her head and thrust her chin toward the screen belligerently. "I don't know why you think you have to keep picking on me. I'm not stupid you know. I'm not a baby," she said with another flounce. "I'm a competent professional."

I'm amazed at the number of women who are accomplished flouncers. I don't know whether it comes naturally to them, or whether there was a flouncing course in junior high school that I missed. Maybe it's just that I'm tall and flouncing works better with smaller, more compact bodies. When you're five eleven, flouncing has an epic quality, a vastness that seems incongruous. Anyway, I've never done it. But Rory was a superb flouncer. She sighed aloud and rearranged herself on the chair, tapping some more keys and taking some notes on a pad.

The competent professional wasn't wearing a bra and her unusually dark nipples showed through the thin fabric. For that matter, much of her breast was exposed through the armholes as she moved around. Maybe I'd misjudged her. Maybe it was a nightgown. Maybe she really had put on a freshly pressed linen nightgown and earrings and bracelets and makeup and high-heeled sandals in the middle of the afternoon to take a nap. "Of course," I agreed. "So knowing that the hotel has screwed up once, you've checked on these . . . and?"

"And I haven't gotten around to it yet."

I checked my watch. "Well, you've got one hour. That's not a lot of time if they have to set up another room, post new signs. . . ."

She yawned, saluting, not covering the gesture with the back of her hand. "Not everyone's going to come to these anyway. We don't need that much room."

"You can't count on that. People have come a long way to attend this conference. They've been off playing all day. Now they're going to be feeling guilty and wanting to get back into a more serious mode. There may even be some local educators who've come for the day . . . we did issue an open invitation, didn't we? . . . which increases the numbers. And after what happened to Martina, we can't afford any more glitches. Things need to run smoothly."

"All right, goddamn it, you've made your point. I'll take care of it. We are not all as perfect as you are, Thea. We're not used to being up to our elbows in blood and gore. Some of us are still affected by things. Did you know that? Now, why don't you get the hell out of my room and leave me alone so I can work?"

I could hear my mother's chiding voice in my head saying, "Temper, temper," and knew if I said it it would aggravate Rory as much as it used to aggravate me. It took some willpower not to but I hadn't come here to pick a fight—even if she was being a hateful, self-centered little twit. I'd come here to do business.

"There's also the luau," I reminded her. "If you can print out the information about that for me, I can take care of those details while you check on the conference rooms."

Rory's reaction astounded me. "You're just like her," she yelled, shoving back her chair and jumping to her feet. "Just like Martina. Give me an assignment and then take it back because you don't think I can do a good job. Let me tell you something, Ms. Thea the Perfect Kozak. Martina wasn't the wonderful, competent, saintly woman you all think she was. She was mean and hateful and manipulative and a user! She didn't give a damn about real girls, just about ideas that she could use to get a lot of press. She was a drunken nymphomaniac. She was crazy as a coot." She burst into tears and fled into the bathroom.

I hoped whoever was in there was a comforting presence, since I seemed to be rather a laxative one. I sent everyone running for the john. I shook my head. Poor Rory. Here was a perfect opportunity to show the world what she could do, and how did she use it? She whined and fussed and made scenes and vanished. I slid into her chair, brought up her luau files, and printed myself copies. Then I left. Rory never reappeared.

CHAPTER 6

I TOOK THE stairs back to my own floor to do penance for my mean behavior. It's true that under stress I can be mean and there's no denying that being confronted with a strangled body first thing in the morning was stressful. Okay. Okay. I was being too flippant. There was nothing amusing about Martina's death, particularly when every time I closed my eyes I saw her face. I was just doing my best not to think too much about it and the way I avoid the awful truths of life is work.

Having Andre around helps. He keeps me more balanced. I eat meals. I get exercise. I can't work all the time. Much of it, but not all. But today he wasn't here. There was no one to massage the knots out of my shoulders or to remind me to breathe or to tell me that the rest of the conference organizers hadn't died and left me in charge. I'm compulsive. I'm obsessive. I'm a worrier. Where was that guy when I needed him?

They're always writing articles telling us professional women that we need to learn to manage our stress. We're supposed to find the time in our days for an hour of brisk exercise plus a wonderfully balanced, nutritious diet, plus all those calming cups of herb tea and aromatherapy, plus quality time with friends and family, etc. It was the etc. that always got to me. I figured the people who wrote the articles worked about two hours a day and had perfectly painted toenails. I managed stress by moving faster and being more aggressive.

As I was going downstairs, a rhyme popped into my head:

As I was going up the stair,
I met a man who wasn't there,
He wasn't there again today,
I wish, I wish, he'd go away.

I wished they'd all go away. I was tired. I wanted to lie down in my fancy linen sundress and take a nap, like Rory. Thinking about Rory meant thinking about Martina, and thinking about Martina led me to thinking about her husband, Jeff. I'd met Jeff Pullman a few times, at board functions and once or twice at other conferences, and I could never understand what had drawn them together. Jeff was one of those men who never seem to lose their boyish good looks. In his fifties, he could have been twenty years younger, and his disposition was as pleasing and appealing as his looks. I knew he had to be more than a fresh-faced all-American boy. He was a tremendously successful lobbyist. But he seemed totally honest and genuine.

He was fun to talk to. He had an enormous repertoire of funny stories. He had instant recall of his last conversation with anyone, regardless of how much time had passed. He was always up-to-date on current issues in education, all the inside the beltway gossip, and lots of other gossip as well. His eyes twinkled. He had a great smile. And he seemed to want everyone to have a good time. He was never grouchy or short with anyone. He gave the appearance of caring about people. A perfect paragon. I would never be attracted to someone without a few snags and edges—I like my men nice and complicated, moody and passionate and filled with obsessive enthusiasms—but I could see where he was an attractive package. What I couldn't figure out was why he'd been attracted to Martina unless opposites truly do attract.

A former assistant of Martina's named Olivia D'Angelo had put it very well when she'd said, "Martina wakes up in the morning with one idea in her head—herself—and spends the rest of the day trying to make everyone else share her idea." Once when I was telling Andre about Martina, he'd asked me why we put up with her if she was so impossible. My first answer was because we didn't have any choice. She was there, she was a fixture, she was just a difficult person we had to deal with.

It was also true that we had our own selfish motives. The rest of us on the board were interested in promoting the ideas, and exploring the issues, surrounding single-sex education. For Martina, single-sex education was inextricably linked with herself. As far as she was concerned, she was the patron saint of single-sex education in the United States. So I suppose that just as she used us, we used her. Lately, as her behavior got more erratic and her ego more insatiable, a rumbling movement in the troops had begun to discuss her ouster. But we'd been thinking about a board vote, not an assassination. And until now, we'd been too busy with our other lives to take any action.

But that brought me back to my questions. Why had a nice guy like Jeff ended up with a woman who was such a user? What had his ulterior motive been? Or was I just being overanalytical. Why couldn't it simply have been love? If what Shannon had said at lunch today was true, he had left his wife for Martina. What were—had been—her plusses? She was attractive. Smart in the same Washington insiders way that he was. She was rich. Well educated. Could be charming. Was eminently presentable. Maybe that was all. Maybe the first Mrs. Jeff had been a stolid little homebody next to whom Martina had seemed like the perfect mate for a lobbyist.

I pushed opened the door to the twelfth floor and headed for my room. Enough of idle speculation. Anyone would think that I was a gossip. I had work to do. Calls to make. Arrangements. Oh, joy! What I'd said to Andre seemed too true. I might as well have been in the Yukon in February for all the difference it made being in Hawaii. Maybe I'd skip the luau and go into town. Get a burger and walk the streets. Feel like I was on vacation. Except that I was one of the board members. I was here as a worker bee, a professional glad-hander. Besides, the people who were here were interesting. I was just feeling a need for some solitude.

At least I got to be all by myself for the forty-five minutes that it took me to track down the person responsible for the luau, a woman named Leilani Leland. Positively alliterative. Lovely and alliterative or not, it took seven phone calls to find her and telephone tag is one of my least favorite games. When I finally did get connected and explained why I was calling, she told me I didn't have to worry about a thing, everything was fine, all the arrangements taken care of. All in a voice designed to soothe the savage breast.

Once upon a time, I used to hang up at that point, reassured, like young Rory, that all was right with the world. Experience has taught me a lesson, so I said, "Let's just go over a few of the details, shall we?"

"Everything's fine, Ms. Kojak."

She couldn't get my name right and I was supposed to trust her with my conference? "I'm sure it is, but it won't hurt to check." She murmured a reluctant assent. "All right, now, you've reserved a private outside space for us on the beach side of the hotel, yes?"

"Yes. Certainly. We always use the same spot."

"Good. Now, let's check numbers. Last night, through some oversight, we had twenty-five guests left without tables at dinner. We can't have that happen again, can we?"

"I can assure you, tonight everything will be fine," she said. In her voice was the certainty that in her department, at least, things went right.

I went right on with my checking. The more cheerful the reassurance is, the more wary I get. "We have one hundred fifty conference attendees, plus one hundred guests, spouses, mostly, and thirty-five children. I make that two hundred eighty-five. Is that the number you have?" There was silence except for the rustling of papers, a sigh, some more rustling. Another sigh. With each rustle and sigh, my anxiety level rose. "Excuse me," I said. "Are you still there? Is something wrong?"

Another silence. Then she said, "According to the papers I have here, your group confirmed for two hundred people. That's the number we've given the kitchen."

Oh, great. Last night they'd forgotten twenty-five people.

Tonight it was eighty-five. Tomorrow they'd probably clean out our rooms and put our luggage in the street. I said, "No."

"Excuse me?"

"I said, no, not two hundred. It's two hundred eighty-five. And we did confirm, to you, in writing. I have a copy of a letter here, from the hotel. . . ." Rory might be irritating, but I blessed her for being so organized that not only had she confirmed the two hundred eighty-five number in writing, she'd scanned their reply letter right into her file, so I had a copy of it as well. Sometimes I hated technology. There were days when I longed to move to a cabin in the woods and grow beans, like Thoreau, but at times like this I thought technology was simply grand. "It's confirming two hundred eighty-five people for a luau this evening, signed on behalf of the hotel catering service by a Mr. Charles Thorsen."

There was another long silence. Actually, it wasn't quite a silence. What I heard, faintly but distinctly, was my sweet telephone contact saying "Oh, shit," followed by the sound of breaking crockery. Then she raised her voice, and I heard that quite clearly. "Can someone find that moron, Charlie, and send him in here. Pronto." Then she was back on the line, her voice simmering with honey. "It won't be a problem, Ms. Kojak. I assure you. Your two hundred eighty-five people will be well fed. Is there anything else I can do for you?"

"No. Thank you." I disconnected without even correcting her about my name. I didn't have the heart to ask whether there would be enough tables and chairs as well as food. I figured she'd take care of that while she was running around for the rest of the afternoon slaughtering coconuts, skinning pineapples, and husking chickens.

It was board policy for each of us to monitor one of the seminars, to be sure that what we said we were offering was what people got. I opened my appointment book to check on which one I was assigned to. Miraculous. I had the afternoon off. But before the devil could find work for my idle hands to do, there was a knock on the door.

When I opened it, the entire doorway was filled with brilliant color. Jonetta Williamson. Our missing board member. Person of color. Woman of size. She would have shamed a peacock. She was magnificent. "I just got in," she said. "I met Shannon in the lobby, pale and staggering after her bout with some feisty cop. She could barely speak. You want to fill me in?"

I stepped aside and let her sweep past. She settled herself in a chair. "Sorry I couldn't get here sooner. We had a missing student. Thirteen. Tiny little bird of a thing. I was dying of fear, imagining some wretched child fancier had snatched her. She disappeared between home and school, you see. Come to find out, she'd run away with her nineteen-year-old boyfriend, and there she is, nothin' more than a baby. They can't start prosecuting those guys for statutory rape soon enough for me. I'd like to string a few of 'em up by their balls right outside the schoolhouse door."

She fanned herself with her hand. "Don't they even have air-conditioning in this place? I am roasting."

"Oh, sure. I'll turn it on. I was on the phone the last hour, so I guess I didn't notice."

"Honey, you are always on the phone, it seems to me. You've got to start takin' it easy and let someone else do the work. You're never going to get your own school to run until you prove you can delegate."

"Truth is, Netta, I don't want a school to run."

She shook her head knowingly. "We'll just wait and see. Time you get around to wanting to marry and have some babies, it's gonna be mighty complicated trying to raise your kids when you spend half your life on an airplane and the other half on the phone. Babies cry on airplanes and as soon as you get on the phone, they go flush your purse down the toilet."

Unlike the rest of the board, who ran nice upper-middle-class establishments in nice upper-middle-class towns, Jonetta was out there on the line saving lives. Single-handedly she had secured funding and a building to start a school for poor black girls. As she put it, "All of you sigh and worry about a girl with good grades and her college money already in the bank gettin' left behind in physics because the boys are more aggressive and outspoken. I'm worrying about the girls with twenty-seven-year-old crack-addicted mothers who are likely to get pregnant and drop out of school, or join a gang and drop out of school, or just drift away because they've got no idea that school can do anything for them. I'm worryin' about the girls who may otherwise be dead or at a dead end if I don't help."

I thought a lot of what we did was important. Not only because we did it in private schools, but because the ideas were getting out and getting used and making a difference in lots of girls' lives. It was exciting to me to teach teachers new ways to help girls feel comfortable with technology, whether it was building bicycles or tackling computers, and it was fulfilling to know that because of what we were doing, many girls would have greater success at science and math. But Jonetta was the person I wanted to be when I grew up. Jonetta had a calling, a mission, and the courage and drive to see it through. I could argue with a caterer and win. Jonetta could argue with the mayor of New York.

The air-conditioning made an instant difference. Jonetta leaned back in her chair and smiled. "Well, good to see that something works. You got anything to eat?"

I passed her the room-service menu. "I'll call down and have them send up some sandwiches. What sounds good to you?"

"The shrimp and avocado salad. And the turkey club. Some fries would be nice, and I think after all the way I've come, that you'd better get me some of that banana cream pie, too." I picked up the phone and ordered everything. I also asked them to send up a pitcher of lemonade and some Maui potato chips. They actually taste just like Cape Cod chips to me, but maybe I'm being a regional chauvinist. I didn't care what they were called, they were good and I was craving salt.

That done, we got down to business. "So, Thea," she said, "you found her?" I nodded. "How did that happen?"

I told her about Rory banging on the door, and about the premeeting meeting being missed. "She was in a state and I knew she wouldn't let it alone until I did something, so I went up to Martina's room and banged on the door. When she didn't answer, we got security to let us in. And there she was."

"Can you tell me about it, or was it too awful?"

I hesitated, Nihilani's flat, cold voice in my ear, commanding me not to tell anyone about the crime scene. But Jonetta hadn't even been here, and anyway, I felt, at this point, desperate for someone I could talk to, and I'd always felt close to Jonetta. "I'm not supposed to talk about it. The cops . . . you know . . . they told me not to."

Jonetta rolled her eyes. "Thea, you know I didn't have anything to do with it. I wasn't even on Maui at the time." When I still hesitated, she said, "Must be some scary cops, to shut you up. Well, okay, what if I cross my heart and hope to die and swear I'll never, ever tell a soul?" I couldn't help but meet her smile. "And anyway," she added, "sometimes, when you've had a terrible experience, it helps to talk about it."

"Cross your heart?" I said, feeling foolish.

She nodded solemnly.

"It was pretty awful. She'd been strangled with her own stocking."

"Stocking?" Jonetta looked puzzled. "You mean, her panty hose?"

I shook my head. "I guess it won't make any sense unless I tell you the whole thing. She was lying on the bed, on her back . . . kind of like she'd been arranged. She was dressed in this absurd outfit—red bustier and garter belt and thong panties and black stockings. Red stiletto heels. And posed on the bed in a very suggestive way . . . and then that bloated, strangled face. . . ." Now I saw it all again too clearly. "It was ugly, Netta. Very ugly." I felt a chill that wasn't the air-conditioning.

She nodded, slowly taking it all in, then patted my arm. "I'm sorry you had to see that . . . but . . ." Her silence was long.

"But what, Netta?"

"I'm ashamed to say this," she admitted.

"But?"

"Better you than most people. Were there any witnesses?"

"Not that I've heard about. But it . . . her room . . . there was food as though she was expecting somebody."

"Any idea who?"

"None. Well, I don't think . . ." Now mine was the long silence.

"Come on girl, spit it out," she said.

"Last night she left the restaurant with Lewis Broder. . . ."

"That little weasel? No way. I might not have liked her, but the woman had taste. Look at that husband of hers. He's a fine piece of work."

"I know. But that's what I saw. . . ."

"You tell the cops?"

"They didn't ask."

"And of course you didn't feel like volunteering anything."

"It wasn't that. But if I told them about Lewis . . . where would I stop? She also had a fight with Rory last night. And for that matter, with me."

"I see what you mean. And then you'd have to go on to the whole board, I suppose."

"That's what Jolene said at lunch. That each of us probably has a Martina story we'd rather not have reported to the police."

She nodded. "No rumors floating around about suspects?"

"Either there are none, or we're all suspects. I don't know. You know how the police work. They pick your bones bare and leave you behind and never tell you anything."

"Oh, honey, do I ever! Given my school's constituent group, I've got gentlemen and gentlewomen from the constabulary in and out of my office daily. Some of 'em are human, but a lot of 'em came from central casting or they've been watching too much TV, or . . . I don't know. They won't tell you anything even if it might help them, you know what I mean."

"I know what you mean. I've spent too much time with cops myself. They have a way of working you over without even touching you." It was true that since my sister, Carrie's, death, I'd spent an inordinate amount of time in the presence of cops. Most of it with Andre, and while that had started as business, it was now mostly pleasure, except when he had one of his pig-headed moments of macho protectiveness, which he would characterize as my pig-headed moments of foolish feminist assertiveness. But there had been other cops, too, not nearly as attractive or personable as Andre. And basically, I don't like cops. I don't like authority figures. I don't like being told what to do.

"Yeah, I saw how Shannon looked," Netta said. "She's some mad at you for managing to escape."

"It's not like I didn't log in my time with the police." Her eyebrows went up. I told her the story of the stolen speech and the Cinderella shoe, the long grilling, the birthday flowers, and the cop's parting warning about not telling anyone anything, as well as his admonition not to make him mad.

She shook her head so vehemently her earrings jingled like wind chimes. "On your birthday?" She spread her arms wide. "Come here and have a hug, honey. You sure have had a bad day." I don't accept hugs from just anyone, but in my book, getting a hug from your hero, getting sympathy from someone who sees life's dark side all the time, is A-okay. I went and was hugged and felt comforted.

"I hardly dare ask," she said, "is everything else all right?"

"Well, this ultraluxurious hotel can't count. Last night we ended up with twenty-five people standing after we'd been seated for dinner, and the luau tonight would have been a disaster if I hadn't called. They'd taken our count of two hundred eighty-five and converted it to two hundred. I think they ought to give me a medal or something. After all, the eighty-five hungry, angry people would have been on their backs, not mine."

"Don't hold your breath. But why were you dealing with that stuff? Isn't that Rory's job? I notice you've barely mentioned Rory. Let me guess. . . ." She touched a fingertip to her forehead and closed her eyes. "Ah, yes . . ." Suddenly her rich voice changed to a perfect Scottish accent. "The puir wee thing has taken to her bed."

I laughed for the first time all day. "Exactly. Well, not exactly. There's something strange going on there."

"I'm not surprised. Working with Martina has made her nuts. What surprises me is that you didn't just give her a swat on the rear and tell her to buck up and get on with it."

"Oh, I did. Her getting on with it worked just long enough to get the files up on her computer. Then she declared that I was hateful and lacked empathy, burst into tears, and locked herself in the bathroom."

Jonetta gave a decisive shake of her head, setting her earrings ajingle again. "Hard to get good help these days." She giggled. "Listen to me! I'm almost as insensitive as you, aren't I? What about the rest of the crew? Shall I show you what a brilliant people person I am and tell you how everyone is behaving?"

"You could, but it's pretty predictable. . . ."

"Sure. Zannah is waxing eloquent. Shannon is ebullient and curious. Jolene is trying to keep the peace, and Rob is protecting himself with sarcasm. Right?"

"Damn, you're good. What does that mean you say about me?"

"And Thea's running around trying to fix everything."

"Double damn."

There was a knock at the door. "Wow," she said, "that was fast. Maybe if they can't count, they can at least cook."

I answered the door and there stood the cop again. Detective Kane Nihilani. I didn't think I'd done anything wrong, but someone must have. He didn't look like a happy camper.

CHAPTER 7

HE MARCHED INTO the room, looking like the wrath of God, and backing me before him like a leaf before the wind. "What were you doing outside Martina Pullman's room at one-thirty this morning?" he demanded.

"Nothing," I said. "I wasn't there."

"That's not what I hear."

I had no response to that. My experience with policemen investigating murders is that they like to play their cards close to the vest, whatever that means. To me, it meant that they liked to ask a lot of questions that I was supposed to answer frankly, totally, and honestly, without being allowed to know a goddamned thing about what was going on. To the old advice about never eating at a place called Mom's, never playing poker with a man named Doc, and never sleeping with anyone who's crazier than you are, I always add, and never let a cop put words in your mouth. Rephrase, qualify, and clarify, if necessary. And where no response is called for, give none. Some of Mother Kozak's rules for life. He was waiting and I wasn't even hissing softly, though that's what I wanted to do. Let him wait.

He was so intent on intimidating me that he still hadn't noticed Jonetta. Either as a courtesy or because she's not used to being invisible, at least not since she became a grown-up and found her voice, she jangled her earrings nice and loudly so he couldn't help but hear. He swung around like he'd been bitten and stared at her. "Excuse me, ma'am," he said. "I'd like to be alone with Ms. Kozak."

"Not on your life," she said. "You come in here yelling at that poor girl and bullying her, after the day she's had, and on her birthday, too, and you think I'm going to walk out and leave you alone with her? You must be crazy!" She got up and sashayed over, planted her hands on her hips, and looked him up and down like he was a tidbit presented for consumption. The she stuck out a hand. "I don't believe we've met. I'm Jonetta Williamson."

What else could he do? He took it. "Detective Kane Nihilani, Maui police. I don't want to be rude, but I do need to speak with Ms. Kozak alone. Police business."

"Why does she need to be alone?" Oh, man, I loved this woman. She did naturally and with ease things it would take me an afternoon of sweating to work myself up to. Maybe it came from dealing with cops every day.

"I'm investigating a . . . an incident in the hotel. Ms. Kozak is a valuable source of information."

She gave an eloquently disdainful sniff. "You're calling Martina's death an 'incident,' Detective? You make it sound so trivial. Personally, I don't find murder at all trivial. I find it depressing and shocking. I find it shakes the foundations of one's self, especially when you know the victim, as Thea and I did." She put a hand on his shoulder and pressed him into a chair. "You seem convinced that Thea isn't telling you the truth. In my experience, Thea is as honorable a young woman as you are ever likely to meet. Too honorable, if anything. I doubt if she'd lie to you. Once we've talked this over calmly, I'm sure a reasonable explanation will be found."

"As to honorable, I won't go into an incident this morning when she stole some papers from the victim's room. I'm not here to have a group discussion," he began. "I merely want to ask Ms. Kozak a few—" There was a knock at the door. "Ignore it," he said.

"Hardly," Jonetta said. "That's my lunch and I'm starving." She lumbered to the door and threw it open, admitting an admiring waiter pushing a small cart. "Thank goodness you've come," she said, "I was dying. Thea, you want to sign for this?"

I was happy to. I would have bought her the whole hotel in return for the past few minutes. The baffled look on the detective's face would stay with me for a long time. Of course, I knew he'd get me later, if he had the chance, but for now, I had a protectress as fierce as any lioness, and I was enjoying myself. I signed the slip, gave the waiter a generous tip, and closed the door. By the time I'd returned, Jonetta was halfway through her first sandwich, and Nihilani was staring in a puzzled way at the glass of lemonade in his hand.

Since the two chairs were taken, I sat on the foot of the bed and waited. He drank some lemonade, set the glass down, and tried again. "Where were you at one-thirty A.M. this morning?"

I patted the bed. "Here. Asleep."

"How do you know?"

"What do you mean, how do I know? I was asleep. All I can say is that I have no history of sleepwalking. No one has ever reported finding me out of my bed when I thought I was in it. And that's where I was when I fell asleep. Here in this bed."

"At what time?"

"About twelve-thirty."

"Alone?"

I bounced to my feet. "What kind of question is that? You talked with Andre earlier, right? Andre, the state police detective? Andre Lemieux, the man I love? The man I live with. You know I live with the guy, right?" If anything, he was looking even more surprised than when Jonetta had lit into him.

People make a lot of mistakes about me. People think, because I work hard and try to be agreeable, that I'm a pushover. People think, because I have a large chest, that I must be dumb. People think, because I'm young and attractive, that I'm sweet. People can be wrong. As my aunt used to say, I have quite a little temper. And here in Hawaii, the land of volcanoes, I was erupting. "You think I nipped off to Hawaii for a little something on the side, is that what you're asking?" Detective Kane Nihilani had pushed the wrong button. "What the hell is this, some kind of weird brotherhood thing? You think you ought to check up on me because he's a fellow cop? Just what are you suggesting with a remark like that? I thought you had a murder to investigate? So why the hell are you wasting both of our time trying to investigate an imaginary person in my bed. Don't you have better things to do?"

I had had a hard day. I'd endured the shock of finding a body, a wrestling match with Rory, the stress of having to give an important speech at the last minute, the duress of a lengthy police interrogation, I'd had a gruesome nightmare, much of the burden of running the conference had fallen on my shoulders, as well as a second unpleasant confrontation with Rory, and a struggle with the hotel's convention planners. I was in no mood to have a stranger marching in, yelling at me and accusing me of being a liar, and topping it off by accusing me of infidelity.

I walked over and opened the door. "Get out," I said. He didn't move. "I know you're not hard of hearing. I'm asking you to leave."

"Look, I'm sorry. I didn't mean it like that . . . I was just—"

"Oh, save it for some sweet young thing who still thinks cops are those nice people who help you cross the street on your way home from school. I wasn't born yesterday. I know you guys, remember? I know how you work. I know that you'll do any damned thing you can get away with if you think it'll help you solve a crime. I know the sorts of things you'll do to shock people into talking. I know you don't care about my feelings and it doesn't matter what you do to me . . . or to anyone else . . . if you think—"

In an unfortunate imitation of Rory, I burst into tears and fled into the bathroom. Thea Kozak. Professional woman. Tough as nails. Sitting on the edge of the bathtub, sobbing into a towel until I threw up. Welcome to Hawaii, vacation paradise. Was I having fun yet?

CHAPTER 8

AFTER A WHILE, sitting in there began to feel silly. It was my room, after all, there was no reason why I had to hide in the bathroom. At least they hadn't banged on the door and tried to get me to come out. For that I was grateful. I opened the door and went out, prepared to face whatever was waiting. No one was waiting. Jonetta's dishes were there, every scrap eaten. Nihilani had finished his lemonade. And they were gone. They hadn't even left a note. I sat on the edge of my bed and pondered. Who might have told Nihilani I was outside Martina's door at 1:30 A.M., and where would someone have gotten that idea?

The murder was ugly and it loomed large on my horizon. I would have given a lot to simply press an erase button and have the whole thing disappear from my memory. But despite the cops camped on my doorstep, and my very firsthand knowledge of the circumstances, there was a way in which I'd been able to treat it as not my problem. I hadn't felt any obligation to jump in and start trying to find out what happened. I was reacting to Martina's death like normal people do. Troubled, saddened, and shaken. A little nervous at the idea of a killer around. I had known her, so it affected me, yet it wasn't my job to figure out who had done it. My problem was that I had a history of getting drawn into murders. Violent death seemed to lurk in my path like a hidden tiger trap.

I'll be walking along, minding my own business and then boom, I've fallen right into the middle of it.

Okay. Okay. Jonetta said that I was an honorable person and honorable people, which is what I try to be, tell the truth. The truth was that I had deliberately involved myself in my sister, Carrie's, murder. I had pushed and pried and clawed and stuck my nose in where it wasn't wanted—almost getting myself killed, talk about cutting off your nose to spite your face—because I wasn't willing to let someone I had loved so much be discarded like a wad of used tissue. To this day, Carrie haunts me. I found her killer but I couldn't save my sister. Maybe we can never do enough for the people we love.

I like to think, though, that I've learned a few lessons from the violent deaths that have touched my life. Principal among them, to stay out of it. To continue to pursue my already overwrought, overfull, exhausting work life and leave murder and death to the professionals. That was my position on Martina's death. I would cooperate when asked, assuming I wasn't gratuitously insulted. I might bat my eyes and try to wheedle the name of the person who'd told them I was outside Martina's room out of the cops, because I can't stand it when people tell lies about me to try and get me into trouble, but otherwise I was staying out of it. I was determined to protect my sensitive, already-broken-one-time-too-many nose. Just thinking about it made my nose hurt. I rubbed the bridge ruefully and promised it, and the rest of my body, a nice, safe stay in Hawaii.

Getting mad, seething, steaming mad like I'd gotten at Nihilani, always leaves me in a shaken and drained postadrenaline state. A nap seemed like a good idea. I called the desk, told them to hold all calls, and asked them to wake me at seven. Then I took off my clothes, put on my nightgown, and got into bed, hoping I wouldn't dream.

I fell into a deep sleep so fast it seemed like my head had barely touched the pillow. I was falling and falling and falling. I opened my eyes and saw the balconies streaming past, the long trails of hanging plants, the astonished faces of people bending over and staring at me as I fell. Dream falling. Not plummeting but drifting, like a feather. It took forever to get down. And as I fell, things floated past me. A chair. A lamp. A suitcase. Shoes and belts and shorts and great, leisurely billowing skirts. A pert little red camisole flew by. Then a pair of red shoes. Red panties. A red garter belt, the garters snapping and jerking as they passed. One long, silky black stocking. I tried to wake up. I knew what was coming.

An icy hand clawed my arm, latched on. Clung. Martina's bulging eyes stared into mine. Hers were vacant, fixed. "What have you learned, Thea? What have you learned?" The icy claw pinched tighter. Tighter. Her face was up against mine, cold, horrible, the voice grating in my ear. I tried to push her away and couldn't. I landed, finally, and her body landed on top of me, stiff and sprawling, pinning me there, the purple face just inches from my own. "Get her off! Get her off!" My own screams woke me up. No. I don't sleepwalk but, boy, do I dream! I wouldn't wish them on my worst enemy.

I staggered into the bathroom and turned on the shower. There wasn't enough hot water in the hotel to warm me up. Half an hour later, my skin was boiled lobster pink and I still felt the chill. I pulled on a robe and went and sat on the bed, too tired to even think about the process of drying my hair. Everyone always says how lucky I am to have long, curly hair. They should only have to live with it. I regularly decide I'm going to chop it all off, but the truth is that even though it's more trouble than caring for sixteen cats, I like it, and Andre loves it. He likes me best, he says, when I'm wearing nothing but my hair. His own private Lady Godiva. Thinking about Andre was nice, but it led to thinking about Nihilani and his remark, and that reminded me of the rest of the day.

Endorphins. That's what I needed. A chemical lift. Running. I threw my hair into a thick braid, pulled on running clothes, zipped my room key into a secure pocket, and took the elevator to the lobby. There was a cement walk along the beach. I could go for miles. I had my Walkman. Bruce Springsteen and Tom Petty and a miscellany of other moving music. I put on my headphones, turned up the volume, and took off.

Five miles later I had sweated out at least a gallon of water and I felt great. Rubbery and breathless, but great. And alive. I no longer envied the little circling jet skis, throbbing like a band of chain saws, out on the water. I no longer envied the parasailers, trailing like human kites behind powerboats. I no longer envied the supine bodies, oiled and laid out in the sun to bake like peculiar loaves of bread. I felt the deep pleasure that comes from pushing a well-conditioned body hard.

That's what living with Andre had done to me. He loved jogging and going to the gym. And skiing and snowshoeing and biking and in-line skating and hiking and walking and playing catch and playing Frisbee and making love. The whole great physical morass. Four months with him and I had muscles on my muscles. I had the kind of back and arms and shoulders I used to admire on women in fitness magazines. I loved it. The trouble was, it took maintenance. Lately, since work always picks up as the school year ends and heads of schools and boards of trustees begin to be anxious about getting projects under way, I'd started feeling the pressure, and wondering if there was any way to exercise while sleeping, or to work while sleeping, or at least to read while sleeping. Sleep seemed to take up time I didn't have.

I was standing in front of the hotel, sweating and blowing and walking in small circles, like a cooling race horse, when a man approached. Very tall. Handsome in a raw-boned, edgy sort of way if you like lived-in faces. Early fifties, with a graying brush cut and very square shoulders. "Excuse me. Are you Thea Kozak?" Cautiously I admitted that I was. He probably thought he looked like Everyman, but to the trained eye, he had cop written all over him. I wiped my sweaty hand on my shorts and held it out. "Detective?"

He ducked his head, like a boy caught out. "Bernstein," he said. "Lenny. And don't you dare laugh. Been running?"

No, I thought, *I'm standing out here with a scarlet face and sweat-soaked clothes, panting and gasping, in an abbreviated costume no proper New Englander would be seen wearing, because I want to be noticed.* "Five miles," I said.

He looked me up and down with an eye that was appraising but not prurient. Now that I've been spending more time in gyms, I can see the difference. People who work on their bodies are interested in what other people are doing with theirs. It's more of an athlete thing, an "us versus them."

"You work out," he said.

I shrugged. "The guy I live with, he likes all this stuff. I keep him company."

"That's what I wanted to talk to you about," he said.

"The guy I live with?"

"And about Detective Nihilani." He pointed to an empty bench. "Would you like to . . ."

"I'd rather walk, if you don't mind. I'm not quite ready to sit."

"Of course," he said. "No problem." Together we strolled back to the walk along the beach, heading in the opposite direction from the way I'd run, so that the sun was at our backs. "Is this your first trip to Hawaii?" he asked. I said it was. "How are you enjoying it?"

"You're kidding, right? I barely get out of the hotel. This isn't a vacation. It's work. As I'm sure the other detective told you, I'm one of the conference organizers, and a member of the board of the National Association of Girls' Schools, which is sponsoring the conference."

He nodded. "Yes, he did tell me that." He hesitated. "I'm sorry things got onto a wrong footing this afternoon. Detective Nihilani didn't mean to be insulting. He only meant was there someone with you, someone you were meeting with, perhaps, who might have been able to corroborate your whereabouts?"

It was sort of an apology, I supposed. "I had already told him that I was in bed, asleep. That's when he asked me if I was alone." Suddenly a big red warning light in my brain began to blink. He might be attractive and companionable, but he was still a cop. I screeched to a halt so fast my shoes squeaked on the pavement. He was several paces ahead before he noticed that I'd stopped.

"What's the matter?" he said.

"Do I need a lawyer?" I asked.

His expression was adorably puzzled. "What do you mean?"

I rolled my eyes. "Let's just skip the games, Detective. I don't know whether you and Nihilani are playing good cop, bad cop, or whether they sent you because they thought that charm might succeed when blunt force hadn't. That's your business, not mine. But you just said Nihilani was looking for someone to corroborate my whereabouts at a particular time. Your words, not mine, but to the innocent layperson's ear, the suggestion that my presence needs corroboration smacks of alibis and suspects. And since the person whose word seems to need corroboration is me, I can only suppose that means I'm a suspect. If I'm a suspect, you should be warning me about that and I shouldn't be talking to you without a lawyer, right?"

He didn't say anything. "What's the magic word switch here, Detective? Something about when the conversation switches from interview to interrogation, it's time to give the subject a Miranda warning?" I waited for his response.

He looked uncomfortable. "Please, Ms. Kozak, you're blowing this all out of proportion. We just asked you if—"

"If I can prove I was in my room alone and asleep at one-thirty A.M. Which leads me to suppose that that's when Martina was killed, although you won't, of course, tell me anything. I don't see that I have any choice here. You won't tell me if I'm a suspect, yet you ask and expect me to be able to answer impossible questions." I brushed my hands together in a dismissive gesture. "I have only one thing to say to you, which is this—I had nothing whatsoever to do with Martina Pullman's death. End of conversation. If you wish to speak with me in the future, please schedule an appointment so that I can arrange to have an attorney present." I turned and walked away.

He came after me, planting himself in my path so that he blocked my progress and invaded my personal space. "Look, you're making all of this much too hard. We just want to talk to you. Now, we can do it the easy way, and have a nice cooperative little talk here at the hotel, or we can bring you down to the station and do it there." He leaned in, his face now grim and menacing.

The woman from the room next door was passing, the one who had stared at me from her balcony. She was staring at me again, obviously wondering what was going on. "Excuse me," I said to her. "Could you come here for a minute?" Lenny Bernstein's breath hissed out through his teeth. If looks could kill, I would have been the day's second casualty. She came over. "This man," I said, pointing at Bernstein, "is from the Maui Police Department. He's being threatening and abusive and he's frightening me. Could you just stand here and be a witness to what he says, because I don't know what to do. Since he is the police, I can't call the police and ask for help, can I?"

The woman looked worried and plucked anxiously at the hem of her shirt. "Well, I don't know if I should. . . ."

"You shouldn't," Bernstein said angrily. "You shouldn't be interfering in police business. You should go away and let me finish my conversation with Ms. Kozak. Nothing is going to happen to her if she just cooperates." It was about what I'd expected he'd say, and it had the desired result.

"What if she doesn't cooperate?" the woman asked in a shaky voice.

I tucked my arm through hers, like we were bosom buddies. "Yes," I echoed, "what if I don't cooperate? I've already cooperated for several hours today, haven't I? Are you going to arrest me?"

"What am I going to do with you?" he said through clenched teeth. "All I want is the answers to a few questions."

"I wish it were that simple," I said. I turned to the woman and dropped my arm from hers. "I'm sorry. I didn't mean to involve you in this. It wasn't fair. It's only that I didn't know what to do. He's the second policeman to come and ask me where I was at one-thirty in the morning. When I told the first one that I was in bed, asleep, at twelve-thirty, he asked me if I was alone. Now this one comes along and asks if I have anyone who can corroborate my story that I was in bed asleep at that time. How do you prove you're in bed alone in the middle of the night? So I asked him if I needed a lawyer and he got very belligerent and when I tried to walk away, he came after me and threatened to arrest me." I knew I was being wicked and manipulative, but Bernstein's use of the word "corroborate" had really spooked me. If my whereabouts weren't a big deal, why were they being so persistent?

"That's all right, dear," she said, patting my arm. "Here comes Eddie. He'll know what to do."

"This is all totally unnecessary," Bernstein said.

"You're probably right, dear," the woman said. This time she patted Bernstein's arm. I was surprised that he didn't say something rude. His face was positively choleric. "Eddie! Eddieee!" She called his name and waved. He gave a brief return wave to indicate his assent.

The approaching Eddie was middle-sized, middle-aged, and portly. His glasses and a slightly abstracted look gave him a scholarly air. He walked with a slight limp. He was wearing one of those awful Hawaiian sport shirts enthusiastic women buy their husbands, the ones with the matching swimming trunks. His were an unnatural shade of bright blue with palm trees and hula dancers and neon green and yellow leis. Despite the ridiculous clothes and the excess weight, he looked perfectly content. A man at peace with life and himself. And I would have bet a bushel of doughnuts that he was cop. Small-town police chief. Or if not cop, at least cop related.

He arrived blissfully unaware of the mess his wife was about to involve him in, saying, "What's this, Marie? I thought you were going upstairs to get another book?" To us he added, "Marie is the world's biggest mystery fan. She goes through them like bonbons." Then he stuck out his hand. "Ed Pryzinski."

Bernstein's reaction was as strange as everything else had been today. I'd expected him to give Pryzinski a brusque brush-off. Instead, he got a strange, kind of awed expression on his face. Then he seized Pryzinski's hand and pumped it vigorously. "Dr. Edward Pryzinski? Author of *Pryzinski's Principles of Investigative Practice*, *Crime Scene Management*, and *Don't Touch That Body unless You Use Your Head?* That Edward Pryzinski?"

The woman beamed and patted her husband's arm, "See, Eddie," she said, "you're famous. Eddie's here to address the annual Maui Policeman's Banquet. He's the keynote . . . oh . . ." Her face fell. "That's you, isn't it?"

"What seems to be the problem?" Pryzinski asked. "Officer . . . uh . . . ." At least, like me, he could spot 'em.

"Detective. Lenny Bernstein, Maui police. Homicide."

"Homicide!" Marie gasped. "Surely you don't think this nice girl has killed someone? Why, just this morning, I saw her saving someone." Normally I bristle at being called a girl, but right now, I was too grateful for Marie's help to be upset.

"The problem?" Pryzinski repeated.

"I just want to ask the woman a few questions."

Ah, at least *he* didn't call me a girl. Cops have so many lessons in political correctness these days that between those constraints and cop speak, it's a wonder they can communicate at all. "Dr. Pryzinski," I said, "you may or may not know that a woman was murdered here in the hotel last night. A woman who was a colleague of mine, who was chairing the conference on Girls and Single-Sex Education. Evidently someone has told the police that they saw me near the woman's room at around one-thirty A.M. It isn't true. I wasn't there, but someone has said so, and twice today I've been interrogated by police officers demanding that I somehow prove to them that I was in my bed, asleep, at the time in question."

I took a deep breath. Dr. Pryzinski had a nice, fatherly face. I wouldn't mind having him on my side. "The first detective, knowing full well that back home in Massachusetts I am—" I searched for a discreet way of putting things. Both "living with" and "boyfriend" weren't very flattering choices—"involved in a serious relationship with a state police detective . . . asked me whether I was alone in bed or whether I had someone with me who could attest to the fact that I was in bed asleep." I lowered my eyes demurely. "I'm afraid I found the question so insulting that I asked him to leave and then this—this—person"—I pointed at Bernstein—"this person comes up to me when I'm just cooling down from a five-mile run, acts all nice and friendly, and suddenly he's saying that they need to 'corroborate' my statement that I was alone in my room in bed. Now, first of all, I haven't a clue how anyone goes about proving they are alone in their room asleep, but second, and more important, I found his use of the phrase 'corroborate my whereabouts' very unsettling. It sounded accusatory to me, his talking about suspects and alibis. So I asked him if I was a suspect and if I needed a lawyer, and that's when he became threatening and said he'd have to take me down to the station if I didn't cooperate."

I could see that I had the doctor's attention, and Marie was giving Bernstein dirty looks. "I should back up and say that I've already given about two hours of 'cooperation' to the police today, despite the trauma of having been the person who found the victim . . . that I'm very tired and upset . . . much of the responsibility for running the conference has now fallen on my shoulders . . . and I would just like to have the police deal with me honestly instead of these devious inquisitions."

Damn Bernstein. I'd just wasted all those lovely endorphins that were supposed to make me feel good coping with the threat of his suspicion. Now I was a jittery wreck again, and on the verge of tears besides. I'm not given to weeping, or emotional firestorms of any sort. No PMS, no mood swings. I'm a delightfully stable professional woman with a clear head and stamina and plenty of drive. And I felt an inexplicable desire to throw myself into Marie's motherly arms and sob.

"I'm afraid I didn't get your name," the doctor said.

"Kozak. Thea Kozak."

"Thea. What a nice name," Marie said. "Is it short for something?"

"Theadora."

"Well, Theadora. I think if you and the detective come into the bar with me and Marie, and we have ourselves a few of those nice piña coladas they make so well here, we can work this whole thing out," Dr. Pryzinski said.

"I can't drink. I'm working," Bernstein said.

"We'll ask for yours without alcohol," the doctor said with a wink.

"But I can't go into the bar dressed like this," I said. Abbreviated shorts and a sweat-soaked tank top were not my idea of the proper garb for a nice hotel bar.

"This is Hawaii," the doctor said. "Pretty much anything goes, but if you'll be more comfortable, Marie would be happy to pop upstairs and bring down one of those muumuu things. She's got one in every color. You wouldn't mind, would you, dear? That teal-colored one, I think. It would suit Thea's coloring."

And thus it was that I was kidnapped and spirited off to the bar for my second round of drinks of the day. Draped in a borrowed muumuu and soothed with alcohol while Ed Pryzinski tried to persuade Detective Bernstein that I wasn't a lethal criminal. I was going to have a monumental headache by bedtime.

CHAPTER 9

IT WAS A rich, velvety black night filled with a warmth and mystery that reminded me of late June in New England, of prom nights and graduation and staying up till dawn, of steamy windows and snuggling in parked cars with the radio on. The patio where we were having our luau was surrounded by shrubbery, rendering it private and secluded. At intervals, tall torches spouting leaping flames stood above the bushes. Drums beat, subtle yet insistent, in the background. The buffet tables, which hadn't yet been opened to the crowd, were heaped with a fabulous feast of barbecued meats and chicken and shrimp, masses of delectable fruits and salads. It looked like my honey-voiced contact in the conference office hadn't let me down.

Though most of the guests now knew of Martina's murder, the mood was upbeat, sustained by the festival atmosphere and the trays of hors d'oeuvres and rum punch that had been circulating for the last hour. All the guests had been greeted by hula-skirted lads and maidens who had dropped flowered leis around their necks and by servers with trays of punch. Up on the stage, a handsome Hawaiian in the world's gaudiest shirt was emceeing a karaoke contest. In the spirit of fun, Shannon, Zannah, and Jolene were acting as the backup shoop-shoop girls while Rob belted out an Elvis song.

I had been asked to join them and declined. It felt like I'd spent enough of the day on stage. Now I was beginning to regret my decision as I found myself cornered by two large ladies in peach-colored sheaths. The Elliot sisters. Identical twins who, in their sixties, still dressed alike, did their hair alike, and even wore identical jewelry. "What's the inside story on Martina?" Ann Elliot asked.

"Yes," her sister, Jan, chimed in. "We were sure you would know."

"I know everyone must be terribly curious," I said, "but I'm afraid the police have asked me not to talk about it. You know how it is with an investigation. It's important to keep the details a secret so that they know when they've actually found the . . . kill—uh . . . perpetrator."

Jan nodded. "Just like on television. Can't you tell us anything?"

I considered. I don't like being a gossip. On the other hand, the Elliot sisters *loved* to gossip. If I gave them a tidbit, they'd immediately be off to spread it around the room. And I'd be free. I told them something I was sure would be in the papers by morning. "She was strangled," I said. I didn't tell them about the stocking, or the costume, or the untouched feast for two.

"Of course, we're all so sorry," Jan said. "I can't imagine who might replace her. No one has, uh, had . . . a better command of the issues than Martina. I wonder how her husband is doing. He isn't here tonight, is he?" She craned her head around, checking the crowd one last time. "No. I don't suppose he would be."

"He wasn't with her," I said.

"Are you quite sure?" Ann said, raising her eyebrows. "I thought I saw him in the lobby last night."

"I understand that the police spoke with him at home in Washington this morning," I said. "He was going to get the next flight out."

"Oh, my sister," Jan said. "All handsome men look the same to her. She swears she saw Paul Newman in Chicago once, and Harrison Ford at a car rental counter. That's what she says. I can't believe Harrison Ford has to rent his own car."

"Just because I notice them," Ann said, "that doesn't mean I can't tell them apart. But it was at a distance, and rather dark. Maybe it was Tom Cruise. Or Dennis Quaid. One of those handsome, dark-haired Hollywood types. Yes, now that I think of it, I'm sure it was Tom Cruise. But the woman with him wasn't Nicole Kidman. She's going to be very upset when she hears my story, isn't she?" She linked her arm through Jan's. "Come along, sister. We'd better get some more of this punch before it's all gone." They strolled off.

"So," a voice behind me asked. "They pry any good gossip out of you?"

"I told them Martina's killer is the same person who sank the *Titanic*. They went away to spread the word."

"Well done. I hope Nihilani hasn't been back to bother you."

"He sent his brother, Lenny. Leonard Bernstein."

Jonetta muttered a lengthy and creative expletive. We stood side by side, watching the ladies up on the stage. "Why aren't we up there with them?" she asked. "Making fools of ourselves like conference organizers should."

"I was offered the opportunity. I declined. What about you?"

"I was hiding," she said. "They couldn't find me. I don't sing until I'm good and drunk. Then I shake the rafters." She looked up at the clear night sky. "Or the stars."

I smiled. There weren't too many places that a six-feet-two black woman who weighed over three hundred pounds, dressed in what looked like a cascade of hula hoops trimmed with crocheting, could hide. "Pretending to be a flowering kale?"

"Centerpiece," she said. "I was hiding among the pineapples and ribs."

"Speaking of which, there they go." There was a moan of pleasure from the crowd as they surged toward the food. "How'd you get Nihilani to leave, anyway?"

"Batted my eyelashes and shook my booty. You want to sit somewhere? My feet are killing me." We retreated to a table in a back corner where a diligent waitress immediately appeared and offered us rum punch. Whooee! The hotel was certainly making an effort to keep us cheerful. I declined, having already had my share of alcohol for the day, but Jonetta happily took both mine and hers. We settled back in our chairs. Things seemed to be going well, though I wasn't going to breathe easily until everyone was served and seated. Something could still go wrong. "Actually," she said, "he was so embarrassed at the mess he'd made of things, he was happy to escape. Behind that scary exterior he's not a bad guy."

I leaned back and looked up at the stars. "Pretty night. With all this going on, it's hard to remember that it was only this morning we found Martina."

"You can't be dwelling on that, Thea."

"So far, I haven't been given a choice."

"Look around you. These people are really having fun. Oh, and I went around to the seminars this afternoon. A dynamite bunch of speakers. If people don't go home from this thinking it's the best conference they've ever attended, they should have their heads examined."

"Any feedback from the field trips?"

"You mean their adventures in paradise? A few of the Mt. Haleakala crew got carsick. One or two of the ones who took the bike trip down got skinned knees. The Napali coast crew loved it but a few of them got carsick, too. Maybe tomorrow we should put Dramamine on the breakfast menu. The snorkelers were all happy except for one who complained that they'd been promised sea turtles and didn't see any. I don't know. I suppose they think the tour operators go out at dawn and sprinkle turtles and other wildlife about. And these are supposed to be the smart people. You've got to wonder sometimes."

I sighed. I'd come to the luau still worked up from the trials of the day, feeling totally unfestive and weary. I'd done my best to get into the spirit of the occasion by wearing a long, flowery sundress and letting my hair down. I'd even taken a rose from Andre's bouquet and pinned it in my hair, and the scent had been drifting across my face ever since like tiny reminders of the good things in my life. Now, sitting here, the night was working some kind of a spell. It ought to have been totally hokey—the artificially fueled torches and the canned drumbeats and the faint scent of Sterno and the karaoke. But the sky was vast and lovely, the air was gentle and perfumed with flowers, and in the distance, there was the resonant sound of waves on the beach.

"I could grow to like this," I said.

"You?" Jonetta laughed. "It would be a total waste to put someone like you in paradise. You'd see the light of day so rarely it wouldn't matter if the sun shone and the balmy breezes blew."

"Hey, this is the new me. I've reformed. Since Andre came to Boston, I've been outside plenty. I've run through rain and sleet and snow. I've skied in rain and sleet and snow and ice. I've skated on—"

"Girl, you've got a twisted notion of fun, you know that? You gonna marry that guy?"

"Questions like that give me palpitations."

"So, we'll talk about something else. Did you know that Martina's husband's first wife is here?"

"Someone said something at lunch but I didn't quite follow it. She's not at the conference, is she?"

"Oh, but she is. I guess when they divorced she was pretty much a homebody, but part of the deal was that he get her a good job. He used his connections . . . that man has more connections than a New York drug dealer . . . and got her a job in the Department of Education. And through some personal perverseness, she's made single-sex education her special area."

"I hadn't heard."

"She's here somewhere. I'll point her out if I spot her. She doesn't go by Pullman. She took back her maiden name, so she's Janovich, Linda Janovich. Anyway, until recently, she was very quiet. In the past year, she's surfaced. She's been at the last two conferences I've attended. Not making any waves. Not calling attention to herself. Just sitting there where Martina is sure to notice. She doesn't say anything. Just sits there and smiles. It drives . . . it drove . . . Martina nuts. I hear they had words in the lobby last night."

"Looks like Martina managed to have words with a lot of people. Me. Rory. Her husband's ex-wife—"

"Drusilla Aird . . ."

"Her, too? How'd you hear that?"

Jonetta grinned. "I get around."

"She have words with anyone else?"

"Well, I wasn't here, so I've escaped the list. What did the two of you argue about?"

"Rory, treatment of. Martina had been drinking."

"What's new?" Jonetta said.

"And she was being loud and obnoxious." Sotto voce, Jonetta murmured "What's new" again. "Rory was trying to get her to quiet down, to stop calling attention to herself, to not, as Rory put it, 'embarrass the conference.' Martina called her a sneaky little guttersnipe in front of the whole bar and told her go upstairs and collate papers or something, since that's all she was good at. Rory fled in tears and when Martina went to the ladies' room, I grabbed her, dragged her down the hall to a place where I thought we wouldn't be seen, and told her to get a grip on herself and start behaving like a responsible adult."

"I'll bet she took it well from you."

"Yep. She suggested I try some anatomically impossible activities and then she said I couldn't fool her, she knew what I was trying to do."

"Which was?"

"That Suzanne and I were trying to take over the board as a way of getting a higher profile and more business for our consulting group. She said she knew we were behind the conspiracy to throw her out." I pushed back the hair that was blowing into my face. Up on stage, Rob and the shoop-shoop women finished a song to a roar of applause.

"Jonetta, up to that point, I didn't know she had any idea of what the rest of the board was thinking, but she was on a tear . . . you know how she could be . . . so angry she was practically foaming at the mouth, and getting more obscene every minute. She said that she was chairman for life or until she decided otherwise, and that any change she didn't want would happen only over her dead body."

"Hot damn!" Jonetta said. "And who do you think overheard that and reported it to the police? That's got to be why they've been breathing down your neck."

"I guess I'm not very good at math," I said.

"What's that mean?"

"It means I didn't put two and two together until just now."

"So you don't know who saw you?"

"I didn't think anyone had but Zannah said something about it at lunch today so I guess I was wrong. And if Zannah and Shannon and Jolene and Rob all know . . ." I trailed off. No need to state the obvious. The tables around us were filling up and the noise level had reached the point where talking was almost impossible. "What do you think? Shall we get some food?"

"You know me," she said, heaving herself to her feet. "I never say no to food. Looks good, doesn't it?"

We left our drinks there to secure our places and threaded our way among the tables to the buffet. There were only about twenty people ahead of us. I could already smell the food, and after my run, I had a healthy appetite. Just like I only have two speeds, I seem to have two states of hunger: indifferent or famished. Suddenly I was impatient with the pace at which things were moving. I wanted to shout at them to hurry up because I was hungry, but the line seemed paralyzed. No one was moving. I stepped sideways and looked ahead to see what the problem was, expecting, with a sinking feeling, that it was because they'd run out of food. It wasn't.

In the space ahead, where the line should have been moving sedately along the food tables, two women were squared off like boxers in a ring. As I watched, one of them grabbed a fistful of grilled shrimp and threw it at the other. The other woman picked up a pineapple and heaved it. The rest of the group seemed paralyzed, watching them. I turned to Jonetta. "If we don't stop them, they're going to toss away our dinners."

"Right," she nodded. "Let's go."

Together we pushed our way through the crowd to the combatants, just as one picked up a whole platter of ribs, about to heave it at her opponent. I sprang forward, grabbed the tray, and slammed it back on the table. "What do you think you're doing?" I yelled. Instead of answering, she picked up a huge wooden candlestick and charged at the other woman. The other woman seized a lethal-looking fork and they dove at each other.

You would have thought Jonetta and I had played college football the way we tackled those gals. I went for the brunette with the wooden candlestick. Just like Clue. The tall brunette with a candlestick at the luau. The plump blonde with a serving fork on the patio. Jonetta took her woman down in one neat tackle, hula hoops flying and all that crocheted fringe jiggling. I had a little more trouble. My brunette was wearing a tight, silky number that made her as slippery as an eel. Hard to get a grip on. I got her down but couldn't keep her pinned and finally ended up having to sit on her. It was about as undignified as it could get. All the while, the two of them kept cursing at each other like a pair of hookers in a lockup.

Over the din, Jonetta leaned toward me and winked. "Something I've been meaning to put on our agenda, Ms. Kozak," she said. "The increase in fighting among girls. It's getting to be quite a problem." Despite the awkwardness of our situation, I had to laugh.

We were rescued at that moment by the arrival of two men in Hawaiian shirts and leis, flashing hotel security identification. Neither of us minded handing our charges over to them and letting them lead the two cursing women in opposite directions to calm them down. Neither of them had uttered a single phrase that was printable but neither of them had said anything worth saving for a rainy day, either. I was disappointed. I'm a great fan of creative cursing.

Jonetta dusted off her dress, planted her hands on her hips, and said to the staring group. "Come on, eat, will ya? We're hungry." Obediently, the line started moving. As we moved back to our places, she gave me a high five. "Well done, girlfriend."

"Who were they? Did you know either of them?" I asked.

She looked surprised. "You didn't recognize them?" I shook my head. "The tall brunette, the one you took down, was Linda Janovich, formerly Linda Pullman. The other woman was Drusilla Aird."

"I thought Drusilla Aird was a redhead?"

"That was last year and twenty pounds ago."

Now some of the things they'd been saying to each other made sense. Stripped of embellishments, each had been accusing the other of the capital crime of killing Martina before she could do it herself. Each claimed that she had had more right, or been more wronged. Each was furious about a missed opportunity. Or so they claimed. And where were the cops when they were needed? Both Bernstein and Nihilani would have found the encounter most enlightening. But they were probably at the Maui Policeman's Banquet, listening to a lecture by Dr. Pryzinski.

"Well, we almost got through this event without incident. Soon as I eat, I guess I'd better sing to these people and settle them down."

"Oh, I think there will be some nubile maidens clad in bits of grass to entertain us. They'll be a good warm-up act for you. Should I ask the guy to get that started?"

"Get yourself some food first," she said. She looked around. Everyone seemed to be tucking into their plates with gusto. "Folks sure are funny. Best fight I've seen in all my years of going to conferences, and it doesn't look like too many people even noticed."

I took enough food to feed the tackle I'd just been and carried it back to my spot. Shannon, Jolene, and Zannah were waiting for us. "What was that all about?" Shannon asked before I could even sit. "Wasn't that Drusilla Aird?"

"And Linda Janovich?" Zannah added. She had a pinched and worried look that reminded me that I wasn't the only one having a bad day. "I knew something bad would happen the moment I saw her in the lobby."

"But last night, when she and Drusilla were in the bar, they acted like the best of friends," Jolene said. "I wonder what happened?"

"Each of them seems to believe the other killed Martina, thus depriving her of the pleasure. Or something to that effect," I said, picking up a rib. I bit into it. Heavenly. But they were juicy and I only had one napkin. I flagged down a passing waiter and asked for more. Across the table, Jonetta was busily engaged in reducing the mound on her plate to rubble. We wanted to eat, the others, having already eaten, wanted to talk.

"Shannon," I said, "maybe you should ask the emcee, or whatever he's called, to get this show on the road. I don't want to give people time to sit around talking about the fight. It's been perfect so far. Let's keep the momentum going." Perfect. An ironic choice of words. But then, it seemed sinful to even think about having a good time, under the circumstances, and yet we all were. Not our good time. Theirs.

"Good idea," Jolene said. "I'll take care of it." She slipped away, deftly threading her way among the tables. I saw her onstage, whispering in the man's ear, and it seemed like only seconds later that he was announcing the beginning of the next phase of entertainment and the drumbeats got louder.

"This food is wonderful!" I said.

"At least they didn't screw up like they did last night."

"Thanks to Thea," Jonetta said.

"When I called them, they'd undercounted by eighty-five people," I said.

"That Rory," Shannon began. "If she'd just do her job. . . ."

"She gave them the right count. I saw the correspondence. It was the hotel that screwed up. But they have more than made up for it."

But Shannon was on a tear. "Well, she didn't follow up on the rooms, you know, and the hotel had us set up in two adequate rooms and two so small you couldn't have fit a mouse convention in them. It was touch and go whether we'd get everything rearranged in time, and then the program had been printed with the wrong rooms in it, so we had to stand there and direct everyone to the right rooms. And Rory wasn't a bit of help. Tell them, Jo."

Jolene said, "When I went to speak with her about it, she said too bad, she was sick, we'd just have to manage on our own. It took me half an hour to talk my way into the room and cajole her into agreeing to try and pull herself together and finish the conference. And she only agreed to that after so much sweet-talking I felt like a cotton-candy machine. I realize this has been difficult for her—she was very close to Martina—but she knows the conference still has to go on. As an educator, I shouldn't say this, but sometimes I worry about what's going to happen to the world when so many of our young people don't seem to have any of what my mother would have called 'guts and gumption.' This attitude that says 'To hell the rest of the world, let chaos reign, I need to pay attention to my own feelings right now' truly scares me."

Maybe the reason I liked Jolene so much was because we shared a common prejudice. My reaction to Rory had been the same. "Is she here tonight? I haven't seen her."

"She said she wasn't up to seeing people. She was going to have a quiet supper in her room and then get some sleep. I asked her if she could give me the backup information about tomorrow. I thought if we'd had two screwups we could probably count on more. She said she'd get to it and leave the information for me at the desk and would I please go away and leave her alone, she'd been hassled enough by our group." She looked at me. "I assume she meant you, Thea?"

"Oh, I'm a world-class hassler, Jolene. Ask anyone. Did you get the information?"

"Not yet." Jolene folded her hands demurely in front of her. "But if it isn't at the desk after dinner, I'm going to demonstrate that even a quiet old library lady like myself can do a bit of hassling when necessary."

"Mind if I join you ladies?" Rob Greene pulled out a chair and sat down. "I couldn't help myself," he said, pointing at his heaping plate. "I had to have seconds. I have to admit I was pleasantly surprised. I wasn't expecting much from a canned luau."

"Guess I'll follow your example," Jonetta said. "That was a nice snack, but if I'm going to have to keep sorting things out physically, I've got to keep up my strength."

Rob stared after her, a puzzled look on his face. "What's she talking about?"

I could have hugged him. If Rob, who didn't miss much, had missed our spectacular assault on the ladies' food fight, that meant most of the others had probably missed it, too. It was the best news I'd had all day.

"Why, Rob," Shannon drawled, in a deliberate imitation of herself. "You didn't see Jonetta and Thea break up that fight in the dinner line? Why, Ahv nevah seen anything lahk it. Spectaculah, darlin.' Were Ah you . . ." She reverted to her normal voice. The drawl just took too long to say anything. "I wouldn't cross either one of them. They are two dangerous ladies."

But Rob wasn't listening. Up on the stage, lovely young women were making their hips do extraordinary things. "How do they do that?" he muttered.

"Practice," Zannah said. "I took a belly dancing course once." We all stared. Zannah was a petite size 2 who would never top one hundred pounds. She barely had hips, never mind a belly. "You'd be amazed at what you can learn to do. . . ." She trailed off, staring at something behind me. "Would you look at that!"

I turned. A dead-drunk Rory in a skintight scarlet dress was teetering toward us on skyscraper heels, clutching a bunch of papers. Her makeup had been applied with such an unsteady hand she looked like a caricature, a dreadful Liza Minnelli clown face. When she got within about ten feet, she stopped and heaved the papers at us, scattering them all over the ground. "There, bitches," she said loudly. "You've got what you want. Now leave me alone." She turned and started to weave her way back through the crowd. Despite the dancers on stage, everyone was staring.

"Go after her, Rob," Jolene whispered. "Don't let her make a fool of herself."

Rob hurried after her, whispered something, and tucked her arm through his. By the time they'd reached the path through the hedge that was the exit, he was half carrying her.

"I wonder what life does for an encore?" Shannon said. We didn't have to wait long to find out.

CHAPTER 10

I HAD JUST sunk my teeth into a succulent grilled shrimp when someone slapped a hand down on my shoulder so hard I almost inhaled it. The shrimp, not the hand. The hand lifted and Lewis Broder landed in the seat beside me. He smelled of alcohol and tobacco and he was breathing both into my face with every angry exhalation. The look on his face would have frightened babies. I considered running away. I already knew I wasn't interested in what he had to say and that whatever it was, it wasn't going to please me. I could tell all that from the way he'd thumped me upon arrival. But running away, even when I should, is not my style.

"You just couldn't keep your mouth shut, could you?" were the first words out of his mouth as he slapped a palm on the table. "What are you trying to do, ruin my life?"

"This is something you want the whole table to hear?" I asked, moving my chair farther away.

"It doesn't make a damned bit of difference now," he said. "Now that you've gone and blabbed to the police."

People at other tables had turned and were staring at us curiously. The last thing we wanted right now was another commotion. "I will not discuss this here, Lewis," I said. "If you want to have an acrimonious discussion based on some wrongheaded assumptions you've made, we're taking it away from the party."

"Oh, 'acrimonious discussion,' " he mimicked. "What's the matter, afraid to have your friends know what you've done?"

I'd had enough of having my reputation tracked through the mud today. Being bullied by the cops I was used to. Being bullied by colleagues was something else. Something I wasn't going to tolerate. It was clear there was no shutting him up. We might as well get this out in the open, before the board members, at least. "I've done nothing, Lewis," I said. "I never mentioned your name or anything about you to the police."

"Like hell!" he exploded. I was surprised the hula dancers didn't stop to listen.

"Get a grip, Lewis," I snapped. "You may not care what people think, but I do. We've got a conference to run and you are not going to spoil everyone's good time with your self-centered display of drunken peevishness." I pushed back my chair and stood up. "Excuse me, I'm going to give Mr. Broder a chance to complain in private."

Jolene pushed back her own chair. "I'm coming with you. You've taken quite enough of today's burdens on your shoulders."

"I don't want *you* butting your nose in—" Broder began but Jolene cut him off. She rarely raised her voice, so when she did, people really paid attention.

"We are all people you have to continue to work with, Lewis," she said, "so consider this carefully. Are you quite sure you want to make an ass of yourself in front of everyone?"

While he was still gaping with amazement, she grasped his elbow and led him away from the crowd. As I followed them out, I heard Shannon's parting remark, "Way to go, Jolene," like we were a sports team and Jolene had just scored.

Jolene found a quiet bench overlooking the water, steered Lewis onto it, and sat down beside him, motioning for me to sit beside her. "Now, then, Lewis," she said, "what seems to be your problem?"

"She is," he hissed, pointing at me. "She sicked the cops on me."

Jolene clasped his pointing hand in both of hers and returned it to his lap. "Very rude to point, Lewis. Didn't your mother teach you that? Now, let me see if I understand your complaint correctly. The police have questioned you about your whereabouts last night because you were seen leaving the bar with a rather intoxicated Martina Pullman sometime around midnight, and you believe Thea is the source of their information?"

"Hey, how did you know about that?" He gave me a dirty look.

Jolene shrugged. "Grow up, Lewis. Thea wasn't the only one who saw you. Lots of people saw you. At least three of them have sidled up to me today and whispered about it in my ear. Followed, in all three cases, by the question, What did I suppose Maggie would think?" Maggie was Broder's wife, Margaret Ellis Broder, heiress to a packinghouse fortune, and the principal source of Broder's income, ambition, and position. Maggie was at home overseeing the preparations to send three small, perfect Broders away to three exclusive summer camps.

He jumped to his feet. "Goddamn it! I was so sure that—"

"Sit down, Lewis," she said. I noticed that she had never once raised her voice but there was nothing soft or wishy-washy about the way she was handling things. It confirmed what I'd always thought about Jolene—that she was the right choice for Martina's job. Jolene had enough vision to lead as Martina had, and far, far better organizational and people skills. "Now, I'm sure you understand, or you would understand if you took the pains to think about it, that all of us who have had close personal relationships with Martina, be they unfriendly or too friendly, are going to be noticed, and questioned, by the police. Right?"

Reluctantly, he nodded. "I suppose so."

"And each of us has a civic duty to cooperate."

"I don't see why," he said. "I didn't kill her. Beyond that, what happened between me and Martina is no one's business."

"I'm not sure Jeff Pullman and Maggie would agree with you, and I'm sure the police wouldn't."

"I already know what the police think. They sent a goddamned sumo wrestler after me. Never once cracked a smile. He just sat and stared at me with these eyes like polished stones and made me feel like a cheap suit. Asking what time I did this and what time I did that, and did I go to Martina's room and what happened there and what time did I leave and was there anyone who could corroborate my story. By the time he was done, I felt like I'd been tried and convicted and he was deciding how I ought to be executed."

I realized, from the way he slurred his words, that Lewis was more than a little drunk. A drunken, self-pitying whiner. There's nothing I like less than a man who gets drunk and whines. Unless it's a man who gets drunk and pounds on me to get my attention so that he can whine that his troubles are all my fault. I went out with a guy a lot like Lewis once. A banker. It didn't last. He thought he was God's gift to women when he wasn't even the booby prize. And boy, could he whine. Andre doesn't whine. He either says what's on his mind or he clams up and withdraws completely. I like it when he does the former and when he does the latter, I sometimes have to kick down the door and drag him out and then we have a nice big fight. But we also have the fun of making up.

"Did you go back to Martina's room?" Jolene asked.

"I had to help her upstairs," he said defensively. "She was drunk."

"So you took her to her room. Did you go in?"

"You sound just like that cop," he said, adding, with satisfaction, "and I didn't tell him anything, either." But it was obvious that he wanted to talk, because then he said, "She's just a big cock-teaser. Martina. There in the bar we were . . . she had . . . she put her hand on my thigh and . . . then she suggested we find someplace more private. I wasn't going to say no, was I? Only we kept getting interrupted." He glared at me. "First that little twit, works for her, hauling her out of the bar and lecturing at her like she was a child. . . ." He stopped. "I ever had someone work for me do that, I'd . . ."

He lowered his head and shook it, like a bull shaking off flies. Then he waved an arm dismissively. "Then Thea does the same thing. Martina was some pissed off, let me tell you. She says just wait until the next board meeting, she's going to have some things to say about that and who does Ms. Thea stick-her-nose-where-it's-not-wanted Kozak think she is." He gave me a malicious smile. "She *really* didn't like you. . . ."

"You were telling us about going upstairs," Jolene reminded him.

"Oh, yeah. Forgot. It's her—" He started to point at me and remembered Jolene's warning. "She's a troublemaker but she didn't stop us. No way. Martina and I, we went upstairs. She invited me in and we were going to . . . we were going to party." He grinned, like we were all guys in the bar together. "We even ordered up a nice little feast for ourselves. But then, she's gone into the other room to . . . you know . . . jus' like inna movies . . . sleep, uh, slip . . . into something more comfortable. . . ."

He was tripping over his tongue now. It seemed almost unfair to let him continue in his debilitated state. I looked at Jolene and raised my eyebrows.

She shook her head. "And then?" she asked.

"The phone rings. I mean, it's after midnight and I'm wondering who could be calling, except maybe that sallow little weasel who works for her. Rory. She's always butting her nose in. Tried to break us up down in the bar, like she was Martina's nanny or something, ya know? So I say, if it's Rory, tell her to stuff it. Anyway, Martina answers the phone . . . all brisk, efficient, she's gonna get rid of whatever pest it is . . . she even winks at me as she goes to answer it, you know what I mean . . . and the next thing I know, I'm being hustled out the door like an unwelcome guest. I tried to talk to her. I tried to kiss her and bring back the mood and all I'm getting is not the 'Oh, Lewis' that I was getting minutes before. Now it's 'Oh, for heaven's sake, Lewis, will you please just go, I'm tired and it's late and I have an early meeting.' I mean, she had the same early meeting five minutes ago, too, didn't she? But no, I'm out in the hall with my hat handed to me and the door is shut and locked and I don't even know what's hit me, ya know?"

Jolene patted his arm. "Poor Lewis," she said. "That was kind of rough."

He grabbed her hand and held on. "You know it."

"Do you have any idea who was on the phone?"

He shook his head. "None. She didn't say a fuckin' word, pardon my French. But it made her happy, I can tell you that. She was grinning like a Cheshire cat when she got off. Grinning and smiling to herself, until she turned around and there I was and it was like she'd stepped in something nasty, ya know? One minute she can't wait to get me up there, she's rubbing herself against me like a cat in heat and the next minute she can't wait to get me out the door. Fickle bitch. I wish Maggie were here. None of this would have happened if Maggie could have come." He was sliding into that peculiar mix of maudlin and vulgar typical of those who have had too much to drink.

"You're tired, aren't you, Lew?" Jolene said. "I know we've all had a long, hard day. Tell you what. Why don't Thea and I walk you to the elevator. You've got that seminar you're leading tomorrow, so maybe an early night wouldn't be a bad . . ." She trailed off as she rose to her feet, pulling him up with her.

He rose willingly enough until his drifting eye landed on me. "I don't want her—" He punctuated by pointing at me again. "Don't want her coming with us. She's mean."

"She's not mean, really, Lewis. She just speaks her mind, like Maggie does. But I'm sure Thea doesn't mind waiting here while I walk you to the elevator, do you?"

"Not at all." I sat back down on the bench, very proud of myself for not demanding an apology or otherwise antagonizing Lewis Broder. Sure, he made me sick, but as Jolene had just adeptly demonstrated, sometimes you catch more flies with honey than with vinegar. She'd gotten the story out of him very neatly and then shipped him off to bed, unless something went wrong on their way to the elevator. And I couldn't have done it. I've got a lot of good people skills, but they tend to be the coercive kind, or the blunt now-it's-time-to-face-the-truth kind.

That's why my partnership with Suzanne works so well. They bring me in for the bad news and the hard cases. When the case calls for charm and tact, Suzanne goes, which is why she was supposed to be here. I knew the issues better, and wrote better speeches, but Suzanne could charm birds out of trees. She was supposed to help the board broach the subject of Martina's emeritus position and a new leader for the organization. I was supposed to stay home, run the office, troubleshoot, get a batch of year-end reports written, and play footsie with Andre. Until an evil virus had foiled our plans. Unless it was a bacterium.

I watched lights on the water and listened to the night sounds.

Music, laughter, splashing from the pool. Footsteps along the walk. The rustle of wind through palm leaves. I thought about my own reaction to the police questioning, and Lewis Broder's, and about what Jolene had said. Wasn't it our civic duty to cooperate? Today I hadn't thought so, and of course, I had more experience with the police than either Lewis or Jolene. But having seen how unattractive Broder's reluctance had been, I began to wonder about my own position. If everyone was unhelpful because they were being so self-protective, how would the police ever solve the crime? And on the other hand, I had given them plenty of cooperation. I'd only gotten difficult when Nihilani had insulted me. Oh, hell, I didn't know. I didn't even know if I had anything more to tell them if they asked, other than pure gossip. And what Lewis had just said. And wasn't that Lewis's business? Only he wasn't going to tell them anything.

I thought maybe the next time they asked me something, I'd dump everything I knew in their carefully pressed laps. But I wasn't sure. Despite the delicate truce that Dr. Ed Pryzinski had wrought over drinks, I was still feeling prickly. The whole question was giving me a headache. And hadn't Jolene been gone an awfully long time? Maybe she needed to be rescued from Broder's clutches. Maybe he thought any woman who was nice to him actually wanted to go to bed with him. It would be hard to misconstrue Jolene. There wasn't anything sexual about her approach, only gentleness.

But men aren't always the best readers of cues, not when they're as egocentric as Lewis Broder, especially when they're drunk. There's still that testosterone-driven, woolly-mammoth hunting instinct that makes some men think, when they get an urge, that it's okay to toss the nearest female over their shoulder and carry her off to the cave. Reluctantly I gave up my solitary perch and went to find Jolene.

CHAPTER *11*

I HADN'T GONE far when I heard a rustling in the underbrush. Call it an overactive imagination or attribute it to the fact that I've led a rather dangerous life of late, whatever it was, I came to a halt and stepped quietly off the path, hoping that I wasn't about to find Jolene in some terrible state. "Hey, you!" a voice whispered. "Come here." It didn't sound especially menacing. In fact, it sounded like a child. But I've learned to be wary the hard way. Some of the most innocent-looking people can be deadly. "Over here." There was some more rustling and then a small, dirty child stepped out on the path in front of me. "Hi," she said, grinning. "From the beach. Remember me?"

The little girl who had rescued me from sunburn. I searched my memory for her name. "Laura, right? Laura Mitchell? What are you doing crawling around in the underbrush?"

She put a finger to her lips. "I'm being a spy," she whispered. "The rest of my family is upstairs watching TV. I got bored. I wanted to have an adventure."

"And? Discovered anything interesting?"

"Oh, sure. There are lots of things going on if you're looking for them." She lowered her voice. "And if people don't know you're there. I don't think you could do it. You're too big. But I'm only a child, and you know what? People don't notice children, so we can sneak around and see a lot. I was watching you guys there on the bench for the longest time and you never even knew I was there."

I was supposed to be rescuing Jolene but this was a lot more interesting. Laura was my kind of kid. She wasn't upstairs watching TV. She was sneaking around the hotel, people watching. "Well, I was going to go look for my friend, the one who was sitting on the bench with me. You want to come along while I look for her, and tell me about your adventures?"

"I know what happened to her," Laura said in a teasing voice.

"Don't make me guess, Laura. It's been a long day."

"Okay," she said. "She walked to the elevator with the man who was walking funny." She looked up at me, frowning. "Was he drunk?" I nodded. "I thought so. Anyway, when they got to the elevator, he tried to pull her in with him, and she tried to push him away, and he tore her dress, so the security man came and took him away, and she went upstairs in the elevator. To get another dress, I imagine. I think he must be an awful man. You don't like him, do you?"

"No, Laura, I don't. But he has a nice wife and three little children and I wish he weren't so big. I'd like to take him over my knee and spank him."

Laura laughed. She had a nice, uninhibited kid's laugh, the kind that when you overhear it, it makes you smile and wonder how your own laugh got so stilted. "I'd give my whole allowance to see that," she said.

"I was wondering if you'd like to come to the bar with me and have a Coke or something, but I don't suppose your parents would like it if you were hanging around with strangers."

"Nope. They don't like strangers. My mother is always warning me about them. But you aren't a stranger. We already met when my mom was there, so how could she complain? She was the one who told me to wake you up, wasn't she?"

"All the same, it might be a good idea to call her and tell her where you'll be. There are some phones right over here. You can do that while I call my friend Jolene and make sure she's all right. Deal?" Laura shrugged and picked up a phone. I called Jolene.

"Hello?" Her voice sounded shaky, as if she feared it might be Lewis again.

"It's Thea," I said. "I hear pointing isn't his only rude attribute. I hear that Mr. Broder grabs as well. Are you okay?"

She laughed nervously. "Where did you hear that? Don't tell me it's going to be all over the hotel by morning."

"I don't think so. My source is an eleven-year-old secret agent. Are you okay?"

"Well, my confidence is a little shaken but otherwise I'm fine. There I was, congratulating myself on what a good job I'd done handling the guy, and suddenly he's trying to"—she laughed, and this time it was a little more genuine—"trying to handle me. I didn't hesitate for a second. I slapped him silly and hollered for help. Poor Maggie."

"Poor Maggie is right. The man is out of control. I don't know whether he needs therapy or—"

"More saltpeter in his mashed potatoes?" Jolene suggested.

"Right. Look, I'm headed for the bar with my secret-agent pal. You want to join us?"

"Sure. Why not. I'm not in the mood for any more hula or karaoke, are you?"

"I only hate to miss seeing Jonetta sing."

"Well, we could sneak back for that, but I'm not up to reporting to the gang on the results of our interview with Lewis."

Laura was waving at me impatiently. "Okay, so I'll see you in the bar."

"Righto."

Jolene was the only person I knew who could say righto and not have it sound silly. "Your mom say it was all right?"

Laura gave an elaborate, full-body shrug that shook her little pink skort. Then she spread her arms wide, like a diva inviting applause. "She gave me a lecture on not being so pushy and keeping my nose out of other people's business, but then she said all right. The thing is that I wear her out so she's happy to have me out of her hair. My big sister, Charlotte, is one of those perfect little doobies who always does just what she's told. She does her homework twice and the teachers all love her. And Geoffrey is so competent! Everyone thinks he walks on water because he understands computers. Me, everyone looks at and sighs." She grabbed my hand.

"Well, let 'em. I'm the one who has all the fun. Can we get some of those strawberry daiquiri things? The ones that look like pink milkshakes?"

"Why not?" Hand in hand, we strolled to the bar. As we went, we got lots of approving looks from people.

"They think I'm your kid," she whispered. "Isn't that cool?"

The hostess thought it was cool, too. Even though the bar was crowded, she founded us a quiet table with two of those great, tall chairs that looked like thrones. Laura was impressed. "Wow," she said. "My dad tried to get a table like this and they wouldn't give it to him. Are you someone very important?"

"No," I said, "I thought you were."

She laughed. We gave our drink order to the waitress and settled back on our thrones. "Where are you from?" I asked.

"Iowa. Nothing interesting ever happens in Iowa. When I grow up, I'm going to be a writer and live in the city and have four cats."

"How many cats do you have now?"

"None. Charlotte is allergic. All I have to do is say the word 'cat' and she starts to sneeze. Then there's my brother, Geoffrey. All he cares about is machines. He's a nerd." She tipped her head sideways and stared at me. "You know what a nerd is?"

"I think so. You have one brother, one sister, one mother and one father, is that all?"

"Nope. I've got two mothers and two fathers, and four grandparents and two nasty little half sisters and one nasty little stepdog that poops on the rug."

"So you're here with your mother and stepfather?"

She nodded vigorously. "He has lots of money and now we live in a great big house and he hates kids. Except he sort of likes Geoffrey because Geoffrey can fix his computer for him. And program the VCR. And make the remotes work. And Charlotte reads poetry and sets the table without being reminded and can spell anything. But me? I'm good for nothing. He wants to give me to the Salvation Army, but my mom won't let him. You want to see my treasures?"

Boy, could this kid talk! I had the feeling no one had listened to her for a long time, but I didn't mind. It was restful, after the day I'd had, to talk with somebody who didn't care about Martina's murder or single-sex education. Our drinks arrived. Hers was topped with whipped cream and a huge strawberry. She tasted it carefully and pronounced it delicious before reaching in her pocket and pulling out a small drawstring bag. She set it on the table in front of her.

"Everywhere we go," she explained, "I bring this bag with me, and I collect stuff that I find to be my souvenirs of the trip. This isn't stuff that I buy, anyone can buy junk in stores. It has to be found stuff. The rest of them are always on my case about picking up trash, but you'd be surprised what I find. Look . . . and this is only from two days." She undid the string and dumped the contents out on the table.

"Mind if I join you?" It was Jolene. I made introductions and she pulled up a chair and sat down. Laura and her treasures had to wait until she'd ordered her drink.

As soon as the waitress was gone, Laura picked up where she'd left off. "Okay," she said. "I was about to show Thea my treasures. I hope you don't mind."

"Not at all. Is there a story behind these treasures?"

Laura explained again about how she collected souvenirs, and then she picked up the first item from the pile on the table. It was a small gold earring. "This one I found at the bottom of the pool when I was diving for pennies. I think it belonged to a woman who had kicked me when she was swimming, but when I tried to tell her about it, she called me an annoying little brat and told me to get lost, so . . . the earring and I got lost together. Pretty, isn't it?" It was pretty. Pretty, and, if the thing that looked like a diamond was real, very expensive.

Jolene admired it and set it in a separate pile. "Next?" she said.

Laura's next treasure was a feather of iridescent blue and green. "Found it in the lobby," she said. "I had to race against that guy with the broom. He's so fast things barely make it to the floor. His name is Clay and he's from Cleveland. Here are matches from the restaurant last night. A shell I found when I was playing in the waves. I had to dive down to get it. There are no shells on the beach. Let's see . . . a Japanese coin I found in the parking lot. This dollar bill had rolled under the Coke machine. Here's a neon green cigarette lighter that still works, and . . ."

The last thing in Laura's pile was a small red satin ribbon, the type that is used to trim lingerie. I picked it up carefully between my fingers as a shiver went down my spine. "What about this one? Where did you find it?"

"Did you see the big fight last night? The one where those people threw furniture and clothes over the railing?" I shook my head. It sounded like the same one Alyce Edgerton had told me about. "Well, they were right downstairs from us and it woke me up. Naturally, I was curious, so I took my room key and went outside to see what was going on. The rest of them didn't even stir. I leaned over the railing so I could see better and that's when I saw her dump his whole suitcase off the railing and so he went back inside, got hers, and did the same thing. Then the security guys came and made them go back in their room, and everything got quiet. But I have this thing where, every time I leave my room, I have to walk all the way around to get back to it. So that's what I did."

"You're on the seventeenth floor?" I asked.

"That's right," she said. "How'd you know that?"

"Oh," Jolene said, "Thea's a very fine detective."

Her words, like the little scrap of red satin, chilled me. "So you were walking back to your room. . . ." I tried to remember when Alyce had said the fight took place. She hadn't been very precise. Around one or two in the morning, that's what she'd said.

"And I found this lying on the floor."

"Any idea where?"

"About halfway around from my room."

"Did you see anyone else while you were making your circle?"

"That's how I think of it, too," Laura said, "That I'm making my circle. Just the tall lady. The one who had hair kind of like yours. Shorter, though. She was going into her room. I don't think she saw me, though. The door was almost shut and she didn't turn around."

"And you didn't see anyone else on the way back to your room?"

"Just a man walking toward the elevator, but he looked puzzled, like he was on the wrong floor, and when he saw me, he turned and went down the stairs."

"Did you notice what he looked like?"

She thought for a minute. "Old," she said.

"Old like with gray hair?"

She shrugged. "Just old. Like my stepdad, Howard, only not so short and fat."

I was about to ask her if the man had had any noticeable characteristics, like a limp or facial hair, when she screwed up her eyes and looked at me suspiciously. "Why are you asking so many questions? You didn't ask a lot of questions about the other things I found."

I thought fast. "Well, if you're going to be a spy, you need to be very observant, right? So, since I used to be a pretty good spy myself, I'm testing you, to see if you measure up."

She sat up straighter and placed her folded hands on the table in front of her. "Well, do I?" she said. "Do I measure up?"

"You're an A-plus spy," I said. "Well, at least an A. And if you can tell me what time this all took place, I'll give you that A plus."

"One-thirty-seven," she said. "And I set my watch by the radio yesterday morning."

I looked at my watch. "Speaking of time, it's about time you went upstairs, especially since you were up late last night." I fingered the little piece of ribbon. "I don't suppose you'd let me have this?"

She considered my request. "Well, I don't know. It's one of my best things. Okay, I'll make you a deal." I got the impression Laura made a lot of deals and that her family was probably pretty sick of them. She pointed at the rose in my hair. "You give me that flower and I'll give you the ribbon."

I unpinned it and handed it to her. She tucked it away in the bag, to which she'd already restored the rest of her treasures. "Don't you want to know the story?" I asked.

She leaned forward, all eager eyes and grin. "There's a story?"

I nodded. "Today is my birthday," I said.

"How old?" she interrupted.

"Thirty-one. And back in Massachusetts, where I live, I have a boyfriend named Andre Lemieux—"

"That's a French name," she said. "Is he French?"

"His ancestors came from France. His family lives in Maine. Actually, that's where he lives, too, most of the time. He's a detective with the Maine State Police."

"Wow! A real detective? Like on TV?"

"Like on TV. And he's handsome, too."

She squinted at me curiously. "Are you in love with him?"

"You bet. Anyway, today is my birthday, and so he sent me a dozen pink roses. Now you have one of them."

"Do you have a picture of him?" I opened my wallet and pulled out a picture Suzanne had taken. Andre and I were on Rollerblades. My first time. He had his arm around my waist so I wouldn't fall down. He looked liked like a million bucks. I looked like a total dork because I'd insisted on wearing every piece of padding I could find and a helmet. No, I didn't look like a dork. I looked like a Martian. She took the picture, studied it carefully, and handed it to Jolene. "He's gorgeous," she said. "You look like a dork."

"Laura," Jolene said, in her headmistress voice, "that's not very nice."

Laura looked crestfallen. "I'm sorry," she said. "I mean, you look cautious."

Jolene handed the picture back. "She's right. He is gorgeous. And now, I think it's time we paid the bill and went upstairs to bed. What time shall we have our premeeting meeting in the morning?"

"Not at six."

"Right. How about seven-thirty, in my room? I'll call the others and let them know."

Laura slid off her chair, tucked her treasure bag in her pocket, and said a polite goodnight. She walked a few feet, then turned back with an impish grin. "You didn't ask if I saw anyone on the other floors."

"Did you?"

"It was the middle of the night," she said. "After the couple finished their fight, everyone disappeared real quick . . . quickly . . .

I did see one woman, though, down on the floor below. I noticed her because she was staring up at my floor with an angry look on her face."

"All right, Detective. What did she look like?"

"Fat," she said. "Well, fattish. You know, with a wide, puffy kind of face and a sort of waddle when she walked. And she had blond hair. I don't think it was natural, though, because looking down like I was, I could see different colored roots. She was holding her hands like this"—she demonstrated by clasping her hands together and bringing them to her chest—"like she was praying or something. Well, gotta go. They're threatening to ground me." With a wave of her hand, she was off.

We watched her go, not speaking until she was out of sight. "Boy, I sure hope she's right that no one saw her," I said.

"What's the big deal about a piece of red ribbon?" Jolene asked. "When she pulled it out, you looked like you'd seen a ghost."

"Oh, hell. The police asked me not to say anything to anyone, but I don't see what difference it makes if you know. You're hardly the type to go around killing people." Even as I said it, a long-ago conversation rang in my ear. I could still hear a voice say, "Everyone is the type to be a killer, given the right circumstances." "It's bound to be in the papers anyway. The cops can never keep things secret. When we found Martina, she was dressed in red. . . ." I couldn't bring myself to finish. Even as I started to say it, the image of Martina's grotesquely dressed and arranged corpse floated before my eyes. "Red lingerie."

"I see." She nodded. "And you think this might have . . ."

"I don't know. But it's possible. It's also possible that that little girl saw something. And if someone saw her . . . and knows she might make the connection . . . then she could be in trouble."

"That's an ugly thought."

"Murder is an ugly thing."

Jolene laid some bills on the table. "Let's go listen to Jonetta sing."

CHAPTER *12*

I DON'T INDULGE in hyperbole—it was a fact—listening to Jonetta sing was one of life's transforming experiences. Trying to describe her voice made me wish I had a bigger vocabulary; it made me dig down into the thesaurus of my soul and pull out magic words. I knew she had sung in a gospel choir since childhood because she'd told me. I knew she believed, like many people of deep and sincere faith, that through singing she could glorify God. I knew that even when she was singing to entertain, as she was now, the power of her voice made a difference. In the movie *Chariots of Fire* one of the characters says that when he runs he can feel God's pleasure. It must have been that way for Jonetta.

The noisy party we'd left earlier had become so still you could have heard a pin drop. No one wanted to miss a note, a word, a phrase. And we'd almost missed it. When we tiptoed in, she was singing an old Tina Turner song, "Midnight Train to Georgia," one of those songs that always revived my secret desire to be a torch singer. Listening to Jonetta always simultaneously rekindled that desire and squelched it. I sat and listened to her, mouthing the words, wishing a magic wand might touch me and make my voice like hers.

I sat in the dark, alone in a crowd of people, and wondered how my life might have been different if I'd been born with some special talent, instead of merely a knack for competence and the will to get things done. Beautiful music, a warm tropical night, another day I wanted to forget. Was it any wonder I was filled with longing for things to be different? For life to be simple, for my path to be straight, for choices to be clear. Yes, I liked what I did, or I wouldn't be doing it. I didn't mind hard work. I enjoyed being good at something, at solving problems, giving good advice, helping people work things out. But my personal life, while rich in love, was otherwise a shambles.

Jack Leonard, Andre's boss with the Maine State Police, had given us a gift. Normally, Andre lives in Maine and I live in Massachusetts, and we manage a stressful, patchy commuting relationship. He'd sent Andre to Boston for a six-month course that had meant we could be together without commuting and distance and uncertainty. Jack's gift had been six months of normal life—breakfast together, dinners when we weren't otherwise detained by work, waking up in the same bed day after day. It hadn't been a surprise to learn that we liked our lives that way. We fight. We're both strong-willed, opinionated people. And we love. And while love may not conquer all, it certainly conquers much. But our time was almost up.

The words of the song were breaking down the barriers of my resistance, sneaking under my skin, making me think about the future when I wanted to avoid it. She sang, "I'd rather live in his world than live without him in mine," and I felt a tightness in my throat and a stinging behind my eyes. Did I? Could I find a way to live in his world? Find a way to blend his world and mine? I'm a workaholic. He's a workaholic. We both loved our jobs but there was no way we could be together and do our jobs without the long commutes that made us both so miserable, the forced spaces apart when one of us needed the other that made us sullen and resentful.

I knew that life was full of choices, not all of them easy. Look at Jonetta. She could have been a singer, that is, she could have been paid big bucks for singing, but she had chosen to educate girls who might not otherwise have a chance. Sometimes she used her music to raise money, and she taught all of the girls to sing. Once she'd said to me, "Sometimes, when you're down, a song is all you got, but it's still something you can do for yourself, and nobody can take it away." How could I not envy someone who had a calling, when I felt so rootless myself?

I sighed and Jolene put her arm around my shoulders and gave me a quick squeeze. Sometimes I thought that included among her many talents was the ability to read minds. Certainly it was a useful talent for a headmistress.

Jonetta finished the song to a roar of applause and bowed, her silly, wonderful dress all aquiver as she did so. Behind the tables, the space had filled up with other hotel guests, and the roar of approval drowned out the persistent sound of the waves. "It's getting late," she said, "and we've all got a busy day tomorrow, so I'm going to stop now. . . ." A moan went up from the crowd. "But I'm going to leave you with a little spiritual enrichment to carry away with you. You all know this song, and I expect you to sing right along with me. Okay?" She bowed her head for a moment, then lifted it and began to sing "Amazing Grace."

Inspiring music, stained glass windows, the poetry of biblical phrases, it was important that the things of religion have some apartness, some difference from everyday life, to remind us to give faith the thought and respect it needed. " 'I once was lost but now I'm found. . . .' " she sang. I thought I was lost and not yet found. " 'Through many dangers, toils, and snares, I have already come. . . .' " I was haunted by death and loss, disconnection and uncertainty, fear and anger and resentment. Stirred by the music. Unbearably restless. I pushed back my chair, the pressure to be by myself, away from people, was suddenly more than I could stand.

"I'll see you in the morning," I whispered.

I threaded my way through the crowd and out to the beach path. There were few strollers out this late and my shoes echoed loudly in the darkness, an irritating little clomp, clomp, clomp as I walked. I slipped them off and padded along barefoot, the tar still warm from the sun, shoes dangling from my swinging arm. I walked until my feet were sore, my mind in a muddle. I was having the birthday blues. Another year older. No closer to having anything settled in my life. No clearer about what I wanted, except that I knew I wanted to be with Andre. I just didn't know how.

Time to head back. Limping now. Where earlier my steps had raced to match the pace of my thoughts, now they moved slowly. I was tired. My knees hurt. My feet hurt. My head hurt. I have the unfortunate disability of getting my hangovers shortly after drinking instead of the next morning, so that all that rum and sweet juice was already taking a toll. Bedtime. It had been a long hard day.

I limped along, no longer enjoying the night. I'd pulled back from the broad focus of what was I going to do with my life to the smaller focus of what was I going to do tomorrow. There was no formal breakfast meeting but the seminars started early. I was going to monitor one on "Girls and Technology: Strategies for Hands-on Learning." Rob Greene was chairing the panel. It sounded interesting. When I got back upstairs, I had a bunch of reading to do. I always had a bunch of reading to do. Sometimes I was so envious of the people who claimed to be bored because they had nothing to do. I hadn't had a minute with nothing to do in so long. I'd love to have a chance to be bored.

Actually, this limping along on sore and tired feet was kind of boring, but I was engaged in a typical Thea Kozak maneuver—thinking about work so I wouldn't have to think about Martina's death. Thinking about Andre and what it meant to live in his world had cast my earlier reactions to Nihilani and Bernstein in a different light. Yes, they'd done typical cop things, some irritating, some manipulative, and some insulting, and yes, dealing with authority figures in situations where everything was one-sided and there was no give-and-take always rubbed me the wrong way. I admit it. I have trouble with authority.

But Nihilani and Bernstein were investigating a murder. There was no uncertainty about that. I'd been there. I'd seen what someone had done to Martina Pullman. Not a nice woman, not a likeable one, but someone who had had a sense of mission, and who had, in her quest for personal aggrandizement, also done wonderful things for thousands, perhaps millions, of young girls. Martina had been one of those special people who were making a difference in the world until someone appointed himself or herself as executioner and left her lying there dead, degraded, and ridiculous.

There is so much violence and death in the world today promulgated as entertainment that it's easy to lose sight of reality. Reality is that when a person dies, they stay dead. They don't pop up again tomorrow on another program, or have nine magical lives. They die and their own particular light goes out and the people who knew them and loved them and valued them are left with holes in their hearts and stories in their heads and the memories and the pain, which don't die. I know. I live with a homicide detective. My own sister was murdered. And yet I still have trouble with the idea that anyone can decide to kill another human being and then act on it.

Someone had killed Martina Pullman and when the police came to me for help, I didn't want to talk to them. I didn't want to tell them all the things I knew about the rest of us, about the problems we'd all had with Martina. I didn't want to get anyone in trouble. It was the completely normal reaction of an average citizen being questioned by the police. But tonight I was thinking about Andre's world, not my own. Living in his world meant looking at things from the cop's point of view. When I looked at myself through Andre's eyes, I saw a defensive, arrogant, and uncooperative woman who might be able to help refusing to do so. I saw a person who knew the inside stories not telling them because I hadn't been asked the right questions.

I didn't much like seeing myself that way. It reminded me of my meeting with Andre at the state police barracks in Thomaston, Maine. Our second meeting, when he was the detective investigating my sister's death. Even as my mind veered in that direction, I tried to turn it aside. There are some things I don't like to remember. Like learning how my sister, Carrie, had died.

I could still see him sitting behind that desk. I heard his voice as clearly as if it were yesterday. We'd been arguing about the very explicit questions he'd been asking about Carrie. Questions I thought were intrusive and uncalled for when applied to my baby sister.

"I'm going to speak very frankly," he said, "so that you can understand. Murder isn't nice. It isn't polite, and murderers are not respectful of people's feelings. The unfortunate but necessary result is that murder investigations aren't nice either. Murder victims don't have a right to privacy. The killer takes their privacy when he takes their life. We need to know as much as possible about the victim to help us know where to look." Then he'd pulled out the pictures. "Do you know how your sister died?"

More than two years had passed and still, when I thought of him reaching for those pictures, I went cold all over. For a long time, the Carrie of those pictures had come to me in dreams. I hurried on, trying to keep them from coming back now. Instead I saw Helene Streeter, my old friend Eve Paris's mother, slashed to death on the street in front of her house, trying to hold her gaping wounds together as she crawled toward her own front door. She smiled when she saw me. "Thea . . ." She held out a hand, dripping blood. You can't close your eyes on the pictures inside your head.

I started to run. An incongruous, desperate escape from all the dead people inside my skull. The path that had seemed so warm and inviting when I started out now seemed punishingly hard and endless. But running helped. It's hard to think when you're gasping and hurting. I ran on and on, surprising the moonlight strollers, ignoring their stares, until I was back in the brightly lit lobby. I punched the elevator button, doing an impatient little shuffle while I waited.

Upstairs I fastened all the locks on my door and closed the curtains against the night. Then I turned on the television, looking for a movie to distract me. Drivel. Trash. Junk. Crap. News. Sitcom. Wait. I went back to the news. Nihilani, looking no more animated on camera than he had in person. The reporter was asking him questions. The first was whether they had any suspects. Nihilani replied that the investigation was ongoing. The reporter said the rumor was there was no sign of forced entry, did that mean the killer was probably known to the victim? Nihilani was noncommittal. So it went for several more questions. The police had no comment other than their opinion that there was not a killer running rampant among Maui's tourist hotels and there was no reason for people to be alarmed.

As news stories went, it was typical and uninformative and boring. And not particularly reassuring. I was about to turn it off when it switched to a picture of Jeff Pullman arriving at the airport. Disheveled, which Jeff never was, wearing dark glasses, his shoulders bowed with grief, waving off reporters with a choked "No comment." My heart went out to him. I remembered those stunned days after we heard the news about Carrie. Planning for her funeral. Choosing a casket. Packing up her apartment. The pain of touching her things, smelling her perfume, seeing her handwriting, wrapping up the bits of jewelry we'd given her as gifts.

I remembered getting the phone call about my husband, David, summoning me to the hospital. Going there, reaching out and touching his body, still warm yet with his spirit gone. I remembered my screaming agony back home in an apartment where I was completely surrounded by his things. I'd spent the whole night curled up in a corner, clutching his pillow, disbelieving, waiting for morning and light and someone to come and tell me it wasn't true. How morning had come and it was still true. David, my husband, the love of my life, was gone and he wasn't coming back and all the wishing in the world couldn't make it so.

If there was anything I could do to help make Jeff Pullman's world right again, anything I could tell the police that might help find the person who inflicted this hurt on him, who had willfully eliminated Martina and left her for the world to mock, I had to do it. Nihilani had thoughtfully left me his card. I picked up the phone and called him.

CHAPTER *13*

NIHILANI WASN'T AVAILABLE. All they'd tell me was that they'd have him call. I waited by phone for a while. When you're ready and willing to spill your guts, not that I had very much to spill, you want to get it over with while the momentum is still there. After an hour, knowing I had another busy day ahead, I gave up, put on my nightgown, and went to sleep. Between the long run and the long walk, I hoped I'd get lucky and I wouldn't dream. For good measure, I took a nice sleepy-time analgesic for the sore knees and feet and it was like rolling off the edge of the earth.

I woke to a pounding on the door so similar to the way the day had begun that I expected to find Rory in the corridor again. In my stunned state, I even expected she'd be taking me to see Martina. With a bleary brain directing my numb fingers, I fumbled with all the locks and finally I got the door open, raising my arm to protect my eyes from the corridor lights. Nihilani and Bernstein were standing there, looking dead on their feet.

"Sorry," I said stupidly. "I was asleep."

It was Bernstein's stare that alerted me to the inappropriateness of my costume. My favorite nightgown. A slip of white cotton gauze, plain except for the million buttons down the front. Andre bought it. He likes to undo the buttons. I snatched up the matching robe and put it on. It wasn't much, but at least two layers of gauze were better than one. On TV people always have their robes laid carefully across the feet of their beds for just such emergencies. But Andre is wiggly. Even if I wore a robe, which I don't unless I'm visiting or in a hotel, and even if I did leave it on the foot of the bed, it would be knocked on the floor or churned into the mass of covers long before the fire broke out or the burglar needed to be chased away.

They took the two chairs, dropping into them wearily. It was 2:00 A.M. and they'd been on the case almost twenty hours. "Sandwiches and coffee?" I suggested, passing the menu to Bernstein. He took it, studied it, and handed it to Nihilani. They gave me their orders and I phoned them in to room service.

We all sat and stared at each other and the silence in the room was leaden. I thought I should have invited them to lie on the bed and sleep. It was one of those king-sized beds hotels seem to like. I always feel strange sleeping alone in something half an acre across. Not that I would have invited them to sleep with me. After my earlier outburst with Nihilani, that would have been impolitic. It was just that they looked so tired, and I had a soft spot for tired, hardworking guys. I had one of my own. There had been days, when he was working flat out on a homicide, when I'd have to literally steer him toward the bed, and he was asleep before I could pull off his shoes.

"It could have waited till morning," I said. I wondered which of them would take charge. Bernstein was more outgoing but I had a feeling that somehow I belonged to Nihilani.

But it was Bernstein who spoke. "First twenty-four hours," he said. The whites of his eyes were red. His lanky frame drooped in the chair like someone had laid a garment bag over it and the bag had sagged to fit the shape of the chair. The lines beside his mouth were deeper and his skin had a pale, dry look. He needed a shave. "So, what changed your mind?"

"Andre."

Bernstein shrugged and looked at Nihilani. "You know. The boyfriend," Nihilani said. "Cop. State cop. Detective."

"So he told you to cooperate?" Bernstein asked.

I shook my head. "He's working a case. Just like you guys. No.

I was thinking about Andre . . . about what he'd think of me, if he was in your position." I shrugged. "I didn't like it much." My eyes wanted to close again. Not even the shock of a sudden awakening and two strangers in my room were enough to jar me into wakefulness. The analgesic must have had some weird stuff in it. That coffee had better get here fast.

"And then I started thinking about my sister, Carrie. She was murdered a few years ago. That's how I met Andre. He was the investigating detective. . . ." I didn't know why I was telling them all this—my censor facilities must have been asleep—but having come this far, I might as well tell all. "So I know how it feels to lose someone you love. Lose. That's a stupid way of putting it. I know how it feels to have someone you love murdered. I know how it felt when people knew stuff about Carrie that they weren't telling the police. Then, on the news, I saw Jeff Pullman. He looked so sad and I thought that if there was anything I could do to help, I ought to. . . ."

They were staring at me like I was a Martian. People did that a lot. Maybe when I talked I was funny looking or my nose bobbed up and down. One of those things we don't see when we look in the mirror. "Why are you guys staring?" They dropped their eyes like an invisible commander had given an order, so that now they were both staring at their shoes. I waited. No one said anything. Oh, hell, I knew better than to wait for an answer. Cops don't talk. They ask.

Finally Nihilani said, "So, what did you want to tell us?" He sounded like he expected to be bored out of his mind. I excused him only because he also sounded the way people do when they're too tired to move their mouths anymore.

"Last night . . . I mean Friday night . . . the night before Martina was . . . look, maybe I'd better back up and tell you about an assumption I've made . . ."

Nihilani's eyes opened a little wider and I understood why Lewis Broder had been intimidated by what he called a stone-cold stare. Bernstein had moods. He got mad and he got kind and he got tough and he got friendly. Nihilani was monolithic. He didn't do anything except be there. It was a lot scarier than being yelled at. I swallowed and pushed the words out. "I'm assuming, because you guys were so interested in what I was doing at one-thirty A.M. yesterday morning . . ." It struck me, suddenly, that Martina had been dead for a whole day. That technically, their first twenty-four hours was over. But maybe it was like in law. Maybe it ran from time of discovery. I didn't have any idea.

Spit it out, Thea. "I'm assuming that Martina was killed around one-thirty A.M."

"So?" Bernstein was getting impatient.

"Let her talk, Lenny."

"So, I don't know. That's what's in my mind—that she was killed around one-thirty A.M. Anyway . . . I have no idea who . . . whom you have spoken with and whom you haven't. From what you've said, you must know that Martina and I had an argument last night, outside the bar. Martina had been drinking. She was becoming loud and out of control. Rory, her assistant, spoke to her and tried to cajole her out of the bar and upstairs to bed. Martina wouldn't go and she was abusive to Rory. She was often abusive when she'd been drinking. Abusive and flirtatious. It seemed like her natural competitiveness toward women and her desire to be attractive to men were both exaggerated by drink."

Bernstein yawned loudly and his eyelids drooped. Nihilani was unchanged. Without any feedback, I had no idea whether I was telling them anything useful or not and there's nothing more depressing than gearing yourself up to bare your soul to someone, only to find that they're simply bored. "Am I boring you?"

Bernstein appeared to be asleep. "Go on," Nihilani said. Neither of them was taking notes.

I stopped my linear account and digressed a little into Martina's character. "Andre says that in order to know the killer, you need to know the victim. Maybe this is extraneous, since you've been talking to people about Martina all day, but people have a tendency to guard the privacy of the victim. . . ." I stopped talking. It was hard enough to spill my guts when someone was eager for the information and leading me along with questions. Trying to give information and tell a story in the face of utter indifference required almost more ertia, more effort, than I was willing to give. "Look, you obviously aren't interested in any of this. There's no sense in wasting your time. Why don't we all quit and go to sleep?"

The only light in the room was the one beside my bed, so I was talking to two figures half-shrouded in gloom. Nihilani snapped on the light beside him. "We're listening," he said. "Go on." I wondered what he did when he wanted to discourage conversation. I wondered why, even when I was making an effort, I couldn't seem to get along with these guys.

I had to nudge myself back into speech. "You know that we're here at a National Association of Girls' Schools conference. Martina was the association director, essentially the administrator for the association. The association also has a board of directors. All of the directors are here except one, Sister Mary Catherine of St. Mary's School. Sister Mary Catherine had to cancel because one of her most beloved faculty members was killed by a hit-and-run driver the day she was supposed to leave." Now I really was wandering and Bernstein was right to yawn.

"The other board members are me and my partner, Suzanne Merritt. We essentially share one board position. Then there is Zannah Wu from the Heights School in San Francisco; Jonetta Williamson, founder of the Refuge School in New York City; Shannon Dukes, headmistress of the Colonnade School in Savannah; Jolene Hershey, headmistress of Caroline Perkins School in Shaker Heights; and Rob Greene, headmaster of the Cantwell School for Girls in Bethesda." I waved my hand in a dismissive gesture. "Forget all that. What is important is that the association is Martina's brainchild. She started it about eight years ago."

Nihilani shifted restlessly in his chair. Like a nervous schoolgirl, I started talking faster. "Everyone acknowledges that Martina was an inspiring leader in many respects. She did a great job for the association, at first. But Martina's interpersonal skills, while superficially deft, leave . . . left . . . a lot to be desired. She was unable to delegate tasks and share glory. She was equally critical of subordinates and peers. She had stopped listening. Lately a lot of balls had gotten dropped and relationships had become seriously frayed. Everyone was frustrated with her, and angry, and the board was planning to sit down this weekend and decide how best to accomplish her ouster. It wasn't something we were looking forward to, but her irritability and outbursts, her abusive behavior, and her drinking problem were all getting worse. We wanted her to retire before she'd done so much damage to her reputation that she would be remembered as a vindictive, unstable, alcoholic crank instead of a visionary leader."

I was shaking and I didn't know whether it was because the room was cold and I was lightly dressed or whether it was because no matter how much I wanted to be frank and open, it was hard to talk about Martina and reveal her flaws now that she was dead. I think there's an innate tendency to memorialize, to want to preserve the memory of the dead in the best possible terms.

"So Ms. Pullman was a drinker," Nihilani murmured. "Can you elaborate on that?"

"She was what I think of as a 'professional alcoholic.' She was sober and hardworking during the day, but when she started to drink, she often didn't stop until she was staggering and incoherent. And along the way, she usually became abusive."

"And she had reached that stage last night? Friday night?"

"She was well on her way. Her speech was still clear . . . relatively clear. But her walk was a little crooked. And her tongue had become vicious."

I thought that I could hear gentle snores from Bernstein, but Nihilani was very awake. "After she yelled at her assistant, what happened?"

"After she'd been called an incompetent slut, Rory had a few choice words of her own to toss back and then she started to cry and ran out of the bar. Martina went to the ladies' room and when she came out, I grabbed her by the arm and hauled her down the corridor to a quiet place where I gave her a piece of my mind about her public behavior, treatment of employees, and not disgracing the group by getting drunk and making a scene in the bar. She told me I was a meddling, obstructionist, empty-headed bimbo and that I would never have gotten anywhere in life if I didn't have a big chest. How that's supposed to have helped me get along with women, I don't know. I realized that I couldn't get anywhere so I gave up and rejoined my group in the bar. About twenty minutes later, Martina left with Lewis Broder."

"About what time was that?" Nihilani asked.

"Midnight or a little after. I was tired, so I finished my drink and went upstairs to bed. . . ."

"That's what you called us in the middle of the night to tell us?" Bernstein said. "I heard she hit you."

So he wasn't asleep after all. Just playing possum. "No. There were a few other things. Besides, I didn't call you in the middle of the night. You *came* in the middle of the night. I'm no more pleased about it than you are. As for her hitting me—" Man did this guy have a knack for getting on my nerves. An attractive piece of human sandpaper. All he had to do was open his mouth and he scratched a sore spot. "She did hit me, if the ineffectual swat of a drunk can be called hitting." I shrugged. "I've played with the pros. It was no big deal."

"Let's see if I've got this straight. Martina had a fight with her assistant, and her assistant went upstairs. Then Martina left with Broder. Then you left, right?"

I couldn't help myself. "Left, right," I said. "But I talked with Broder tonight . . . after you spoke with him apparently, since he was convinced I was the one who had sent you. He cornered me to complain that I'd set him up, and to find out what I'd told you. I said I hadn't told you anything . . . which was true . . . but he was intoxicated . . . it sounds like we're much more of a hard-drinking crew than we are . . . and he wanted to talk, so Jolene Hershey and I plunked him down on a bench and . . . and asked what had happened."

"Which was?"

"Well, he was defensive at first, defensive and belligerent. He's a married man, and his wife is the one with all the money. All the brains, too, I expect. Anyway, he wanted to tell us how shabbily Martina had treated him, and we were willing to listen if it meant he'd stop sulking. . . . Stop me if you've heard all this before."

Nihilani surprised me by giving out an actual piece of information. "He told us that he walked her to her door because she was a bit unsteady on her feet and then he went to his room and went to bed."

"Well, he's going to hate me for this, but—"

There was a knock at the door. I admitted the room-service waiter, a well-trained lad who didn't bat an eye at finding me entertaining two gentlemen in my nightie at 2:00 A.M. He gave me a quick tour of what was on the tray. "Coffee. Three cups. Cream and sugar. One hamburger, medium. One cheeseburger, well. Potato skins. Two strawberry cheesecakes, one chocolate cake. Is that everything?" I nodded. "Do you need anything else?" I signed the check, crossed his palm with green, and he disappeared into the night.

I gave Nihilani his cheeseburger and Bernstein his hamburger, and divided the potato skins onto two plates, one for each of them. I poured coffee. Bernstein took his black; Nihilani had cream and two sugars. When my guests had been served in a manner that would have made my mother proud of me, I poured myself coffee, added lots of cream and sugar, and took my coffee and cake back to the bed. This time I leaned against the headboard and pulled the bedspread up over me. They both had sports jackets on. I was cold.

Nihilani nodded. "Go on." I told my story while they ate with the practical determination of men who might not get another meal for a while.

"Broder says he went back to Martina's room with her. They engaged in a little hugging and kissing and promises of things to come. They ordered themselves a little feast from room service. Champagne and caviar and berries. That Martina had gone into the other room to change into something more comfortable when the phone rang. She didn't tell him who it was, and he says he couldn't hear any of the conversation, but when she came back, she seemed very happy about something, and eager to see him gone as quickly as possible. He left, but his ego was badly bruised."

Bernstein sat up a little straighter. "Looks like we need to have another talk with Mr. Broder."

Nihilani nodded, finished the last of his potato skin, and stood up. "Thank you," he said. No follow-up questions. No "Good job." No "Sorry for interrupting your sleep."

I supposed I should be grateful for the grudging thanks, but I wasn't. I was cold and sleepy and my knees ached and my feet hurt and what I had just forced myself to do was hard. I'm as egocentric as the next person. I liked to be appreciated for my sacrifices and for doing my civic duty. "I'm not finished." Stuffy, head-mistressy tones. Maybe some day I *should* have my own school.

"Oh?" He sat back down, folded his hands in his lap, and waited. He was so astonishingly incurious I wanted to hit him. I want to yell. I wanted to know what mattered and what didn't, what he needed to know, what he already knew, and what he cared about. And he wasn't telling me anything. They'd happily let me buy them a meal—which maybe meant I wasn't a suspect—but they hadn't even shown they'd appreciated it, and they certainly hadn't shown anything else. Someone might have dumped two big lumps of clay in my room for all the human company they offered.

I got up, found my purse, and pulled out the little scrap of satin ribbon I'd gotten from Laura Mitchell. I handed it to Nihi-lani. He took it carefully between two fingers and then looked up at me. "Where?"

"Apparently from the hallway outside Martina's room."

"Apparently?"

"I didn't find it. Someone gave it to me." Now I was on dan-gerous ground. I wanted to tell them about Laura. At the same time, I was reluctant to send two such insensitive people after a lit-tle girl.

"Someone gave it to you," Bernstein said. "That's very inter-esting. Who might this someone be?"

I had a question of my own. "When you interview juveniles, do you do it yourselves or do you use a juvenile officer?"

"In this case?" Nihilani asked.

"In this case."

"We'd do it ourselves. What's the big deal? You got it from some kid?"

"Detective, I don't know if it's a big deal or not. The big deal/small deal choices are yours, not mine. What I do know is that on the one hand this child may have seem something which puts . . ." I wasn't ready to say him or her, so I amended it to, "which creates a dangerous situation. And that means you should be aware of the issue and prepared to protect the witness. On the other hand, from my own experience, it doesn't seem like either of you is . . ." I searched for words, though I was already in too deep to bother with much tact.

"Come on, Kozak, spit it out," Bernstein said. "You don't think we've got the tact to handle a child. You can say it. We've got hides like alligators, after all the years we've spent talking to people like you."

Bernstein and I were truly simpatico, weren't we? It seemed unfair, when I was trying so hard, but maybe our mutual antagonism was insurmountable. It looked like all that time Dr. Pryzinski had spent trying to negotiate a truce had been wasted. I was tempted to run next door, knock on his door, and drag him into it again. But it was almost three in the morning. "Right," I said. "People like me. People who are willing to give up a whole morning and a night's sleep and endure gratuitous insults just to try and help you out, and who go to the extra trouble of feeding you into the bargain. You should only be so lucky that you have to run into people like me. You could have a whole passel of Lewis Broders instead."

"Don't mind Lenny," Nihilani said. "He always gets crabby when he's tired. Trade him the chocolate cake for the cheesecake and he'll cheer right up."

I looked at my luscious piece of chocolate cake, the thick icing gleaming in the light. Oh, man. I wanted that cake. I picked it up and held it out to Bernstein. "You wanna trade?" Damn my mother for raising me to be so nice.

He stood up, picked up the cheesecake, crossed the room, and set it beside the bed. Then he carefully took the chocolate cake from my hand. "Thanks," he said. He sat back down in his chair and took a big bite.

"Okay. Who's the kid?" Nihilani asked.

"I don't know what room she's in. There's a little girl . . . about eleven . . . named Laura Mitchell, in one of the rooms on the other side of Martina's floor. She woke up because of the fight last night. You have heard about the fight?"

Nihilani nodded. "Newlyweds," he said. Bernstein went on eating my cake.

"After the fight, she wandered back to her room. She says she has a ritual that whenever she comes out of her room, she has to go all the way around to get back in. On her way around, she found the ribbon on the floor near Martina's door."

"She see anything?"

"She says she saw a woman with dark hair, not as tall as I am, going into one of the rooms. She didn't see a face. And that's all she says she saw but I didn't press her. And a man who went down the stairs. And on the floor below, she saw a woman who, judging by the description she gave me, might have been Drusilla Aird. There might be things she doesn't remember or things she saw that she doesn't even know are important. That's why I'm worried about her. About something happening to her, if the word got out. I don't even think her family knows she was out wandering. I gather she wanders a lot. She says she's a spy."

"Laura Mitchell," Nihilani said, and wrote something in his book. Then he raised his head and gave me a dose of those cold eyes. I shivered under the covers. "Drusilla Aird. What can you tell me about her?"

"Very little. All I know are the stories other people have told and I'm sure you've heard those."

"Humor me," he said, tapping his pencil against the pad.

I thought I would. Sometimes I imagined I detected a shade of warmth in the man but mostly he scared me to death. I thought of his kind of coldness as reserved for the bad guys. The ones without consciences. True, he had fetched me water, inquired after my well-being, and been sort of understanding when I stole the speech, but still there was that something. That cold, hard something. It made me glad I wasn't a bad guy. I repeated the lunch-table gossip about Drusilla Aird, plus what little I knew on my own, ending with the tale of Drusilla and Linda Janovich having their knock-down, drag-out melee at dinner. When I was done I got a nod. Profuse thanks considering the source.

"This Linda Janovich. The ex-wife. What can you tell me about her?" He had his pencil poised.

"Nothing. I've never met her. Formally, I mean. She's the one I tackled tonight. People say she's nice."

Nihilani snorted. "Getting back to this kid. Laura Mitchell. What's she look like?"

Bernstein finished the last few crumbs of my cake and set the plate aside. He looked a hundredth of a percent more cheerful. He reached for the pot and poured himself more coffee. He didn't offer to pour for either of us.

"Laura? A sprite. She's very thin, with reddish hair and pale skin. Short. Appealing. A nice, nimble mind. Everywhere she goes, she collects a bag of found treasures. The ribbon was in her bag."

"How'd you happen to see it?"

"We're buddies. We were having drinks in the bar, and she showed me."

"You were having drinks in the bar with an eleven-year-old?" Bernstein said.

"Oh, give me a break, Lenny. I'm trying to protect her from you, remember? I'm hardly the type to go out and corrupt the young. She had her parents' permission and she was drinking a nonalcoholic strawberry daiquiri. You can check my bar tab if you want. And there was a witness present."

"Don't trust us much, do you?"

"My own personal cop, Andre Lemieux, I love. But, Lenny, you and your buddy here have hardly been candidates for Mr. Congeniality, have you? When you've dealt with as many jerks as I have, you get a chip on your shoulder. I'm doing my best here, okay? So give it a rest. Or go downstairs to the lobby and kick the potted palms or something."

Nihilani was back on his feet again. "I don't suppose you have anything else in your bag of tricks to pull out? You aren't about to unveil the identity of the murderer, just to show us up?"

I gave him my best smile. "I would if I could."

"I believe you," he said, and they left.

I wasn't sorry to see them go. Even when I did my best to be a good little doobie and cooperate with the police, I lost my temper. Maybe there was a fundamental truth I was avoiding here. Maybe I wasn't a good citizen. Whatever the truth was, I wasn't going to discover it tonight. I had less than three hours to sleep before it began all over again. My only regret was that Bernstein had eaten my cake.

CHAPTER 14

MY WAKE-UP CALL was delivered by a woman born to be in the wake-up business. Her voice was light and bright and cheery, soothing and gentle as she nudged me out of sleep and into the day. I thanked her and finished crawling out of my cocoon. The untouched strawberry cheesecake was sitting by the bed and it didn't look any more appetizing than it had three hours ago. The topping looked like dried blood. Just the sight of it turned my stomach. I picked it up and threw it in the trash as I dashed for the bathroom.

My whole body felt stiff and sore, even after a shower, and I did a bunch of stretches trying to work out the kinks and make things limber again. What did I expect? I was a year older, in a high-stress situation, and woefully short of sleep. I pulled on a T-shirt and the new sage green jumper that had landed on my desk after Suzanne's last shopping trip. I looked good in green. It made my eyes glitter. Unless that glitter was residual irritation at my nocturnal visitors. For years, I relied on my partner, Suzanne, to buy my clothes. She liked to shop; I didn't. She had good taste; I could never tell what was going to suit me or fit me. Then Suzanne got married and had a baby and suddenly she was too busy to shop.

Lately I'd been looking pretty ragged, but things had taken a turn for the better when a nifty discount store opened up within walking distance of Suzanne's house. Now she goes for evening strolls while her husband Paul takes care of Paul Junior, or some-times she even puts Junior in a stroller, and off she goes. It's magic. Suddenly I have clothes again. They appear on my desk. I write checks. The world is a better place. Andre may like me as Lady Godiva but the business world expects consultants to wear clothes. I've never tried showing up naked but chances are it would make it hard to get much business done.

I did the best I could with my hair. Inside the hotel it was all right, but outside, the damp tropical air made it even curlier than usual and it was like a big cloud of knots. Oh, what the hell. I was the one who wanted it long. I opened the door and stepped out onto the balcony. It was early and things were still quiet. No jet skis buzzing. No catamarans. No sailboats with brightly colored sails. No children splashing and shouting. It was nice. The last taste of dawn was still in the sky.

"Good morning." I turned and there was Dr. Pryzinski on his balcony, reading a book.

"Good morning. Looks like a lovely day."

"It does," he said. "Marie and I are taking a boat trip to Molokini today to do some snorkeling. Maybe you'd like to join us?"

It sounded like fun and I was dying to get away from the hotel. "What time are you going?"

He checked his watch, a funny habit many of us have when thinking about time. "It's a two o'clock boat," he said, "so we're leaving here around one. Marie hates being late. We've got room in the car and we'd love to have you."

I did my own quick calculations. The seminars were starting at nine, which meant that everyone would be done by eleven-thirty and then off to their fun events. According to a memo that had been slipped under my door, the board was meeting with the hotel manager at seven and our public relations person at seven-thirty, so we should be able to take care of business before the seminars. Yes. I was free. I could do it. "I'd love to," I said. "Do I need to make a reservation?"

"No problem," he said. "I'll give the concierge a call and have you added to our party."

"I don't have any gear."

He smiled the paternal smile of one who knows all the tricks. Ed and Marie had children. "That's no problem either. They said they'd have lots of it on the boat for anyone who didn't bring their own. We'll just knock on your door on the way out, shall we?" I had the feeling that I was being taken up, or taken in, or however you'd put it. Being taken care of. It was kind of nice. Dr. Pryzinski might spend his days up to his elbows in blood, but he hadn't lost his humanity. Maybe it was a Midwest-versus-the-East kind of thing. Whenever I leave the East Coast to visit schools, I feel like I'm entering a nicer, simpler world. The problems may be much the same, but the people rev at lower RPMs.

From inside I heard Marie's voice. "Eddie? Are you out there talking to yourself?"

"I'm talking to Thea, dear. Come on out and say hello. I've invited her to come snorkeling with us."

She stuck her head out. It was still done up in big pink foam rollers. "Hi," she said. "No more trouble with the police, I hope?"

"They dropped by at about two A.M. Stayed an hour and went away. I get the feeling they don't like me much."

"Oh, I wouldn't worry about it," she said, shaking the rollers wisely. "It's not you. That's just how they are, isn't it, Ed?" Ed nodded. I got the feeling that Ed nodded a lot, whether he agreed with her or not. But then, I also got the feeling that Ed really liked Marie, and that pleased me. I'm always happy when I see older couples who visibly like each other. It gives me hope.

"Bernstein's touchy," he said. "He's a good cop, though. You can trust him and he's smart. As long as you're straight with him, you don't have anything to worry about."

I thought I'd been about as straight as a person can be with cops. "I've done my best," I said.

When I bent down to pick up my earrings, I noticed that the message light was blinking. I hadn't checked it since I'd told them to hold my calls yesterday afternoon. It was incredibly irresponsible and not at all like me. I picked it up and followed the instructions. The first message was from Andre. Very brief, he didn't want to disturb me, giving me the number at Jack Leonard's and at the local station where I could reach him if I needed to. He hoped I was out on the beach working on those tan lines. He'd call later. The second was from Jolene, changing where we were meeting and confirming the times.

The third one began with a long silence, and then a little voice, saying, "Hi, this is the spy. Meet me by the blue parrot in the lobby at noon and I'll make it worth your while. P.S. The police are taking me to breakfast and Geoffrey is green with envy. How did you ever manage that?" Poor Laura. I hoped the police would be gentle with her. I had so little confidence in Bernstein's self-control, and Nihilani might have a side I hadn't yet seen, but so far, he seemed to have no warmth. Yes, I said to an imaginary Andre, I know the police aren't supposed to be warm and fuzzy, but Laura, for all her precocity, was only a child. And a sensitive one.

Had it not already been curly, the fourth message would have curled my hair. Just a man's voice, no greeting. "You bitch. You told them! If I ever get my hands on you, I'll wring your fucking neck."

"And a gracious good morning to you, too, Lewis," I said as I hung up the phone. I carefully saved the message. I thought I might want to play it for my friends from the Maui police.

I couldn't remember whether Jolene had said it was a breakfast meeting or not. I hoped so. I'd been snatched away from the grilled shrimp in midbite so it felt like I'd never finished dinner. I don't like things left unfinished. They haunt me. I'll come back hours later to a half-finished cup of coffee, and woe to the person who throws it out in the meantime. I'll spend the rest of the day with a restless sense that something still needs to be done. Probably I have a bit of the obsessive-compulsive personality. Then again, who doesn't? Just like there are no functional families, there are probably no people around without some quirks that qualify as defined disorders. We can only hope to keep them sufficiently in check so that we still function.

I hurried into the meeting room and followed my nose directly to the coffee urn, fortifying myself with a cup before I said good morning to anyone. Since I knew the others, I figured the dapper Asian man at the head of the table must be the hotel manager. He looked like he was already having a bad day. I set my coffee on the table, but before I could sit down, Jolene grabbed my elbow and pulled me aside.

"I saw Lewis Broder a minute ago," she whispered. "At the desk with a suitcase. Checking out, I suppose. He gave me the dirtiest look! As if I was responsible for doing him some harm. And he left an awful message on my machine, accusing me of reporting him to the police. After what he did last night, I *should* have reported him. But I didn't. And see what I get for my forbearance?"

Forbearance was Jolene's kind of word. Tolerant. Patient. She was sharp enough to know that goodness didn't require being a fool. "Don't worry about it," I said. "He left me one, too. Did he threaten to strangle you, too?"

"Yes." She seemed relieved that I'd gotten the same message. "You don't think he—"

"I doubt it. Whoever killed Martina planned it. If Lewis ever were to kill someone, it wouldn't be premeditated. It would be impulsive and inept. He'd probably leave his wallet behind in his haste to escape, and then whine 'Poor me, she made me do it' all the way to jail."

She shook her head sadly. "This is all so ugly. Did you see the paper this morning?"

There had been one outside my door, but I'd just carried it in and tossed it on the bed on my way out. I hadn't even looked at the headlines. "Bad?"

"Not too. Well . . . the whole business is bad, but the story doesn't say much about the crime, probably because the police don't know much. And it was very positive about what a wonderful person Martina was."

"Billy Berryman," I said. William Berryman, known to everyone as Billy, was our public relations guy. Billy was young. He looked like a geeky twelve-year-old who ought to be in his room making explosives with his chemistry set, but appearances can be deceiving. In my opinion, Billy was brilliant. He could read minds and he could telegraph thoughts and ideas to the press so well they never knew what hit them. He also possessed the magical ability to seduce cameras, so that on the screen, his geekiness fell away and he looked young and earnest and winningly sincere.

"You bet. Where'd we find the guy, anyway?"

"Oh, those gals at EDGE Consulting. Once in a while they do something right."

She was surprised. "You and Suzanne found him?"

"Nah. We made him in the back room from excess body parts."

"This morning, that doesn't seem at all funny."

"You're right." I switched to another topic. "Is there going to be food?"

Shannon leaned into the conversation in time to hear my question. "Honey, if there is one thing we headmistresses know, it's that tragedy and food go hand in hand. Never leave anyone alone to discuss disaster without a sandwich, right, Zannah?"

Zannah, in a pink dress, looked like she'd been spit polished before leaving her room. Every hair was in place—not that that would be true of mine even if I used a gallon of shellac—and her outfit was impeccably pressed and accessorized. "Maybe it's the Jewish mother in me," Zannah said, "but I don't think you can have a conversation without food."

I stared. "Jewish mother?"

"You didn't know? I was adopted when I was four by Mel and Sarah Steinberg."

"People!" Jonetta rapped on the table. "People. Time's awasting. Let's get this show on the road." Like the nice girls and boy we were, we took our seats. I wondered why she was running the meeting instead of Jolene. She nodded toward the man at the head of the table. "This is Denby Inashima, hotel manager." Mr. Inashima bowed and said good morning.

The second we were in our seats and Mr. Inashima had bowed, a brisk cadre of servers spread placements before us and set down steaming plates of food. This was no muffins-and-coffee buffet. This was a meal. An eggs-and-bacon-and-potatoes-and-toast meal, the kind no one eats anymore because it pushes all the bad-for-you buttons. I sighed and smiled and waited for Mr. Inashima to continue. "On behalf of the hotel, I apologize for the problems there have been with some of your arrangements," he began. "There have been some miscalculations, which I deeply regret." He bowed again. "However, we are meeting this morning to determine how we may all work together to ensure that despite this . . . tragedy . . . which has occurred, the conference can proceed as smoothly as possible. First of all . . ."

On cue, a tall, slim, middle-aged woman with her hair in an efficient chignon, entered the room. "This is Mrs. Sato, our assistant manager. She will be working with you on every detail to ensure the success of the remainder of your convention. Mrs. Sato will be going over all of the details with you, as she would have with Mrs. Pullman. I can assure you that everything will be given her personal attention." Mr. Inashima bowed again. "There is no one better than Mrs. Sato." He said a few more consoling and reassuring things, and then checked his watch. "Unfortunately, I must now attend another meeting. Please call upon Mrs. Sato for your every need." He rose gracefully from his chair, bowed again, and departed.

Mrs. Sato did a liquid slide into his seat, pulled some papers from a leather folder, and spread them on the table before her. "This morning you have scheduled four conference rooms," she said. "Yesterday there was some confusion. . . ." And we were off, taking care of business. Room sizes, PA systems, signage. Tour buses and boat trips, snorkel trips, and bike trips. This evening's banquet. Our PR person would be meeting with their PR person. There would be no more glitches. The hotel would align their press releases with ours. A one-page letter from the manager would be slipped under every door. They did not, any more than we, wish to have anyone's vacation/conference marred by dwelling on violent death.

Seven-thirty came. Mrs. Sato ran a red-lacquered fingernail down her checklist. "There is one remaining thing," she said. "The guest count for this evening's dinner. If I could have that, please, we can be sure there are no problems such as have occurred before."

She waited. None of us spoke. It was an uncomfortable silence. Finally Jonetta broke it. "I'm afraid Ms. Pullman's assistant has that information and she isn't here this morning. We will have to get that information to you later."

Ms. Sato looked down at the list again while she evicted displeasure from her face and reinstated placidity. "Certainly," she agreed. "As soon as you can." She slid out of her seat and glided away.

Billy Berryman took her place. Billy was neither quiet nor graceful. Papers spilled from his hands and words spilled from his mouth and after the peaceful approach of Mr. Inashima, it was like being sucked into a whirlwind. Names of newspapers and contacts poured out. Details of press releases. Suggestions about damage control. More suggestions about damage control. Billy was reassuring. If such a thing had to happen, better that it should happen here than in Washington, where Martina and Jeff were well known, while here we were transients and it was the aim of the tourist industry to keep a lid on things and not scare the customers. As he spoke, he was passing things out. Copies of the press coverage "back home." Copies of what he'd released, what he was planning to release.

"I'd like to get something on the record from Jeff," he said. "Could you fix that up, do you think, Jonetta?"

"Shouldn't we leave the poor man alone?" Jolene said. "He's just lost his wife. Surely this is no time to be worrying him with our concerns."

Billy shook his head. "Don't forget, Joly, Jeff's a pro. Tragic mourning for murdered wife will get him some sympathetic ears when he gets home. And from our point of view, Martina's loss as a spokeswoman for America's girls is a headline we don't want to pass up."

"That's ghoulish," she said.

"Au contraire," he said. "It's memorializing. It's press inches. Martina loved press. You wouldn't deny her in death what she so cherished in life."

"Billy, darlin," Shannon said, "you could get a serial killer of children a job in a day-care center, you know that? You positively scare me sometimes."

"Sometimes I scare myself. Okay. Jonetta, you're going to get me some time with Jeff, right? And Thea, I need a copy of that speech you gave yesterday and about half an hour of your time. And what are we doing about tonight? Who's going to introduce

the speaker? Thea, I think that's you as well. We'll work on it together. Something nice and juicy about the next big area of focus,
the hot-button issue for the millennium, whether public schools
can offer girls the opportunity for single-sex education or whether
they'll run afoul of the separate-but-equal problem. I love it!
Nothing is more fun than being on the cutting edge."

Rob Greene was edging his way toward the door. "Hold it!
Rob! Don't try and get away. We've got some brainstorming to do.
Think memorial service. Think memorial acts. We handle this
right, and Martina can be even bigger in death than she was in
life."

"Billy, that is utterly tasteless," Jolene said. "Can you at least
pretend not to be so enthusiastic? More than any of us, you should
know that appearances count."

"You bet, Joly. But hey, I'm among friends. The second I walk
out of this room, I shall assume the solemn mask of tragedy. Oh,
yeah. Almost forgot . . ." He started digging through his bag. I
didn't want to give him half an hour to write an intro to the dinner speech and talk about spin. I wanted to slap him upside the
head and tell him to cool it for a while. I wanted to remind him
that good as he was, no one is irreplaceable, especially if they of-
fend the client. I wanted to remind him that in business, you are
never among friends. Your clients are your friends only as long as
it is expedient.

He pulled out a stapled stack of photocopied sheets. "Get a
look at these, will you? Makes you wonder if maybe we can't stop
looking suspiciously at each other, doesn't it?"

I took the bundle and scanned it to see what he was referring
to. It was a bunch of newspaper clippings about murders. All the
murders had taken place in resort hotels. In no case was there a
suspect. And the killer, if indeed there was a single perpetrator, was
being called, in one of the stories, the lingerie killer. In each case,
the victim was dressed in revealing underwear—bustier, thong
panties, garter belt—and strangled with a stocking.

CHAPTER 15

SHANNON WAS THE first to speak. "Is this one of those cases where bad news is good news?"

"If a serial killer can ever be considered good news," Jolene amended.

Billy just shrugged. "I don't know if that's what we've got here or not. That's for the police to say. The others were in Florida, Colorado, and California, but they were all at resorts. For that matter, I don't even know if the Maui police know about this stuff. I found them by playing on the Internet. And it took me a long time." He raised his eyebrows at me, which meant I was supposed to understand that he was billing for all that time. *Sure, Billy*, I thought, *anything you want*. He might have just gotten the police off our backs. I, for one, would kiss the ground he walked on if that was the case. My vacation fun would not be diminished if I had no more visits from the midnight twins Bernstein and Nihilani.

"Oh, sure," Zannah said. "They're all on the Internet these days. Don't they just tap into their computers and call up the FBI or something? You know, 'Dear Mr. FBI, we just had this crime. Do you have anyone on your serial killers list who fits the bill,' that sort of thing?"

Jonetta shook her head. "Girl, you've been watching too much television. Okay, is everybody cool for this morning? You got your new seminar room assignments that Mrs. Sato handed out? Everyone knows where they're going?"

"Jonetta, most of us will never know where we're going," Rob Greene said. He was rumpled and disorganized this morning. Very unusual for him. Even his mustache was unkempt.

"In the short-term, Rob. In the short-term," she said. He nodded. "All you have to do is introduce the panels and then be there to troubleshoot in case all hell breaks loose." No one said anything. "Fine," she said. "That's it for now. If anyone sees that Rory, rope her and hog-tie her and deliver her to Jolene. She won't answer her door, she won't return phone calls, and I can't get at her files. There are all sorts of things I need from her and I can't get anything. That stuff she delivered so dramatically last night? It was crap. It was for the two days we've already gotten through. We still have nothing for the rest of the conference. Nor for next month's board meeting, nor the articles we're supposed to be considering for the next newsletter, even though Martina promised Rory had all that stuff with her, right on her handy-dandy laptop."

She paused, and we assumed we were all dismissed. Then she said, "May I have a resolution of the board to fire Rory? Effective immediately?"

"I so move," Shannon said.

"Second the motion," Zannah said firmly. That surprised me. Zannah was usually our bleeding heart, the voice for giving everyone second and third chances, for trying to understand why people did what they did. Maybe that's why she'd been able to get along with Martina.

Billy leaned forward and opened his mouth. "Maybe we should . . ." We waited to see what he had to say, but after a few seconds hesitation, he shook his head and leaned back, folding his arms across his chest.

"All in favor," Jonetta asked.

I was the only dissenting vote. Not because I had any respect for Rory. I didn't. I thought she was being an incredible wimp. Her behavior was tiresome and irresponsible. I dissented because I know how confronting the dead body of someone you're close to can knock you off your feet and make you behave in abnormal ways. In fact, I was glad the vote went against me. Being able to replace Rory quickly, while it might give us a bit of down time at first, was a good first step toward a new regime.

Jolene was the first one up. "Running to the ladies'," she said, "Be right back." She hesitated at the door. "Before I forget. Jonetta, Thea . . . if you do find Rory . . . will one of you, please, just take her laptop so we'll have it? Never mind if she screams and hollers. This constantly trying to track her down and wrangle every piece of necessary paper out of her is tiresome and unproductive. Much as she treats the darned thing like a special pet, it doesn't belong to her. It's ours. The association's, I mean." She turned and walked away, shoulders slumped, as though the speech had been hard for her.

There was a noticeable change in everyone after Billy's announcement. It was only as they filed out that I understood what had just happened. All the caution, all the restraint, all the unnaturally formal behavior or unusually boisterous camaraderie, and all the strain I'd seen on everyone's faces had resulted, in part, from a fear—a suspicion—that one of the group had killed Martina and killed her in a particularly vicious and ugly way. Billy's information that it might have been the work of an anonymous stranger really had been a cause for relief. It made me feel rather naive and trusting that I hadn't assumed it was one of us—unless Lewis Broder counted as one of us—and I was the one most familiar with murder.

The group dispersed and I stayed behind with Jolene and Billy to work on the introduction to the speech. Billy also wanted my advice on a number of other things, and there was stuff he wanted faxed from my office back in Massachusetts.

"But Billy, it's Saturday. There's no one in the office."

He shrugged. "Call someone. Surely you must have staff."

"Your problem is that you work in Washington. You think the world revolves around putting the right spin on everything. Back home in Massachusetts, we don't like our names in print. And we still take the occasional day off."

"Maybe they do, but you are a workaholic."

"Not me. I'm even taking the afternoon off. Going snorkeling at Molokini."

He looked surprised. "Maybe in Hawaii you'll play, but if I were here and you were there, I'd be able to get what I wanted, Saturday or not."

"Not anymore. I'm busy on weekends."

"The burly cop?" I nodded, I knew who he meant, even though I never would have called Andre burly. "Pity," he said. "Well, isn't there someone you can call who can get in there and fax us some stuff?"

"Let's make a list of what you need, and then we'll see."

Jonetta stuck her head in. "Sorry to interrupt. When you're done, Thea, let's pay a call on Rory, shall we?"

I checked my watch. "If we have time. Where will I find you?"

"In my room."

Billy had a list in front of him, and he went straight down it, giving instructions and telling us what he needed. Suddenly he snapped his fingers. "Damn!" he said. "I forgot. While the board was all together, they should have appointed Joly here as acting director." Jolene lowered her eyes and stared at her intertwined fingers. "Don't look so modest. It's not like this is news or something. You know it's what the board wants."

"Not now, Billy," I said. "It would look terrible to replace Martina so quickly."

"I only said 'acting' director." He sounded sulky. He even looked sulky.

"Don't sulk," I said. "It's not becoming. Let's get to the speech. If only we had Martina's papers, this would be a cinch. I put the stuff together for her because we found the speaker. But it's just an introduction."

"You don't have her papers?" he interrupted.

"Of course not. The police have her papers. This is a homicide, Billy. They take everything. I had to steal back my own speech yesterday. They weren't going to let me have it. You can imagine what a disaster that would have been. They made me give it back afterwards."

He nodded and moved his chair closer, then said, in a lower voice, "You think I'm callous, don't you? You think I'm taking this too lightly, right?" I started to shake my head. "Don't deny it," he said. "I read minds, remember? Anyway, for the record, I'm not. I'm doing exactly what you're doing."

"Which is?"

"Getting immersed in the job so I won't have to think about what happened to Martina. That's what we're all doing, isn't it, Joly?"

Jolene nodded cautiously, as if she didn't quite trust what she was agreeing to. "I've been thinking, maybe if I'd tried harder, I could have worked with her," she said. "I've been wondering how much our disapproval, which she has to have known about, contributed to her downfall. . . ." She trailed off and for the first time I noticed how pale she was and how unlike herself she looked. There was nothing flashy about Jolene, but she always had a quiet luminosity, a way in which the good person and the good intentions showed through. Today she looked plain and tired, as though someone had turned the internal light off. We all looked plain and tired.

"You didn't fail her, Joly," Billy said. "She failed all of you. All of you and all the girls whose brighter futures depended on her success."

"Let's not get too dramatic here, Billy. Setting aside the idea that we mustn't speak ill of the dead, it isn't true that Martina was a failure, she'd just . . . she was in a slump," I said.

"Like a baseball player?" he said. "You think a good batting coach could have nudged her out of it? Give me a break, Thea! Martina Pullman had a good, maybe a great, cause to work for. She used that cause to promote herself . . . no, wait!" He held up a hand to keep me from interrupting. "I know you think you've got to protect her, but let me finish, okay? We are . . . were . . . all of us . . . you, me, Joly, Jonetta, Shannon, Rob, Zannah, your partner Suzanne, and even poor Rory, props of Martina Pullman, Inc. Why? Because we got paid to be? Some of us, some of the time. Me, I'm a very good hired flack, but—"

"Billy—"

He reached out and put a hand over my mouth. "Let me finish," he repeated. "Thea, my lovely, you are a beautiful, intelligent, thoughtful, caring, more than hardworking stand-up gal, but even in your perfection, you are not always right."

It was a sentiment my own hardworking, gorgeous stand-up guy, Andre Lemieux, had voiced as well. I exerted self-control and stopped trying to get my own oar in. Maybe, for once, I should listen. I nodded to indicated my cooperation. Jolene was watching the two of us with a shocked look on her face.

"As I was saying . . . people like you and me, like Suzanne and Rory, we're here because we get paid to be here. The others are on the board because they believe in the mission of the association. But even the two of us, you and I, also do this because we think that equity in education, or finding better ways to educate the underserved half of our population, is important, right?" He didn't wait for a reply. "I don't know whether Martina once passionately believed in the education of girls or whether she had just found an issue that she could successfully manipulate. I like to believe it was the latter—"

"Excuse me," Jolene interrupted. "Where are you going with this, Billy? We all know that Martina was committed to educating girls—"

"Then why did she stop paying tuition for her stepdaughter, Melissa, at a private girl's school, forcing her back into a coed public school?"

"Maybe that was Jeff's decision, or the mother's. Maybe Melissa wasn't doing well and was asked to leave."

"Can we get on with this meeting?" I interrupted. "I've got things to do."

"Thea, you will die with things to do," he said. "We all will. I just want to get this out on the table, okay? For the record, Melissa was doing fine, and her mother wanted her to stay there but couldn't afford it, and Melissa loved the school and wanted to stay. My point is that Martina could easily have kept her there but wouldn't . . . a classic case of not putting your money where your mouth is. But that's not what I wanted to say."

He cleared his throat, waiting to see if I would interrupt again.

Looking at him, I realized that like the rest of us, Billy was getting older. He no longer looked like a gawky teenager trying to figure out how to be a grown-up. He was a grown-up. Still geeky, but he'd matured, while I'd looked at him once, formed an opinion, and stopped noticing. "For the past eighteen months, two years, Martina has been coming apart, drinking heavily, forgetful, erratic, abusive not just to co-workers like you two and subordinates like Rory, but to people she needed as supporters and friends," he said. "She's made an ass of herself at parties and dinners, called press conferences and then forgotten what she wanted to say. Wrapped herself around other men when Jeff was present."

He stared down at the table. He wanted to tell us this but it wasn't easy for him. "Poor Jeff has been carrying a terrible burden. He and Rory have worked their tails off, trying to keep her from ruin. Plenty of nights, Rory had to see her home and put her to bed. She was practically living there, from what I hear. I've pulled Martina back from the brink, played wetnurse, scraped the mud off, and made the best of things so many times I've lost count. I have read her press releases while she stood there barely staying on her feet, breathing her fetid alcoholic breath in my ear."

"Billy, she's dead," I said.

"Goddamn it, I know that!" Billy Berryman, Mr. Cool and With It, Mr. Manipulation and Spin Control, started to cry. "Shit!" he said. "I can't believe this. I didn't mean . . . I used to admire her so much. When I started working with her, I used to think she was a shining model of exactly how a person should be. . . . She was one of my heroes, you know? I thought I was so lucky to be able to work for one of those rare people who can make a difference." He unbuttoned the top button of his collarless linen shirt and pulled it away from his throat like it was choking him. I passed him some tissues.

"This is ridiculous . . . I can't believe I'm sitting here crying about this," he said. "There was a time, a few years ago, when I used to think I was in love with Martina, when I'd listen to her speak and I'd listen to her ideas and it was all so inspiring and then . . ." He blew his nose and apologized. "Then I began to see what was really going on. How she stole from people, how she used them . . . how she was never willing to give credit where it was due, never wanted to share the spotlight. It was like lifting the cover on a beautiful box and finding the inside crawling with maggots. . . ."

He turned his face way to hide the tears, but he was with the two of us, instinctive comforters. Jolene and I moved in and put our arms around him. "I'm a hired gun," he whispered. "I'm not supposed to care . . . but I cared so much for what I thought she was . . . and when I saw what she truly was, I . . . I . . . I hated her. And now she's dead and she died while I was still hating her and I don't know what to do."

A couple of deep breaths and sobs and sniffs. We kept our arms around him. Finally he shook us off. "Let's get on with it. We've got work to do."

We gathered around the papers again. Billy gave me the list of things he wanted and gave Jolene another list. Then Jolene left, I opened my laptop, and Billy and I hashed out an introduction together. "This should do," he said, scanning the screen. "Maybe Rory's got the stuff you need to fill in those spaces."

We both stood up. It was only 8:00 A.M. and if the way I looked matched the way I felt, I was going to go out there and scare babies and small children. "Billy," I said, "I know how you feel. The best you can do, once someone is dead, is to try and remember the good stuff. The process of dealing is bad enough without filling your head with—"

He turned away. "Don't bother," he said. "Nothing is going to make me feel good right now."

"Billy, I've been there. You know how, at weddings, they tie a string of cans to the car and when it drives off, the cans come rattling along behind? Well, I've got a string of sad, complicated muddled deaths tied to my ankle, and everywhere I go, they come rattling along behind me. I'd give anything to be able to cut the string and leave it all behind but life's not like that. Your memory comes with you. You have to do your best to keep it from pulling you backwards and weighing you down. You gotta keep on walking. . . ."

"I've got work to do," he said in a strangled voice.

"Me, too." I left him alone with his grief.

Jonetta was waiting outside in the hall. "Shall we tackle Rory now?"

I shrugged, not looking forward to another emotional confrontation. "Might as well." I patted the laptop. "I just want to stop at my room and drop this off. It seems to weigh a ton today."

I wasn't eager to confront Rory again. I knew that shock took different people different ways. Unfortunately, the ways it was taking her were all the ones I scorned most. Hysterics, hyperbole, self-pity, drunken exhibitions, and a complete abandonment of responsibility. Maybe because they were the weaknesses I feared most in myself.

Sometimes I felt like I'd been hanging on by my fingertips for years, about to fall off the ledge, and only willpower kept me from letting go. Sometimes I longed to let go, to stop being logical and controlled and disciplined and responsible. It was lovely to fantasize about throwing myself into Andre's arms and letting him take care of me. I imagined quitting my too-hard job and settling down with novels and bonbons. But not for long. My fears of the loss of autonomy and being dependent were too great.

"It's going to be just like yesterday," I said. "She won't answer the door and we're going to have to get security again."

"We'll do what we gotta do," Jonetta said. "There are so many people depending on us for a successful conference. We can't be letting one person screw up the whole thing because she's upset. Who *isn't* upset? Shannon's getting wilder by the minute, Rob's muttering dark threats about quitting, Jolene looks like someone drank a quart of her blood in the night, and our quiet Pollyanna Ms. Wu from San Francisco is nibbling off her nail polish and looking over her shoulder every five minutes. Even little devil-may-care Billy is upset and I didn't think he had feelings, only circuits and sound bites."

She stabbed the elevator button with an angry finger. "Damned media hog. The woman can't even die quietly."

"She didn't choose the way she died, Netta."

"I know. I know. Don't mind me. This thing wears me down,

that's all. I thought I'd be walking through this weekend with my eyes shut, know what I mean? I was looking forward to some informative talks and good food and some lying in the sun. Plannin' on doing some thinking there by the pool. Closin' my eyes and plannin' out the future. Girl, I have got a lot of thinking to do, too. If I can't raise another half-million dollars in the next few months, we're going to be closing our doors, all those poor babies back out on the streets again. Makes me feel like a criminal, taking them in and giving them hope like I've done and now maybe I can't live up to my promises."

The elevator opened and we got in. The door rolled silently shut. I pressed twelve. Jonetta stabbed seventeen. "Thing was, I thought we had that money. Martina had promised me. She had sources, she had grants, she was going to put something together. It was cool as long as she'd get the credit." Jonetta spread her arms, bracelets jangling. "What did I care who got the glory, if I could save some kids? Then she says no deal. I know that I was dumb to have trusted something that wasn't in writing, but we've been colleagues a long time now, and I let down my guard and relied on her word. Expanded the school on a little seed money and a promise of the rest, and then, just two weeks ago, she calls me up and says she's ever so sorry but she had to divert that money somewhere else, she knows I'll understand."

She banged her fist against the elevator wall. "I told her I damned well didn't understand. I told her that real girls who were in a life-or-death situation were counting on that money and that it was a damned sight more important than funding some study or other. She said I was out of control and she'd discuss it with me sometime when I was calm. Well, I told her that when the issue was throwing desperate black girls back in the street, kickin' 'em in the teeth and telling them we couldn't give 'em an education after all, when that was what we'd promised, I'd never be calm. She said there was nothing in writing, so how was I ever going to show that promise, when she was the one who said we didn't need to put it in writing, her word was as good as a promise."

The door opened on twelve and we got out. "Of course, I did

calm down. I knew it was my mistake, not getting it in writing. I wasn't born yesterday. I know that in business, nobody is your friend, so I let it go."

She paused while I got out my key, let myself in, and dropped my laptop on the desk. On our way back to the elevator, she said, "Well, I let the money issue go. Didn't seem like there was anything else I could do. But I came here determined not to leave until Martina had been replaced, whatever that took."

We rode in silence up to seventeen. Got off and walked to Rory's door. Jonetta raised a big hand and knocked sharply.

I didn't want to have heard what I'd just heard. We all should have sat down and talked long ago. I wondered what Rob's story was, and Zannah's. The wrongs that Martina had been committing were piling up like snowdrifts, covering all the good she'd done. So many evil, hateful, selfish acts. I didn't think any of us realized how much harm been done in the name of the organization. "Does everyone have a story like this?" I asked.

"I think so," she said. "There have been some dark hints, but no one is saying much. Especially now." She knocked again. "Damn that girl!" she muttered. I felt a black sense of foreboding steal over me. A powerful sense of déjà vu. I wanted to run away and leave Jonetta to deal with it this time. But even as the urge to flee was rushing through my mind, I saw a maid come out of a room two doors down. I hurried to her.

"Please," I said, "could you open this door? Our friend was ill last night and now she doesn't answer. I'm afraid she may need a doctor."

She didn't ask any questions, or dither, or suggest we call security. She simply put her key in the lock and opened it. None of the security locks were on. The door opened into a deadly quiet darkness. The curtains were drawn. The air-conditioning had dropped the temperature so that a blast of icy air came rushing at us as the door opened.

Jonetta marched in, calling Rory's name. No one answered. The maid turned on the light. There was no one in the bed, although it appeared to have been slept in.

"We have to check the bathroom," I said. I didn't move. I couldn't move. "No. Let's get out of here. Let's call security and have them check."

"What's the matter with you, girl?" Jonetta said. "Suddenly you lost your nerve?"

"Yes."

"Well, get a grip." Jonetta crossed to the bathroom and yanked open the door. Rory lay on the floor between the toilet and tub, surrounded by towels. With the white towels and her white dress and her white skin all splashed with blood, she looked like a pile of bloody laundry waiting to be collected. "Sweet Jesus!" Jonetta said.

I pushed past her and reached down, feeling Rory's neck for a pulse. "She's alive," I said. I ran for the phone. Behind me, I could hear Jonetta murmuring as she bent to see what she could do for Rory. It probably wasn't the first time she'd had to deal with a girl who'd slashed her wrists. The maid was screaming, a peculiar rising and falling wail like a distant fire engine. I picked up the phone and asked for the manager. The operator tried to shunt me aside.

"Mr. Inashima," I insisted. "Please tell him that he has an attempted suicide in Room Seventeen-eleven, the young woman who was assistant to the woman who was murdered, and we need a doctor and an ambulance. He might also want to contact the police."

"I'll take care of it," she said, "and I will have him call you back."

I put down the phone and waited, my own wrists aching. I closed my eyes but all I could see was a picture of myself, crumpled in the driver's seat of my car, feeling the hot rush of blood from my own wrists, feeling my own life ebbing away, helpless to do anything about it. I wrapped my arms around my body and rocked, shaking with the cold, and with memories that clung like tin cans to my ankle.

CHAPTER 16

LIKE A CONTESTANT on the $64,000 question, I was in an isolation booth. I couldn't hear anything that was going on around me. I kept my arms wrapped tightly around my body and I rocked. I rocked and I shook and I rocked and the pain in my wrists was so great I felt like screaming. Someone had tried to kill me once by slashing my wrists to make it look like suicide. Seeing Rory brought it all rushing back. I was as mired in those awful memories as a tiger in a tar pit. I felt like joining that damned hysterical maid who was imitating a fire engine. I left all the hard work to Jonetta and I didn't do a thing except sit there. Jonetta had to call me three times before she penetrated the fog.

"Thea. Thea. Thea!" The third time shook the rafters. Having a powerful voice has its advantages. I shook off the cloak of shock that trapped me and went to the bathroom door. She looked up at me. "Help me get her to the bed," she said. "I want to wrap her up. We don't know how long it will be until help arrives."

"I'll take her feet." It meant stepping over her body and the blood, but at least it kept me away from those wounded hands.

Together we carried Rory's limp form to the bed, propped her head and feet up on pillows, her arms folded on her chest, and covered her with blankets. Jonetta had wrapped her wrists in towels. Arranged like that, she looked like some warrior princess, killed in battle, laid out for her funeral pyre. Her skin waxen and pale, her dark hair pooled on the pillow. I turned off the air conditioner and opened the door to let some warm air in.

Jonetta finished, planted her hands on her hips, and stepped back. "Good thing we're forceful women. If we hadn't come up here, if we'd waited for her to come to us, who knows what harm a few more hours might have done? I knew she was upset. I never thought she'd do something like this." She shook her head. "I wonder why?"

"Yesterday she was sure that they'd blame her. Maybe she still thought that. People can be pretty crazy."

"Unless she did it. Someone did it." Jonetta shifted her attention to me. "Girl, you look like you've just seen a ghost. What's wrong?"

I didn't want to talk about it. I didn't want to think about it. Sometimes things happen to you that you don't want to remember. The inside of my head was becoming my own personal Madame Tussaud's of violence and crime. I shook my head. "Nothing. All that blood. Finding the two of them . . . like this . . . I . . ." Maybe I was becoming the world's biggest wimp, but I had to get away from the smell of blood, the bloody bathroom, the trail of scarlet drops across the carpet. "Would you mind if I left . . . can you . . . There isn't anything more I can do. . . ." I hated to run out on her. It didn't seem fair to leave her deal with such a mess on her own.

"Honey, this isn't the first time I've picked some poor girl up off the bathroom floor. I don't mean to sound like a hard-ass, but you might say I'm kind of used to it. You go along. You've got a seminar in a few minutes anyway." Obediently, gratefully, I headed for the door. "Wait!" she said. "Remember what Jolene said. Take her laptop. We're sure gonna need it, all the stuff that's on it, and if the cops come, you can bet it'll go right downtown and we'll be up the proverbial creek." Mechanically I crossed to the desk and packed the laptop into its case.

"Wait," she said, "better take the printer, too, or they'll wonder why in heck she had a printer with nothing to print from."

And so I left, lugging the laptop and portable printer before anyone could arrive and say nay. I carried it down to my room, put it on my desk, plugged it in, and took a quick break to throw up. I've learned to work a lot of stuff into my routine. I could walk and chew gum. I could talk on the phone and type. I could work on two major reports at once and not mix up the data. I could skate and kiss Andre without falling down. And now I was learning to download data and throw up without missing a beat. Still, when I got home, it was time to see the doctor. Whether it was mono, hepatitis, a parasite, food poisoning, or an ulcer, I was losing meals at about the same rate that I was eating them. Eventually, like the all-celery diet, this could lead to starvation.

Only a few minutes left before I had to go downstairs and introduce Rob and his panel of speakers. Just time to get the banquet stuff except that Rory's computer wouldn't let me in without a password. All I could tell from the row of asterisks was that it was a five-letter word. It could take the rest of my life to crack the code. I closed my eyes, cursed the poor girl roundly, and tried to put myself in her shoes. I tried Martina, even though it had six letters, and NAGS though it only had four. I tried Aurora, which was Rory's real name. And then, as I sat there with hands poised over the keys, it came to me. I typed "bitch" and the computer let me in.

Quick as a wink, or as quickly as the poky little printer would let me, I made a copy of the stuff in her banquet file. Two minutes. I had figures for the dais and for the number of attendees. I picked up the phone and tried to reach Mrs. Sato. The helpful person I reached at the number we had been given announced that it was Mrs. Sato's day off. Someday I'm going to be sitting on the phone, one too many stupid messages is going to pour into my ear, and I'm going to die instantaneously from steamed brain. As it was, I could feel the ire rising.

"Where are you located?" I demanded. I did not use my polite voice. She told me. "Good. I'll be there in five minutes. This morning Mr. Denby Inashima told me that Mrs. Sato would be attending to all of our conference problems today. If, when I get there, she isn't available, I will go directly to Mr. Inashima." I slammed down the phone and headed for the door.

Oops. A last-minute glance in the mirror showed blood down

the skirt of my nice new jumper. Not the best way to appear before a group already made skittish by violent death. A quick change was required and no time to do it. Good thing I loved jumpers. I had a black one in the closet. Off went green. Off went my blouse. As I slipped off the blouse, I inhaled traces of men's cologne on the sleeve that had been around Billy. The same as the scent in Rory's room. When Billy supposedly hadn't even been here.

Stop dawdling, Kozak, and don't even think about playing detective. No time. No interest. No inclination. Let George do it. Or Nihilani and Bernstein. On went fresh blouse. On went black. And out I went. Loaded for bear. Actually, it was a good thing I didn't carry weapons. In my present state of mind, people were at risk.

I ducked into the seminar room, whispered my predicament to Rob Greene, and said I'd introduce him but then I had to leave for a few minutes, so please not to have any crises until I could get back. He promised that he would do his best. Then, the appointed hour arrived, I marched to the mike, gave everyone a warm welcome, said I hoped they were all enjoying themselves so far, and asked who had attended the luau. Most of the hands went up. "Well," I said, "I'm the one who didn't sing last night. But at least they let me talk." Then I introduced Rob and his panel and left them to talk about introducing girls to technology. Little did the crowd know that in about fifteen minutes, Rob and his co-panelists were going to be passing out kits and everyone in the room was going to be assigned to a team, the teams were going to assemble little motorized cars, and then there would be a race. This was hands-on learning.

I wanted to be back in time to build my car, so I was hurrying. I rarely get to play anymore. Following the directions I'd been given, I went to something called the conference offices. Mrs. Sato was waiting for me. She looked pointedly at her watch. "You said five minutes."

I thought the customer was always right. I looked at my own watch. "How nice to find you in," I said. "Your office said this was your day off. Look, I've just come from dealing with an attempted suicide. We had to wrap her up, call for EMTs and an ambulance, and then I had to find the files she couldn't help me with because she was unconscious. That involved figuring out the password to her computer, printing the files, changing out of my bloody clothes, and introducing a panel of speakers. All in the past fifteen minutes. And I threw up my breakfast. The sight of blood can do that to you. I am not in the best of moods, so let's just skip the pissing contest about who has kept whom waiting and discuss the banquet details."

Mrs. Sato, with whom we were supposed to be much pleased, inclined her supremely stiff and upright body in a mockery of a bow and swept an arm toward the corridor behind her. "If you'll step into my office." I wondered, as I followed her erect back, whether the Japanese had a term equivalent to "steel magnolia."

Since we clearly did not share a mutual admiration, I was glad she didn't waste any time on chitchat, but got right to the heart of things. She held out her hands for the papers. "May I see?"

She studied them and nodded. Compared them to a file of her own. Nodded again. "May I take copies?" she asked.

I inclined my head in a vestigial bow of my own. The conversation reminded me of Antioch dating rules. May I hold your hand? May I kiss you? May I unbutton your shirt? "Do our records agree this time?"

At least she was honest. "Sadly, no," she said. "Despite our written confirmations, we seem to have consistently undercounted. I shall have to change the room, which is a problem because . . ." She didn't finish the sentence. "It is of no matter. Things will be rectified. All will be well. . . ."

"Except that nearly everything in our printed program is wrong. People are constantly being sent to the wrong room, through your error. . . ."

"The hotel's error," she murmured. "I shall have all of the changes reprinted and delivered to your rooms, shall I?" She rose to her feet, signaling my dismissal.

I didn't rise. "The predinner cocktails? Is that room large enough? And you will check with food service as well? This isn't merely a matter of space, you know."

"You may confidently leave all of those details to me." Clearly she wasn't used to having her authority questioned, her dismissals not dismissive.

I stood. "Mrs. Sato, perhaps by your standards I am being overly cautious. On the other hand, by my standards, if I were to leave without your verbal assurances on each of these subjects, I would be overly careless. You run many conferences, I am sure. I am running only this one, but this particular one has had more than its share of disasters, both on your end and ours. I need to do everything I can to ensure that nothing more goes wrong. Nothing. I'm sure that we understand one another." I bowed most politely this time, giving her no choice but to reciprocate, and left, eager to go build my toy car.

I was rushing along the corridor, ticking over in my mind all of the things I might have forgotten, when someone called, "Thea, you going biking down the mountain today?" An acquaintance from Baltimore who had been standing beside me at the activity board when I was chosing my outing. "That's Sunday. Today I'm snorkeling," I said, "out at Molokini." I was looking for room numbers instead of where I was going and I ran full tilt into Jeff Pullman, who was folding up his phone.

"Thea," he said, steadying me. "I didn't know you were here. I thought your partner was coming." He shoved the phone in his pocket. His appearance shocked me. He was neatly dressed and freshly shaved, but he looked older, as if overnight he'd aged twenty years. There was even some gray in the thick, dark hair.

"Pneumonia," I said. "She's home in bed. I'm awfully sorry about Martina."

"Why?" he said bluntly. "She didn't like you. She didn't trust you. She knew you were out to get her."

It was a very un-Jefflike remark but his were trying circumstances. I shrugged it off. "I long ago got over the need to be liked by everyone, Jeff. I admired Martina. She was doing very important work."

"Yes, she was. I don't know if any of you realize how important. Nor am I sure that you can carry on Martina's level of achievement without her. She was a brilliant spokeswoman."

He's bitter and grieving, I reminded myself. *Don't take this personally.* I lowered my eyes and nodded. "None of us will be able to handle the press like Martina. That's true."

He continued as though I hadn't spoken, not so much talking to me as talking at me. It seemed to be a speech he had to give. "She knew what you were planning to do. She was aware that you were planning to vote her out of her directorship. She was terribly hurt by that. Terribly hurt. The association was her baby, her brainchild, she'd put you all on the board, and there you were, scheming to take it away from her. She wouldn't have let it go without a fight . . . but I guess that problem is solved for you now very neatly, isn't it? I wonder how you're going to live with that."

He turned on his heel and stalked away, but maybe ten feet down the hall he stopped and wheeled around. "Have you seen Rory? I've looked all over for her. I've left messages. I've called her room and gone up and knocked, and she's not answering. I know she has to be taking this very hard. I thought I'd"—he paused for a long time, then said—"comfort her. I thought she might need someone to talk to about . . . what hap—about Martina."

Talk about emotional seesaw! First he's laying the entire guilt trip for Martina's demise on my head and then in the next breath he's asking me if I know where Rory is. I didn't know what to say, given his emotional state. He seemed so volatile I wasn't sure he could handle another psychological blow. On the other hand, despite my nefarious deed concerning the pocketing of a speech, I do try to be an honest woman. I feel compelled to answer a direct question.

From what he'd said, it didn't look as though my image could be rehabilitated in his eyes, but I supposed, knowing what he was going through, that he deserved the truth. I didn't know quite how to deliver it. "Jeff . . . she's . . . she's not here . . . in the hotel. . . ."

"Oh, so she's left?" He sounded so eager, as if leaving was the perfect solution for Rory.

"Not exactly."

My hesitation made him belligerent again. "Well, spit it out, Thea. What's going on? Has something happened to her?" His phone rang. He pulled it out, barked hello, listened, then said,

"I'm in Maui, Joe. It'll have to wait." He shoved it back in his pocket and glared at me. "Well?"

We were standing in one of the main corridors of the hotel, leading from the lobby to one of the connecting buildings, and lots of people were going past. I wasn't going to deliver the news about Rory in a loud voice to someone ten feet away. I pointed toward a bench, off in a corner out of the flow. "Let's sit down there and I'll tell you."

"No!" he said, in such an explosive voice that at least ten people stopped and stared at him. "No. I'm not going to sit down and have a nice little chat with you after the way you treated my wife. Forget it. Just tell me where to find Rory."

Okay. He wanted to play hardball. He was refusing to be civilized. I was sorry but I'd done my best. I will cut people a lot of slack when they've been wounded by life, but when it comes to shouting and public abuse, I draw the line. In private, between the two of us, he could say anything he wanted. Before a whole hotel full of people, it was different. I had other people besides Jeff Pullman to think of. Rory's suicide attempt was not something I wanted broadcast all over the place and I was sure Rory didn't, either. Besides, I had always treated his wife fairly and decently. She'd been the bad actor.

"If you will lower your voice, stop the abuse, and come close enough so we can speak in civilized tones, I will tell you where to find Rory."

"Abuse? Abuse! You're one of a pack of witches who have just conspired to murder my wife and you're complaining about being abused? Just give me the goddamned information and I'll get the hell out of here."

I was beginning to wonder if Jeff, as well as Martina, had a substance abuse problem. He certainly had a self-control problem. "Maui Memorial Hospital," I said. I turned and walked away.

That was a tactical mistake. Every warrior knows that you never turn your back on the enemy. Unfortunately, I was no warrior and despite his strange behavior, I hadn't realized how unbalanced Jeff Pullman really was. I heard running footsteps behind me, but by the time I could turn to see what was happening, he had launched himself at me in a flying tackle that slammed me to the floor, carried me along the slick stone and smashed both of us into the pot of a large plant. Plant, dirt, and pot came crashing down on top of us.

"Witch!" he yelled. "Traitor! Murderess!"

I slapped him hard, hoping to knock him out of his hysteria, but it only made him madder.

He was attempting to disembowel me with a chunk of broken pot when a large man seized him, set him on feet, and said, "Enough!" in a voice that brooked no opposition.

I had never expected to look upon Detective Nihilani with favorable eyes, but at that moment, he was elevated to hero status. I had never been disemboweled but it seemed like something I would be particularly averse to. As it was, prior to Nihilani's arrival, Jeff had managed to get in a few good whacks. I wrapped my arms around my battered middle, curled up in a ball, and groaned. I had dirt in my mouth, dirt in my eyes, dirt in my nose, and dirt in my ears. And by the time I got changed and cleaned up, I would have missed my chance to make a toy car.

Andre thought I was here for sea and sand and fun. He thought I was going to be coming home with tan lines. It looked as if I was going to be coming home with bruises instead. Someone was talking to me. Of course. The other midnight twin. He was being nice and calm and reassuring and trying to get me up off the floor and onto my feet. An anxious security guard stood right behind him, moving fretfully from foot to foot. It was bad for business to have guests brawling in the hallways and knocking over the plants. Single-handedly I was turning the resort hotel into a vacation nightmare.

I carefully levered myself to a sitting position, blinking the dirt out of my eyes. "You got a handkerchief?" Some time ago, I'd vowed to reform and start carrying one myself. One of the nice big sturdy cotton ones guys carry, not some dainty little lace number. Like most of my proposed reforms, it was languishing at the bottom of my in box. I'd get around to it just as soon as I got all the other stuff done. Unfortunately, new stuff never stopped coming.

He pulled it out of his pocket and handed it to me. "Are you okay?" he asked.

"Don't be a boob," I said. "The last time some maniac jumped on you, knocked you to the floor, and hacked at you with a piece of crockery, how did you feel?"

He shook his head. "Never happened."

"Some people have all the luck." I took his outstretched hand and let him pull me to my feet. "How do I file assault charges?"

"Cut the guy some slack, can't you? He's just lost his wife."

I wanted to play hardball. I was mad as hell. A second outfit had just bitten the dust, or at least the dirt. I ached from head to toe and I didn't give a damn about poor Jeff Pullman's feelings anymore. But Jeff believed that I was somehow responsible for Martina's death. I remembered my husband, David's, friend coming to see me after he'd taken David for a ride his new Camaro and wrapped David around a tree. He'd come to apologize but there's no way you can apologize for killing someone's beloved. I'd given him a broken nose and two black eyes. So, mad as I was, I did understand the impulse.

"There's a ladies' room just down here," Bernstein said. "Why don't you wash your face and then I'll get you a cup of tea."

I didn't want to leave the wall, which was all that was holding me up. The morning had been one shock after another. I felt drained and unsteady. He put an arm around my shoulders. "Come on. Lean on me. Let's go."

Cops are trained to take over for us when our own systems shut down, so Bernstein was doing the right thing. I just wasn't a very good victim. Except for my few dearest friends, Andre, Suzanne, and my second-favorite cop, Dom Florio, I don't let people take care of me. I don't like the fuss. I don't like the attention, and I can't stand feeling helpless or out of control. I don't panic when I'm hurt; I panic when someone tries to help me *after* I'm hurt.

"Careful," I warned in a shaky voice. "I'm very bad at being a victim."

"So I've heard," he said. "Here's the ladies' room. Clean up. I'll be waiting right here."

Suspicion of the brotherhood arose in my mind. "Have you been talking with Andre?"

"Clean up," he repeated.

Damn them all. I limped into the bathroom and went to work removing all traces of the potted plant and trying to restore some sort of order to my appearance. It felt like a bruised rib. The rest was just the kind of thing I used to get playing basketball, when someone "accidentally" jabbed an elbow into my stomach. It would hurt. I'd be bruised. I'd live to play another day. Still, I was battered enough so that I walked with the cautious, bent-forward shuffle of an old lady.

I grimaced at the woman in the mirror, straightened up, and tried to walk easily. The effort brought a wave of pain and curses to my lips. Maui. Fun spot. Vacation paradise. I couldn't wait to see the last of it disappearing through an airplane window. I went out, hoping that Bernstein had been called away to more important business. There he stood, holding a Styrofoam cup with the telltale tag and string of a cup of tea.

He crooked his free arm like a prom date and gestured toward the exit. "Shall we?"

CHAPTER 17

I SAT ON a bench, staring out at the water, and sipped my tea. I could feel each warm sip hitting my empty stomach. I felt like a displaced person. Hotels do that to me anyway. It was intensified by the aura of violence and death and everyone around me going crazy. I may rush around and work all the time and appear to live in my car, but at heart, I'm a homebody. I need a base to return to. A place to recharge. Being here where I had none of that jarred me and put me off my stride. Normally, I'm so tough a little thing like being tackled and battered in a public place wouldn't faze me at all.

Bernstein, in what seemed to be the interrogative style of the Maui police, wasn't saying anything. He sagged back against the bench in that almost boneless way he had, eyes closed. Once again, he appeared to be asleep. I didn't blame him. He probably hadn't gotten any sleep and the warm sun and gentle breezes made me want to put my head on his shoulder and snooze myself. I sipped some more and thought about how good it would feel to immerse myself in a hot tub or just to curl up in a ball and moan.

"You get any sleep last night?" I asked.

His head moved slightly in what I took to be a negative gesture. "Pullman," he said finally. "What happened?"

"It was weird," I said. "Jeff has always been so warm and genial and charming and now, suddenly, this. Just before he . . . just before it happened, I was wondering if he was on drugs or something."

"Shock takes people in different ways."

"Jeff is a professional lobbyist, Detective. A spinmeister. His public persona is his stock in trade. His job requires iron self-control and managing difficult situations. Have I used enough clichés yet?" Bernstein didn't say anything. "Maybe it was just shock but I have to think there's more to it. Drugs or alcohol. Maybe he's taking some kind of tranquilizer to cope and is having a bad drug reaction. Everything about him was different. To use another cliché, it was like Jekyll and Hyde."

"Tell me."

Brisk, efficient, a man of few words. I guess he'd used up his caring response getting me back on my feet and loaning me his handkerchief. Normally that would have been fine. I wasn't one to expect pampering. But right now, I wanted some TLC. I didn't understand it myself, this need to be cared for and reassured. It wasn't like me. Normally, I wouldn't have expected it, especially not from a cop. The old adage, "You catch more flies with honey than with vinegar," wasn't something they taught at police academies. And yet, if Andre had been here. But then, Andre was my lover, Bernstein my inquisitor.

He didn't say anything, but the slack body had straightened and his posture had a listening edge.

"I was rushing down the hall, late as usual. Tending to Rory—"

"Wait a minute," he interrupted, "you know about Ms. Altschuler's suicide attempt? You were up there?"

"I nodded. Someone had to help Jonetta. And if we hadn't gone . . ." But then I let it drop. I wasn't interested in tooting my own horn or in discussing Rory. The whole business depressed me. "But then I had to leave because I was covered with blood and I was supposed to introduce the speakers and then I had to meet with Mrs. Sato about the banquet and—"

"Doesn't anyone else in your group do any work?"

"Sure. Everyone . . . it's just that I'm . . ." I skipped what I was going to say about Ms. Fixit. "We've lost Martina and Rory, and they were in charge, so we're racing around plugging the holes as best we can. I was rushing back to the seminar room and I was thinking about what had happened and not looking where I was going and I ran right into him. Jeff, I mean."

"Literally?"

"Literally. I wanted that chocolate cake, you know."

"I know. I'll buy you another one. Nihilani's right. When I'm tired, I get grouchy. It helped. You ran into him, and then?"

"I said I was sorry about Martina. He said why was I sorry, Martina had never liked me. Then he said that she, Martina, had known what we were planning to do to her. . . ."

"Which was?"

"I've told you this. Or maybe it was Nihilani. Replace her as director of the association."

"And . . ."

"And he accused me . . . accused us . . . of conspiring like a bunch of witches to oust her. He implied that we had conspired to kill her to solve our problem. That her death was some sort of planned assassination."

"And that's when he attacked you?"

"Then you are willing to acknowledge that he attacked me, even if you won't let me bring assault charges?"

"Christ, Kozak, you had ten or fifteen witnesses. You want to file charges, you go right ahead. Can we get on with this?"

"Only if you call me Thea. You sound very grouchy when you say Kozak."

"It's a pretty name," he said. "Thea, I mean. Kozak is tough and gritty. Russian?"

"Ukrainian. Cossack." This guy had better watch it. He'd had a couple of human moments there.

"Then what happened?"

"He said he wondered how I was going to live with myself after what we'd done. I didn't want a fight so I didn't bother to argue that we hadn't done anything. I just walked away. Then he called after me, as though we'd had a normal conversation instead of his litany of virulent accusations, asking if I knew where he could find Rory. He thought she might need comforting. We were standing about ten feet apart at that point, in the middle of the hallway, surrounded by people. I didn't want to have to shout out what had happened—that she'd tried to commit suicide—so I tried to get him off to a quieter place. I invited him to sit on a bench. . . . He refused, then started shouting and calling me names. I wasn't going to allow him to abuse me like that, so I just said, 'Maui Memorial Hospital' and walked away. That's when he jumped me."

Bernstein nodded, his blue eyes fixed on the water, not looking at me. "It might not be a bad idea if you went home early."

"I thought I wasn't supposed to leave town. I believe that's what Detective Nihilani said."

"Detective Bernstein says you may go."

"Thanks. I wish I could. There's nothing I'd like better. But there's still a lot to do and—"

"You wouldn't be the first person in history to be suddenly called away," he interrupted. "I know you like to take the weight of the world on your shoulders but you don't always have to." He checked his watch and stood up. "Just think about it, okay? Think about getting away from this thing before something worse happens."

"What's that supposed to mean?"

"You have a reputation as something of a crime solver, right? People here know about that. It could . . . you know . . . cut both ways."

I didn't understand what he meant, but there was something else about this conversation that bothered me more. "Wait a minute," I interrupted. "How did you hear about this so-called reputation?"

Bernstein didn't look at me. He stared out at the water, his eyes narrowed as if what he was saying pained him. "You know how it is," he said. "Like it or not, cops stick together. Look, don't be mad at him, okay? I'd do the same thing myself, if I was tied up and my girlfriend was involved." I took a deep breath, ready to argue, but he waved his hands defensively. "Now, don't get all steamed up until you've let me finish. When I say involved . . . I mean the way you are involved . . . tangentially . . . I mean you knew the victim and you found the body. No one thinks you had anything to do with this despite what Nihilani and I may have suggested by using the word 'corroborate.' So yes, your boyfriend called us up. You want to know what he said?"

I wasn't sure. Probably. It was such an odd idea to think of him trying to take care of me from thousands of miles away. A year ago it would have sent me into fits. Like I said, I'm hard to take care of. I'm as stubborn and independent as they come. But I also love the guy, and I've been through some scary times with him. Coming close to losing him taught me how important he is, and our arguments about my putting myself in danger have given me insight into how he feels and how he works. He rights wrongs and makes the world safe for a living. There's no way he's not going to do it for me. "Sure. Tell me what he said."

"He said you're more impossible to control and care for than a two-hundred-pound Newfoundland. He said you're slow to get mad and you'll put up with a lot but that when you do get mad, people better step back." He laughed. "I guess I found that out for myself. He said you're a lot like us . . . you have a deep sense of right and wrong and you keep trying to make the world right. He said you're a real champion of the underdog, the little guy, that you think it's your job to take care of people weaker and more helpless. As to your so-called detective abilities, he told us about your sister and the others. He says if you didn't have so much trouble with authority figures, you'd make a good cop."

Bernstein swallowed and looked down at his shoes. "He says that you are beautiful and good. That he worships the ground you walk on. He says he's going to marry you, make you the mother of his children, and grow old with you, and that if we let anything happen to you, he's going to come out here and skin us alive. And we're not doing a very good job of taking care of you. So will you please go home."

By this time, I was dabbing at my eyes with his dirty handkerchief. "I wish I could," I said. "It's so nice of you to ask. Usually I get asked to be the staked goat."

"The what?"

"The tiger trap. The bait. You know. It seems like one of my callings in life is to stay around and be provocative until I impel the murderer to come after me. Thea Kozak, goat girl. The human target."

"Not on my watch," he said, still talking to his shoes. "Why don't you just go home?"

Click your heels together and go back to Kansas, I thought. I could see him being sucked up and carried away. He wouldn't fit in any better in Kansas. Bernstein was born restless and edgy. He must have driven his mother crazy, lying there in his carriage, watching the world with those restless blue eyes. "I can't leave," I said again. "Do you really think I have to be careful? I don't know anything. I haven't seen anything. . . ."

"Phooey," he said. "People tell you stuff. You know more and you've seen more, or at least told us more, than any of your colleagues. And you've been seen with us."

"So has everyone else." I changed the subject. This one was making me too nervous. There were too many reasons why I couldn't leave. Some of them involved my responsibilities to the board. We represented the organizing group of the conference and therefore had to set an example. If I were to turn tail and run, others would wonder if they should do the same, while some would wonder what I'd been up to that made me run away. So in addition to actual responsibilities with running the conference, I also had to stick around and be a role model, demonstrating that things could go on successfully in the face of tragedy.

There was a second reason not to flee that was also business related. This was a conference attended primarily by people associated with independent, or private, schools. I was a partner in a consulting firm that made its living doing work for independent schools. I had my reputation to worry about. If I suddenly vanished from the conference after Martina's death, it could give rise to two future problems—doubt about my character in case the murder wasn't solved, and doubt about my fortitude whether it was solved or not. Since helping schools in tough cases was becoming my personal specialty, it wouldn't look good if I bailed out when confronted with a situation that was tough on all of us. There was no way I could explain this to Bernstein.

"Laura Mitchell," I said. "The little girl you took to breakfast—"

"Do we ever do anything you don't know about?"

"Probably. Did she have anything more to tell you?" Bernstein didn't answer. "Oh, for heaven's sake, Detective. Does this always have to be a one-way street?"

"Leave," he repeated. "Go. I'll drive you to the airport myself."

He seemed to be regretting his lapse into humanity. Maybe it had just been a ploy to soften me up so I'd be more amenable to his suggestion when he urged me to leave. I just didn't understand the man. The incredible frankness followed by a complete stone wall. Did he care? Didn't he care? What was an act and what was real? Sure I had trouble with authority figures, but I'd tried hard this time. I'd been as cooperative as I could possibly be. I was prone to blame myself for lapses in human interaction, but wasn't it just possible that it was him and not me this time?

"I'm sure you won't understand this, but I can't leave. Not now. Not right in the middle like this. I'm a working girl and this is where I'm working right now. If you think I'm at risk, how about a bodyguard?"

"Spare me," he said, rolling his eyes. "It's not like we've got personnel pouring out our ears. We're always running short and right now we've got a murder to investigate."

"Then I'll just have to be careful. More careful than I was this morning. But Lenny . . ." I gave a secret, internal smile when I used his name. "I never would have expected Jeff to behave like that. He's always been so nice." He was acting like he wasn't listening again. "By the way, what's the story with Rory Altschuler?" I didn't expect him to answer. He never answered my questions. This time he surprised me.

"Maui Memorial is about thirty minutes from here, ambulance speed. She'll just be getting there now. We have people there who will let us know what's happening." He'd closed it, but now he flipped his notebook open again. "Tell me about finding her."

So I told it as best I could, and got through it without letting my own memories derail me. Got through it without getting upset. But I needed to be moving again. Sit too long and the stories in my head jump out and grab me. I couldn't take that now, being pulled into a wallow of my own awful memories.

I got up to leave. Then, since Lenny and I were temporarily sort of friends, or at least there was a truce in our acrimony, I reached in my briefcase and pulled out the clippings Billy had given me about the lingerie murders. I handed them to Bernstein. "I assume you guys know about these?"

He took them and started to read, his face growing red as he did so. "Where did you get these?" he demanded, assuming the neatly neutral position of neither confirming nor denying that he'd had the information before. I thought the red face probably meant that our truce was over—the red face and the extremely displeased look on his face.

"Our public relations guy. Billy Berryman. He got them off the Internet."

"I'm trying to like you," he said through clenched teeth.

"I'm trying to be helpful," I said, not sure what his problem was.

"Who else has seen these?"

"The other board members. He gave them out at the meeting this morning."

"I thought I told you—" Whatever he'd been about to say, he thought better of it. "Who will probably have shown them to half the Western world by now." He got up, anger visible in all the lines of his long, lean body. "Try to stay out of trouble, okay?" He flipped a card into my lap. "My phone numbers. The bottom one is my pager. Use it. I do not, I repeat, do not . . . want to have to call a brother officer and tell him something's happened to his girl—uh—lady friend."

Being treated like a burden irritated me. I really was trying to help. I hadn't even tried to stick my nose into his investigation. It wasn't fair for him to be mad at me just because I knew things. "I'm going snorkeling out at Molokini this afternoon. Maybe you'd like to send someone to watch my back."

"I'll see what I can do." He turned and strode away, the clippings swinging vigorously at the end of his arm.

As I watched him go, realization hit me like a ton of bricks. No wonder he was so mad at me. He thought I'd told Billy all the details of Martina's murder—details the police had held back—thus enabling Billy to do his search and come up with the lingerie killer stories. Stories that Billy said he'd spent hours on. The problem was, I hadn't. I'd told Jonetta a lot, and Jolene a little, and sworn them both to secrecy. I'd told Billy nothing. And as I sat there, staring with unseeing eyes at the restless ocean, I wondered. How had Billy known?

CHAPTER 18

I STOPPED IN the lobby and called Billy's room. He wasn't in so I left a message asking him to call me. I was tempted to also tell him that the cops were looking for him but I didn't. I'm a slow learner, but I do learn. Messages are accessible. The cops can read them. And the cops were already mad at me. Unfairly, but what the heck. Who ever said life was going to be fair? Besides, I had a few questions of my own I wanted to ask Billy. Similar to the ones the cop would ask. Maybe none of us would get any answers. Maybe Billy had vanished into thin air.

That's something I've always wondered about—expressions like that. Why *thin* air? When I'm running on too little sleep and too much tension, my mind tends to wander to questions like this. I lose my balance and begin to feel like an alien, as though life goes on for everyone else on a normal plane, and I'm connected to it by a stretchy cord that lets me drift far away and then snap back. I get to all the same meetings and conduct the same business, but in the spaces between events, I find bodies and attempted suicides and spend the wee hours of the night being interrogated by cops who don't seem to like me. Wee hours—that's another of those expressions. Why are the hours late at night considered wee? Is it because of those little bitty numbers? Or maybe because we never get enough sleep and therefore have to lay the blame somewhere. It was those damned short hours!

Well, it was time to snap back and go to Rob Greene's seminar. I got to the seminar room just as the groups were finishing their cars. Judging from their expressions, everyone seemed to be having a wonderful time. It was precisely the kind of learning I liked best—the kind where you have so much fun you don't notice that it's a learning experience. When we first approached the subject of girls and technology, many teachers hadn't noticed how much the girls hung back and let the boys do the hands-on work or how often the girls were reluctant to take on tasks that involved building and working with their hands. We had put together a one-day workshop designed to break down those barriers for teachers and give them techniques they could take back to the classroom. This seminar was a shortened version of that.

Rob was standing at the front of the room with a stopwatch, while his co-panelists circulated around the room, helping groups put on the finishing touches. "One minute," he called out. There was a chorus of protests. "All right," he said. "Two minutes."

I was glad to see that the session was being videotaped. Most of us were book-and-word people and we tended to forget how valuable preserving a good seminar session could be. A picture really can be worth a thousand words. Learning from our experience at prior events, Suzanne and I had insisted that part of the conference organizing include provision for videotaping some of the segments. Indeed, one of the concerns about moving rooms had been making sure that the video equipment got moved and was usable in the new locations. People always think they're going to be too nervous if cameras are present. Our experience has been that after the first few minutes, they forget the cameras are even there.

I helped lay out the race track, a long roll of green vinyl flooring with white lines painted on it. The corners had to be secured to keep it from rolling up again. Then we set up a strip of red tape attached to two sand-filled soda bottles, to mark a finish line, and Rob pulled out a starter's flag made from a dowel and a bandanna. Everything except the car kits, which were ordered, was made from readily available materials so that the group could replicate the exercise at home. We were ready to roll.

There were four races, followed by semifinals and then finals, after which the group returned to their seats for an analysis of the exercise and presentation of a trophy to the winning team. The whole thing ended with a burst of applause and everyone filed out of the room with smiles, the conversation eager and lively. As he passed me, Rob muttered in a low voice, "Well, at least something's finally gone right. And now I'm going to go sit on the beach and no one had better disturb me."

"Did you hear about Rory?" I whispered.

"What now? More public hysterics when she learned that she'd been fired? She dropped her precious laptop in the pool? What?"

"She slit her wrists. Jonetta and I found her. They've taken her to the hospital."

All his merriment fell away. "Is it bad?"

"It wasn't pretty, but Jonetta thinks she's going to be fine. Have you seen Jeff?"

He shook his head. "Not yet. You?"

"I'm afraid so."

"Afraid so? He's taking this badly?"

"Badly? He thinks we killed her. He literally tackled me and pummeled me when we met in the hall."

He looked down at my dirty dress. "You mean physically attacked you? That doesn't sound like Jeff." His face was twisted with distress. "I wish I understood what was going on here. Did you tell him about the lingerie killer?"

"I didn't get to tell him anything, Rob. He was . . . well . . . it's hard to describe. He just wasn't anything like the Jeff we know. He was wild and . . . and violent. And so angry at all of us. If I were you, I'd stay out of his way."

But Rob was shaking his head, still struggling to understand. "I can't believe he attacked you, Thea. You mean—"

"I mean he jumped me from behind, knocked me to the floor, and we both smashed into one of those big plants out in the hallway. He was trying to carve me up with a piece of the broken pot when the police hauled him off."

Now he was really paying attention. "That's awful!" he said. "Really terrible. Are you all right?" He peered into my face. "You don't look like you're all right."

Never tell someone who is trying to keep her spirits up that she doesn't look well. It's an instant downer. "To be honest, Rob, I'm not very well. I'm battered and bruised and feeling terribly sorry for myself. I think I'll go upstairs and wash the rest of the dirt off and then go lie in the sun, just like you." He looked so distressed that I was sorry I'd told him. It was mean to have spoiled things for him when he was on such a high.

I changed the subject. "Your seminar went so well! Everyone came out of there with huge smiles and talking a mile a minute. I'm glad it's one of the ones we got on tape."

"Me, too," he said. "I had a great team and we really pulled it off. We've already been asked to do it again at three different schools."

"Uh-oh. Success is going to your head. Next thing I know, you'll be resigning and going on the lecture circuit."

"No way, José," he said. "I'm finally beginning to get things at my school running the way I want them. This is no time to bail out." He smiled wryly. "I'll do it in all my spare time."

"I didn't know there was any."

"There isn't. Well, gotta get me some of that sun. No one is going to believe I was in Hawaii the way things are going." He swung his tote bag onto his shoulder and picked up the roll of vinyl. "Catch you later."

"I'm going on the snorkel trip," I said. "See you at dinner."

"So long. Have fun. Forget all about this, if you can."

I went upstairs, threw my briefcase on the bed, and took off my dirty clothes. Then I took a warm, soothing bath, slathered myself with sun screen, and went outside to lie in the sun. I didn't have much time to get those tan lines. In the end, I'd probably have to resort to artificial tanning stuff. I didn't want my sweetie to be disappointed, not after he'd gone to all the trouble of calling up the Maui police and reading them the riot act on my behalf. On reflection, though, it didn't seem to have made Bernstein and Nihilani much more protective. Other than a clean handkerchief, a cup of tea, and a warning to get out of town, they didn't seem to have taken the assault very seriously, though Bernstein had been awfully adamant about the get-out-of-town part.

My body, on the other hand, had taken it very seriously. I had three very ugly bruises and a collection of smaller ones, so maybe it wasn't such a bad thing that I rarely got to lie around in my bikini. People by the pool were bound to notice. At least on the snorkel boat, I could wear my T-shirt and no one would see. I decided on a room-service lunch. I was not feeling especially sociable. My room-service bill was going to be horrendous! Luckily, I only had to justify it to myself—I was a partner. No one except the accountant looked over my shoulder.

I checked my watch. A little past noon. I had almost an hour. And back home it was five o'clock. I might find Andre at one of the numbers he'd left. I was reaching for the phone when it rang and because he was on my mind, I almost said, "Hello, Andre," but I didn't. I just said hello and waited, listening to some breathing on the other end. But Lewis Broder had left the hotel. Was it Jeff? Was it someone else, one of the unknowns about whom I'd been admonished to watch my back. I have no patience with silly phone games. "Speak now or forever hold your peace," I said.

There was a choking sound and a little giggle. "It's the spy," she said. "Where were you?"

"Oh, Laura, I'm sorry. I had such a busy morning I forgot all about our rendezvous. Will you forgive me?"

"If you meet me later."

"Later when? I'm going snorkeling this afternoon."

"You are?" It was a squeal of delight. "Me, too. I mean, all of us. Are you going to Molokini?"

"Mm-hmm."

"So I'll see you on the boat," she said. "I can't wait to tell you all about breakfast with the cops. Geoffrey and Charlotte are barely speaking to me, they are so jealous. Oops, there's something I have to check out. Catch you later." And she was gone. My little hit-and-run friend.

I tried Andre, didn't find him, and left messages at both numbers. I picked up my book and went outside onto the terrace. I hadn't even gotten it open when the phone rang. Let it ring, I thought. But I am a slave of duty. I hoisted myself out of the chair and stumped inside. It was Jolene.

"Thea, I heard what happened this morning. I think perhaps you ought to go home." She was at her most prim and head-mistressy.

"Why?"

"So many bad things are happening, and you always seems to be at the center of—"

"Are you suggesting I'm making them happen?" Whoee! I was edgy, wasn't I?

"I'm just worried for you, Thea. There's no ulterior motive here. . . ." Was it me, or did she sound defensive?

I could expect her to understand what Bernstein hadn't. "Jolene, if I run when things get tough, if I head for home when the whole board is dealing with a crisis, what do you think that will do to my reputation?"

There was a long silence. Finally she said, "I don't think it will have any effect. After what you've been through, no one would blame you for—"

"Maybe they won't blame me, but will they still respect me in the morning?"

Another silence. "Just think about it, okay? If we have to, we can muddle along without you." She hung up without waiting for a response.

I couldn't worry about this now. Start pondering on what she'd meant, on what her motives might be, and all my free time would gone. Deliberately I shut my mind and went back out to the balcony.

It was positively illicit, sitting out there in the sun, eating my salad and drinking lemonade and reading an actual novel. I have to do so much reading for work that I rarely get the chance to sit down and read for pleasure. Suzanne had given me the book when I stopped by her house to drop off some tea and pick up last-minute instructions. Dumped it into my bag, gaily wrapped in silver paper, saying, "You're going to love it. You have to love it. It reminds me of you."

So now I was lying in the sun reading Barbara Kingsolver's *Animal Dreams* and loving it, but every time I came to Loyd Peregrina I got distracted thinking about Andre, who, like Loyd, had so many attributes of the perfect man, and who could be so romantic and yet so independent, and then I'd get to a sad part and start to cry. The truth was that I needed to cry. I didn't do it much and so I had lots and lots of stuff bottled up inside. There were only two acceptable ways to let it out. Sad books and sad movies. Catharsis. Despite the past two days, when I'd been reduced to tears so often it felt like chronic PMS, I was always too busy to cry. Also, until I'd come here and fallen into this wallow of anger and emotion, I'd been fairly happy. In the short-term, anyway.

I sat in the sun and munched on lettuce and was brilliantly entertained and enchanted by my book and cried my eyes out. By the time that Ed and Marie knocked on the door to collect me for our expedition, I had scarlet eyes and a much calmer soul. I had also, in a bit of perversity I couldn't explain, stuffed Rory's laptop into the stack of towels under the sink in my bathroom. In a hotel potentially full of murderers and inscrutable constabulary, I couldn't help feeling a little bit paranoid. I felt silly doing it, but who's to say that a person can never be silly? I hadn't yet taken the time to download the rest of the materials we needed and my plan, assuming I could find the right equipment, was to simply link the laptops and copy her files onto mine. In all my spare time. Maybe I could get Billy to do it. He was good with computers.

Marie instantly homed in on my red eyes. "What's the matter?" she demanded.

I pulled the book out of my tote bag. "I was reading this."

She nodded approvingly. "I read that in my book group. Cried my eyes out. Then I went back and read it again and cried in all the same places. I wish she'd hurry up and write another one like it."

Ed shook his head and looked pointedly at his watch. "We'd better get going," he said. "It's a beautiful place but traffic on this island moves like molasses."

I followed them to the elevator. Marie had a huge straw tote bag, a net bag with a bottle of spring water, and a wide-brimmed hat. Ed had a bulging duffel bag filled with snorkeling gear and a second bag that seemed to be stuffed with towels. They looked like they were going away for a week. I had my book, a spare T-shirt, a towel, my own bottle of water, an elastic to tie back my hair and heavy-duty waterproof sun block. Let the fishes beware.

Ed apologized as I squeezed myself into the backseat of their rental car. "I reserved a midsized car and all they had was this. Midsized only to a child of six. I believe there is a bus going, if you'd rather not have your knees in your ears."

"This is fine," I assured him.

After a lifetime living with Boston drivers, it was a pleasant surprise to ride with Ed. He drove carefully, used his turn signals, allowed people in in front of him, and never once leaned on the horn no matter how stupidly the car in front of him behaved. We arrived safely and in plenty of time and he hadn't even worked himself into a frenzy. It was very restful. Even I, despite my mother's attempts to make me a lady, curse when I'm driving. Sometimes, when things heated up at work, I'd get so tense I started grinding my teeth. My dentist was threatening to make me a mouth guard. He told me half the women in his practice were wearing them. Part of the equal opportunity stress women had fought so hard for.

"That must be the boat," Marie said, as I slowly worked my way out of the car. Getting out was a lot harder than getting in, and Ed Pryzinski didn't miss the grimaces as I twisted and turned my bruised torso. His eyebrows went up in an interrogatory way but he didn't say anything. Shortly after we went on board and got ourselves settled, a big snorting bus pulled up and most of the people I'd been looking forward to getting away from climbed off.

First Jolene, who seemed to be carrying a lot of luggage. Then Shannon and Zannah got off together, laughing about something, and I heard Shannon's voice, "This had better be fun. I need some fun." The bus was like a clown car, disgorging many more people than it looked like it could hold. So far, besides Rob who'd said he was going to sit on the beach, the only person missing was Jonetta. I assumed that she had gone to Maui Memorial Hospital with Rory. Laura Mitchell got off, looking small and pale next to the rest of her family. There was her scholarly brother, Geoffrey, her perfect sister, Charlotte, the red-haired woman in polka dots with the big hat must be her mother, and the man hovering protectively behind the polka dot lady must be the stepfather, Howard. He looked like a Howie to me.

Laura's family, along with about half the people from the bus, crowded onto our boat. The others headed for a second boat at the other end of the parking lot. Shannon, Zannah, and Jolene went with that group. As it filled up, I was glad that we'd come early and staked out our spots. After my close encounter with Jeff Pullman, I needed my space. I needed enough room to stretch out. My body was not keen on being folded as it had been for the past hour. I scanned the crowd with my cop-seeking eye but I didn't see anyone whose demeanor said "cop" to me. It looked like Nihilani and Bernstein agreed with me that I didn't need a bodyguard for my fun excursion.

The last person off the bus was Jonetta. Last but not least. She was wearing a tie-dyed muumuu in neon colors, topped by a hat with a black center and a bright yellow brim that looked like an enormous sunflower. As I sat and watched, it seemed to me that the crowd parted before her, as before some juggernaut, making way for an obviously superior being. Last off the bus, but sooner onto the boat. My boat. The whole craft dipped in response to her arrival.

"In another time," Marie whispered, "the Hawaiians would have made her a queen."

"She's something," I agreed. "She's every bit as imposing as she looks, too."

"You know her?"

"She's on the board of the association with me." Everyone was staring at her. Jonetta didn't seem to notice. She settled herself on a seat in the shade, pulled out a book, and started reading. The rest of the passengers were loaded, the crew made several announcements about fitting us with equipment, where we were going, and what the protocol would be, and we were off.

I pulled out my own book and was luxuriating in a steamy scene in some natural hot springs when someone tapped me on the leg. I quickly closed the book. It's embarrassing to be caught reading

sex scenes. Once, during a very boring meeting when I was await-
ing my turn to speak, I pulled out a book and started reading and
suddenly realized that I was sitting in a whole room full of people
while I was absorbing one of the most erotic passages I'd ever read.
Even though reading is a private thing that takes place between the
eyes and the brain, it was not the kind of thing to read in a room
full of people. My whole face got red and I quickly put the book
away, hoping the people sitting on either side of me hadn't been
reading over my shoulder.

Laura Mitchell was standing there looking forlorn. "Hi," she
said. "Can I sit with you?"

"Of course you can, dear," Marie said. "We'd love to have you
join us." She took her big bag off the seat and set it down by our
feet.

Laura squeezed herself into the space and gave Marie a winning smile. "I'm Laura Mitchell," she said, holding out her hand.
"I'm a friend of Thea's."

Marie shook the offered hand. "Marie Pryzinski," she said.
"And this is Eddie."

Laura shook hands again. "I get so bored with them. Geoffrey
is always playing with his video games. Charlotte always has her
nose in a book, and my stepdad spends all his time fretting about
my mom." She leaned forward and said, in a conspiratorial whisper, "She's pregnant."

She settled herself back on the seat. "Where are you from? I'm
from Iowa."

"Cleveland," Marie said, "so we're both midwesterners. Is this
your first trip?"

"Yeah," Laura said. "I thought it would be more exciting than
this. I was expecting giant waves and erupting volcanoes and stuff,
not that skinny little beach in front of the hotel and you have to
make reservations and pay big bucks for everything you want to do.
But I'm looking forward to the fish. I've only been snorkeling once
and it was great. That was when we went to the Virgin Islands.
Since my mom married Howie, we go lots of places. Howie wishes
we'd stay home. Hey . . ."

I liked Laura but I was beginning to wish she'd go back to her family. I wanted to sit quietly and read my book. She was like a little whirlwind, causing a swirl of commotion around her. I was weary of commotion and conversation and questions.

She bent down and rustled around in her backpack, murmuring to herself as she sorted. I hoped we weren't in for another trip through her treasures. When she did straighten up, she was holding a newspaper, the *Maui News*. She opened it, folded it to display the thing she wanted to show me, and thrust it into my face. "Did you see this?"

I took it and stared at the picture she was pointing to. It was a picture of me, looking like death warmed over, coming out of a hospital emergency room, leaning heavily on Andre's arm. Laura was pointing, not to me, but to Andre. "That's the guy you showed me the picture of, right? Your boyfriend the cop?"

"Yes. That's Andre." My voice was practically strangled by anger and surprise. Not because there was a picture of Andre. Because there was a picture of me. And a caption, identifying me. And a little story beside it—"Private School Detective Attends Education Conference"—describing my involvement in resolving the death of a student at the Bucksport School, and querying whether my presence at a private school conference where an attendee was murdered might be more than mere coincidence.

A lot of words inappropriate to utter in the presence of a minor bubbled to my lips. I clamped my jaw tight and didn't say anything. Dr. Pryzinski reached over and took the paper out of my hand. Read the story, shook his head, and whistled. "My, my," he said. "There's more to you than meets the eye."

CHAPTER 19

"I DON'T KNOW where they got this," I said, "or how they got it. But if I ever find out it came from someone I know, I'm going to dismember them with my bare hands."

Marie looked shocked. "You're a detective? A sweet young girl like you? I never would have imagined. . . ."

It took a major effort not to roll my eyes or explode. At least she hadn't said "little," and people made the mistake of thinking me sweet often enough so I ought to be used to it. Besides, this time it was my own fault. I had played the ingenue when I wanted to get Bernstein off my back. As ye sow, so also shall ye reap. "This is a bunch of hogwash," I said. "I'm here as a board member of the National Association of Girls' Schools. I'm here as a participant, as a speaker, as an organizer. I made my reservations months ago . . . or at least, my partner did. . . ." Here my irritation did spill through. "It doesn't say here that I'm supposed to be a psychic detective—that back in January we were anticipating something might happen to Martina."

"In a way you were, though," Ed Pryzinski said. "Your board had planned to oust Martina."

How did he know that? Would the stolid Nihilani and grouchy Bernstein, who refused to talk to me, confide in him because he was, in effect, "one of them"? "Not quite so dramatically. Besides, what does that have to do with price of eggs in . . . oh, never mind! Look, this is filler. Drivel. Inflammatory junk. I am not involved in this investigation. I don't want to be involved in the investigation of Martina's death. Every time I get involved in an investigation, I end up getting hurt. I'm sick of being bruised and battered. I'm sick of being scared and worried. I just want to do my job and go home." I broke off. They didn't need to hear this, and I risked my protests having the opposite effect—the "methinks she doth protest too much" problem. But I couldn't resist adding, "I'm not even supposed to be here. My partner is. I only came because she got sick at the last minute. This afternoon I don't even want to think about work. All I want to do is float around in the water and look at fish. I'm going to forget about Martina, and single-sex ed-ucation, and girls' schools . . ."

Laura, bored by our adult conversation, wriggled off the seat. " 'Bye," she said, and wandered away. She quickly struck up a con-versation with the cute brown-haired college student sitting be-hind us. They were talking about the kinds of fish they were likely to see, looking at a chart the boat had provided. I was sorry to have disappointed her but too caught up in my own sense of vio-lation to set it aside and give her the attention she craved. That's what her family was for.

The article had singled me out in an unwelcome way. I don't mind being known for competence. I've tried to earn a good rep-utation—but not as a detective. Because of this, for the rest of the conference, people would be staring and pointing and watching me expectantly, waiting for the "private school detective" to do her thing. We were moving briskly through blue water, the island looked lovely and the sun was beating down warmly. I ought to have been having a good time. Instead I had an anxious tightening in my chest and a rising uneasiness I couldn't quite explain, except for the unpleasant knowledge that the bad guys can read just like the good guys.

Maybe Bernstein was right—much as I hated to admit such an irritating guy could be—maybe I should just go home. Of course, no sooner did I think about leaving than I began making a mental list of all the things I'd need to do first. Thea the Obsessive. Ms.

Fixit. Go back to the hotel and print out the rest of the stuff we needed to finish the conference, transfer the rest of her files over to my computer, and then give Rory's to the midnight twins. Who knew what they might find? I hated to do it. Turn over the computer, that is. Who knew how long they'd keep it, when Rory's successor was bound to need it.

Jonetta and Jolene had been right that we should take it, but Rory's peculiar behavior, more than her suicide, made me think I ought to give it to the police. It was just the stuff that needed to be done first, things that became more work for me. Every day, in every way, I was getting better at delegating, but who was I going to pass this chore along to? My life was always so much to do, so little time, and people would be expecting me to add crime solving to my list of tasks. I sighed, feeling my shoulders hunch defensively as I thought about how things would be at the banquet tonight.

"I don't blame you for not wanting to get involved," Ed Pryzinski said as he folded up the paper and stuffed it in his bag. "Nice-looking guy, that Andre. Marie, did you happen to bring those pictures of the children?"

She nodded. "I think so," and began digging through the enormous bag. After a minute, she made a triumphant sound and held up an envelope of photographs. She pulled them out, shuffled through, selected one. "That's Eric," she said, pointing to a tall, langy kid in his early twenties. He didn't look anything like his parents. "He's twenty-four. Works as a climbing guide in the Rockies. It's such a dangerous job. I never stop worrying about him. But our Eric is kind of a Peter Pan. He doesn't want to grow up. This way, he works with kids, and he thinks he'll stay a kid forever."

Ed pointed to the girl in the picture. "That's Martha, his girlfriend. She's got enough common sense for the two of them." Martha was short and rounded and sturdy. She had a pleasant, friendly face. The Pryzinski men, I thought, liked solid, regular, homey women. "They're getting married in August. Marie is already in a twitter about what she's going to wear." He shifted to the next picture. "And this is Marietta, our daughter."

Marietta was Asian. Tiny and perfect, with waist-length hair. "Your children are adopted," I said.

"We're so lucky!" Marie said. "So many people have trouble getting children these days, and we were given two of the most perfect children in the whole world."

"You get the idea that she likes her kids?" Ed teased.

"I get the idea that you both love them very much," I said. "My sister, Carrie, was adopted."

"Was?" Ed said. "Never mind. Here's a picture of the kids at Marie's fiftieth birthday party." Bless Ed. He was still looking after me, even if I wasn't a helpless ingenue. The picture showed tall, gangly Eric with his arm around his tiny sister. She was holding a paper in her hand and it was evident that they were reading some sort of tribute to their mom. Ed shifted to the next picture, a smiling Marie holding a tissue to her eyes. "They wrote a tribute to the world's best mom." He reached across me and squeezed Marie's hand.

I thought of Andre and his hope that someday we would be surrounded by strong brown girls and mischievous boys. Crazy, wild, insolent, headstrong girls is what he'd actually said. Would we ever be like Ed and Marie, content and comfortable together, showing people pictures of our kids? Going home looked more appealing all the time.

The loudspeaker was blaring again, announcing our impending arrival. We were informed that there might be several boats at the location, to try and stay with our group, not to touch the coral, and a number of other instructions that I ignored, including something about how if a wind came up, the water might get choppy and more easily wash us onto the rocks. When you have trouble with authority, it extends in many directions. I just wanted to slip my sun-heated body into that cool water and paddle about. Rest my list-filled, work-obsessed mind. I did not want to listen to boring instructions aimed at morons.

At one end of the boat, a small group was struggling into wet suits and hefting scuba tanks. If Andre had been there, that's where he would have been, joining the ranks of what I thought of as "rubber space men." So far, though he'd managed to enlist me in a number of sports, I refused to try one that required me to breathe underwater. Not me. I have the land animal's natural aversion to being under water. Besides, given the trouble I have getting clothes to fit, it would probably be impossible to find a wet suit.

I piled up my mask, snorkel, and fins, wove my hair into a braid, and started to take my T-shirt off. It was halfway over my head when I remembered the bruises. Not a good idea. I let it drop again, but when I'd picked up my stuff and straightened up again, heading for the rear of the boat where they were helping us into the water, I saw Ed looking at me thoughtfully. Good old Dr. P. didn't miss much.

Getting into the water with fins is never graceful. Oh, maybe on TV. Those cool scientists on the Discovery Channel and NOVA and National Geographic specials always make it look like a cinch. I expect they spend hours flopping gracelessly into the sea to get one good shot. In any case, I flopped gracelessly off the rear of the boat, pulled down my mask, paused, treading water, while I got my hair out of the way so the mask wouldn't leak, and stuck the tube in my mouth. Watch out, fishes, here I come.

With my breath whooshing in my ears like Darth Vader, I paddled away from the boat, found a relatively unpopulated spot, and hovered there, watching the fish. Way down below, the rubber space men were getting up close and personal with some pretty big fish. All the more reason why the surface was fine with me. Someone tapped me on the shoulder and I jumped, losing my snorkel and taking in a mouthful of water.

"Sorry," Laura said. "I wanted to show you the eel." I put myself back together and looked where she was pointing. An eel's head was just visible in a crevice, its mouth opening and closing, opening and closing, filled with about a million teeth. Yessiree, it was a thing of beauty and a joy forever and I was happy to be many feet above it. When I'd seen enough of the eel, I raised my head and looked around.

Laura was paddling about five feet away, but I couldn't see the rest of her family. It irritated me. I wanted to find that complacent, pregnant, polka-dotted princess and whack her upside the head.

Laura was a competent little girl, but she was still a child, and some adult or older sibling ought to be staying close to her. Snorkeling was quite a benign sport until something went wrong. But when you're out on the water, the things that go wrong happen fast. The water beyond Laura stirred and the cute college girl surfaced.

"Thea," Laura said, "this is my friend Robin. She said I could swim with her." Robin and I exchanged greetings. "Did you see the eel?"

"I did. Thanks."

"Did you see the barracuda?"

"No."

"Neither did I," Laura said, "but some people over there said they saw one. Robin says not to worry." She paddled away and I went back to rocking in the waves and watching fish. Up closer to the rocks there were some lovely bright-colored ones. I was happily following a neon blue-and-yellow one when I bumped up against a rock. Picking my head up, I saw that I'd drifted far from the group and right up to the edge of the rocks. Oh, well. So much for following orders. My watch said I still had plenty of time and the fish around here were nice. Still, just to be on the safe side, I moved back toward the rest of the group.

I floated along, just off the edge of the rocks, watching a myriad of different colored fish, small groups, big groups, big fish, little fish, flitting around among the rocks and coral. About twenty feet away, Laura and Robin lifted their heads at the same time I did, and waved. Molokini Crater was a little crescent of land that created an enormous fishbowl for our viewing pleasure. I was having a lovely time puttering along. With my head in the water, I occasionally checked the rocks, but otherwise I wasn't paying attention to the people around me. I wasn't feeling sociable. I was chasing fish. When someone tapped me on the shoulder, I assumed it was Laura again and waved her off. I wasn't feeling sociable. I was enjoying being alone. Laura tapped again, and when I raised my head to ask her to leave me alone, a hand swept across my face, knocking out my snorkel tube and sending the tube and my mask flying.

I saw a black rubber arm and then it wrapped around my neck and I was being pulled down into the water. I clawed at the arm, trying to pull it loose. My assailant was strong and flailing underwater, I couldn't get any purchase on anything. No leverage. I struggled but it was like being in a weightless state. I was strong, yet I couldn't move my arms or legs through the water with enough force to help myself. If I kicked back, the body behind me merely floated away. If I struck out, by the time the blows landed they were ineffectual.

Around me, big fish circled and I had panicked visions of sharks attacking. But the only shark around here was a human one. I turned, trying to get a glimpse of a face, but my captor turned, too. Like dancers, we moved in harmony, twisting and turning and writhing in a grotesque water ballet. The pressure in my lungs expanded until they felt like they were exploding, so that I fought not only my captor but my own instinctive need to inhale. I tried to claw my way free, breaking my fingernails on the smooth rubber, hacking and digging until I found a space between the glove and the sleeve. I sunk my nails into the skin, clawing, gouging and tearing, trying to cause enough pain to lessen the grip. I was not going to let this person kill me without putting up a fight.

I've been scared before. Lots of times. I've wondered if my life was over. I've felt that gut-wrenching fear that turns me cold and sends waves of adrenaline flowing. This was different. The hardest part of being afraid was feeling helpless. I could be scared but hopeful, scared but angry. This was scared and trapped. Trapped because I couldn't use my environment to help me. Trapped because while I was fighting my attacker, my body was fighting me. Soon it would give up and the demand for oxygen would get so great I would inhale. My desperate lungs would haul in seawater and I would start to drown.

The wise, experienced survivor in me kept up a steady litany. *Stay calm, relax, look for an opportunity. Try to attract the attention of other divers. Of people on the surface.* But my terrified instinct was to thrash, to fight, to force my way to freedom. *Relax,* I told myself. *Go limp. Pretend to be giving up.* If nothing else, controlling my frightened impulses would lessen the need for oxygen. An agitated person breathes more. I needed to breathe less, much less, not at all. I went limp. Relaxed against the arm, let my body float. It took all my willpower.

It seemed to work. The arm around my neck slackened. Instantly I forced my head forward and down, against the hand, the wrist, the weakest part of the hold. I broke free, jerked the bastard's regulator out, and began pushing frantically toward the surface. I wasn't fast enough. Two hands grabbed me and pressed me down, down, down, forcing me face first against the sand, and held me there. I struggled to turn, to rise, to escape again. I managed to twist my head sideways. There was a dark shape on the surface. Was it swimming toward us? Frantically, I waved my arms and legs, hoping to attract attention. My whole being a silent, desperate scream for help, all the while battling with my lungs, fighting my own urgent need to breathe.

I lost the battle. My assailant suddenly struck me in the side with a heavy object, and I instinctively reacted by taking a breath. Choking, gagging, coughing out the water, but when I opened my mouth, more water poured in. I was swallowing it, gasping, gasping. Trying not to take another breath. I flailed around like a fish on a line, pinioned there, my face against a rock, trying to twist, to turn, to get to that close but unreachable surface.

My life did not flash before my eyes. I was too damned busy fighting Mr. Death to think about what came next. I got a hand around and clawed at the arm and wrist again. Clawed hard enough to get between the sleeve of the wet suit and the glove and sink my nails right into the skin. Did enough damage to draw some blood, I could see the tendrils of it floating past my eye. Oh, God. Someone. Notice! There were at least a hundred people in this little fishbowl with me, yet I was drowning and no one noticed. If I'd been an eel they would have gathered in a group. But I was only human. No cute black-and-white speckles, just black-and-blue spots. No gills. Oh, damn. What I wouldn't have given for gills.

I kept struggling to turn, to get loose. Digging a knee into the sand, I tried to get a foot up under me but the damned fins kept folding and bending and slipping. Gasp. Gasp. Cough. My lungs hurt. They hurt when I didn't breathe and they hurt when I did breathe. The black shadow was spreading. It wasn't just overhead now. It was all around me, surrounding me, gathering me in. I was tired. So tired. Tired of fighting. Tired of the struggle. Tired of wrestling with the pressing hands. Relax. That's what I wanted to do, wasn't it? Why didn't I just relax and let go? Just take in that water. Join it. Become one with it. I didn't want to fight anymore.

Poor Bernstein. Poor Nihilani. Bright optimists who hadn't thought my back worth watching. I hadn't thought it needed watching. Andre would skin them alive. A small revenge for the loss of those brown-haired girls and boys, a lifetime of love and happiness. I knew just how he'd feel. I'd been there myself. Lost a loved one. Been down in the blackness of a grief that won't let up. Known what it was like to spend three months sleeping with an old shirt because it still smelled faintly of David. When Suzanne had taken it and washed it, I cried like a baby. Inconsolable. Shattered.

Do not go gentle into that good night. I had tried not to go gentle. I had tried my best not to go. I didn't even know who had done this to me, so I didn't know who to come back and haunt. If I could come back. My last thought, as the ocean took me, as I fell down into the endless black of eternity, was about my mother. How a second child of hers would die with a breach unmended, with anger unresolved, leaving only Michael out of the big family she'd planned to have.

CHAPTER 20

IT FELT LIKE someone had reamed out my lungs with a file. I'd coughed until my back and chest and stomach ached with the effort, until my cough had grown weak and feeble. My throat had been singed with a hot poker. Rhinos had been dancing on my stomach. Heavy, sharp-hoofed, ponderous. I was god-awful ghastly sick and wondering whether I would have been better off dead. At least when you're dead you don't have to wake up again and suffer. I would have moaned but I had no voice, not even a whisper. I was lying on my side, curled up in a fetal position. I had utterly collapsed. I was one with the puddle on the deck beneath my body. Shivering despite the blazing sun.

Once I opened my eyes but there were people around. Nosy, staring people assaulting me with their ugly curiosity. People looking, talking, pointing as if my ordeal, my terror, was simply entertainment for them. I imagined them telling it when they got home—We saw sea turtles, dozens of kinds of fish, and a woman who almost drowned. Want to see my pictures? I went away again. Back inside my head where there was less confusion. Not that things were much better there. I kept feeling the rough fabric of that wet suit against my throat, the press of hands on my shoulders, the exploding agony in my lungs. I stirred restlessly, trying to get away from those thoughts.

Warm hands touched my head, rearranging it, sliding a towel underneath, smoothing the hair away from my eyes and mouth. Gently. Very, very gently. A soothing voice spoke in my ear. "Don't try and speak now. Just rest. Rest. You're going to be fine." I thought it was Dr. Pryzinski.

Fine. Such a crazy idea. How was it going to be fine? I was supposed to be back at work in a few hours and I couldn't even sit up. I was supposed to be able to have a little bit of fun in my life, but some asshole had pointed a big red arrow at me and said, "Amateur detective," causing our renegade conference killer to wreck my one free afternoon by trying to kill me. I no longer put any stock in the idea that this could be the work of the lingerie killer. Why would he stick around to come after me? Dumb as the thought was, I considered this attack simply unfair. I didn't know anything. I wasn't involved. True, other times I had stuck my nose in other people's business, but not this time. I'd done nothing more affirmative than answer questions. I had not played "Thea Kozak, girl detective." I had been restrained, and look where it got me. I wanted to ask the people who always urged me to be careful how I was supposed to have avoided this.

Fine. They said things were going to be fine. Call me clueless in lavaland, but I didn't see how. I didn't know who was after me, but I would have to spend every minute I had left in Hawaii looking back over my shoulder while trying not to run into anything. Fine. What crap. What bullshit. What a load of baloney. I needed some new expletives. Maybe I'd retire from work and spend my days making lists. Maybe I didn't want to be a nineties woman. Maybe being strong and forthright and independent weren't all they were cracked up to be. If I spent my days at home reading dictionaries, no one would pin me down at the bottom of the sea and wait for me to die. Maybe the thesaurus was a girl's best friend?

I would have felt better if I could have told people what had happened. I would have felt better if I could have groaned and moaned and complained. We're given the capacity to groan for a reason—it is very therapeutic. There is no satisfaction in being able to make a wheezy hissing sound, unless you're a snake, and any self-respecting snake would have found mine pathetic. I would have felt better if I felt better. If I wasn't so weak, so cold, so dazed, so completely exhausted. If so many things didn't hurt. If I could stop coughing. If everyone would go away and leave me alone. If someone would give me something to drink.

A loud female voice, quite close to me, said, "Such a terrible accident." I wanted to tell her it was no accident. How could anyone believe what had just happened was an accident? Of course. Because they were all blind and deaf and optimistic and they'd been out ogling the fishes, just like me. Because even those of us who ought to be more cautious can't imagine living our lives in a constantly wary state. It's not human. It's not normal. I raised my head and tried to tell her it wasn't an accident. Raising my head reminded me of the weight machine that was supposed to work my arms and chest. The first few times I used it, I couldn't move any weight without help from the attendant. My head was just as intractable. "Not an accident," I whispered.

The cute college girl who'd been snorkeling with Laura leaned down and whispered in my ear. "Patrol Officer Robin Dunn. We know it wasn't an accident. Don't try and talk now."

I wondered how long it would before I'd be well enough to go after Bernstein and Nihilani. No need to watch my back, eh? They'd thought there was and for that important mission they'd sent this incompetent baby not yet old enough to ride her bike off the sidewalk. I didn't even have enough strength to be angry. I tried to speak again and she bent her head, all perky and attentive. "Go away," I said.

"I'm not supposed to leave you alone," she whispered.

"Then where . . . the . . . hell were you . . . when I . . ."

I wanted to say "needed you," but there wasn't enough air. Or strength. I wanted to critique her competence and her credentials. I wanted to scream in her face, to tell her about my agony, to let her know how it felt to be dragged to the edge of the abyss and shoved over. I wanted to ask her how it felt to have been responsible for another person's life and to have almost lost it because she wanted to play. But I couldn't. I'd been reduced to a human pudding. A great big slug. A spineless, gutless, gormless wonder. My only remaining talent was my ability to drip. I seemed to be able to shed more water than there was in the sea, and it all stayed right beside me, in a faithful puddle, making me colder. I closed my eyes and threw up in her general direction. A visceral demonstration of what I thought of her abilities.

Someone, warm hands again, wiped my face. A gentle voice. Marie's voice. "Poor thing. You feel just rotten, don't you?"

Someone said something. The policewoman. I thought of her as the policegirl, but that wasn't politically correct. Of course, could I have spoken, I would have defended myself by noting that her performance had not been competent or efficient. Girlish. Not womanly. Sent to watch over me, she'd gone off to play with Laura. Oh, hell. What did I know? Maybe in her educational experiences, she'd been shortchanged. Maybe life had caused her to step back from the hands-on experience and let the boys do it. Maybe she was well trained but instinctively unable to step up to the plate.

Funny. I could spend many of my life's hours worrying about what we needed to do to help young girls become strong, confident, forthright women. At all levels, there were ways in which the educational system, and, indeed, our social system, shortchanged girls, handicapped the women they became. I studied it. I thought about it. I worried about it. I saw it changing and was glad.

Still. Understanding is one thing. Being sympathetic when your life has been put on the line is another. I still expect competence from professional women. I groaned. Better to move on. To not dwell on the negative. Wasn't I lucky to be alive, even if I didn't feel particularly lucky right now? Shouldn't I be bouncing with glee, suffused with joy, ecstatic in the knowledge that someday soon I would stop coughing and retching and heal and be as good as new? Thinner, perhaps, paler. Left with another notch on my soul, another dark place in my psyche. The bright, sparkling ocean another place where danger lurked, another place I couldn't go as easily anymore. Would the restless rustling of the waves outside my condo, something that now served as a pleasing backdrop to my days and nights, become tainted with this evil? Had the nameless, faceless figure who had seized me and carried me down to drown not stolen my life but taken my peace of mind? And might I get it back by giving that evil a name and a face?

We all dream of drowning sometimes. The fear of drowning may go back to our watery beginnings, to that traumatic moment when we're pushed violently out of our warm, dark, watery cradle and into a bright cold world. We cry and suck air into our lungs and can never go back. I had almost gone back. I had felt the tug of it, been drawn down into the water's dark embrace, been lured from the frenzied pain and terror of gasping, choking, filling lungs—I had no words for that experience, it had been a fearful, ghastly shriek from the body itself, a body in desperation and a mind closing down—to the peaceful, comfortable cradling of that surrounding darkness. A part of me regretted leaving it. It had been quiet and painless while the world surrounding me now was chaotic, noisy, and painful.

There was commotion all around me. People were grabbing me, lifting me, moving me. I being taken from my puddle, dumped on a rough, dry surface. A stretcher, probably. Carried. Oh, dear. All this bumping and moving was not pleasant. Staying still. Very, very still. That was the key to survival. Leave me alone, curled up in my little ball, long enough, and I would be fine. Life never does that. The powers that be, the helpful folks who aid those of us in distress, usually long after the time when they would have done the most good, are an intrusive lot.

I have often wished for a magic wand, or for the supernatural power, to put someone in my place, especially when I am a patient. If all of those willing and opinionated helpers could know what it feels like to be the piece of meat on the table, they might act differently. I am learning to be a better patient, to endure without fuss until I'm stable enough to get my feet on the floor—either literally or figuratively. But it's always agony. Like right now. They ought to know I'd been repeatedly sick, and carry me tenderly. My balance was off and my stomach so fragile, yet they transported me with all the care they'd give a canned ham. I'm not good at being passive. This enforced passivity was one more torture being inflicted on my already battered self.

Someone was talking to me. I ought to pay attention. What would my mother think? Dr. Pryzinski. He was walking along beside me as we bobbed our way across the deck, through the sea of curious faces. Rude, staring faces. Nosy, curious, eager faces. I wanted to hit them. Couldn't even curl my hands into a fist. Hands, I thought. Something about my hands that I wanted to tell him.

"Thea, they're moving you to another boat," he said. "A smaller, faster boat. It will take you to an ambulance. They're going to take you to the hospital." His face loomed over me, blotting out the sun. "It's just a precaution. Because of all the water in your lungs. You're going to be fine." His hand was warm and solid on my arm. I wanted to grab it and hang on, to beg him not to leave me, to ask him to protect me from hospitals.

It made me seasick to watch him. Not because he was moving, but because I was bobbing and weaving and dipping and drifting and had I not felt sick already, I certainly would have by the time they got me transferred. I closed my eyes, felt the accelerated, exaggerated motions as they moved me onto the other boat.

"Ms. Kozak?" I opened my eyes. A neat and eager EMT was waiting for me, his uniform crisp and fresh. He told me his name, which was Tim Thomas, and asked me how I felt. Tom Tuttle from Tacoma. Ted Turner from Truckee. Tyler Teehee from Tuskeegee. Turtle Turkle from the Tyrols. Oh, help. I was losing it. I couldn't speak. After all that motion, I felt fearfully sick. I threw up on his nice clean shoes. He retaliated by getting out his needles and sticking some into me. That's medicine for you. Find a person who has been through a bad time and make them feel better by punching holes in them. I believe this is directly descended from the primitive custom of bloodletting.

Just in case I wasn't feeling sufficiently helpless and dislocated, he also threw on a cervical collar and a few straps to hold me down. Yessirree. The best way to help a person who has just been traumatized by being held down and nearly drowned is to tie them down. The best way to calm and reassure a person who has been the victim of an attempted murder is to depersonalize them, talk over them like they're deaf and dumb, and surround them with mechanical devices, like you were trying to revive a roast. I wasn't a roast and I didn't need reviving. I just needed rest. And warmth. And peace and quiet. Quiet so I could think. Quiet so that, as my frightened and fragmented brain went back to work, I could start remembering things that might be useful, start assessing what I knew, start adding detail to my anonymous attacker. No one around me was quiet. The people working on me were keeping up a regular barrage of talk, to each other, to the policewoman. Through the radio.

I said, "Pryzinski?"

The man bending over me looked puzzled. He turned to Patrol Officer Robin Dunn. "She doesn't speak English?"

Robin leaned in to listen, tilting her little shell pink ear to catch my utterances. Dammit, Dunn, I thought, tell the man that I speak English so he'll stop with the zombie looks. It's the least you can do. If you'd been more attentive, I wouldn't be here. I said, "Pryzinski?" again. I knew what I wanted to tell them. Be careful of my hands. I had scratched that arm, gouged that wrist. I might be carrying evidence.

She nodded. "Dr. Pryzinski stayed behind on the other boat."

I swallowed. Gathered myself for another attempt. "Hands," I said. She looked blank. "Hands. Evidence. I . . ."

"You didn't have anything in your hands when I brought you up," she said.

May the Lord preserve us from fools. Why did everything have to be so hard? I didn't have the strength for this. These were the times when I longed for telepathy. "Fingernails," I whispered. "I scratched . . . skin. . . ." I closed my eyes. Tired of doing other people's work for them.

I opened them again. Saw the gradual dawning of recognition. "You scratched the person who tried to drown you?" she said. "You think there may still be blood and skin under your fingernails?" Bright girl. Now, what would she do with this information? Of course. To complete the depersonalization, they tenderly and carefully unwrapped me, pulled out my hands, and bagged them like a corpse, making me so glad I'd called it to their attention. They wrapped me back up, strapped me back down, and went back to chatting. I went back to fighting my claustrophobic panic. The boat sailed on.

CHAPTER *21*

I WAS A prisoner at Maui Memorial Hospital. Imprisoned by tubes and needles. Imprisoned by the fact that my only clothing consisted of a bikini and a T-shirt. I didn't even have shoes. Imprisoned by my traitorous body, still so weak and unwilling I couldn't get up and walk out. Otherwise I would have, even barefoot. Even in my hospital johnny. I would have hiked to the nearest hotel, rented a room, and taken a shower. I hate being weak. I hate being helpless. I hate hospitals.

The more they cut back on nursing care, the less hospitals can do for their patients. They can save your life but they don't bother to wash your face. My skin was sticky and stiff. The rough braid I'd made in my hair lay like a wet log beneath my head. My face still tasted salty. My teeth needed brushing. I would have given a year's salary for some mouthwash. Two year's salary for a blanket and a cup of tea. I was cold and damp and itchy and miserable. My hair smelled. I hurt. Weariness lay so heavily on me that it seemed like a chore to breathe. And I was enjoying the pleasure of a visit from the midnight twins.

So far the conversation had been pretty much one-sided. Bernstein had sat there looking miserable. He needed a shave, an iron, a shower, and Right Guard. I knew the look; I'd seen it on my own guy. He sat close enough to smell, but he wouldn't look at me. Could he actually be worrying about what he'd say to Andre? Feeling guilty about the incompetent Robin?

Nihilani had no such problem. He paced the floor, ponderous and implacable as a rhinoceros, and snapped out questions. I wished he'd sit down. Commotion was abrasive to my senses. I was still longing for peace and quiet. My mind felt like a spilled puzzle that had to be picked up piece by piece and put back together. They had come to me directly from their interview with Rory. Reported that she was doing fine—I knew what that meant—and immediately launched into their questions. It must have been an unproductive interview. I was getting the benefit of the bad mood she'd left them in.

I had had only one thing to say. I said it as soon as they came into the room, and it was not a remark calculated to make relations between us smooth. "Staked goat."

"What's that supposed to mean?" Nihilani came to a halt. Even though hospitals are sturdily built, I wondered what his thudding footsteps were doing to the people downstairs.

I didn't think it needed explanation. I turned my head sideways and burrowed into the pillow.

"Come on, Thea, you've got to talk to us. We know you can talk. The doc said you were okay. This attitude of yours is getting us nowhere. You know that, don't you? We're trying to catch a killer. We can't do it if you won't cooperate." He paused. Gave me one of his stony looks. *Save it for someone who cares*, I thought. *I've been eyeball to eyeball with Mr. Death.*

"Your killer . . . almost . . . caught . . . me." I'd given hour-long speeches that took less energy. He was trained to be observant. Couldn't he see what was happening here? I wanted to suggest he go run fifteen or twenty miles and get run over by a truck and then come back and we'd talk. Maybe then he'd understand that I wasn't just being stubborn.

"Nothing was supposed to happen," Nihilani said. "That's why we sent Dunn."

"Good . . . choice." *Jerk*, I thought. Murder and attempted murder are never supposed to happen. I pulled the sheets up over my head. They smelled like pizza for lunch. It made my stomach twitchy. It set my fuzzy little teeth on edge.

"What can you tell me about your assailant?"

"Mean . . . SOB." Wasn't this police harassment? But what could I do? Even if I rang for the nurse, I couldn't explain what I needed. If I'd had the energy to explain, I would have just answered his questions. Where was mental telepathy when we needed it? I was so cold my teeth were practically chattering. I closed my eyes and tried to think of warm things.

He grabbed the covers and jerked them down. "Look at me, goddamn it!" he said. "This is important."

I looked at myself. Down past the faded blue-and-white johnny, rucked up to my waist. At my cheerful bikini bottom. At the bruises on my exposed stomach. At the bandages on my knee, gouged when I'd tried to dig it in and push myself away, down there at the bottom of the sea. At my pale white faraway feet with the hopeful pink polish I'd put on, thinking about wiggling my toes in the sand, trying to convince myself that the trip might be fun. No tan lines. I hadn't wanted to come to Hawaii. It meant missing most of a week with Andre. But with Suzanne sick, I'd had no choice. I've never been able to walk away from a job that needed doing. Could anyone seriously have thought I'd come to play detective? But why else would someone attack me?

"Picture . . . in . . . paper. Whose idea?"

Nihilani looked at Bernstein. Bernstein looked at his shoes. I looked at both of them. Of course they wouldn't tell me anything. I wished he'd put the covers back. I was so cold I felt blue. I wondered if they really believed the doctor who had proclaimed me fine. People around me kept throwing the word around with such abandon. Didn't fine mean A-okay? Hunky-dory? Peachy keen? I wondered if they really believed I could sit up and chat like nothing had happened. I wondered if they had any idea how I felt? If they knew that I could barely string two words together? I wondered, as I stared at them across the great void of my exhaustion, how men trained to be observant could be so dense.

I even wondered, given the picture in the paper, the setup I suspected, if hauling off my blankets and leaving me cold and exposed was part of their strategy. An odd strategy, to torture the victim, but the world works in devious ways. There are those who believe that the end justifies the means.

"Look," Nihilani said, "you must have noticed something. We know how clever you are. How observant. Experienced. Can't you give us something? Anything? We've got people dropping like flies around here and not a hell of a lot to go on."

I buzzed and flapped my wings. Then I held out my hand and flapped my fingers feebly at him. "I tried. Evidence. Fingernails. Marks. Torn suit. What more? Please. I'm cold."

The door had opened while I was delivering this lengthy speech. Dr. Pryzinski, in a borrowed white coat, stethoscope over his shoulder, entered, followed by Marie. Ignoring the twins, he came directly to me, felt my skin, peered into my face, and pulled up the covers. Then he rang for a nurse. "Don't worry," he said, "we'll get you some blankets. Do you think you could drink a little tea? Marie noticed a kitchen down the hall. I'm sure we could fix you something." I nodded, and Marie hurried out.

"I feel terrible about this," he said. "Responsible. If I hadn't invited you . . . pressured you . . . to come with us, none of this would have happened." Only then did he acknowledge the detectives, greeting them by name and shaking their hands. "She's doing pretty well, considering the circumstances. I suppose her weakened condition frustrates you, when you want so much for her to talk. It frustrates her, too. You can see it in her eyes. She's dying to spill her guts. . . ." He noticed my reaction.

"Oops. Sorry. Unfortunate choice of words, under the circumstances. I mean, she's anxious to talk to you and tell you what she knows, and she can't. She's a strong, healthy woman, though, and you're going to see dramatic improvement over the next few hours—"

"The ER doc said she was fine," Nihilani said. I thought I detected a trace of uncertainty in his voice. Might just have been wishful thinking, though. Experience has been a cruel teacher, but I still like to believe the cops are the good guys. It gets hard sometimes.

"Barring postimmersion syndrome, that's exactly right,"

Pryzinski agreed. "He meant no long-term damage. He didn't mean she'd be ready to jump up and go dancing two hours after such a traumatic experience. Why do you suppose they admitted her, in this era of managed care, instead of sending her back to the hotel to rest?" He studied Nihilani's face. Bernstein was still studying his shoes. Boring brown wing tips. In need of polish. "Oh, no! You think she's playing hard to get, don't you? You think she's being uncooperative. Honestly, Detective! Sometimes I think you guys can't tell the good ones from the bad ones. We should all be thanking our lucky stars that this little gal isn't spread out on an autopsy table instead of resting up so she can talk to us."

He turned to me, caught the look on my face, and winked. "Marie is going to fix Thea some tea and make her more comfortable. Why don't we go get some coffee? Maybe by the time we get back, she'll be feeling a little livelier. I know she wants to talk about it, don't you, Theodora?" His use of my full name reminded me of my father, and for a minute, I felt a rush of sadness at my estrangement from my parents. I feel it most in those moments—those rare moments I try to guard against—when I want to be safe and cared for again. When, like now, I'm helpless and needy and far from home. When it's scary to be a grown-up. I forced myself away from self-pity and back to the moment. Once again I got to watch Pryzinski's effect on his fans. If I'd been able to tell them to go away, they would have stayed put, picking at me like a pair of hungry crows, but when he suggested they leave, they were as docile as sheep. It wasn't just that they admired him. He had, despite his genial manner, an air of absolute authority. He made his request very politely but he didn't expect to be turned down.

He paused at my bedside and took my hand. "Count on a good hour," he said in a low voice. "Marie will take care of you." Then he left and I was alone. Rescued before I could be pecked to death.

Marie did take good care of me. Despite my dysfunctional relationship with my own mother, I seemed to have a knack for acquiring other motherly persons to care for me. Dom Florio's wife, Rosie, was one. She was like my mom and my big sister and my best friend all rolled into one. Marie was another. She came back with tea and Jell-O.

From my too frequent contact with hospitals, I've developed quite a taste for Jell-O. Also curiosity. I wonder what the annual medical Jell-O budget is for the nation's hospitals. And what the company would do if it were ever declared unhealthy. Most hospital refrigerators contain little else. Pink Jell-O. Orange Jell-O. Red Jell-O. Rarely green Jell-O. Maybe green isn't an encouraging color. Maybe green is too much like the way patients feel. It was certainly a lot like the way I felt.

She fed me sips of tea and bites of Jell-O. She smoothed the sheets. Washed my face and hands and arms and legs. Unbraided my hair and did her best to comb the snarls out. Found an extra pillow and two blankets. Propped me up and wrapped me up and then sat back to admire her work. "Pretty as a picture," she declared. "Is there anything else I can do?"

I felt ungrateful asking for more. Thus far, no nurse had ever appeared. If it hadn't been for Marie, I'd still be a smelly, sticky, freezing mess. But there was one more thing. "Toothbrush?"

"Let me see what I can do." What she did was reappear with toothbrush, toothpaste, a basin, and a bottle of ginger ale. Pretty soon I was so spiffy I almost could have gone dancing. If I could have stood up. "Your little friend Laura was awfully upset," she said. "She thinks it's all her fault because she was distracting the police officer. I told her that it wasn't her problem and it wasn't her fault. She was just a kid. It was up to the adults to decide how they would behave. She's a very engaging child, isn't she?"

I nodded. "Oh, listen to me," Marie said. "You're supposed to be resting and I'm babbling on like an idiot. Here, have some ginger ale. That's good. Now close your eyes and get some rest. I'll be right over here with my knitting."

Far better than an armed guard was Marie with her lethal knitting needles. No wonder she and Ed carried so much luggage. She was from the be-prepared school of travel. She sat in a chair by the window, humming softly to herself, the needles clicking rapidly. And I, warm and clean and finally feeling a little bit safe, closed my eyes and went to sleep.

I expected they'd only give me a little nap before the crows were back, pecking away, but when I opened my eyes again, the sun was low in the sky and the sweater Marie was knitting was nearly finished. "Oh, hi," she said. "Feeling any better?"

"Much." It was true. The restorative powers of peaceful sleep. I didn't feel great but I did feel slightly human. "How long have I . . ." I wasn't in full voice, but at least I could speak.

She looked at her watch. "A good two hours. They came back a while ago and were going to wake you, but then they got paged. That little girl. Laura. She had something she wanted to tell them. So off they went. And a good thing, too. They didn't need to wake you. That little sleep has done wonders." She laid her work aside and came over to the bed. "Yes. You're much better, aren't you. I wouldn't be surprised if they let you go." She hesitated. "If that's what you want, I mean. I know I never spend a minute in a hospital that I don't have to . . . when I'm not working, I mean. I expect you're the same way."

"I hate hospitals."

"Right. Eddie's gone to see if he can find you something to put on. He should be right back. I'll just go and see about getting you discharged, shall I? Oh . . . I forgot. We've got your stuff. From the boat. It's in the car. So we've got your shoes." She giggled. "Eddie did a good job getting those detectives out of the way, didn't he? He's such a good man. When he likes someone, he'll do anything for them. And he really likes you. He says he hopes that Andre knows how lucky he is."

I nodded. Where did she get the energy? She was wearing me out just listening to her. When she was gone, I closed my eyes again and relished the peace. I tried not to think about all the things back at the hotel that I ought to be worrying about, like introducing the dinner speaker and reassuring the board that they hadn't lost another member. And letting Laura know I wasn't mad. As Andre had pointed out, I wasn't the only member of the board. I hadn't been left in charge alone.

While she was gone, Eddie came back clutching a plastic bag. "Found you this," he said, pulling something out. "I'm afraid it's not the greatest, but just to get you home, uh, back to the hotel . . . it ought to do. I hope. I'm not much of a shopper but Marie didn't want to leave you." He held it up. It was a long, shapeless green dress. A pale, pleasant green. Rather like my complexion right now. "Sorry about the green. It was all they had in large and Marie said I had to get large. I'm used to buying things for Marietta and for her, nothing can ever be too small. She's such a little bit of a thing."

He laid the dress on the bed. "So, I'll get out of here and you can get dressed. I go see if I can rustle up a wheelchair. It's kind of a long walk to the car." He hesitated. "I suppose I ought to call them and let them know that you're returning to the hotel so they don't have to drive back here. They get very unhappy when they're stressed, I've noticed. No sense in antagonizing them." We both knew who "they" were. I nodded. He left.

The phone rang. Jolene, sounding worried. "Thea, are you all right? I . . . we . . ." She hesitated so long I was afraid she'd called to report another disaster. "We heard what happened to you . . . on the boat . . . and when we called the hospital, they said you were going to be fine, that they were just keeping you a little while for observation, and then I just ran into that detective, Bernstein, and he said you were still in the hospital."

"I'm just getting ready to leave right now."

"Are you going to be here in time to introduce our banquet speaker?" she asked.

Oh, how much they loved and valued me. Her overwhelming concern for my welfare was touching. And this was Jolene, the most human. The one I saw as a leader. Get up close and personal with Mr. Death and all she wants to know is who will introduce the dinner speaker. "I can't," I said. "I'm . . . I just can't. Look, the introduction that Billy and I drafted is on my laptop, which is on the desk in my room. Get someone to let you in . . . you can use the printer that's right there to print it. It's filed under DinSpch. Have Zannah do the intro."

"Great," she said. "Great. I'll do that right now. Have you heard how Rory is?"

"Not really. They just said she'd be okay."

"I'd better go find that speech," she said. She hung up without ever learning how I was.

All the care and attention I got was from Ed and Marie, who

were practically strangers. Nothing from my colleagues and so-called friends. It just confirmed what I already knew—that in business your friends aren't really your friends. I had no reason to be surprised. What did surprise me was my reaction. I'm supposed to be tough and cynical and well defended, and here I was longing to be cared for. Clearly I hadn't been eating my Wheaties. I needed more mental gymnastics to toughen up my mind and spirit. Next I'd be wishing Andre were here to protect me from the bad guys, when I believed in taking care of myself.

I rested. Marie came back with a nurse, got me unhooked from my bottles and tubes, and helped me dress. Then, equipped with my wallet and my health insurance card, I signed my life away in return for a discharge with sheets of instructions about what to watch out for. And I was free. But before I left, I wanted to see Rory.

Eddie and Marie were reluctant. They didn't think it was a good idea. But I insisted. I needed to know how she was. Maybe my visit was prompted, in part, by knowing how it felt to have no one asking about me. She was irritating and irresponsible, but she was also obviously disturbed enough by what had happened to have done herself serious harm. Having judged herself so harshly, she didn't need any more judgment from me.

They wheeled me to the door and I pushed myself into her room and up to her bed. Her eyes were closed and she was as pale as the sheets. Her arms were wrapped in bandages. Tubes dripped various fluids into her veins. "Rory?" I said.

Her eyes fluttered open. "Thea!" She looked like she'd run if she could.

"I came to see how you were."

"Wish I was dead," she said. "I tried to be." She closed her eyes.

"Why did you do it, Rory? No one was blaming you."

"You don't know anything," she said. "They will. You'll see."

"But why? Why would anyone blame you?"

"I'll never tell. Not you. Not cops." She trailed off and closed her eyes, a look of pain on her face. "They were here, you know."

She gave a faint, ironic laugh. "Did you know that suicide was a crime? We're so damned powerless! Even our lives aren't our own. Oh, God! I've been so stupid. I never thought this would happen. Never expected . . . I was a fool, you know. So naive."

I touched her arm. "Talk to me, Rory," I said. "Tell me what happened. I know you didn't kill her. . . ."

She moved away from my hand. "Go away. Just go away and leave me alone. I don't want to talk about it. Besides, you know too much already."

What was she talking about? What did she know? What was she hiding? And what on earth did she think I knew? "You're wrong," I said. "I don't know anything. This is the craziest, most paranoid group on the planet. What is it that I'm supposed to know, Rory?"

"Don't try and play dumb with me. I know what a clever, manipulative bitch you are, remember?" She sighed and turned her head away. "I don't know," she said. "Do I need a lawyer or the coroner? I don't know. It's too confusing right now. I never thought . . . this . . ." She sighed again. "My laptop. Who has it? Jolene? Jonetta? I know the cops don't." There must have been something in my face, because she said, "It's you, isn't it? Ms. Finger-in-every-pie, right?"

"I have it."

"With you?"

"Back in my room. What's on it, Rory?"

She sat up suddenly. "Nothing. There's nothing on it. Just my own private stuff. I just don't want anyone looking at my stuff. You know how it is. My personal life is none of their business. None of your business. Don't let anyone look at it, okay?"

Actually, her personal life had become their business—them being the Maui police—when she'd attempted suicide. A corollary to Andre's rule. You try to take a life, any life, even your own, and you lose your privacy. But this wasn't the time to tell her that. We'd had a murder and she knew something about it. That's what I wanted to talk about. A complex person, Rory. Bad at doing her job and bad at letting someone else do her job. She was bad at lying and bad at telling the truth. Amorphous. Pinning her down was like trying to catch fog. I could imagine how much she must have frustrated Nihilani and Bernstein.

Yet I was exactly as bad as they were. I knew just how she felt, which they probably did not, and yet I wouldn't leave her alone either. "If you're involved in this, you're a lot better off if you work with the police than if you go ahead and protect Martina's killer, and that comes out." I waited. No response. "You know something, don't you, Rory? What do you know?"

She opened her eyes and looked at me. It was a look of sheer hatred. "Why . . . did you . . . have to come and not . . . Suzanne?" She was too tired to talk much more. I knew how that felt, too. I was barely holding up my end of this nearly monosyllabic conversation.

"Suzanne got sick."

"And pigs can fly." She closed her eyes again. I was glad to be free of that fierce glare. "I'll never tell," she whispered. "Never. I can be trusted. I made some mistakes. Yeah. But I can be trusted. I can. I'm not like Martina."

"Did you help her killer?" I asked again.

Rory opened her eyes. Earlier she had looked like a warrior princess. Now she looked like an evil witch, as though Martina's evil mantle had fallen on her. "Everything I know stays with me. Dies with me, if necessary. I'm not some maudlin, slobbering drunk, like Martina. They can trust me. I'm reliable."

Her self-centered drama, combined with her hostility, finally got to me. My resolve not to be judgmental dissolved. *Oh, please spare me*, I thought. I'd intervened for her on Friday when Martina was drunk and abusive. Gone with her to rouse Martina and discovered a body on Saturday. Kept her from jumping off a balcony and summoned help for her today and of course all she could think of was herself, and even then, not with any eye toward helping herself by digging out of this mess. The kid needed counseling. She needed to understand that she wasn't the center of the universe and that all of us, whether at the center of the universe or not, must at some point take responsibility for our own actions.

"Oh, grow up, Rory," I said. "That's exactly what you were last night—a slobbering drunk. Martina's death is a terrible thing, but life goes on. Your life is going on. You need to start thinking about how you want the rest of it to be! About taking charge. All this dramatic living and dying stuff. It's so adolescent!" Any second now, a cadre of caring therapists was going to burst through to door and start beating me with Prozac bottles. I was being monumentally unsympathetic to the plight of this poor, unhappy girl.

The dark eyes blazed. "You'll be so sorry you said that! You don't understand anything. You don't know anything. What's going on. What people really think. What I really think. Maybe I have good reasons to be upset; maybe I really did want to kill myself. Maybe if you hadn't come to Hawaii, everything would have been fine. But no. You had to come along and stick your nose into everything; well, I don't want you nosing around me. Those two Neanderthal cops were bad enough. You don't even have a right to be here."

With difficulty, because what I wanted to do was spank her, had both of us not been too weak, I returned to the original purpose of my visit. "I just came to see if you were all right . . . as a board member. . . ."

"Oh, screw the fucking board," she said. "Of course I'm not all right. But I will be. They'll take care of me. Now get out of my room or I'll call a nurse and have you thrown out."

I wheeled myself slowly out of the room. At the door I hesitated, as a thought occurred to me. "Rory," I said. "If you had anything to do with the people who killed Martina, don't assume you can trust them. They've already killed once. . . ." I was going to suggest she think of her own safety, perhaps even suggest a cop outside her room, but she cut me off.

"Shut up," she said. "Shut up and go away. Whatever it is you have to say, I don't want to hear it." As I wheeled away, I wondered if Bernstein and Nihilani had gotten anything more out of her than I had. From their behavior toward me, I thought not. Rory was a real puzzle. What had she done that was so terrible? That had driven her to suicide and to these fantastic protestations? Had she actually helped kill Martina? Was she the killer? It was possible, I supposed. But if Rory was the killer, why had someone tried to kill me? Did she have an accomplice? She had said "they," at some point, hadn't she? Thinking about all this hurt my brain. I was happy to close my eyes, relax, and let the Pryzinskis wheel me to their car.

But partway there, I began to focus on something else Rory said—that I knew too much. I wondered what it was that she thought I knew, what possible basis she could have for accusing me of sticking my nose into things. All I'd ever done, with respect to her, was routine conference business, except for rescuing her from Martina's drunken abuse. I knew she was very protective of Martina, but interfering with some masochistic role didn't logically connect with the things she'd just said. The threats and dark hints. So what was it? Something even I didn't recognize? Or maybe the girl was simply crazy.

Her confused and agitated state was so upsetting I wished I could evict all thoughts of her from my mind. But I have a terrible flaw in my character. I am the self-appointed rescuer of those who can't seem to help themselves. And unlikeable as Rory was, she couldn't take care of herself. I worried that she might try and harm herself again. Wondered what the hospital was doing about that. When I got back to the hotel, I'd ask the midnight twins to keep an eye on things. Maybe call the hospital as well.

I shook my weary head. None of it made any sense. This whole business didn't make any sense. I knew too much and understood nothing. Of course, to me, murder had never made any sense, yet it happened. For once, maybe Rory was right. Maybe it was time to take my nose back to the hotel and tuck it into a nice, safe bed. Right after I ordered up a delicious batch of tea and toast, took a hot bath, and tried to reassemble my brain. And then something else occurred to me, popping into the thought window like a message in a magic eight ball. Once I had my brain back, I was going to take a look at Rory's computer. No longer just to download files. Now I was wondering what she didn't want me to see. Whether there were clues there to all the nonsense she'd been babbling. Maybe in the process, I'd be able to figure something out.

CHAPTER 22

MARIE INSISTED I sit in front on the ride back to the hotel, which made me feel guilty but I was glad not to have to ride with my knees in my ears. It was a peaceful ride. Dr. Pryzinski asked if there was anything I wanted to know, medically, about what had happened. I asked a few questions. He gave simple, thoughtful answers. It made me wonder why a man who was so good with patients, which is sort of what I was by adoption, had chosen pathology, so I asked him.

"Revenge," he said.

"Revenge?"

He nodded. "Back when I was in high school I had a friend. She was a girl but she was a friend, not a love interest, named Shirley. Shirley was just a little bit of a thing, kind of like our Marietta, and very shy, but she was smart. Back then, it wasn't very easy for a girl to be smart . . . I guess, being in the business you're in, I don't have to tell you about that. Shirley put a lot of effort into not being smart, but sometimes she couldn't help herself. Anyway, Shirley wanted to go to college. No one in her family had ever gone to college and they didn't understand why it was important to her."

He chuckled. "You're going to be very sorry you asked. I never make a long story short."

"He's telling you the truth," Marie piped in. "When Eddie starts to tell a story, you have to be prepared to sit back and listen."

"I'm prepared." I was interested, and it sure beat thinking my own thoughts or remembering my day.

"Shirley had a boyfriend. Guy named Joey. Did I tell you that Shirley was pretty? Well, she was. Little bitty blond thing with the biggest, bluest eyes. Anyway, Joey wanted to marry Shirley as soon as she graduated, while Shirley, she wanted to wait until she finished college. They used to fight about it a lot. She'd tell me about it and cry on my shoulder when we did homework together. I never would have gotten through math without Shirley. She had an instinct for math and a real knack for teaching. What a loss to the world that was . . . but, I get ahead of myself."

He cleared his throat. "Joey didn't like it that Shirley and I studied together. He came by my house one night and told me to keep away from her. He said that Shirley belonged to him. I hadn't met Marie yet, nor had a daughter, and I wasn't educated about feminist ideals back then, but it seemed quite clear to me that Shirley ought to be able to study with anyone she wanted to study with. I told him that. I also told him that Shirley and I were only friends and I was no threat to their relationship. But the next time I called Shirley and asked for some help, she wouldn't talk to me."

He slammed on the brakes as a vivid orange Volkswagen beetle ducked out in front of us, and just like every parent since cars were invented, he threw out his arm to protect me. Marie laughed. "He's whacked more people in the chest that way. I'm beginning to wonder if it's really accidental."

"After that, Shirley avoided me. She just sort of drifted around at school, looking lost. One day she had a black eye and I asked her about it. Back then, we didn't know so much about battered women, either. She gave the standard reply, that she'd run into a door, and hurried away. The next week it was bruises on her arm. But she was still planning on college, as far as I knew. The school year ended and graduation came. No one was surprised that Shirley was valedictorian. No one was surprised that she declined the honor of making a speech. No one was surprised that she'd been accepted at a really good college and offered a generous scholarship."

"Hurry it up, honey," Marie said. "We're almost to the hotel."

"Two weeks before she was supposed to leave for college, Shirley disappeared. When the police went to talk to Joey, he told them that he and Shirley had been parking on one of the local lover's lanes, that they'd had a fight, and Shirley had gotten out of the car and walked away. They found what was left of her body two months later at the bottom of a ravine. The coroner determined her death was an accident."

He snapped on his turn signal. "It was no accident. When I was in medical school, I had a pathologist for a teacher who truly loved what he did. He used to say, 'They talk to me and I listen. The ones who have killed them think they're silenced forever, but I'm their translator. I'm their spokesman. I interpret for the dead and give them the voices that their killers have tried to steal away.' I listened to him and I thought, someone like that could have proved that Shirley's death was no accident. I decided to become a champion of people like Shirley."

"Isn't he wonderful?" Marie said. "Other people may make more money, but Eddie makes a difference."

They pulled up in front of the hotel. "Why don't you get out here," he said, "and then I'll go park the car." I got out of the car and stood for a moment, testing my shaky legs. "Can you manage?" he asked. "Marie could . . ."

I shook my head. "No, really. I'm fine." Damn! Now I was saying it, too. I was far from fine. I just hated being fussed over.

After the cool austerity of the hospital and the soothing ride in the Pryzinski's air-conditioned car, entering the lobby was like walking into sensory overload. I stood in the entrance, gathering myself for the long hike to the elevators, assailed by the mingled scents of earthy, tropical vegetation, the faint salt tang of the ocean, and the perfume of flowers and scented women. Faint music, chattering voices, children splashing in the pool. Phones ringing. Welcome back to the world.

Jolene, done up in a long-sleeved shimmery blue dress, was

arguing with someone at the desk. She abandoned the argument and came running up to me. "Thank goodness you're here," she said. "They won't let me into your room, dinner is in an hour, and I need that speech."

"Why didn't you get Billy to write you another one?"

"I would have, of course, but with your accident and the incident with Jeff this morning, and Martina . . . well, when I got back from the snorkel trip, Billy was working and couldn't be disturbed, and now I can't find him. I've asked everyone." She was moving rapidly toward the elevators as she spoke. I couldn't keep up. Normally, yes, but I was still a wee bit under the weather, if feeling like I probably wouldn't make across the lobby could be described that way.

"Slow down," I said.

"But we don't have time. . . ."

Long-forgotten words came tumbling out. College Shakespeare. The most exciting teacher I'd ever had. Obviously, I'd carried the fear of drowning with me then, as well.

" 'Lord, Lord! methought, what pain it was to drown:
What dreadful noise of waters in mine ears!
What sights of ugly death within mine eyes!
Methoughts I saw a thousand fearful wracks;
A thousand men that fishes gnawed upon.' "

That stopped her. "What on earth is that?" she asked, turning to stare at me.

"*Richard III*, I think."

"Shakespeare? At a time like this?"

"Seemed to fit the moment." I didn't bother to tell her that it was always time for Shakespeare. Shakespeare and the Bible. That I still kept both within reach for ready reference, at work and at home. We made it to the elevators. Conference attendees were buzzing around the lobby, colorful as butterflies, talking and laughing. Despite our series of disasters, we hadn't managed to put a damper on everyone's good spirits. The elevator arrived. We got in. I leaned against the wall and closed my eyes.

"Now that you're here, maybe you could still do the—"

Without opening my eyes, I said, " 'Full fathom five thy father lies; Of his bones are coral made: Those are pearls that were his eyes: Nothing of him that doth fade, But doth suffer a sea-change into something rich and strange.' "

"*The Tempest,*" she said. "Have you gone mad?"

"Suffered a sea-change. No. I'm *not* giving the speech. Two hours ago I couldn't speak at all. Now I can speak but I can barely stand. I'm not pushing my luck. You wouldn't want me to. It would do the conference no good if I collapsed into my dinner plate before I got our speaker introduced. We've had quite enough drama for one weekend."

"You're right," she said. "I'm sorry. I'm afraid I'm letting all this chaos get to me. I should know better. The headmistress's life is pretty much constant chaos, at least at my school, hard as I've worked to change it. I don't know why I think this should be different. Or why I'm not coping."

"You'll do fine."

The door opened and we got out. Two women were waiting to get on. Women in identical blue dresses. Of course. The Elliot sisters. They smiled and waved and didn't even stop to ask questions. The open bar only lasted for the first half hour of the cocktail party. When the door had closed behind them, I said, "I saw Rory at the hospital. I thought I should."

"And?"

"She says she wants to die. I can't tell whether it is just hysteria and late-adolescent angst or whether she had something to do with Martina's death and now she can't handle the guilt. She drops these dark hints but she won't say anything. If she hadn't been so helpless I might have whacked her. But it worries me. The whole situation. A kid, alone in a hospital in a strange place . . ."

I was hoping Jolene would pick up the ball and put herself or someone else in charge of Rory's welfare, but all she said was, "Guess we'll have to put off telling her that she's fired, won't we?"

"I guess." I stuck the key in the door and opened it. The room seemed very dark and I was sure I'd left the curtains open. I snapped on the light and stared. It looked like a tornado had hit.

My clothes and papers were flung helter-skelter all over the place, mixed with crumpled bedding and pulled-out drawers. The coup de grace was my laptop, which I had left on the desk. It had been dismembered and the pieces were scattered everywhere. My recovery suffered an immediate and serious setback. I sat down in a chair, gasping. I had once again lost my powers of speech.

As if they'd been summoned by my telekinetic powers, Bernstein and Nihilani arrived at the door, invited themselves in, and surveyed the damage. Out popped a radio and technicians were called. Dr. Pryzinski and Marie arrived and wanted to carry me off to their room. Bernstein and Nihilani didn't think so. Jolene looked like she was about to decompensate.

I have been Thea the fixer for too long. Despite the shock, despite my anguish at losing my computer, I summoned back my powers of speech, begged for ten minutes grace from the midnight twins, and went to her room with Jolene to compose a speech. I felt dissociated from myself, as though one Thea, the battered, confused, exhausted one, was watching another composed and coherent Thea perform. Luckily, I had invited the speaker. I had collected background materials and written the speech for Martina. I had written it again for myself. By this time, I could practically recite it from memory. I talked. She wrote. My voice held; her fingers flew. At last, I said, "Therefore, it is my great pleasure to introduce Dr. Noreen Van Norden, whose courage in pioneering single-sex math classes in the public-school setting, and the positive results of that experiment, has, and will continue to have, lasting importance for the lives of young girls everywhere. Dr. Van Norden."

She put down her pen. "You're amazing, you know that?"

I didn't feel like being complimented. I didn't feel angry. I felt on the verge of complete collapse. Visions of warm blankets and soft pillows danced before my eyes. "I only wish I could hear her speak. She's going to be wonderful."

"So come. It's not too late."

"I'm tired, Joly. I'm beyond tired. And I've still got the mess that was my room to deal with. I don't even have a place to lie down." I picked up her phone and called the desk, explained what had happened, and asked for another room. All they had left, he said, was a suite. I said a suite would be just dandy. He hesitated and then informed me that it was next door to the, um, room where a woman, um, had, um, been, um. I thought that if he said "um" one more time that I would crawl down to the lobby and strangle him. It seemed like justice to me. I asked if he could send someone up with the key. At that he hemmed and hawed and hesitated.

"Look," I said, "here in your hotel, while I was at the local hospital being revived after nearly drowning, someone broke into my room, trashed it, and destroyed a very expensive computer. In case you have missed the irritation in my voice, let me point it out to you. I'm very tired, physically unwell, and extremely upset. Send someone up with the key." I banged down the phone and leaned back in the chair, exhausted. My eyelids felt like there were little lead weights on them.

Jolene was hovering by the door. "I'd better get downstairs with this. Do you mind? You're okay . . . I mean . . ."

"Go," I said. "Go ahead. I've got to get back there and see what I can rescue anyway. I'm not spending any more time than I have to in this." I plucked at the shapeless green sack I was wearing. Ed Pryzinski was a wonderful, generous man but he had no fashion sense. As she reached for the doorknob, the sleeve of Jolene's dress pulled up and I saw a Band-Aid on her wrist. "What happened to your wrist?"

"Coral," she said. "Or lava. You know how things are closer than they look in the water, kind of like side-view mirrors? I reached out and bingo. Big scrape and blood pouring everywhere. I headed for the boat so fast I practically walked on water. Ran on water. All I could think of was sharks." She opened the door. "See you in the morning. We'll miss you."

I trudged back to my room. The destruction was being photographed like a serious crime scene, instead of merely nasty vandalism. This time I noticed, as I hadn't before, that my birthday roses had been shredded. That hurt. I sat in a chair and put my head in my hands. It never seemed to stop, did it? "They're giving me another room," I said. "Could I get some of my clothes and stuff and go up there?" I only asked permission because I was too weak to argue.

The midnight twins exchanged glances. "Sure," Nihilani said. "Long as we know where to find you."

"Someone's coming up in a minute with the key." I knelt by the pile, picking through it, brushing aside the petals of my brutalized flowers. Found some clean underwear. A nightgown. A skirt. A T-shirt. Some shoes. The sandals I was wearing hurt my feet. I decided to switch to the shoes. When I stuck my foot in, a piece of paper rustled under my toe. I pulled the shoe off, took the paper out, unfolded it. A cash receipt for the purchase of lingerie. The top, which would have listed information about the store and purchase date, had been torn off. It made no sense, but so little of what was happening did. I handed it to Bernstein, my extended arm shaking with the effort of holding it out. "Here," I said. "It was in my shoe but it's not mine. I wore these shoes on Friday."

Bernstein took it, looked at it, and handed it to Nihilani. Nihilani frowned and pointed at the door. Then the two of them went out into the hall. At this point, I didn't even care if they arrested me. There were beds in jail and I longed for bed. There might even be hot showers or cups of tea. Right now I had no amenities. I took advantage of their absence to go into the bathroom. For some reason, the vandals had neglected to do their work here. I collected my cosmetics bag and vital stuff like toothbrush and hairbrush. Then I checked the stack of towels to see if Rory's laptop was still there. It was. I wrapped it up in the bundle of my clothes and stuck everything into the tote bag I'd been carrying.

A bellboy came hurrying in and stopped in shock when he saw the mess. He held out an envelope. "Ms. Kozak?" he asked. In his voice were the words "What the hell happened here?" but he didn't say that aloud. He only stared. I opened the envelope and read the room number.

"Thanks," I said.

"I'm supposed to ask if you need any help with your, um, things," he said.

Maybe "um" was a part of the Hawaiian language, but I doubted it. "I'm beyond help," I said. "Maybe tomorrow." He left.

I followed him out, gave the number of my new digs to the midnight twins, and took the elevator up to seventeen. Maybe, if I was really lucky, I'd get a fruit basket. What I wanted to do was to drink the entire minibar and fall into a mindless stupor. But my stomach was in no state for such indulgence. What I wanted to do was call Andre, cry on his shoulder, and ask for advice. But I didn't know how soon the twins would arrive and I didn't want to be interrupted in midcry. When I finally got around to crying about this, I wanted to give it my all. I wanted to get into it, immerse myself in it, to wallow in self-pity.

I called room service and ordered tea and soup and toast. Then I wrapped myself in a blanket, lay down on the couch, and waited, letting myself drift into a senseless doze. Eventually they came. Pulled up their chairs and sat down. Took out their notebooks. Clicked their pens. Looked at me hopefully. "Mind if we call room service?" Bernstein asked. "We didn't have time for dinner."

I waved in the general direction of the phone. "Be my guest," I said. What the heck. The bills were already so insane what difference did a little bit more make? My regret was not that I had to feed them again—I like feeding people, especially, sexist as it is, hungry men—but the fact that it meant they'd be staying awhile. Visions of bubble bath, warm and soothing, danced in my brain. I'd spotted some in the bathroom.

I was so into my vision, I almost missed it when he said, "We'll reimburse you, of course." Of course. All I'd have to do would be complete seven hundred different forms, pressing hard so my writing would get through all five copies of each. So now we'd observed the formalities, but as far as I was concerned, they could eat for free.

While Bernstein ordered up a feast for the two of them, Nihilani began to go through the questions he'd asked earlier. Step by step he walked me through the entire attack. What I did. What the attacker did. I told him everything I could remember, which was very little, struggling against the anxiety remembering brought. While I was describing being pinned to the bottom and trying to wiggle free, my lungs started to ache. I felt like I was choking again.

"I kept trying to turn but I couldn't. He kept twisting and turning out of reach."

"He? Then you think it was a man?"

"A man. Or a strong woman. Someone pretty big, I think. He, or she, stayed behind me the whole time."

He nodded. "We checked out all the people on your boat, particularly the scuba divers. No one had an arm or wrist injury."

I shrugged. "There were other boats."

"Who knew you were going snorkeling?"

I thought about that. Who had I told? Laura. And of course Ed and Marie knew. And I'd told Rob Greene when we were talking after the panel. And Billy. Hadn't I told Billy? "Maybe I said something at breakfast. I can't remember. And I told someone in the hall, when there were who knows how many people around. The hotel might have had my name on a list . . . one that anyone could have checked." It was only a suggestion. I didn't know whether my name had appeared on any lists anywhere or whether I'd been part of Pryzinski, party of three. "I suppose anyone could have seen me leaving the hotel, but I didn't get on the bus, so how would they know where I was going?"

Nihilani was giving me his stone-cold stare again. "You say you have absolutely no idea why someone might have wanted to hurt you?"

"Not hurt," I corrected. "Kill. None. I've gone over everything that's happened in the past few days and I don't come up with anything. Well, other than something so vague I can't make any sense out of it. I went to see Rory before I left the hospital—"

"You what?" Bernstein's narrow face tightened, the frown lines deepening.

"I was there. She was . . . is . . . one of our employees. And Jonetta and I were the ones who found her. I wanted to know how she was so I could report to the others when I got back. I thought she might like to see a familiar face. And I wanted to ask her why she did it. Just like you guys."

"Yeah," Bernstein said, "but we're detectives."

"Thought I read in the paper today that I'm a detective, too."

"Amateur," Nihilani said. He rolled his eyes. "Dumbest thing in the world a person can do, thinking they're better than the police at solving crimes."

That stung, but I wasn't getting into a pissing contest. "I couldn't agree more," I said. "That's why I'm leaving it all up to you. But it looks like you haven't got a clue, either."

"I wouldn't say that." Bernstein. He was more vulnerable to insults than Nihilani. I think I could have called Nihilani every bad thing I'd ever heard, going all the way back to the misconstrued epithet I'd hurled at my brother, Michael, when I was five, calling him a "piece of hell," and the man wouldn't even have blinked. "What else did Ms. Altschuler tell you?"

"Nothing. She was upset that I had come to Hawaii instead of my partner, Suzanne, who was supposed to come until she got sick. Rory seemed to think my presence was deliberate. . . ." I stopped. "Because of that article in the paper, perhaps? I assume you guys were responsible for that."

"Not us," Bernstein said. Not only more emotional but more comfortable with lying. Nihilani didn't like to communicate but I thought he also didn't like to lie.

"Staked goat," I said. I had no evidence, but I was sure they'd set me up. Thinking that I'd draw the bad guys, like moths to a flame, while they carefully watched and swooped down for the capture. Nice plan. Poor execution. Might be seen as an interesting bit of police work, if you weren't the goat.

One of the tortures they'd inflicted on the Salem witches was called *pressing* where they piled stones on the person until eventually she was crushed or suffocated because she couldn't breathe. I felt like that was being done to me here. I was trying to stay uninvolved, just trying to do my job and get out of here in one piece, but this business wouldn't let me alone. Things kept getting piled onto me by everyone—my co-workers, the bad guys, the cops—until the burden was starting to crush me, until I felt like I wasn't going to be able to breathe. Everyone, it seemed, made assumptions about me and lied to me.

"Look, if you guys are going to set me up like this, you've got to do a better job of protecting me." There was a lot more I could have said on the subject but it wasn't worth it. They knew how I felt. They knew what had happened. They knew they'd let me down. Or so I thought. Not on very good evidence—the presence of Robin Dunn on the boat, Bernstein's determined study of his shoes at the hospital, Nihilani's restless resettling in his chair when I accused them. Call it woman's intuition. But I had to let it go. If I dwelled on it, I'd get too upset to talk. And then they'd hang around longer and I'd get wearier and and and.

But I did have one question I'd like answered. "Did Officer Dunn notice anything?" I asked, adding, "anything helpful?" Nihilani looked at Bernstein, who shook his head. Why was I not surprised.

"You were telling us about your conversation with Rory Altschuler," Bernstein reminded me.

"Rory said sooner or later you'd end up blaming her," I told them. "I asked her why? She wouldn't say anything, except that I already knew . . . how did she put it? . . . oh . . . she said I knew too much already. I asked what she meant. She wouldn't answer. She said some dramatic thing to the effect that she'd carry her secret to the grave or die trying. She said, 'They can trust me.' "

"What is this too much that you know?" Nihilani asked. Actually, he didn't so much ask as growl.

"Beats me," I said. "I've gone over everything that's happened since I got here, and I can't figure it out." Bernstein smothered a yawn. "Look, if I'm boring you, why don't you leave?"

"Haven't eaten yet," he said, trying for lightness.

Nihilani made no such effort. "We'll go when we're done with our questions," he said. "What did she mean by 'They can trust me'?"

"I don't know."

"You sure?"

Bastard, I thought. "Do you think I'm just waiting till you leave so I can go solve the crime myself?" I said. "Of course I'm sure."

"Were you aware that Ms. Altschuler was embezzling money from the association accounts?" Nihilani asked.

"Rory? You're joking."

"Do I look like I'm joking?"

Nihilani looked like he'd never heard, or told, a joke in his life.

I shook my head. "How do you know she was embezzling?" I thought about Rory's computer, lurking in my bag. Were her records on her computer and did she have an accomplice who had destroyed my computer, thinking it was hers?

To my surprise, Nihilani answered the question. "Mr. Pullman told us. He said he was going through some association records, looking for an expense his wife thought had been improperly entered, and he kept finding things that didn't make sense. Repeated bills for identical amounts and consulting fees paid to Alt Corp. He was planning to spend the weekend going over accounts, but he'd barely begun when he got the call from us. By that time, though, he'd determined that Alt Corp. was nothing more than a bank account kept by Ms. Altschuler."

CHAPTER 23

ROOM SERVICE ARRIVED and there was brief halt in the action while we ate. Not that I consider tea and soup eating. Tea and soup are culinary resting points. But the guys ate in a seriously hungry way. Watching them made me think of Andre, the man who loved his food. It always surprised me that Andre could be such a sympathetic guy when he was basically a creature of appetites. For food. For fun. For sex. For adventure. For solving crimes. It was true, I realized. Andre approached his work the same way he approached everything else, wholeheartedly, with determination and a fierce passion. Whatever the hour, as soon as they were gone I was going to call him. What the heck. He was used to being interrupted in the middle of the night.

We went all around Robin Hood's barn—or perhaps it was Davy Jones's locker—a few more times without finding anything more of interest. I'd been too busy fighting for my life to be observant. Short of a developing conviction that my assailant was either a man or a large woman, I had no insights. Despite the efficiency with which I'd put together the introduction with Jolene, I was in a frustratingly vague and dazed state. I was a 78 played at 33 RPMs. I didn't think I'd develop any insights unless I was left alone long enough to get my brain back in order. I said as much, hoping they'd go away. "Why don't you look at who signed up for scuba on those other boats?" I suggested. I remembered the threatening message I'd carefully saved. "And what about Lewis Broder? He left me a message saying he was going to get me."

"Say what?" Nihilani said. "Someone threatened you and you didn't tell us?"

I gave an airy shrug. "I'm so used to being threatened I hardly pay attention anymore." I couldn't resist a slight dig. "I mean, what would you have done if I told you? Send someone to watch my back? I did save the message, though. But I don't know what may have happened to my messages now that I've changed rooms. You can check."

Nihilani nodded to Bernstein. Bernstein picked up the phone. "Anything else you've neglected to share?" Nihilani asked. There was a definite growl in his voice, like he wished he was gnawing on my bones. *Go ahead*, I thought. *Gnaw.* I could hardly feel worse. But there was something scary about him. Expressionless people make me uneasy.

"Other than Rory promising I'd be sorry? Nothing that I can think of. Except that if you think I told Bill Berryman the details of the, uh, crime . . . you're wrong. I had neither seen nor spoken with him before the meeting at which he handed out those clippings." They exchanged meaningful glances. Meaningful to them. I had no idea what was going on. But then, why should anything have changed? I gave. They took. I stayed in the dark. "Is there something going on that I should know about?" I asked, not expecting an answer. Of course I didn't get one.

We sat in uncompanionable silence while Bernstein tracked down my messages, listened intently, and then held the phone out to Nihilani. "Here, you should listen to this."

Nihilani listened and then disconnected. "This the last you heard from him?"

I put my head on the arm of the sofa and closed my eyes, wishing someone would bring me a pillow and a blanket.

"Hey," Bernstein said, "don't go falling asleep on us." He repeated Nihilani's question.

"Jolene said she thought he'd checked out. She got one of these calls, too. He was just angry that you'd heard about his lie. She won't want to tell you this, but last night, when she walked him to the elevator, he tore her dress trying to get her to go upstairs with him. Give him a few drinks and the man's an animal."

Nihilani nodded. "We heard about that from your little friend. Now, what about that receipt, the one that was in your shoe? How could it have gotten into your shoe if you didn't put it there?"

I raised my head. He sat, staring and monolithic and I felt returning tendrils of the anger I'd felt on the boat and at the hospital. Small, random flashes, like heat lightning. With these guys, I always felt used and abused. *Easy, Kozak*, I told myself. *Assume he's not accusing you. Pretend that security at the hotel isn't as tight as a sieve. Assume it's a fair question.* I thought about it. Who had been in my room? "Quite a lot of people have been in my room," I said. "There's the person who trashed it . . . that's your simplest explanation, of course . . . and Rory, before she became hysterical and tried to jump off the balcony. She was alone for a few minutes while I went to get her some water. Jonetta was there, but of course, so were the two of you. Eddie and Marie Pryzinski? You guy are detectives, so you tell me. Can you get fingerprints from a piece of paper like that?"

He got up and headed for the door. "You've got Lenny's card, right? Don't go anywhere without telling us. Just a precaution," he said.

"No. Lenny's card is somewhere in the mess downstairs. You'd better give me another. I know I'll feel safer knowing you're watching over me."

I didn't share my thoughts with him, burbling, angry thoughts that seemed to be rekindling some of my lost energy. Given his track record, checking in might give me a false sense of security that could get me killed. I just nodded, held out my hand, and took the new card. Andre, the man who sometimes advises me to button my lip in the name of public relations, would have been proud. A thought occurred to me as I watched their departing backs. "Do you have someone watching Rory's room?" I asked.

"No."

"Not that it's any of my business, but if I were you, I would," I said. "If she is a part of this, her accomplices might not consider her too reliable. . . ."

Bernstein's shoulders had stiffened in what looked like a prelude to resentment. "Oh, never mind," I said. Nihilani grunted. One of those nondescript sounds that could have been yes or no or Oops, I forgot to take out the trash this morning, or even gas.

Their reaction to my suggestion about Rory was so positive that I kept my next one to myself—that if someone was going around attacking potential witnesses, they should keep an eye on Laura Mitchell. Still, I had to have the last word. "Do what you want," I said. "You always do. I don't know why you keep bothering me." Another grunt. Then they were gone and I was blissfully alone.

"Screw you," I told the chairs they had occupied, half surprised they hadn't suggested I was actually the murderer and I'd faked my own drowning to throw off suspicion.

I back-burnered my plans to take a bath, locked the door as many times as it would lock, and got out Rory's computer. First item of business was to check on tomorrow's arrangements. I couldn't print but at least I could take notes. Four workshops requiring four conference rooms—surely Mrs. Sato would have anticipated that—followed by our closing lunch. All carefully confirmed in writing. Again, it seemed like a no-brainer to me, but compulsive that I am, I called and left a message on her voice mail reminding her to check on the details.

Rory's suicide attempt puzzled me. The Rory I was used to was careful, detailed, compulsive, serious, and hardworking. In my experience, in times of extreme stress, people reverted to their most conservative behaviors. Quiet people stopped talking altogether. Depressed people got more depressed. Compulsive people, like me, got more compulsive, taking refuge in the familiar. Workaholics worked harder. But Rory had fallen apart. Maybe it was just that she was young, but that was being a bit condescending, considering that I wasn't so much older. It had to be something else.

They had told me she'd been stealing money. That didn't sound a whole lot like Rory, either. From my observation of her, I would have said that while Rory was ambitious and aspired to bigger than things than being Martina's assistant, she was basically the assistant type. Given direction, she would perform brilliantly within her normal sphere. But Rory was not an innovator. For all that she'd accused me of being like Martina in giving her an assignment and then taking it away, when she'd had the chance to step into Martina's shoes and prove herself by running the conference, she'd buried her head in the sand and failed to do anything. In fact, not only had she not done anything, but she'd whined and acted like it was terrible imposition when asked to do something. Not leadership behavior.

If I'd been in her position, I would always have been nosing up against Martina's domain, appropriating pieces, taking over whatever I could. I've often described myself as the perfect second-in-command. Put me there and I'll always be trying to seize power. Give me power and I get nervous. Actually, that's how I used to describe myself. Over the years, I've gotten more comfortable with power and responsibility. I've gotten used to being in charge.

Going back to Rory, I pondered. Was being a shrinking violet consistent with concocting a scheme to embezzle money from the association? Was it the kind of behavior a smart but chronically oppressed and ill-used person might resort to? A sly and underhanded revenge? Maybe it was. Maybe Rory's self-pitying declarations were only anticipation that someone would discover her fiscal irregularities, not fear that she'd be accused of Martina's murder. But that's not what I'd seen. I'd seen a girl who believed she was going to be accused of murder. Who expected to be caught and thought she deserved it. And yet I couldn't see Rory as the murderer. Only as the murderer's assistant.

I stared at the glowing screen. As long as I was here, I might as well see what else I could find. I browsed through her meeting notes. Nothing of interest. Her correspondence. That, too, was just more business. I poised my fingers over the keys and closed my eyes. Where was the secret heart? Where would there be anything personal, revealing? Where would I find Rory in this little metal-and-plastic box? I decided to check her E-mail files.

Bingo. Some very interesting correspondence between Rory

and someone called Fox. Among other things, this Fox had advised Rory on the fine points of stealing the money, including making the suggestion that she type up Alt Corp. invoices and get them copied at Kinko's, the papers she'd need to set up a corporate bank account, and how she should keep the amounts small so they wouldn't be noticed. Rory's responses to the Fox were equally revealing. Rory was going to rendezvous with the Fox here in Hawaii. Alt Corp. would purchase a ticket to Maui and one from Maui back to Honolulu. There, presumably, Fox would lie in wait for Rory. Until. Until what?

Had Fox come to help Rory with a murder? Come to perform the dastardly deed? Or just come to enjoy some sun and fun? Was Fox an accomplice to murder or just a larcenous boyfriend? I needed to know when Fox had flown in and when Fox had flown out. Difficult if I didn't know Fox's name. But not so difficult for the police. We had Fox's E-mail address. It wasn't much of a challenge to convert that back into a name. Maybe for an ordinary citizen, but not for a cop. Probably not for a good hacker, either.

Once again, I'd set out to do conference business and found myself back in the middle of Martina's murder. I'd taken the laptop because it was important for business. Now, swept away on a wave of anger and curiosity, I'd gone beyond the bounds of business and learned—learned what? More about Rory than I wanted to know. Clearly it was time to turn this baby over to the midnight twins. In just a minute. It obviously held information relating to a crime, even if not the crime of murder. On the other hand, it was bound to mean endless hassles for our post-Martina, post-Rory transition. Once we let it go, it would be hell getting it back. And maybe there was more stuff here that I really ought—

Wait a minute, Kozak, I told myself. Wasn't I the reformed, risk-averse, don't-get-involved Thea Kozak? Professional woman. Nobody's detective, even if I did get onto elevators and have people call me Sherlock.

Why was I hesitating? Why didn't I just beep Lenny and hand the damned thing over? Maybe it had something to do with the way they'd treated me. Or my conviction that they'd set me up, pointed me out as a detective to see what might shake loose.

I've been accused by my beloved of being pigheaded and reckless. And the man is sometimes right. It's not that one of us is from Mars and one from Venus. Our problem is that we're both from the same planet, but the behavior that is appropriate for him is inappropriate for me. Well, in a minute, after I'd finished playing with Rory's laptop, I'd get back in touch with my fragile-blossom side. Turn this thing over to competent professionals who would know what to do with it.

I browsed a little more. Aha! There was a more romantic correspondent called Bilbo who got fairly risqué in the comments he made. I recognized some of Rory's physical characteristics from the descriptions. Others were new to me and rather more personal than I would have liked.

I wouldn't have saved them on my machine. The wisdom of living defensively suggested the same rule for one's personal files as for one's person. Never wear anything you wouldn't want to be caught dead in. Never leave a message in your E-mail files that you don't want someone else reading after your death. But then, Rory wasn't dead, just out of commission. So maybe the moral was, don't write anything you wouldn't want the police, or your boss, to see. Well, the police were about to see this one. After all, whoever had smashed my laptop might have thought that they were smashing Rory's. They might have thought that all this stuff had been destroyed. The way news traveled in this group, it would have been no secret that I had Rory's laptop for the benefit of the organization. Heck, it belonged to the organization.

Though I'd stayed perfectly calm about it downstairs—calm because I was too weary and distracted to be anything else—the loss of my laptop really made me furious. I used it so much it was practically a prosthetic device. My synthetic brain. Once I'd gotten over my technophobia, it had become the mainstay of my workday. It was so easy to keep it open at meetings and tap in all sorts of useful data. Its destruction would have meant the loss of tons of irreplaceable data if I hadn't downloaded the entire hard drive onto a tape just before I left, in case I died in a plane crash. Whoever had done this to me was the same person who had tried to drown me. Or an accomplice. Maybe there was a whole horde of them out there, stalking my every move.

Was the attack on me because of what I might have seen on Rory's laptop? So far, I hadn't seen anything worth killing to protect, but then, I was a poor judge of what was worth killing over. I believed nothing was. No. That wasn't quite true. I could imagine killing to protect someone I loved.

If I kept this up, I could fall into a real paranoid funk. Threatening people with bodily harm or attempting to take their lives is supposed to put them out of commission. To remove them from the picture. Especially when the victim is a helpless female like me. Right now, after my ordeal, I ought to be cowering in my boots and packing my bag to depart. I couldn't pack my bag, it was part of the unsorted mess downstairs. As for cowering, I wasn't the type. It is one of my peculiar failings that when I get scared, I get angry. And the thought of someone trying to take my life, trying to asphyxiate me, to dispose of me like unwanted goods, made me mad as hell.

Okay, so this time it took a while. On other occasions I've come up screaming and swinging. This time I'd let them get me down. But not for long. As I once told someone who wanted to know why I hadn't taken to my bed with aspirin and tea, instead of getting back on my feet and into the fight, you can't keep a good woman down. I wrote down Fox and Bilbo's addresses and went to the phone. Sure enough. Rory had logged in a local number. I sent a message to Fox, saying: "Fox: I have Goddess's laptop. You want it? Mermaid." Goddess was Rory's nom. I sent one to Bilbo, too. Probably stupid. No doubt Nihilani and Bernstein would have my head.

Stupid, but something I couldn't resist. I was sure one of these assholes had tried to kill me. The midnight twins weren't the only ones who used me as a staked goat. Sometimes I did it to myself. There's a reckless side to my character that sometimes scares even me. A reckless, cocky, go-ahead-and-push-me-and-see-what-happens part—like the guy at school who's always getting right up in the bully's face. Go ahead, I say, try me and see what happens. Probably I need therapy. My second-favorite cop in the world, Dom Florio, says it's post-traumatic stress disorder and that I ought to get some help. And he loves me dearly. The way he puts it, it doesn't sound healthy. Nice girls don't act like me.

I disconnected and turned off the laptop, ready to call Lenny and turn over this hot little item. Before I could do anything, the phone rang.

A quick voice, barely audible. "Hey, it's me. The spy? Are you all right? I'm sorry about what happened. It was all my fault, I know. Will you ever forgive me?" She didn't wait for me to say yes or no. She went right on talking. "I wanted to give you a present. To say I'm sorry. My mom says it's all right, so can I come over now and give it to you?"

Bath postponed again. "Sure," I said. "Why not?"

"See you in five," she said.

While I waited, I thought about Bilbo and the Fox. And, with the kind of curiosity that killed the cat, I just had to know whether a civilian could crack the code. Despite the lateness of the hour—or the earliness—I called back East and woke up Bobby.

Bobby was one of our employees at EDGE. A fine writer and researcher. Good-humored and the heart and soul of the office. Well connected to a number of wily computer types. And Bobby owed me big-time, since I'd sublet my condo to his friend Roger who had proceeded to trash the place. When Bobby's sleepy mumble came on, I said, "Bobby, it's Thea. I need your help."

"It's the middle of the night," he said. "Is it an emergency?"

"Someone tried to kill me today, Bobby."

"It's an emergency." He sighed. "Your whole life is an emergency. What can I do?"

Bobby was big and bearlike and had the world's sweetest nature. I felt a twinge of guilt at what I was doing. But only a twinge. I told him what was going on and about the messages on Rory's laptop. I gave him the E-mail addresses, the names of the servers, and the names of every male even tangentially related to the conference.

He hummed a little as he wrote them down. "Give me your number," he said. "I'll get back to you as soon as I can. Say, did you hear? Paul's been offered that headmaster's job up in Maine after all." There was a click as he hurried off to start my research.

I sat staring at the receiver. Hell and damn! If her husband, Paul, got a new job, my partner, Suzanne, would be moving north. Another major crisis and hassle, figuring out what we'd do with our business, but I couldn't deal with any more stuff right now. I shoved the thought into a mental closet and slammed the door. Then I called Bernstein's page number and left a message for him to call me.

A few minutes later there was a knock on the door. Circumstances have taught me to be a cautious sort, so I looked through the little spyhole before I undid the locks. It was Laura, a bedraggled, badly sunburned Laura, holding an enormous box with wrappings and ribbons. She came in and dropped dejectedly onto a chair, holding out the box. "Here. I can only stay five minutes," she said. "They're timing me."

"Why?"

"Cuz hanging around with you might be dangerous."

"They think someone's going to attack us right here in the room?"

Her eyes grew wide. "Do you think they might?"

"I doubt it."

She held out the box. "Here. You'd better hurry up and open it."

"You don't seem very enthused," I said. "Does that mean you didn't pick it out?"

"Exactly!" She sighed and hunched further down in the chair. "My mother and Charlotte did the shopping. They love to shop. They would spend their whole lives shopping. Sometimes I feel like I dropped from the moon and landed in the midst of a bunch of strangers who claim they're my family."

Another reason why I liked this girl. All kids feel like they must have been adopted but not every girl of eleven finds shopping a bore. "I know what you mean," I said. "I hate to shop, too. I have a partner named Suzanne who doesn't mind it and she buys my clothes. Just brings them to the office and leaves them on my desk."

"Lucky," she said. "I wish my mom would do that. She makes me go with her and try things on." She stirred restlessly, as if the sunburn was painful.

"You got a sunburn," I said.

"My own dumb fault. I hate those icky sticky sunscreens that make you smell like toasted coconuts so I didn't wear any."

"I've got one you would like a lot," I said. "And something for that sunburn, too." I went in the bathroom and brought out both. I showed her my favorite sunscreen, which she duly admired, and then I gave her what I called the "blue goo," with aloe and painkillers, the world's greatest stuff for sunburn. "Smear this on and I guarantee you'll feel better in no time."

She poured a little into the palm of her hand and looked at it dubiously. "It's blue," she said.

"And you're hot pink. Try it."

She rubbed it on her sore-looking skin. "Ooh! It's cold." She made some faces but went on applying it. When she was done, she sat up straighter. "The person who attacked you came off one of the other boats," she said.

"How do you know?"

"When we saw you there on the bottom, Robin went down to help. I saw the guy swimming away, so I tried to follow. I couldn't get close. I'm not a great swimmer so I couldn't keep up, but I kind of followed the shape through the water and saw him haul himself onto the boat. I was going to swim over and get a better look but then my mother turned up, yelling at me for being off by myself, and by the time I got her calmed down, three or four more scuba divers had climbed back on the boat, so going out there wouldn't have done any good. I wouldn't have known which one he was."

"But you're sure it was a man?"

"Pretty sure. Aren't you going to open your present?"

"In a minute. What you just told me, is that what you wanted to tell the police?" She nodded. "Since you're our resident spy, is there anything else I should know about what's going on around here?"

Laura pondered. "Do you suppose room service delivers ice cream sundaes?"

"That sounds a bit like extortion," I said. "And you've only got two minutes."

"But they'll never notice," she said. "They're watching a movie."

"What about honor?" I asked.

"Honor?"

"Doing what you're told because it's the right thing to do."

She considered. "If they meant it," she said, finally. "But they're always making rules and then forgetting they've made them. Where's the honor in that?"

I would have bet money this kid would grow up to be a lawyer. I passed her the menu.

She looked up, her eyes glowing. "They have a four-scoop banana split extravaganza." Then her face fell as the impact of my words sank in. "But you don't have to get it for me. I know I've been bad."

She looked so pitiful I was sorry for my remark about extortion. It's hard to remember, with precocious, outspoken kids, how young they are and how literal-minded they can be. Besides, ice cream sounded good to me, too. I must be recovering. I picked up the phone and ordered two of them. Laura looked like a little kid at Christmas. "I love room service," she said. "It's like magic!"

"Okay, kid. Your bribe is on the way. Now spit it out. All the dirt on everyone. Now!"

She started to giggle. "You are so funny," she said. "I'm really glad you didn't drown."

"Me, too."

"And I'm sorry that I distracted Robin so that she couldn't look after you. She was very upset."

"She should have been. Even though hanging around with you might be a whole lot more fun than swimming after me, she was out there because the police thought that someone might try and hurt me."

"Why?"

I shook my head. "I'm not sure, Laura. Maybe because of that picture in the paper. It might have made some people think I was here to try and solve a crime. If the people who did the crime thought that, then they might have gotten worried and wanted me stopped. Kind of like something you'd see on TV."

"Are you here to solve a crime?"

"Far from it. I'm here doing my best to stay out of it, but things keep coming to me. Like you and that little red ribbon."

She nodded solemnly. "The man I was watching at the elevator last night, that one who tore the lady's dress, was in the bar with a guy called Billy tonight. We were at a table pretty near them, getting those funny drinks like you bought me. They were laughing and having a very good time."

So Lewis Broder hadn't left the hotel after all. Interesting. "Could you hear anything they were saying?"

"Not much. It was noisy. I did hear your name, though. It sounded like the elevator man had said something nasty and the other guy, Billy, said you weren't so bad. Your problem was that you were good at whatever you did, whether other people wanted you to be or not. What did he mean by that?"

I shrugged. "I don't know, Laura. Sometimes people get angry if I can do my job and they can't do theirs, because they think it makes them look bad. Maybe that's what he meant." I didn't try to explain about the times when I've been hired because someone wanted me to fail, and I didn't. That was pretty complicated stuff even for a smart kid.

"There's something else," she said, "but I'm not going to tell you until you open your present."

"All right." I picked up the big box, tugged off the ribbons, and pulled off the gaudy paper. The slick white box inside was embossed with a pastel woman on tiptoe, twirling in an ephemeral dress that swirled around her attenuated limbs. She reminded me of a New Age Barbie doll. The shop was called The Blue Wave. There probably already was a Crystal Barbie. Maybe this could be Angel Barbie. Damned hard fitting those dresses around the wings, though. I lifted the cover, and found swaths of purple tissue paper. I rolled my eyes and looked at Laura. She giggled. I burrowed through the paper and pulled out a lovely shrimp-colored gauze sundress. I stood up, held it against me, and twirled, like the lady on the box.

"Cool," Laura said. "Look again. There's more. . . ."

"My birthday was yesterday," I said.

"I'll take a present anytime," she said. "Though I'd rather have a book."

The phone rang and someone knocked on the door. "You get the door," I said, "I'll get the phone. No. Wait." I couldn't risk sending Laura to the door. "You get the phone and tell them to hold on. I'll get the door."

As I went to the door and peered through the spyhole, I heard Laura say, "Oh, you must be Andre. I've heard a lot about you. I'm Laura Mitchell, her sidekick. She's gone to answer the door. Can you hold on for a minute?"

Meanwhile, I opened the door to admit Ed and Marie. Marie was carrying a foil-wrapped container. They were both dressed as if they'd been to dinner. "Come in," I said. "Please. Sit down. I've got a phone call and then I'll be right with you."

Laura held out the phone. "It's Andre," she said.

"Hi, handsome," I said.

"You having a party without me?"

"Hardly. Without you, it's not a party."

"I miss you," he said. He hesitated. "I can't believe how much I miss you. If you were alone, I'd tell you in great detail, but I wouldn't want you blushing in front of other people."

"I wish I were alone."

He laughed, that rich laugh I like to hear with my head on his chest. "You catch your bad guy yet? I caught mine."

"I thought I was supposed to be a good doobie and stay out of trouble."

"Supposed to. But when did my girl ever do what she was supposed to do?"

"I've been trying." It was true. Until moments ago, when I fell from grace at the keyboard, I really had been trying. Behind me, I could hear Laura telling Ed and Marie about the ice cream that was supposed to be arriving. I figured I might as well tell him about my accident that was no accident. "This time it seems like the bad guy is trying to catch me."

There was a longer silence. "What's that supposed to mean? I told that guy, Bernstein, to keep an eye on you."

"I went snorkeling. There was someone there . . . a scuba diver, who grabbed and held me underwater and I—" It turned out I couldn't say it. You can't tell someone you love about something so awful in a phone call. Especially when you've got a room full of people listening. "I could have drowned."

"What happened? What's going on? Are you all right? Do I need to come out there?" Before I could answer, he said, "You've got to come home. Right now. This is crazy! Those guys said something about using your reputation as a detective to try and flush out their killer, but they promised they'd be watching every minute. And now you tell me this? Pack your things and go to the airport. It's not safe for you to stay there." Then, before I could say anything, and I was almost too flabbergasted to speak, he said, "What does the doctor say? Are you sure you're all right?"

"You want to talk to him?"

"The doctor is there?"

I looked over at Ed and pointed to the phone. "Sort of."

"Does that mean you only have part of a doctor there, or does that mean whoever is there is only sort of a doctor?"

"I mean one of the guests at the hotel is a doctor and he's sort of adopted me. . . ."

"Oh, so you mean, this guy isn't one of the doctors who treated you at the hospital?"

"Right. All he did was rescue me from the hospital. But he's a very nice guy."

"How old? How nice?" Andre's voice had dropped to a growl. Jealousy and passion did that to him. Too much testosterone, poor fellow. I could almost hear his beard grow.

"Middle-aged. Very nice. He's here to speak at the Maui Police Department annual dinner. His name is—"

"I don't want to know."

"Yes, you do. His name is Ed Pryzinski." I waited for the light to go on. It did.

"You don't mean Dr. Pryzinski, author of *Don't Touch That Body unless You Use Your Head?*"

"I do."

"But he's a pathologist."

"I'm still breathing."

"Put him on," Andre said.

I held the phone out to Dr. Pryzinski. "It's Andre," I said. "He wants a full report on my medical condition."

Ed took the phone and I watched as they went through the phone equivalent of a hand-slapping ritual. Then Ed settled into a chair by the phone and began to reassure Andre about my physical condition. He was just as calm and patient and comforting with Andre as he had been with me. As I watched, I imagined Ed as a father, guiding his big, gangly son and his tiny clever daughter through the perils of their youth. Lucky kids. Beside me, Marie chatted with Laura about snorkeling. Despite my dramatic interruption to everyone's day, they'd still managed to go on and have fun. My life, full of high drama as it was, was just a little blip on other people's screens. It helps to put things in perspective, most of the time. But not now. Life and death, especially my own life and death, is too immediate to disregard.

I drifted back to the conversation as Ed was saying, "No. If she's doing this well this many hours after the incident, I think we can relax about the possibility of secondary effects. She looks fine. She's walking and talking and I understand she's just ordered herself a four-scoop ice cream sundae, so ability to take nourishment isn't an issue."

He listened to something Andre said and laughed. "Me, too. I always admire a girl with a healthy appetite. She's going to be just fine and there shouldn't be any problems with the baby."

CHAPTER 24

EVIDENTLY ANDRE HADN'T completely lost his powers of
speech, as I had, because then Ed said, " 'What baby?' Thea's baby.
Your baby, I presume." He listened for a while and then said,
"Well, hard as it is for me to believe, from the look on her face,
she's just as surprised as you are. I thought young people these
days got sex education courses. Some of this stuff is pretty basic,
son." He listened again and then held the phone out to me. "He
wants to talk to you."

I took it cautiously. I was so stunned by what I'd just heard I
wasn't sure I could speak. I tried "Hello?"

"Why didn't you tell me?" Andre demanded. "Didn't you think
I'd need to know?"

"Andre . . . I . . . I didn't . . . I don't . . ." *Spit it out, Kozak, the
man is waiting.* I could picture the anger and confusion on his face.
With something so intimate, something so stunningly earthshak-
ing, life altering and life affirming, I would never have delivered
the news in public. "I don't know what he's talking about. I've been
awfully tired and I get sick sometimes, but I just thought I had
some low-level illness . . . food poisoning, parasite, mono. Something I was going to check out with my doctor when I got home.
I wasn't trying to keep something from you. . . ." Was a woman
ever placed in a more awkward situation? "I don't even know why

he thinks I might be pregnant. He's only listened to my heart and lungs . . . look, hold on. I'll ask him."

I turned away from the phone. Ed Pryzinski looked like a kid caught with his hand in the cookie jar and Marie was giving him her best quelling stare. I held the phone out, helplessly. Marie said, "He's always had an instinct for pregnancy, Thea. He reads it in women's faces. He's never been wrong, either."

"There's another phone in the bedroom. You'd better get in on this, Ed. My beloved thinks I've been keeping something from him that I didn't even know myself."

Ed went in the bedroom. I heard a click and then his slightly twangy voice on the line. "Detective? I am truly sorry about this. I can assure you, from the look on this little gal's face, that she had no idea."

"She didn't tell you?"

"No, sir, she did not. It looks like I just told her."

"But when you examined her—"

"Detective, I am feeling terribly guilty for speaking out of turn like I did, especially since I have no medical information on which to base my diagnosis. It is purely instinctive."

"No medical information," Andre said, "so you don't know for sure." He sounded terribly disappointed.

"I don't know from conclusive medical tests," Dr. Pryzinski said carefully, "but I know for sure. I hope this news is happily received by both of you. Your Thea is a great girl, and from all I can see, she loves you very much."

I put down my phone and went in the bedroom. "I'll take it from here," I said. "You go out and hang up the other phone."

"Guess I'm signing off now," Ed said. "Best of luck, Detective."

He left the room and a few seconds later I heard a click as the other phone was put back in its cradle. "So," I said, "that was a bolt from the blue. I don't know what to think, do you? We're not ready to be parents. We can't even decide where to live. Our lives are crazy. When would we see it? Where would we keep it? Who would take care of it? I don't think we could even agree on a name."

"If it's a boy, he's called Oliver, after my father, or Mason, after my uncle. If it's a girl, her name is Claudine."

I didn't know what to say. Weren't women the ones who kept lists of names for their future children? I didn't have any names on my list. I didn't even have a list, while Andre had it all worked out. "I can't even think," I said. "It's all too much for me. Let me get rid of all these people and I'll call you back."

"Thea . . ." He hesitated so long that I'd thought of five different, terrible things he might say before he spoke again. "If you don't like those names, we can think about others."

"Just as long as we don't call him Ollie. I love you," I said. "Good-bye."

"Stay safe," he said. "Be well. I'll talk to you soon. You can call me in the morning."

"Yours or mine?" I asked.

"Either one is fine. I love you," he said. "Good-bye."

I cradled the receiver and sat there, breathless, speechless, and utterly stunned. I had never been so surprised in my life. I went back to the sitting room and found Laura happily eating ice cream while Ed and Marie sat looking guilty and embarrassed.

"I can't believe he did that," Marie said. "Eddie isn't usually so tactless. Blunt and straightforward, but not utterly tactless. We're so sorry if we've caused problems for you, Thea."

I sat down and picked up my spoon. After a day with nothing but tea and toast and salad, suddenly I was ravenous. "Oh, well. I hope little Mason or Oliver likes chocolate." I raised a dripping, gooey spoonful to my mouth. "Unless it's Claudine."

Ed and Marie got up. "We'd better be going," Marie said, leaning down to give me a hug. "Seems like every time we try to do something for you, we mess things up worse than before. I can't remember a time when we've managed to do so much harm through good intentions. We're going to go back to our room and see if we can stay out of trouble."

I walked them to the door. Laura went on eating. Obviously, the subject of pregnancy was not one that interested her. She got enough of that at home, with her stepdad Howie dancing attendance on her polka-dotted mother. I sat down and picked up my spoon. "This was a good idea. Now, what was the second thing you were going to tell me?"

"Something I heard from the security guards." She grinned. "It pays to be a kid sometimes. I sit down and open my book and everyone thinks I've disappeared. But I'm still right there, listening. I heard these two guys talking about the couple that had the fight. The newlyweds who threw their luggage and stuff? Turns out that they left the next morning. Because they were so embarrassed, you'd think, right? Well, the hotel checks their registration information and guess what? Nobody by that name existed at that address. They were fakes. I guess the guy who was talking was the one who'd done the detective work. He was the blue-blazer type, not the work-shirt-with-security-patch type. Then the cops go through the hotel trash. . . ." She gave me a curious look. "You're a detective, Thea. Did you know that they did that?"

I nodded. Skipped reminding her that I wasn't a detective. The one time I was following advice and not getting involved, and no one around here believed me. "I've heard. I wouldn't want that job, would you? Especially not with a place as big as this. That's a lot of trash. And?"

"And they found two discarded boarding passes, Honolulu to Maui, for people not registered at the hotel. So guess what? This guy tracks them down and it turns out they were an actor and actress from Honolulu who were hired to came here and have that fight. But the security guy says they don't know who hired them because it was all done by phone and letter. All they can say is that it was a woman who told them to show up at the hotel and gave them false names to use. Why would you hire someone to go to a hotel and have a fight? Isn't that the strangest thing you've ever heard?"

I'd heard an awful lot of strange things in my life. People's reasons for abandoning morality. People's excuses for inhuman behavior. People's justifications for discarding other people's lives. Compared with that, this didn't seem strange at all. Obviously the couple had been brought in to create a disturbance to divert any attention from Martina's killers. What I found strange, and disturbing, was how carefully planned and orchestrated her killing had been. This was no spur-of-the-moment crime of passion, though that's how it was supposed to look.

"Thea? Thea! Are you awake?" Laura was staring at me nervously. "Is something wrong? Are you getting sick again? Maybe I should call that nice doctor back?"

I had retreated so far into my mind that I'd frozen in midbite. The spoon hung in midair between the dish and my mouth, dripping hot fudge sauce onto my ugly green dress. I stuck the spoon in my mouth. What had been delicious a minute ago no longer seemed appealing. Too many shocks. Too much to think about. When I get distracted, I always lose my appetite. Maybe that's why I'm not fat. Maybe it isn't exercise and hard work. Maybe it's all the meals I skip, all the food I don't get around to eating.

"I'm fine, Laura. I was just thinking about what you said. And about what people do to each other. Ugly thoughts." I stood up and reached for the new dress. "Maybe I'll go put this on. I seem to have ruined the other one."

"Oh, it will wash," she said seriously. "I'm a spiller myself. I know."

I didn't know about this baby, if there even was a baby, but if someone had told me I could have Laura Mitchell, half-formed and delightful at age eleven, I would have taken her in a second. It seemed odd that tomorrow night I was flying back to Boston, and soon Laura would go back to Iowa and I would never see her again. I went in the bathroom, stripped off the green dress, took Bernstein's card out of the pocket, and dumped the dress in the sink to soak. I picked up the clean dress, then set it down again and stood in front of the mirror, staring at my body. It looked just the same to me. Was it really possible that there was another life lurking inside me?

I clasped my hands over my belly. Did it seem rounder? I turned sideways and dropped my hands. Nothing looked any different. What was it that Ed Pryzinski was reading in my face and body that had led him to his shattering declaration. I wasn't ready for motherhood. It was something I wanted to plan. Something I wanted to anticipate. I wanted to affirmatively discard birth control and sleep with Andre, full of the delicious knowledge that what we were doing might lead to the creation of life. I didn't want to have a baby thrust upon me like this, without any say in the matter. And the cool, logical part of me couldn't help wondering why this was such a surprise. As Dr. Pryzinski had said, I was supposed to know about sex and reproduction. Yet I hadn't even suspected. Had I completely overlooked a missed period? Was this denial? Repression? Or just the quirks of a busy life?

A lost and bewildered-looking woman in a flowered bikini stared at me from the mirror. A pale, unhealthy-looking woman with intense green eyes and a wide, chapped mouth. Shaking my head, I turned away and picked up the dress. I'd had some days that I thought were record setters for the amount of emotion and the number of shocks my system had been exposed to. The most terrible had been waking up to learn, from the television news, that Andre was being held in a hostage situation and that probably he was seriously wounded. That day, it felt like I held my breath for twelve hours. And did some heroically stupid things. Today might be a close second. I felt like I could run a mental tongue over the jagged edges of my emotions and come away with the taste of blood.

Laura banged on the door. "Thea! Are you all right? Are you ever coming out?"

"Be right there." I dropped the new dress over my head. It was perfect. That was one positive thing about people who liked to shop. Often they were good at it, too. The shrimp color suited me. I looked like someone had turned on a light beneath my skin. I brushed my hair and twirled like the woman on the box. For the first time since we'd found Martina's body, I didn't look like death warmed over. *A lot you know*, I told the mirror. *Appearances can be deceiving.* I opened the door and stepped out.

Laura was standing there in the gloomy dressing area, waiting for me. She followed me into the living room. "Oh," she said, "you look wonderful. But you need to finish opening your present."

"There's more?"

She nodded. "This stuff, I picked out, so maybe you won't like it as much."

"Never apologize in advance for a present you're about to

give," I said, reaching into the box and fishing around in the purple paper. I pulled out two small packages. Inside the first was a pair of earrings that were carved wooden fish painted in gaudy tropical colors. In the second, a matching necklace. I put them on. "At least I can look at these fish without worrying," I said.

"Funny. That's just what I thought," she said. "I wanted you to have something good to help you remember the trip. And the fish were great, weren't they?" She studied me carefully, in that unselfconscious way that children have before they've learned to stare covertly. "Come here," she said, getting up and taking my hand. She led me back into the dressing room and turned on the lights. "Look. You're beautiful. No wonder that man was watching you on Friday night. Though he didn't look like he was happy to see you."

Little warning flags dropped all over the playing field. "What man?"

"The old man in the bar. The one I saw heading for the elevator after that couple had their fight. I told you. He saw me and he said 'Too slow' and went down the stairs."

I didn't remember an old man in the bar. Maybe, if I got a better description, someone else in the group might. And, of course, old to Laura might not be old at all. I didn't even remember Laura in the bar. "I didn't see you in the bar on Friday."

"Nope. I was outside the windows, trying to catch a frog. But I was looking. I like to watch people. Especially when they don't know they're being watched."

"How old?" I asked. "And what did he look like?"

"As old as Howie," she said. "He's fifty-four. But grayer. Not as fat, though. Kind of tall. He had a mustache. And he was sitting with a tall, skinny woman with long dark hair and the weirdest glasses you've ever seen. The ones shaped like cat's eyes with sequins on the corners. They were way back in a corner where it was dark, like they didn't want to be seen. But the spy sees all."

I put my arm around Laura's shoulders. "I think it's time for us gal detectives to go to work. I know you've already been in the bar once tonight, but could I interest you in another drink?"

"You can't have alcohol," she said disapprovingly.

"Neither can you. We'll get us some Shirley Temples and do a bit of sleuthing. What do you say?"

"Christy and Company," she said, raising her hand.

"Nancy Drew," I said, slapping her palm.

I tucked Rory's laptop in my bag—no way I was trusting it to hotel security—and arm in arm we headed out, two tough dames on the job.

CHAPTER 25

THE BAR WAS nice and quiet but that wouldn't last. If there was one fundamental thing to be counted on at conferences, it was that sooner or later, everyone would end up in the bar. Bars are where most of the actual conference business takes place. We got a good table where we could spy on the whole room and settled in for a spot of girlish detection. Despite the enormous ice cream she had consumed, Laura decided that she was hungry and we asked our waitress for some menus. Meanwhile, Laura ordered a strawberry daiquiri and I got a piña colada. Nonalcoholic for both of us.

Looking at the menu stirred a primitive craving for meat that could only be satisfied by an enormous hamburger. I took it as a sign that I was feeling better, unless it was a sign that Oliver or Claudine was a carnivore. Laura was more restrained. She went for the grilled chicken sandwich. It was clear which of us would live forever. Of course, my earlier adventures couldn't be discounted, either. I'd already had an encounter with Mr. Death, while Laura had only met an eel. Through some strange correspondence in my brain, the thought called forth another bit of Shakespeare. "Thou mettest with things dying, I with things newborn." *A Winter's Tale*. Yet both were met in me.

"I'm sure he's long gone," I said, "but if you see someone who looks like the man in the elevator or the tall woman he was with, let me know."

"How do I do that? My mom says it's rude to point."

Before I could answer, a voice boomed in my ear. "Well, goodness me, Thea, don't you look nice? You're as pretty as a picture. Your mother is going to be so pleased to hear you're looking well. She worries about you." Alyce Edgerton, without being invited, pulled out a chair and sat down. "Haven't got much tan, though, have you. Harry won't be joining us. He's gone to bed. That man is such a party pooper." Her curious eyes lighted on Laura. "And who is this young lady?"

"This is my friend Laura Mitchell." Mentally I beamed messages to Laura not to say anything about what we were doing. I needn't have worried. Laura was an astute reader of grown-ups and Alyce absolutely reeked of busybody. "Laura, this is Mrs. Edgerton. She's a friend of my mother." Laura dutifully stuck out a small hand.

"Well," Alyce said, looking around. "I hope we can get some service. The last time I was in here I had to wait hours for my food. It isn't at all what I would have expected from such an expensive hotel. Not that anything has been as I expected. First that couple having the awful fight and then a murder! The woman who was killed was part of your group, wasn't she, Thea?" I nodded. "Did you know her?" I nodded again. "Terrible thing," she said. "I hear she was waiting for her secret lover and she let in the wrong man. There was something on the news about a serial killer who does this at resorts all over the country. I keep wondering if I should tell the police about that man I saw."

She started waving her arm vigorously. "Ooh. Over here. Ooh! Over here," she said. I watched the flab rock and mentally vowed to do more pushups.

I assumed she was calling for a waitress, but she was waving at a slim, dark man in a security guard's uniform. He came reluctantly toward our table, as if weighing the importance of shutting her up against the possibility of making a quick escape. When he was within moderate shouting distance, Alyce said, "This is my friend Raoul. He knows everything that goes on at the hotel." She patted the empty fourth chair.

I winked at Laura, who was very deftly converting a giggle into a yawn behind her hand. Tedious as Alyce was, she had a talent for collecting gossip, and Detective Mitchell and I were here to collect gossip. I gave Raoul my best smile. "Please join us," I said, "we don't want to interfere with your duties but we're awfully curious about what is going on."

Cautiously he lowered himself into the chair. I could see why Alyce had attached herself to him. In her youth, she had fancied herself a great beauty, or so my mother had told me. In Alyce's mirror, time stood still. Her blond hair was not colored and permed and teased and sprayed, it still cascaded in shiny waves to her prom queen shoulders. Her smile still lit up rooms. And Raoul was a thing of beauty and a joy forever, if you liked the dark graceful types with liquid eyes and sensitive mouths. He perched on his chair so tentatively he reminded me of a caged bunny.

"Tell them what you found in the men's room," Alyce said importantly.

"There's an ongoing police investigation," Raoul said. He had a soft, gentle voice. Across from me, Laura was falling in love. "I'm not supposed to talk about it."

"It's all right," Alyce said. "Thea's a detective. She's used to this stuff, aren't you?"

I thought Raoul would be more likely to tell his story to an ingenue in a shrimp-colored dress than to a tough female PI. I twisted a wayward curl around my finger and lowered my eyes. "Not really," I murmured. "But I am curious. What did you find in the, um, men's room?" Now I was saying "um." A bolt of lighting should strike me if I ever did it except for effect.

"Yes," Laura said eagerly, "what did you find? Was it a gun?"

Alyce couldn't wait for the reluctant Raoul. "It was a can of silver hair spray, like you might use to make yourself old, and some of that spirit gum that actors use to stick on false beards and things. And a pair of latex gloves. Whoever used the stuff didn't want to take a chance on leaving any fingerprints."

I looked at Raoul as though he'd divulged the information. "Really?" He nodded. "What about the gloves? Didn't I read somewhere that the police can sometimes get prints from gloves. Or right through them?"

Now he lowered *his* eyes and looked demure. "I wouldn't know about that."

Be proud of me. I didn't yell, "In a pig's eye," or any of a thousand other disbelieving epithets. I looked around for a waitress. "Do you have time for a drink with us?"

"Raoul is extremely busy," Alyce interrupted. "Last night, at that luau you had, he literally had to break up a fight between two women! First they started throwing food, and then these other two women, a great fat black woman and this other Amazon, jumped into the fight and sat on the first two, and poor Raoul had to break it up. You know what he told me?"

Raoul looked like he wished he could crawl under the table and disappear. "I really should be going," he said. He stood up and patted the radio on his nice, slim hip. "I'm supposed to be working."

"Oh, just let me finished this story," Alyce said, oblivious, as usual, to what was going on around her. "He says that once the two women were away from the party, one of them started crying, and then said, 'at least she's dead.' and they walked away, arm in arm, like lifelong friends. Have you ever heard anything so bizarre? Imagine four women fighting. Why, in my day . . ." Raoul took a step backward.

"Nor in my day," I agreed. "Not that I spend much time with fat black women and Amazons." I held out my hand to Raoul. "It was nice to meet you. I'm sorry my conference has given you such a hard time." He took it with a gesture that was half handshake and half bow. Very appealing. He repeated the gesture with Alyce, who simpered, and with Laura, completing the winning of her heart. Then he went away, leaving two ladies staring after him and one wondering how to get rid of Alyce so that Laura and I could talk.

"I ought to tell the police about that man I saw," Alyce repeated, when Raoul was finally out of sight. "I thought he looked too young to be so gray and Raoul's story explains it."

"Where did you see this man?"

"He came out of the elevator on sixteen and then went immediately to the stairwell. It was right when that couple was having their fight."

"What did he look like?" I asked.

Alyce shrugged. "A middle-aged man with gray hair and a mustache. It was the way he moved that didn't match his hair. It seemed youthful."

"Height?" I asked. "Was he tall or short? Thin or heavyset?"

She shrugged again. "I didn't notice."

"Was he wearing glasses?" Laura asked.

Alyce considered, then nodded. "I think so." Then she shook her head. "No, I don't think so." She'd make a great witness.

"And was he about as tall as that man?" Laura pointed to a man who had just come in who was about Andre's height, or six feet one.

"No. Yes. I'm not sure. He wasn't a shrimp but he didn't strike me as particularly tall. You know, I don't think we're ever going to get a waitress. Things are better in the other bar." She stood up and gathered her things. "I'll tell your mother I saw you," she said. She swept out of the room.

Laura giggled. "You really don't like her, do you?"

"Does it show that much?"

She shook her head vigorously, her red hair bobbing. "Only to me with my keen professional eye."

"When I was your age, she was always telling tales to my mother and getting me in trouble. Would you like someone like that?"

"No. She doesn't know you don't like her, either. She thinks you two are friends." Her grin was enormous. "And you're the Amazon, right?"

I nodded. "So, where were we? I was about to tell you how to let me know without pointing—"

"—if I spot the man or the woman I saw that night," she finished.

"Here we go, ladies." Our waitress put a plate in front of me with enough food to have fed the Russian Army for a week or

Andre Lemieux for a day. She set down Laura's food and smiled. "Sorry about the delay. I was waiting for that woman to leave."

"Thanks," I said. "But how did you know?"

"I'm not clairvoyant," she said, smiling. "I was thinking of myself. I've waited on her before. It's like rubbing sandpaper over a sunburn. I hope you didn't mind too much."

"We're very grateful, aren't we, Laura?" Laura nodded. Her mouth was too full for speech. "We were also waiting for her to leave." Halfway through my burger I suddenly became very sleepy, like a predatory animal after it has eaten all it can of its kill. Of course, a normal, sensible person would have taken to her bed hours ago but I'm not a normal, sensible person. Or I am, but I'm also impulsive, headstrong, and determined, qualities my mother has been hoping I'll outgrow for thirty years. Worse yet, I become more impulsive, headstrong, and determined when I've been threatened with bodily harm. Sheer edgy energy had brought me down here. Now it seemed to be ebbing away. Soon I'd have to give up detecting in favor of sleep.

I yawned. "I'm going to have to go to bed soon," I said. "And we haven't made much progress."

"True," Laura said. "But we did learn one thing. I guess that's something. Isn't that the way detectives work anyway? Gathering information bit by bit?" She looked at her empty plate. "I win."

"The eating contest? Yes, you do. If Andre were here, we'd both lose. The guy eats like a horse."

"That's speciesist."

"That's truth." The bar was filling up. When our waitress checked back to see if we needed anything, I asked for the check. It would have been nice to linger and gather gossip, but one gathers very little gossip while asleep. As we were heading for the door, Jeff Pullman came in with Billy Berryman, talking earnestly. Jeff looked 100 percent better than he had in the morning. Pulled together, neat, relaxed. He passed me without speaking, but Billy caught my arm.

"Thea! I thought you were still in the hospital . . . after that terrible experience . . . and here you are looking like a million dollars. How on earth do you do it?"

"Gene pool, Billy. I come from a bunch of really tough folks. How was the dinner?" What I wanted to ask was where he'd found out how Martina died, but this was neither the time nor the place.

"I'll wait for you outside," Laura said. She looked so agitated I assumed she was rushing to the bathroom.

"Dr. Van Norden was dynamite," Billy said. "The woman would have made a great general. You made a super choice, inviting her. And Joly got through the intro without a hitch. I heard you had to rewrite it?"

"Yeah, a slight accident when my laptop got smashed into a million pieces."

"That's terrible. I couldn't live without mine. What's with you and Jeff, anyway? He saw you and it was like he was seeing a ghost."

"You didn't hear?" He shook his head. "Well, I'm not on his list of favorite people these days. We had a little run-in this morning."

"Run-in? You mean argument? That's too bad. I was hoping I could get the two of you together for a press conference tomorrow . . . you know, get some good looks and good minds out there in front of the cameras. . . ."

"I don't think so, Billy. By run-in, I mean he knocked me down and attempted to carve me up with a piece of broken crockery. Something about avenging Martina's honor or some such thing. At least he said it had to do with our . . . plot . . . I think that's what he called it, to oust Martina from her hereditary position."

Billy shook his head. "That's bad. Very bad. Look, I'm sure it was just the shock of everything. I'll talk to him. He can't possibly think the board had anything to do with this, or you, in particular."

"He seems to think exactly that. He expressed his personal disgust that I had come instead of Suzanne. I think he saw it as a deliberate choice to send the warrior instead of the peacemaker, though he didn't say that. Don't waste your time trying to bring the two of us together, okay? I'm pretty easygoing but when people do what Jeff did, it takes me a while to get over it. The distance between Boston and Washington, D.C. is the minimum amount of space I want between me and Jeff at the moment. Truth is, I didn't want to come here in the first place. I wouldn't be here if Suzanne hadn't gotten sick, and I can't wait to leave."

He looked so unhappy that I patted him on the shoulder. "Relax, Billy. I'm not going to do anything that will hurt your public relations campaign. However I feel about Jeff Pullman personally, the board will continue to present a united front. Good night."

"Look, Thea, maybe we should talk about this—"

"It's been a long, hard day, Billy. I'm going to bed." I displayed my arm, with the bandages where the IV had been and where they'd taken blood. "I just got out of the hospital."

"By the way," he said, making a face, "no thanks for sending the cops after me. I lost some valuable hours convincing them that I'm not a bad guy—"

"I didn't send any cops after you, Billy," I interrupted. I didn't use my Pollyanna voice, either. "First Lewis Broder, before he left, and now you."

He looked puzzled. "Lewis Broder didn't leave."

But I didn't want to waste any breath on Broder, nor did I want to get sidetracked from the point, which was that I did not set the police on people. "And I'm tired of hearing complaints about me and the police. Other than doing my minimal civic duty by answering their questions, I don't like them any more than the rest of you, my relationship with Andre Lemieux notwithstanding. So, to return to our earlier subject, you can do what you want to make things nice-nice, so long as you don't ask me to get near Jeff Pullman, understood?"

I left him staring after me, wondering how he could possibly put a positive public relations spin on a knock-down encounter between a board member and the husband of the deceased. On the other hand, if he hadn't heard about it already, it couldn't be making big waves on the gossip circuit. Billy was a magnet for gossip. Everyone wanted to tell him what was going on.

Laura was waiting in the hall, dancing impatiently from foot to foot. "That was him," she said. "That was the man. I'm sure of it."

Billy Berryman? A killer? I couldn't believe it. I grabbed her arm and hauled her over to a bench among the potted palms. "Speak," I said. "Talk. Spit it out. Why do you think he's the one?"

She shrugged, trying to seem casual, but my reaction had frightened her. I had to remember that even though she was a great companion, she was still just a kid. "It just is, that's all. I mean, he just is. You know, Thea, I only saw him for a minute, when he came out of the elevator. But I'm sure it's the same guy. He has the same shoes on."

I'd been angling for a description so I could explain why she was wrong, since Billy hadn't even been around on Friday night. But shoes were a different matter. "Laura, lots of guys wear the same shoes."

She nodded. "But they're very fancy shoes. Come on. I'll show you." She jumped up and tugged at my arm. Right. Now we were going to go out and lurk in the night and spy on people through the windows while we pretended to catch frogs. Something she was experienced at, something new to my detective career.

Together we slunk through the garden until Laura grabbed my arm and whispered, "There." She pointed. I supposed, since we were outside and we were alone, Emily Post wasn't going to come along and strike us from the social register for our faux pas. I followed the line from her finger. She wasn't pointing at Billy. She was pointing at Jeff Pullman, who was wearing very shiny black tasseled loafers. At that moment, he looked up and saw us.

"Run!" Laura said, and scurried away. Stupid me, I ran right behind her. I didn't even pause to point out that Billy had on fancy black shoes as well.

CHAPTER 26

WE ENDED UP at the elevator, leaning against the wall, breathless and giggling like a pair of fools. "This is the O.J. Simpsonization of America," I said. "Now everybody goes around looking at people's shoes."

"That was fun," Laura said.

"Probably not for long. He didn't look the least bit pleased," I said. "And he's already mad at me. It's too bad he isn't the guy you saw on Friday night. I used to like him but now I wouldn't mind if he got into trouble. But he was at home in Washington, D.C., when the murder happened. He flew in the next day after the police called him."

"How do you know?" she asked, and then, "Are you okay? You don't look good."

"I saw him on the news getting off the plane." I ignored her second question. I felt like I'd just hit the wall, and was a little bit worried about making back to the room, but I didn't want to worry her.

"Oh. Right," she said. "But what if—"

"Not now, please, Laura. I'm tired."

The elevator arrived and the doors rolled open. Jolene and Shannon got off, engaged in what sounded like a good-hearted argument. "Thea Kozak," Shannon said. "I thought you were tucked up in bed with tea and toast, all wan and weak and unable to come to the banquet, and here you are wandering around the lobby, looking like a million dollars. We're on our way to the bar. You want to come have a drink with us?" She sounded like she'd had a few drinks already. She also sounded aggrieved, as if my being up and about offended her.

I only looked like a million dollars if she was thinking counterfeit money. And anyway, as my brother, Michael, used to say, "tough munchies." Sometimes "tough nuggies." I had no idea what either one meant but they sounded good. Maybe it was too bad that I wasn't adept at being a victim. It didn't mean I hadn't had a hard day. "I'm afraid I'm turning into a pumpkin," I said. "My baby-sitter here says I've got to go to bed. How did the dinner go?"

"Oh, Jolene was brilliant. And that speaker you guys got for us was dynamite. She's the best. Honestly. I have never listened to someone more inspiring," Shannon said. "She made me want to go out and change the world."

Jolene took her arm. "We're starting in the bar."

"Have fun. I'll see you tomorrow." Once again, neither of them asked how I was. Or about Rory. It bothered me. I'd looked in the mirror. I knew I looked good in the dress. But there were scratches on my face, bruises on my neck, and bandages on my hand. I was feeling rather green, and usually, when I feel green, I look green, too. I walked with a limp. And, though they couldn't see this, lots of gauze and tape on my knees. Plus big, serious, dark bruises on my psyche.

Maybe it was my own fault. It could be that I've played the tough, independent role so long and so well that everyone is convinced. Stuff rolls right off me. Bodies, threats, attempts on my life—it's all in a day's work for the professional. Smashed computers? A trashed hotel room? Mere bagatelles. Why not? A year ago, I'd believed it myself. Now I wasn't so sure. Now I felt a suspicious need for comfort. Was this the price I paid for love? For letting Andre get close to me? Open the door a crack and the whole world pours in? Admit to the occasional need and become needy?

I stepped into the elevator, which Laura had been holding impatiently, and away we went. As the doors closed, I heard Shannon say, "She didn't look one bit sick to me. Are you sure that story about the drowning is true?"

"Of course it is," Jolene said. "Didn't you see those bruises on her neck? I saw her when she got back from the hospital, and she looked terrible. She could barely stand up. And then she found her—" The rest was lost.

Laura finally looked tired. She leaned limply against the wall and her eyelids were drooping. "Wow," she said softly. "This detective stuff is hard work. Must be time to call it a day."

"You bet, kid." I knew just how she felt. As I watched her, able to allow herself to be totally, visibly tired, or joyous, or whatever the emotion was, it occurred to me that she'd been with me for a hell of a lot longer than five minutes and yet no one had come looking for her. No one, even though they regarded my company as dangerous. Which meant there really wasn't anybody looking out for her. I looked at her small figure, drooping against the wall, and debated the wisdom of warning her about the very real, though remote, possibility of danger against the risk of scaring her. I decided Laura deserved to be in the know. Better safe than sorry.

"Look, I don't want to worry you, but if I were you, I'd be careful from now on. There has been some seriously bad stuff going on around here, and you've been seen hanging around one of the intended victims. You want to stay alive, kiddo, you've got to use your noggin, eh? No more running around the hotel tonight without grown-ups."

"My mom says the hotel is very safe. That's why she lets me go where I want, but don't worry." She could barely speak between yawns. "I'm going right to bed. All that food and fun and sun and swimming. I'm done for." The door opened and she scampered out. "I'll tell my mom that you liked the present, okay?"

"Please do. It's great."

I was equally weary. I'd been running on adrenaline and false courage too long. I trudged to my door and let myself in. Carefully. Cautiously. Not wanting any surprises. I wanted a long hot bath and a dreamless sleep. I was afraid that what I'd get was memories—the shock of having my mask grabbed and flung away, of a neoprene arm around my throat and the agony of my lungs desperate for air. The claustrophobic feeling of being strapped to a stretcher while I was bounced around like a piece of flotsam. The infuriatingly helpless feeling of being poked and prodded and questioned when I was too weak to answer. Hamlet had it right with those musings about the problems with sleep and the fear of dreams.

I got my things and took them into the bathroom. Turned the water on high and let the tub start to fill. Poured in a big measure of bath oil and sat on the edge of the tub, letting the soothing roar of the water drown out everything else. And then I remembered. I was supposed to call Andre. I turned off the tap and went to the phone.

I curled up on the couch and listened to the rings, imagining Andre lying there asleep in the warm darkness of our bed. It was after ten here. He'd be deep into his dreams. Sleeping on his stomach with his arm flung out. I was supposed to be tucked under that arm. When I am, I rarely dream. He's the best cure for nightmares a woman could ask for. Good for a lot of other things, too. The ringing stopped as someone fumbled with the receiver and said, "Lemieux." Brisk, authoritative, ready. A good cop, he's awake and alert while I'm still struggling to clear the cobwebs from my brain.

"Hi, handsome."

"What took you so long?"

Did he sound just a teeny bit aggrieved? "Took a while to get rid of everyone and then I was overcome by the need for a giant hamburger."

The overpowering need to eat was something he could relate to. "Eating for two, are we?"

"Well, *you've* always eaten for two. I'm just beginning. I guess. I wish I were there instead of here. . . ."

"Me, too. I'd scoot right down to the all-night drugstore and get one of those little kits that turns, what . . . pink? Blue? Some baby color. And tomorrow morning . . . well, it's almost morning here . . . you could pee in a little cup and then we'd—"

"Hey," I interrupted. "How do you know so much about this? Baby names. Pregnancy tests. This is a side of you I never imagined."

"I'm a very complicated guy. Look, you know I can't stand waiting. Isn't there an all-night drugstore where you could . . ."

I might be confused and conflicted but this guy was ready, even eager, to jump on the parenthood train. "You stand waiting just fine, Lemieux, and you know it. Waiting is your game, remember? And I'm out here in the middle of a clump of tourist hotels, miles from town. It's late at night and I have no car."

"Call a taxi. Call the cops and get them to take you. They're supposed to be watching over you anyway."

"I hardly think it's the job of the Maui Police Department to drive me to the drugstore for a pregnancy-test kit. I'll go in the morning. Look, all we have to go on is the word of a keen-eyed pathologist, Andre. I don't want you to go getting your hopes up."

"When I think of you, I get more than my hopes up," he said. Actually, it was more like a growl. A lovely deep growl. If I'd had my head on his chest, I could have felt it rumbling through his body. I could have smelled his nice, soapy smell. The hair on his chest would have tickled my ear. Suddenly I was very lonely and much too far from home. I wanted to reach out and touch someone, not telephonically, but truly. In reality. Right now. I didn't care about finding Martina's killer. The police could have that job. And as for running the conference, someone else could do that, too. I'd done my share.

"Let George do it," I said.

"What?"

"I miss you. I'm lonely. It's scary here by myself when there are bad guys around. When we hang up, I'm going to call the airport and see how soon I can get a plane out of here. I've been gone long enough."

"That's my girl," he said.

"You bet." I'd resisted being his girl for a long time. I hadn't wanted to be anyone's girl, or woman, or anything. But I'd changed. I might still find myself humming "You Don't Own Me" from time to time, but our connection was strong. What had someone said once? That we were connected by a bungee cord and no matter how far apart we got, we'd snap right back together again. It was our fate. It didn't seem like a bad fate to me.

"Thea . . ." There was a long silence. I waited, listening to him breathe. Respiration at long-distance rates. It was worth every penny. "Be careful," he said finally. "Be very, very careful. Murderers are bad people. You know that."

"I know it better than most people."

There was another silence. "Not that I'm trying to tell you what to do," he said, "but maybe it would be a good idea to stay in your room with the door locked until it's time to leave for the airport." He was walking a fine line, knowing how prickly I could be about being told what to do. Some of our biggest fights had been when he wanted me to be careful and I didn't see how I could do my job and still do what he wanted. I was learning to listen better; he was learning to give advice more carefully. Patching together a relationship, stitch by stitch. In our case, those stitches were sometimes in ourselves. I could hear the worry in his voice.

"Great idea. Except most of my stuff is still in my old room."

"Right. So when you go down to pack it up, take someone with you. Better yet, take several people with you. A small army, even. Okay?"

Why argue? It seemed like good advice. "Okay."

"Call me when you have your flight schedule. I want to be at the airport to meet you."

"Yessiree," I agreed. "Someone to carry all my luggage."

"Someone who can't wait to get his hands on you is more like it."

"Someone who will have to behave in public."

"But I don't have to behave in the car."

"Whooee!" I said. "I can hardly wait. It'll make me feel like a teenager again."

"Are there things you haven't told me? I thought you were wonky and unpopular."

"I was a smart girl with a big chest. I spent four years with my arms folded protectively and my chin jutting out. But I could imagine the fun other people were having."

"Wish I'd been there."

"Me, too. We'll just have to make up for lost time when I get home."

He made a satisfied sound. " 'Bye," he said.

" 'Bye." I sat there with the buzzing phone in my hand, wishing he weren't gone. I dug around in my briefcase until I found my tickets and called the reservations number. Good news. I could get a flight out of here at 6:00 A.M. I called Andre back, gave him the times, and headed for the tub, hoping it wouldn't be too cold.

It wasn't. It was nice and warm. I got one whole foot in before panic seized me. Something I hadn't even considered. My body simply refused to be put into water. I stood there naked, shivering, with one foot in the warm, inviting water. I couldn't move. This time, I didn't even have to wait for sleep. The nightmare was with me while I was fully awake. I pulled my foot out, put on the robe, and huddled there, pondering, fearful, distressed. Baths had always been my salvation. My refuge. My comfort in a world that was too hard.

At the end of a long, hard day, lowering my body into a tub of lavender-scented water was often the only thing that kept me going. A shower just wasn't the same. But tonight, that's what it would have to be. The fear had chilled me. The day's trials had left my body aching, and my hair was still stiff with salt. Sadly, I let the water drain out, turned on the shower, and stepped in. I could barely tolerate that. When I let the water roll over my face to rinse my hair, the moments when I couldn't breathe terrified me. The suffocating feeling of water pouring down my face, over my nose and mouth, made me want to scream, jump out of the shower half-rinsed, and run out onto the balcony where I could be surrounded by air. I stayed in only long enough to rinse my hair and run a bar of soap over my body, and I was out, huddled back in my robe and shaking uncontrollably, even though I knew the room was warm.

I couldn't even stay in the bathroom long enough to comb my hair. I took my comb into the bedroom, where my meager luggage was, and snapped on the light so that I could get dressed. I took one step into the room, toward the chair where I'd left my clothes, and stopped, arrested, staring at the bed. It was the same bed. The same spread. Same color, same everything, as Martina's room.

Memory ran through me like an icy finger on my spine. I looked down at the rug, expecting to see one red shoe lying on the floor at my feet. When I looked back at the bed, I could see her as clearly as if she was still there.

Her head lay against the covers, hair spread out around it, wreathing that dusky purple face. The bulging eyes still stared blankly at the ceiling, the protruding tongue still poked out between her shiny red lips. What a commercial it would make—Color that won't fade, even when you're dead. The stocking around her neck seemed jaunty, like a scarf tossed casually over the shoulder. One hand still reached its scarlet talons toward me; the other—something I hadn't noticed before—was tucked behind her head, in imitation of a bathing beauty. Now, as I remembered, I saw that the legs almost looked like she was in the middle of a frog kick, as though she'd kicked off her shoe as she swam across the bed. Except no one did the frog kick on their back, not even frogs.

I closed my eyes but Martina wouldn't leave. She hovered there, plastered against the inside of my lids, in life-sized living color. My imagination supplied shadowy figures to dress and arrange her, joking as they worked. The scene showed so much anger. Profound hatred simmered around the cold reality of death.

No way I was sleeping in this room. No way. I wasn't staying here another minute. Cautiously I edged past the woman who wasn't there and grabbed my clothes. Clutching them against my chest, I hurried out to the living room and curled up on the couch, wrapping myself in a blanket. Eyes open or eyes shut, the image of Martina lingered there—the single strap tugged down, the artfully bared breast, the single shoe dangling from her foot, the vulnerability of those bent legs, the exposed crotch covered only by a bit of red satin thong. Martina had been a proud woman. An impeccable dresser. Someone who affected great dignity. The arrangement of her body had been deliberately degrading.

My hair needed to be combed or it would end up a rat's nest but I was unable to summon the energy to start working on the knots and tangles. Delayed reaction. Shock. All my bravado had gone down the drain with the bathwater. I couldn't get her out of my head. She lurked there like an oncoming headache, growing and pressing and filling all the spaces of my mind. Whoever had done this had hated her. It felt like a long-festering hatred. A planned assassination. But who was the assassin? Could Linda Janovich have hated her replacement enough to do this? Could she have done it on her own? And who had made the phone call that sent Lewis Broder packing and had Martina happily bathing in anticipation of a visit? None of it made sense.

The corners of the room were dark. The bedroom was inhabited by memories. Outside the windows it was dark. I wasn't scared of the dark. I just wasn't moving away from the nice, safe patch of light I was in. Hugging my knees, I folded myself into a tight little ball, closed my eyes, and buried my face in the blanket. Trapped in a luxury hotel room with a dead woman who wasn't there. Unable to leave the room because somewhere out there were the bad guys or bad gals and I had no idea who they were. I didn't think I could trust anyone here. I didn't feel safe. I wanted to be at home.

Well, I couldn't go home unless I packed, could I? And I couldn't pack my things if I couldn't get off this couch. Gradually I got myself unwrapped enough to comb my hair. It was a start. But my clothes were waiting on the floor beside me. *Goddamn it, woman*, I told myself. *Time to get going.* I couldn't get off the couch. An emotional vampire had sucked out all my drive. I was inert. Yeah, yeah. I'd had a hard day. I'd almost died. I was entitled to some down time. But not this wallowing. This cowering in fear. Didn't I believe that when the going got tough, the tough got going? Hadn't I been scornful of Rory for being a wimp? And what, exactly, was I being right now?

It didn't work. A brutal little pep talk only made me fold back up into a ball again. At the end of the couch, the phone sat on a little table, the message light blinking like a red-eyed Cyclops. I could go that far, at least. I slid down the couch, picked up the receiver, and followed the instructions.

"You have . . . two . . . new messages," the canned voice intoned. I waited. There was a click, some heavy breathing, and then Rory's voice, sounding small and angry and scared. "Thea? Thea, if you're there, pick up. Please." A silence. Then, slightly louder,

"Please? Please pick up the phone. Where the hell are you? I need you. I need to tell you this before it's too late." She was crying. "Why isn't anyone ever there when I need them? It's always someone wanting something from me, isn't it? No one wants to give me anything. Not just Martina. People I thought I could trust. Can you at least call me back when you get this? You're the one who needed so goddamned badly to know what was going on, aren't you? Are you there listening to me? Laughing at me? Thea . . ." There was agony and something like terror in her voice. "Thea, please. Pick up the phone. They're coming to get me. I know it. I thought they were my friends, you know, and I was wrong. . . . Thea . . . Please! I don't know what to do. Now that I realize I don't want to die, I'm going to."

There was another long silence. "Are you there? Thea? Please, please, please! Call me as soon as you get this. I can't run away and I'm afraid to be here. Help me!" There was a click as she hung up the phone.

CHAPTER 27

WHEN HER VOICE had gone, the silence in the room was deafening. It closed in around me like air rushing into a void, whirling and swirling and pressing on me, squeezing my aching head and ringing in my ears. My imagination gave that emptiness a voice. A cry for help, escalating, rising, increasing in intensity until the silence following Rory's message was an invisible scream that filled the room with her desperation. Yet I couldn't move. I sat on the fancy little sofa in the elegant room with only a cellophane-wrapped tower of fruit for company, reaching out for the silent beige plastic box that would connect me with the rest of the world, and my arm wouldn't move.

Nothing made any sense. I was a woman of action. I didn't sit, paralyzed, in fancy hotel suites when other people needed help. I hadn't been encased in plaster or frozen by a ray gun. Rory was scared and alone and asking for help and I was sitting here staring at the phone. It felt like I was breaking out of that invisible plaster as I forced my arm toward the phone. I didn't want to get involved. I wanted to move only to pack. I picked up the receiver and asked for the number at the hospital. Asked them to dial it. Asked for Rory's extension. Sat in my small pool of light in the cavernous room and heard it ringing and ringing and ringing. No one answered.

I called hospital central again. Explained that Rory wanted to speak with me. Explained that she wasn't answering. Got transferred three or four times, the way hospitals always do, until I got a woman who sounded like she'd just eaten a year's supply of Thorazine. She informed me, in mechanical tones, that Rory was unavailable and offered to take a message. I pressed her for a more human response, explaining that Rory had called me in a highly anxious state, asking for my help. That brought a longer silence, punctuated by whispering voices and words I couldn't discern. Finally she came back to me and informed me that there was nothing I could do for Rory "at the moment." I tried arguing, avoided cursing or screaming, but got only a mechanical repetition that she was sorry, and then she hung up on my next round of protests.

This was a job for Superwoman. It was time to leap to my feet, find the card with Bernstein's beeper number, and call it. Or rush downstairs and seize a taxi. Leaping seemed beyond the realm of possibility. Even getting to my feet and shuffling the short distance to my clothes seemed impossible. My body might have been cloaked in lead. Everything ached and was turgid, sluggish, unresponsive. I had become my own grandmother. I had been secretly transformed into slow-mo woman.

Slo-mo woman rose to her feet. A tall, trembling creature on long, long legs with unreliable, wobbly knees. Shuffled to the clothes and fumbled through the bundle to find underwear. Got one foot into the panties, staggered, caught herself, dropped the panties, bent down slowly, slowly and retrieved them. Got the second leg through. Wonderful. At this rate, I would be dressed by dawn. Getting a bra on when I couldn't lift my arms seemed even more daunting. My partner, Suzanne, helping me get dressed once in the hospital, had said putting a bra on me was like capturing wayward cantaloupes. Slo-mo woman captured what she had to capture and got all those damnable little hooks hooked. Fingers fumbling. Rory's voice lingering in my ear.

The dress was easy. All I had to do was raise my arms and drop it over my head. Raising my arms was about as hard as learning to fly, something I've never been able to do. Finally I got it over my head and settling around my body while I tried to put two arms through two holes, neither of which was supposed to be the neck. Did that. Bravo. Told my feet to go find the bathroom where I had left Bernstein's card lying on the sink. Shuffle. Shuffle. Shuffle. I wondered how bare feet could sound so much like I was wearing slippers. I hated slippers. The sound of slippers on the floor made me feel a thousand years old.

I found Bernstein's beeper number. Back to the phone. The bedroom phone was closer but there was no way I was going in there. Sure. It was irrational and I pride myself on being a rational person. But those who've never shared space with dead bodies don't understand how death haunts a place. All the while that my body was moving, as we New Englanders say, slower than molasses uphill in January, Rory's desperation echoed in my ears. Wait. This was a luxury suite. There was a phone right here in the bathroom. Shuffle. Shuffle. Shuffle. I picked up the phone and punched in the number. Then I'd done my bit. All I could do was hang up and wait.

Andre says he's no good at waiting. I'm a hundred times worse. Normally, I'd pace the floor or do some work while I was waiting, if I didn't just take matters into my own hands and go fix it. I'm a natural-born fixer. It was my job in the family, growing up, and it's stayed with me. That made the waiting even harder. I'd been betrayed by my own body. Even if I'd wanted to get in a taxi and go find Rory, I was moving so slowly and I felt so weak, I'd be practically useless when I got there. There had to be something I could do besides sit here and wait.

I picked up the phone again. Called the hospital again. This time I asked for the nursing station on Rory's floor. No one seemed puzzled or asked me any questions; they just put me right through. When someone on the floor answered, I didn't give them a chance to speak. "My friend Rory, in three-ten, she called me all upset and left a message. Is she all right?"

"I'm sorry," the voice said, "I can't—"

"Yes, you can!" I insisted. "I just need to know. She's alone. She's in a hospital and she's scared out of her wits. Is she all right?"

There was what felt like an endless silence, the kind of silence we fill with our worst imaginings. "I'm sorry," the person said finally. "She's dead." There was the clatter of the phone being dropped and then I was listening to a buzzing line. This time, reality was worse than anything I'd imagined.

This was not a case of a failed suicide waiting for another chance and then succeeding. The Rory who had called me had had something she wanted to get off her chest. Something to tell. Something that she'd been killed to keep her from telling. She had called me for help and I had gotten the message too late. Poor kid. She'd been a bad judge of people. First she'd hitched her wagon to Martina's star, and that had brought her misery and humiliation. Then she'd attached herself to someone else. Someone who had used her against Martina and then discarded her when she was no longer useful. But who?

I thought back over the past few days. Everyone, it seemed, had a grudge against Martina. The list of her crimes against her colleagues was long. She had mortified Shannon in front of her entire school by failing to show up as promised. She had blithely rescinded a promise and destroyed Jonetta's chances of saving more desperate girls. She had stolen Jolene's ground-breaking, career-making idea and claimed it as her own. Even worse, she had used Drusilla Aird's manuscript without attribution and seriously damaged Drusilla's reputation. She had stolen Linda Janovich's husband. I didn't know what she'd done to Rob Greene or to Zannah, but they had nodded when the matter of grudges against Martina had come up, so I assumed they, too, had stories. Perhaps Jeff had grown weary of her drunken misconduct. And there was Billy, who had loved and hated her. But who, among them, had cherished a grudge so strong, a hatred so powerful, that it had motivated him or her to commit murder or hire someone to do so? Not a spur-of-the-moment passion crime, either. A carefully planned murder, complete with the dramatic distraction of the newlyweds' fight. That was why it couldn't have been Lewis Broder. Because it was planned. Unless he was a superb liar, and he'd lied when he spoke with me and Jolene. But I didn't think he was capable of planning a murder.

No. Not murder. Murders. Martina hadn't been the only victim. Rory was a victim, too, and I would have been. I looked around at the bland, banal decor of my room. Infinitely reproducible. In the room next door, one just like this, Martina had admitted, perhaps even welcomed, her killer. Been overpowered, manually strangled, and then dressed and arranged. No blood and gore. When the police were finished, the room would be straightened and cleaned and opened to guests again. Maybe the hotel would get a new bedspread. Otherwise, life would go on. People would dress and undress, rub on sunscreen, watch TV, and make love right there where Martina had died.

It was a brilliant bit of depersonalizing, killing her in a hotel. Killing Rory in a hospital. Drowning me in the sea. All of us temporary guests with no connection to the place. Easily dismissed. Wiped away. Forgotten. And in a place where people were always coming and going, where everyone was a stranger, the killer wouldn't stand out. Another hotel guest. Another hospital visitor. Another diver in a neoprene suit. It wasn't like killing in a town or a neighborhood, where someone might notice.

All right. Who was this killer, this careful, diabolical planner? Or who were these killers, for Rory had said "they." If I couldn't answer the question for Martina, or for Rory, could I answer it for myself? Martina was the target, Rory the disposable accomplice. But what was I? How did I fit in? I didn't believe I'd been selected simply because I'd solved other murders and that made the killer nervous. Unless all of my fellow board members were in on the conspiracy, and they'd tried to kill me because they feared that eventually I'd find them out. There had to be something more. Something specific. Something I knew that had made the killer target me. But what? Had I seen something? Heard something that I wasn't aware of? I traversed the room, back and forth, back and forth, with my pitiful shuffling walk, too tired, really, for even this meager exercise, but unable to sit still.

As I paced, I pondered. I tried to recall everything that had happened since I'd arrived on Maui. What seemingly innocent or trivial conversation might have given someone the notion that I was the woman who knew too much? The man in Rory's bathroom? That didn't seem likely. Try as I might, nothing rang any bells. There were no startling insights or flashes of revelation. I could beat on my chest and howl to heaven about the unfairness of it all, but I couldn't figure out what I knew or what someone might believe I knew.

Stop thinking, I told myself. *Relax. Let the mind drift.* Oh, sure. I was alone in a hotel room identical to one in which I'd encountered a grotesquely strangled body. Someone out there wanted me dead. The only person who knew what was going on had just been killed. It was not a scenario for relaxation, for letting the mind drift. It was time to panic. Time to hand Rory's laptop over to the cops, pack my bag, and run.

I seized the phone and called Jolene. No one answered. I tried Shannon, Zannah, and Jonetta. No one home. They must all still be in the bar. I left a message for Jolene that I was leaving, detailing my few remaining responsibilities and apologizing for dumping them in her lap, and one asking Jonetta to call me. Now I needed to go downstairs and pack but for that I needed help. I have a friend, a very wise therapist, who keeps reminding me that it's all right to ask for help, that people are glad to be asked. So I called the Pryzinskis, apologized for the lateness of the hour, and asked if I could leave the laptop with them while I packed. They were watching a movie, not at all bothered by being disturbed, and happy to help. Ed insisted on coming with me, "just to be sure," exactly as I'd hoped.

He sat on the foot of the bed, watching his movie, while I plucked my clothes and papers from the mess and put them in appropriate containers. Packing is so strange. It always seems to take me days to get ready for a trip and minutes to pack up at the end. Maybe that's hotel rooms again. There are so few places to put things and anyway, I tend to live out of my suitcase instead of stowing things in drawers and closets. I hate those foil-the-thief hangers that require fitting the little hanger tops into the loops on the rail, a dexterity exercise I'm always forced to do either late at night when my eyes are half-shut, or early in the morning when my eyes aren't open.

I checked the drawers anyway, and under the bed, in the bathroom, behind the door. I threw the last of my things into the suitcase and zipped it shut. "Ready," I said.

"Fine," he said, getting up and turning off the TV. "They were about to have a commercial anyway." He reached out and took the suitcase from me. "So you've decided to go home early?"

"First thing in the morning."

"Smart girl."

"The only good thing about this trip has been meeting you and Marie."

"We've enjoyed it, too," he said. "I hope you'll stay in touch."

We stopped at his room to retrieve the computer and then he walked me back to the elevator, rode up with me, and walked me to my door. Cautious and protective. I didn't mind a bit. We found Jeff Pullman standing in the corridor outside my room.

He came toward us with long, purposeful strides. Gave me a carefully measured smile that seemed forced. "Thea. I've got to talk to you about this morning. I owe you an apology. I'm afraid I . . ."

He reminded me of a kid whose mother has sent him to apologize. Insincere and under duress. I would have expected better from a pro like him. I shook my head. "I have nothing to say to you."

"Look, Thea, please, I need to explain. . . ." He reached for my arm, but at the first sign of motion, I stepped quickly backward. He dropped his hand but stayed there, too close, unable to keep the irritation off his face. "Cut me some slack, okay? I was upset about Martina. I wasn't thinking. I've never done anything like that before."

"Lucky me," I said, stepping past him and slipping my key card into the slot.

He grabbed my wrist, trying to make me look at him, trying to force eye contact. He wasn't used to being ignored and resisted. Charm was his stock in trade. "At least give me the chance to apologize and explain. Surely you owe me that."

Idiot! I hate being grabbed. And I hate obnoxious, entitled people who believe they're "owed" the right to excuse their unacceptable behavior. I pulled my wrist away. "I owe you nothing, Jeff. You're lucky you aren't in jail on assault charges. I'm surprised you have the nerve to speak to me, after the way you behaved this morning. The slack I'm cutting you is that I didn't file assault charges. Now go away and leave me alone before I call security."

But he was too used to getting his own way, to having life made easy for him because he was charming and handsome, or to being able to talk his way into or out of anything. "Oh, come on, now, Thea. It wasn't all that bad. You must listen to me."

I wondered what he would consider bad, if knocking me to the floor and hacking at me with chunks of a terra cotta pot was not. I didn't bother to ask. It met *my* definition of bad.

My good buddy Ed had been very patiently standing there with my suitcase, being ignored, but he had heard enough. "Sir, the lady says she doesn't want to talk to you. She has asked you to go away and leave her alone. Is there something about that you don't understand?"

"Look, Grandpa, this doesn't involve you. I'm talking to the lady."

Where was the famous Pullman charm? He sounded like a character from a bad gangster movie. Ah, the lengths a person has to go through these days to be called a lady.

"And the lady has had enough," Ed said. The Grandpa remark had pierced his naturally tranquil facade. His face was ruddy and he had a dangerous look.

But Jeff wasn't listening or noticing. He was staring at the computer. "That's Rory's laptop," he said.

Trust no one, I thought. He might have tried to claim it for the business and I didn't want to have to fight to keep it for the cops. I shook my head. "It's mine. She has the same model." I kept it present tense, too. Not letting on that one of the identical computers, and one Rory, were no longer with us. I wasn't interested in discussing anything with him. Not me, not what he'd done this morning, not Martina, not Rory, not computers.

"But it looks exactly like—"

"Thousands of other computers of the same make and model."

"Look, Thea, I'm sorry. I'm approaching this all wrong. I didn't come here to argue with you, honestly. I came to say I'm sorry . . . to make up for my churlish behavior." He manufactured a charming smile.

But it was too late. The little light on the lock was flashing green. I opened the door. Ed stepped into the room with my suitcase. I followed. "I'm sorry, Jeff, but no. You need to understand that you can't commit violent acts and expect others to behave as though nothing has happened." I closed the door firmly in his face and left him trying to charm the doorframe. I shuffled across the room and collapsed on the couch.

Ed held up the suitcase. "Where do you want this?"

"Bathroom? I've got some stuff in there to pack."

"Delightful fellow," he said.

"Isn't he? I used to think so. His wife is the woman who was killed on Friday night."

"What was he trying to apologize for?"

"Attacking me with chunks of a broken planter."

Ed nodded thoughtfully. "Charming," he said. "Odd, after that, that he should believe you owe him the opportunity to apologize."

"My sentiments exactly. Look, you don't have to hang around and be my baby-sitter. Go back to your wife and your movie. I'll be all right."

He looked at the door and back to me. "Will you?"

"I promise to admit no strangers, okay?"

"I'll go only if you promise to admit no one. That guy wasn't a stranger."

"Not even the cops?"

"All right. The cops." He stuck out a hand. "Deal?"

I shook it. "Deal."

"And don't leave your room for any reason until you go downstairs to go to the airport."

"Yes, Uncle Ed."

"Don't get smart with me, young lady." He smiled. "You mean Grandpa, don't you?"

It was nice to have a lighthearted moment. I knew that as soon as he left, the darkness would start closing in again. I gave Ed a hug and he left. I locked all the locks behind him and retreated to my couch. Sure enough, the corners of the room began creeping toward me at once. Traditionally I take refuge in bourbon, action, or work. Tonight all three were denied me. I couldn't drink, didn't know what action I might have taken even if the flesh was willing, and for once, I had no work. Bobby hadn't called. Bernstein hadn't called. There was nothing to distract me from my thoughts.

I sat in the gloom and stared at my hands and pondered again about who wanted to kill me. And why?

CHAPTER 28

I NEEDED ANOTHER person to act as a sounding board. I would have used Bernstein. Despite our differences, he was a cop and could be trusted, but he was also unavailable. He'd had plenty of time and hadn't called me back. I assumed he was tied up with Rory's murder, but his lack of response certainly didn't make me feel any safer. Between what was happening inside my head, and what was happening outside it, like Rory's death, I felt terribly unsafe. But what good were the police? If I'd been in danger when I called him, I'd be long dead by now. Still, I needed to talk to someone. Now. Soon. I'm always an impatient person. Times like these make me more so. Maybe, running my ideas by another person, I might be able to see what I was missing. Might finally figure something out. All this conjecture was wearing, like being forced to juggle and not allowed to stop.

Jolene was good and solid, but when last seen, she'd been happily drinking. And in my new risk-averse avatar, I wasn't inviting anyone into my room who had bandages on their wrists. Not no one. Nobody. Shannon was too loud and boisterous, when I was feeling fragile. Zannah was too upbeat and optimistic, when I was feeling neither. And Rob Greene was a man, as I presumed my attacker to be. That left Jonetta.

Of course, in my darkest moments, my most paranoid Agatha

Christie moments, I could imagine a conspiracy they were all in together, even Jonetta—they had all hated Martina and they all seemed unwilling to get involved in finding out who had killed her—but I couldn't think of Jonetta as a killer. She was too committed to life, too dedicated to doing good to risk the fate of all her girls. I picked up the phone and called her room. I expected they would all still be in the bar and I'd have to leave a message, but I got lucky. She was in. The instant I heard her resonant voice, I started to feel better.

"Netta? It's Thea. I need someone to talk to. Can you come up?"

"How are you doin', child?" she asked. "You've had yourself one tough day. I got your message about going home. I think you're doing the right thing, you know. This place is just too dangerous for you. Who ever would have thought that Maui, vacation paradise, would turn out like this?"

"Not me, that's for sure. I brought bikinis and sun screen, not splints and bandages. Look, I know it's late but can you come up?"

"Happy to," she said.

"I've moved. I'm up on seventeen now." I gave her the room number.

"Just let me get out of these damned uncomfortable shoes and I'll mosey on up."

I put down the phone with a feeling of relief. Normally I would have said two heads were better than one, but tonight I wasn't sure mine counted for anything, so it was more like one head was better than none. While I waited, I paced. While I paced, I fretted. Bobby hadn't called back yet. Neither had Bernstein. In a few more hours, I'd be gone. There were two ways I could look at it—it could mean that I only had a few more hours to solve the case or it could mean that if I put off figuring things out just a little longer, I'd be out of here and it would be someone else's problem. I leaned toward the latter. Other times, other places, I'd flung myself into the fray, but not this time. This time, whatever it might say in the paper, Detective Kozak wasn't on the case. I wanted the killer found because I didn't believe in killing, but I wanted someone else to do it. Andre would be proud of me.

I wanted to be gone, to be back home with Andre, and, despite what the paper had suggested, I wanted to leave the detecting to the people who got paid for that sort of thing. But there was one small problem—I didn't much like the idea of going off without knowing who had tried to kill *me*. What if they followed me home and tried again there? At least here I was on my guard. I wasn't going to let anyone but the good guys into my room. At least, that's what I thought. The trouble with not having any idea who the bad guys are is that it makes you pretty paranoid. What if it was Jonetta? What if I was such a bad judge of character that I'd just invited my killer to tea?

I marched into the bathroom and looked at myself in the mirror. "Kozak, you are a good judge of character, remember?" I told the reflection in the mirror. Besides, I knew the person who'd grabbed me at Molokini Crater hadn't been Jonetta. No one could have missed a three-hundred-pound woman in a wet suit. Even to the most oblivious, some things in life are unmistakable. Jonetta was an unlikely suspect because she was too big to hide. Besides, she hadn't been around on Friday night, when Martina was killed. She hadn't flown in until Saturday. I was only bothered by paranoia and irrational suppositions because of the day I'd had. Pain and fear and serious physical abuse can affect anyone's judgment. That's why I had called Jonetta for help.

Still, as they say, discretion is the better part of valor. I could be wrong. I have been wrong about people before. I would take out a little insurance just in case I'd made a serious misjudgment this time. Feeling a bit like a fool, I called Ed and Marie, apologizing for disturbing them again. "I feel like a ninny," I said, "but I'm trying to be careful. I need to talk with Jonetta . . . so I'm letting her into my room. . . ." I trailed off, feeling awkward and incoherent.

"What do you want us to do?" Ed asked. "I could come up."

"Oh, I don't know. I guess I just wanted you to know she's here . . . in case . . . in case I don't know what. Call me in half an hour, okay? If I don't answer, send in the troops."

"A lot can happen in half an hour."

"A lot can happen in a minute. But I'm not expecting anything to happen at all."

"I don't like it," he said.

"But you'll do it?"

"But I'll do it."

I hung up feeling foolish. Feeling like I'd blown it. That my people skills were as smooth as crunchy peanut butter today. The phone rang. "Eenie, meenie, miney, mo," I said as I crossed the room and picked up the receiver. "Is it friend or is it foe? Hello?"

It was Bobby. "Hi," he said. He sounded excited. "We've been having some fun with this. Luke is still working on it but I thought you might want what we have so far."

"You bet." I grabbed pen and paper. "Shoot."

"Bilbo was easy. Your guy's name is William Berryman. You want an address?"

"Got one, thanks." So the graphic admirer of Rory's body had been our own Billy Berryman. Poor guy. I wondered if they were still an item. I wondered if he knew what had happened. I wondered that he'd been able to sit by so coolly when we discussed firing Rory. I wondered if he'd been the mystery presence in Rory's bathroom. That was before our Billy was supposed to have arrived on the scene, but perhaps they'd had a secret rendezvous. The cologne matched. And it would explain the source of Billy's information—a babbling Rory.

It made me feel a little better about Billy until two other things occurred to me. Billy was brilliant at presenting a synthetic public persona. Maybe I didn't really know him at all. What if Billy and Rory had plotted this together? Billy had admitted that he hated Martina. Billy was in love with Rory. But someone had killed Rory. It was too much for my befuddled brain.

"What about Fox?"

"The account is for an Alan Grinnell who works for Alt Corp., which has a Washington, D.C., address. But there is no Washington, D.C., corporation called Alt Corp. The address which the imaginary corporation uses is the residence of an Aurora Altschuler. However, the credit card to which the account is charged doesn't appear to belong to Alt Corp. or Aurora Altschuler. Luke is trying to figure out who it does belong to. You want him to keep digging?"

"You bet. While he's at it, see if he can find airline records showing Alan Grinnell flying in to Maui on Thursday or Friday, and flying out again on Saturday? From D.C., I imagine, although I don't know about that."

"We're on the case," Bobby said cheerfully. He was so dear. How many people would be cheerful if you got them up in the middle of the night and asked them to rouse their computer hacker friends? Not too many. But then, though the movies and TV are full of them, not many of us real people actually have friends who can hack their way across America. "What's this about, anyway?"

"Catching bad guys."

"Suzanne's not going to like that. Neither, need I add, is Andre."

"I'm being very, very careful this time, Bobby. I'm doing only this from behind closed, locked doors, and only by phone. The cops are doing the chasing."

"Yeah, right. And if I believe that, you've got a bridge you want to sell me, right?"

"Sure, Bobby. Out in the middle of the Arizona desert. You interested?"

"I'll pass," he said. "Gotta get back to the keyboard. I'll keep you posted." He didn't hang up. I heard him take a deep breath, gearing up, all those thousands of miles away, to say something he was nervous about. "Thea, you don't need me to tell you this . . . but please be careful. We need you around here. We all . . ." This time the silence was even longer. "We all love you." Embarrassed by this confession, he hung up before I could say anything.

My last response to Bobby, "I'll be here," was delivered to an empty line. Someone knocked on the door.

I crossed the room and peeked through the spy hole. Jonetta was standing there, a vision tonight in purple and scarlet. I undid the many locks and let her in. She swept past me, settled herself on the couch, and touched the scarlet turban she wore. "The great Carnac says 'To get to the other side.' "

"I hope Carnac has more insightful things than that to say."

"You should have been at dinner tonight," she said, leaning forward, her big hoop earrings jingling. "The troops were very restless and giddy and talking out of school."

"At dinnertime, I still felt like a puddle of melted ice cream. I don't feel much better now. What do you mean, talking out of school?"

Jonetta had a satisfied smile. "Girlfriend, if you're anything like me, you've been wondering what their stories are . . . what Martina did to everyone that made them so determined to get her off the board. You heard my story, yesterday, when we were on our way upstairs to . . . when we found Rory. And we all know Shannon's story. And Jolene's. But I've been dying to know what happened to Zannah. And to Rob Greene. And I heard how Martina stole him away from his wife."

"I still don't believe grown men can be stolen, Netta. They have to want to be taken before it can work."

Jonetta shrugged. "Maybe so, honey. Maybe so. So why'd you bring me up here this late at night when my bones were aching to go to bed?"

"Wait a minute. Aren't you going to tell me the stories?" I skipped the reference to aching bones. I had a lot more than bones that ached.

She feigned surprise. "I thought you wanted to get right down to business?"

"Maybe the stories are business."

"Maybe. Maybe not." She touched the turban again. "Carnac sees no connections. But perhaps you will. You're our detective, after all."

I winced. "Don't remind me, Jonetta. That article has caused me nothing but trouble. Actually, that whole business at the Bucksport School has caused me nothing but trouble."

"But you did a good job," she said with a firm nod of her head. "A job that needed to be done." She settled herself on the couch and folded her arms. "Rob's story won't surprise you much. It's a lot like Lewis Broder's story, except that Rob wasn't interested in playing. No. I take that back. It's a lot different from Broder's on Rob's side. And sadder, too. Hotel conference. Martina has too much to drink and asks Rob if they can go back to his room where they can talk privately, you get the picture. Rob calls his wife, who isn't in but expected shortly, asks that the wife call him back. Martina makes her moves, gets graciously rebuffed, and when the phone rings with Rob's wife calling back, Martina answers the phone and does a surprised sex-kitten thing before she hands over the phone. You can imagine the rest. He got things straightened out but he was furious. That was the day Martina lost his vote. Sometimes she had a lot of trouble seeing the forest for the trees." She looked around the room. "You got anything to eat?"

"Fruit," I said, waving at the cellophaned tower. "And the mini-bar is full of overpriced goodies. How about a jar of macadamia nuts?"

"Sold." She nodded affirmatively. "So that's Rob's story. You want to hear Zannah's?"

"Sure." I didn't think this was going to get me any answers but it was a brief diversion and I was curious. And still wondering why she found Rob's story so sad. Maybe there was more.

"Zannah introduced Martina to Jeff Pullman."

"Ugh! She must feel guilty, having put him in the path of a black widow like that."

"What makes her feel guilty is that Linda Janovich was . . . and is . . . Zannah's friend. She thought she was being kind to Linda's husband, who was at loose ends because Linda had gone back to school and was up to her ears in work for a master's degree, and Jeff was feeling lonely and neglected. It was just a casual dinner . . . you know the type. Zannah was in Washington, she made some phone calls to put Linda and Martina together. She thought she was going to help Linda get a job when she finished her degree. Instead, she delivered her friend's husband into Martina's clutches. And he stayed there."

"I still say you can't—"

"Yeah, yeah, yeah." The earrings jingled. "And never in your perfect life have you been tempted to sleep . . . or get close to . . . or confide in or whatever . . . any man other than the one you were involved with? Never in a fit of pique or loneliness or need? Come on, honey. Everybody's human. Even Jeff Pullman."

"That prick is all too human. Or at least, all too physical."

"I heard what happened. It was a surprise, though, wasn't it? Out of character. But we both know how a major shock like that can change a person completely. I've always liked the guy," Jonetta said. "Even if he did leave a nice wife for the Black Widow. . . ."

"Was she nice? Linda Janovich, I mean?"

"I didn't know her then, but the way I hear it, she was awfully nice. Subdued and sweet natured and generous. She's changed a lot since the divorce. It can't be easy, having your husband dump you like that, especially after almost twenty years. Especially when you worked to put him where he is." She sighed. "It's an old story, isn't it? But you didn't bring me up here to be filled in on the evening's gossip, did you?"

"No. I'm still trying to figure things out. I needed another head, hopefully one clearer than mine."

"That ain't me, babe."

I rolled my eyes. "Jonetta, you are always a cool head."

"Not when I got this thing on. But all right, honey, I'll give it a try. What exactly is it that I'm supposed to be doing with this-here cool head, anyway?"

"Help me figure out why someone is trying to kill me. Why they've already killed Martina and Rory and now they're—"

"What did you just say? That silly little girl is dead? Why'd we waste our time tryin' to save her, getting ourselves all covered with blood like that, when she goes and does it again anyway? We could have been out in the sun."

I knew she didn't mean it. Jonetta was an instinctive saver of lives. She didn't debate the worth of the effort. I also realized she hadn't heard what I said. "She didn't kill herself, Netta."

"What do you mean?"

"Listen to this." I picked up the phone, summoned back my messages, and passed it to her. I watched her face grow solemn as she listened. When the message ended, she hung up the phone.

"So you called her back, and?"

"And I couldn't get through. Got stonewalled. Tried three times. Finally I called the nursing station. I told them about Rory's call and demanded to know if she was all right. That's when they told me she was dead. Now, I know that, yes, she did try to kill her-self. And yes, when I spoke with her before I left the hospital she was still in a deep funk and speculating about whether she should try again, but that phone call is not a farewell message. It's a cry for help. She wanted to talk. She wanted to clear the air. And she was definitely afraid of someone."

"Too bad she was so determined to try for drama. We'd be a lot better off if she'd just spat it out, wouldn't we? But the girl always was one to muddle as often as she clarified." She shook her head. "We're not supposed to speak ill of the dead, are we? So what are you going to do about this?"

I nodded at my packed suitcase. "I'm going home. Turning tail and running. Even before the dawn breaks over the mountains, I'm going to be winging my way toward the East."

"Very poetic, girl," she said. "And in the meantime?"

"We are going to put our heads together and see if we can figure out what's going on around here."

She tipped her head and stared at me. "Why? Why don't you just go on home and leave this to the experts?"

It was a fair question. "Well . . . let's say someone killed Martina because they hated her. . . ." Jonetta nodded. "And suppose that Rory was an accomplice, and she was killed because she wasn't going to hold up. . . ." She nodded again. "But, Netta, why did they try to kill me?"

This time she shook her head. "I see what you mean. Better break out those macadamia nuts, then. I can't think on an empty stomach."

I got out the jar, broke the seal, and handed it to her. "Thanks," she said. "Now where do we begin?"

"When I got here, I suppose. Rory hinted that my problem was I knew too much. And more than one person has suggested that I'm here because I'm a detective, not because Suzanne got sick and I had to come in her place."

"Like who? Who said that?" Jonetta demanded.

I thought about that. "Jeff Pullman, for one. He was incensed that I was here instead of Suzanne."

"That's weird. Anyone else?"

"Billy Berryman, I think. And there was someone else. I just can't recall. . . ." The phone rang.

"It's Bernstein," a tired voice said. "I hope you're not in trouble. All hell's been breaking loose."

"I know. Look, if I was in trouble when I called you, I'd be long dead by now. I know about Rory—"

"How the hell—"

"She tried to call me. She had some things she wanted to tell me. I tried to call her back, couldn't reach her, and finally found someone who told me what had happened. Well, not what had happened . . . but that she was dead. However it looked, Lenny, she didn't kill herself."

"We know that. So, to what do I owe the pleasure of this call?" His speech was thick and slow and he sounded like he was on the verge of collapse.

"I have Rory's laptop. I had both of them. Hers got mixed up with mine and mine is the one that ended up destroyed. There's stuff on it that you should see."

He sighed wearily. "Tomorrow."

"Tomorrow at the crack of dawn I'm out of here. Shall I leave it for you at the desk?"

"No!" An explosive sound. Moderated by his next words. "Shit, no. Sorry. I'm so tired I can't even think anymore. No. Just hang on to it. I'll come and get it as soon as I can. I don't want to take any chances. Just hang—"

"Lenny, it doesn't have to be you. It's just carrying a computer. Isn't there someone else you can send for it?"

"Yeah. I guess it doesn't have to be me, does it? Good idea. Yeah. I'll send a uniform over." He spoke so slowly I could almost hear the thoughts forming in his head. "Don't open your door to anyone who isn't wearing a uniform. And don't open it unless you've seen some ID. This job over here . . . whoever it was dressed like staff."

"Male or female?" I asked.

"Woman," he said. "Nurse. Shit. This is gonna raise hell with our crime statistics. The Chamber of Commerce gonna have a bird. Don't you go getting killed, too. You hear me? I gotta go." He didn't so much hang up the phone as smash it. I could hear the clatter and rattle of plastic as he fumbled it home.

"It was a woman," I told Jonetta.

"What was a woman?" she countered. "I mean, who?"

"Oh, sorry. Who killed Rory." It felt like some of Bernstein's weariness had rubbed off on me. I was getting fuzzy. And why not? I'd had a long hard day, too, and a night with too little sleep. "I'm fairly sure a man attacked me. And we don't know about Martina. Looks like we've got ourselves a tag team."

"Tag team? Girl, you are the last person on earth I would have expected to say that. You don't watch wrestling?" I shook my head. She jerked her chin toward the phone. "You got another message on there, you know. The voice said two. Maybe you oughta listen to it. Maybe the bad guys called up and confessed."

"Not bloody likely."

She picked up the phone, pressed the buttons to retrieve messages, and held it out to me. "Here."

I put the phone to my ear, knowing that now that I'd heard the outcome, Rory's message was going to be even more painful than it had been the first time. I tried not to listen. Tried instead to start rehearsing stuff in my head for the discussion Jonetta and I were supposed to be having. Finally the desperate voice faded away and I got the operator again, that accentless, upbeat, disembodied female voice. I've always imagine that somewhere in the world there is a woman who is kept in a cave, far from any societal influences, who spends all her days and nights recording bland, upbeat things to go on tapes. I imagine that she's taking heavy doses of mood-altering drugs that make her insufferably cheerful. I imagine her in there with gnomes—no human interaction to interfere with her daily chores—who record each word so that it can be rearranged at will to produce the necessary tapes. No inflection. No rise and fall. No emotion. Her voice is a teeny bit breathy today. Maybe she has to climb many stairs or a steep ladder to get to the recording apparatus. "Second message," she enunciates, oh so clearly. I wait.

A breathless little whimpering sound, then Rory's voice, muffled, almost incomprehensible. "I rang for help, but no one's coming. I should have told you before. Now it's too late. It was Linda. Linda and—" The last was just a garbled sound, a G or a J. There were sounds of pleading, pitiful sounds, and a dull thud. Then the phone disconnected.

I pushed the button to repeat the message and handed the phone to Jonetta. She listened closely and then set down the phone. "I got the Linda," she said. "But what about the other. It's just noise to me."

"Linda Janovich," I said. "Linda Janovich and someone else. Sounded like a G or a J but I can't be sure. It could just be a grunt. Jonetta, Jolene . . . uh . . . whose name starts with a 'juh' sound?"

"Jeff."

CHAPTER 29

"JEFF PULLMAN?" I said. "But he's been a patient and long-suffering . . . and anyway, he was home in D.C. when the police called to tell him about Martina's death. I mean, sure, I'd like to believe bad things about him, after yesterday, but—" A thought hit me as suddenly as a football tackle and I stopped speaking to consider it.

"But what?" Jonetta asked, staring at me curiously.

I felt like I'd been dizzy for days and my head was finally clearing. "But I think I've figured it out."

"Figured what out? Girl, what are you talking about? You're not making any sense. I didn't say Jeff was involved. I said his name began with a 'juh' sound."

"No, Jonetta, I think I'm finally beginning to make some sense." I fished around in my briefcase and found my address book. Started thumbing through the pages. "All weekend long, everyone has been telling me that Jeff Pullman is a saintly, long-suffering man who has had to put up with a terrible load of grief from his out-of-control, alcoholic wife. You've heard the same stuff, right? But what's a guy to do with a wife like that? He's already had one divorce, he's not sure he can afford another and in Washington, you need a wife who can be a player . . . which might be why he married Martina in the first place. But what do you do when the player becomes a liability?"

"Hold on," Jonetta complained. "Hold on. You're going much too fast for me. I don't have the faintest idea what you're talking about."

I found the number that I wanted, stopped pacing, and swung around. "I'm sorry. Suddenly this brain which has been sluggish all day just took off like a greyhound after a rabbit."

Jonetta put a firm hand on my shoulder and led me back to the sofa. "Well, child, you just let that rabbit hop off into the sunset, set yourself down here, and explain what's going on."

"Okay." I took a deep breath and tried to slow down. "The night she died, Martina got a phone call from someone whose impending arrival made her very happy. That we know from Lewis Broder. Lewis thought they were going to get it on and suddenly Martina was showing him the door. The fact that she took a bath and had her nightclothes laid out suggests she was expecting a man. A familiar man." I stopped, trying to figure out how much I needed to tell her.

"There's something else we knew about Martina. She'd been drinking. When she was drunk, she became more difficult and abusive but she also became more physical and more attuned to men. It was as though her feminist side fell away."

Jonetta was getting impatient with my story. "So? What does this have to do with the identity of her killer?"

"I think it was Jeff."

"But he was in Washington. You said so."

"That's what we've—or at least I've—assumed. But only because we believe the police called him there and he flew here. Look, Netta, I'm know I'm doing a terrible job with this. I want to try a little experiment. You know Jeff never has his phone far from his side, right? So I want you to call this number. . . ." I handed her the address book. "It's their home number back in D.C., and see what happens. If he answers, pretend you're a friend and ask for Martina."

"He's here in the hotel," she said. "He isn't going to be answering a phone back in D.C."

"Will you just try it, please?"

Shaking her head, she lifted the phone and dialed the number. Waited very patiently, listening with a dubious expression. She was about to hang up when something happened. I watched astonishment spread across her face. Then she said, "This is Verbena Swinburne calling. I am sorry to disturb you so early but we've got a bit of a crisis on here at the school. May I speak with Martina, please?"

She listened attentively for a moment, then murmured, "Oh, Mr. Pullman, I am just devastated to hear that. Devastated. You have my deepest sympathy. I don't know how any of us will go on. Yes. Thank you. I'll wait to hear about that. Good-bye."

She set the phone down with a shaking hand and stared at me. "I called Washington and Jeff Pullman answered. But he's not in Washington. He's here."

"Right," I agreed. "Call forwarding."

"Call forwarding?"

"You can have your calls sent wherever you're going to be. You can make them follow you around."

"But why didn't he turn it off?"

"Maybe he forgot."

"Or maybe he turned it on again."

"Or maybe he just turned it on and the poor guy is innocent."

"Maybe. The police can probably check phone records."

She leaned forward, staring at me intently. "You think he came here, killed Martina, flew away, waited for their call, and then flew back?"

"Something like that. We know Rory was helping at least as far as to purchase the tickets. And in the message that she left, Rory says her attackers were Linda and Jeff . . . well . . . she didn't actually say Jeff, but it all fits. . . ."

"How sweet. A reconciliation over Martina's dead body."

The phone rang. It was Bobby. "Okay," he said. He sounded like he'd just come in from running several miles. Part of Bobby's charm was the way he got caught up in his work. "Okay. We've got the name of your credit card holder. It's Jeffrey Pullman." He read off the familiar address. "Luke's still working on the reservations, but I thought you'd like an update. He shouldn't be much longer. I'll call if we get anything."

I hung up and nodded to Jonetta. "My office. They've confirmed that the mysterious correspondent on Rory's laptop, who goes by the name of Fox, and carries the account in the name of Alan Grinnell, charges the account to Jeff Pullman's credit card."

Jonetta shuffled her ruffles and gave me a settle-down look. "Slow down, girl. You're not making sense. You lost me about four names ago. What do this Fox character and Alan Grinnell have to do with anything?"

I was too revved up to slow down. "Oops. Sorry. I jumped the gun again. You remember that I took Rory's laptop—"

"I told you to, remember?" she said. "But Jolene said the laptop was destroyed when someone broke into your room." Jonetta looked confused.

"That was *my* laptop. We had the same model." I resisted the urge to digress into a self-pitying riff about my own laptop and stuck to trying to keep my explanation coherent. Not easy, the way my thoughts and words were tumbling around in my mind. "Anyway, on Rory's laptop, she has E-mail correspondence with someone called Fox. Fox has been advising Rory about how to embezzle money from the association."

"Wait a minute," she ordered. "That sniveling little weasel was stealing our money?" I nodded. "And this person called Fox . . . Fox? . . . was helping her?"

"Right," I said. "This Fox character was supposed to fly in to Maui and then fly out again to Honolulu for some unstated purpose. I assumed it was a rendezvous. Rory made the arrangements. Now I'm thinking maybe it was Jeff, flying in to kill Martina and then flying out again so he can be at home when the police called. Except, of course, that he wasn't at home. He was sitting in a hotel in Honolulu waiting to fly back to Maui on a plane arriving at the right time—the time he would have been arriving if he was coming from the East Coast."

"Hold on," Jonetta said, shaking her scarlet turban slowly. "I don't know. It seems too neat, somehow. Too easy if you can sit around and figure it out in ten minutes. Jeff Pullman comes all the

way to Hawaii to kill his own wife? When it would have been so
easy to arrange some drunken fall back home? And how'd he get
on the plane using someone else's ticket? I have enough trouble
using my own ticket. What if you're wrong?"

I shrugged. I didn't think I was wrong. I thought I'd figured out
what it was they believed I knew. Rory thought I'd asked about the
phone and the police because I was suspicious about Jeff's whereabouts; suspicious about the fact that he'd gotten the call on his
home phone instead of his cell phone when he was never home.
"Then I'm wrong. But everything fits. He could have used a false
license for ID. Anyone can get one."

"And what are you going to do with this neat theory, Thea?"

I didn't understand why she was arguing with me. What did
she care? Didn't she want the murder solved? Wasn't she relieved
that it wasn't one of us after all? "Take it to the police," I said,
reaching for the phone. "Tell them what I know and let them take
it from here." I was proud of myself for being willing to let it go.
Normally I want to have a hand in things.

"Hold on a minute," she said, taking the receiver out of my
hand and returning it to the cradle. "Let's talk about this. You're
angry at Jeff Pullman," she said slowly, "because of what he did to
you. I don't blame you," she added quickly, catching my angry
look, "but before you do something that could prove seriously embarrassing, even damaging, to his career . . . and yours, if you're
wrong, let's look at other . . ."

Didn't she understand? I wanted to drop this and run. "You got
a better theory?" I stuck out my chin, childish and truculent.

Jonetta folded her hands over her stomach and settled more
deeply into the couch, like a storyteller getting ready to spin a tale.
Her dark eyes fixed on my face. "Maybe I do," she said. Unspoken,
behind the words, was the command to settle down and listen.

I felt a prickle of fear, followed by uncertainty and a growing
sense that something important was coming. It was so unlikely
that she was about to confess, but there was something about her
manner that was unsettling. She was silent for a long time, just sitting and thinking and nodding. It was a credit to the force of her
presence that I sat quietly, too, and kept my mouth shut. I do not

wait well. On the other hand, Jonetta was one of my few heroes. If she confessed to some complicity in this, it would shake me as few things have done. Maybe I didn't want to hear this. Maybe it was better left unsaid? I considered telling her to stop. But no. I was a slave of duty and a high priestess of truth. I believed in the ultimate value of truth over most things. Still, I felt like a kid at the dentist as I waited.

Finally she said, "What if it happened like this? Suppose that Rory is stealing the money, not for herself, but because she's hopelessly in love with Jeff Pullman?"

"I thought she was having an affair with Billy Berryman. Certainly in the E-mail I've seen, they were plenty intimate."

Jonetta grunted. "I think that's been over for a while. Did you look at the dates?" I had to admit that I hadn't. On the other hand, I had reason to believe that it wasn't over. Still, I was amazed that she had known about them and I hadn't.

"Why does everybody know all this stuff while I'm in the dark?" I complained.

"Everybody doesn't know all this stuff, Thea. Everybody knows bits and pieces. And everybody talks to me."

I didn't have to ask why. I'd confided in Jonetta, too. That was why she was here. We confided in her because she was wiser and more experienced, and, at least I believed, more real. Because we knew she could keep secrets. Because we all felt comfortable talking to her. She was a good listener. And yes, maybe I was a little jealous. I was used to people confiding in me. I was used to being the one in the know. "Okay, so you know everyone's stories. Why would Rory steal money for Jeff Pullman? Were they planning to run away together?"

"So his daughter, Melissa, could go back to private school."

"Give me a break! You've got three professional people with three professional salaries and they can't afford private school?"

"Three not all that big professional salaries, Thea. Supporting the necessary trappings of a fast-track lifestyle. Linda's is a government salary. Jeff's is bigger, sure, but the divorce cost him big bucks and he's paying for two houses, child support, and his son's college. The only one with any money was Martina, and she wouldn't pay for Melissa. I know you heard that story from Billy."

"What kind of a marriage is it where you can't just ask—"

"A crappy one," she said.

"I should have sent those nosy cops to you, Jonetta. You're the one who knows everything."

"I'm glad you didn't." She leaned forward and took my hand. "Don't tell me your nose is out of joint because you wanted to be the one to know everything? I thought you were eager to get out of the detective business. And I thought, as board members, we were all working toward the same goals."

She read me like a book. "Sorry," I said, pulling my hand back. "This is so confusing."

"It is, isn't it? Shall I continue?"

There was more going on here than our talk about possible suspects. Jonetta was asking me some fundamental questions about trust and openness, and about competition or cooperation. This conversation was also about how our relationship, as well as the board's relationship, would go in the future. Jonetta had laid down a challenge without saying a word. Was I going to trust her and work with her or was I going to hold back and play the Lone Ranger because I wanted to be right and I wanted to be in charge.

But I didn't think this was about the board anymore. For me, this was about finding Martina's killer and getting the hell out of here. I couldn't operate on all these levels, I just wanted this to be over. Didn't she understand I was too tired for this? Probably not. Go around acting like Superwoman and people being to treat you that way. No one thought they needed to cut me any slack. "Yes, please. Go on."

She gave a sharp, affirmative nod. "Good. Now, you know that we are sitting in a whole hotel full of people with their own agendas regarding Martina. For the past few years, that woman has been like poison in the water supply. There are so many people here with reasons to hate her. Suppose one of them decided to act on it?"

"It wasn't a spontaneous thing, Netta. Whoever killed Martina had planned it. Knew about the lingerie killer. Bought the costume, hired the actors . . ."

She nodded. Vigorous. Decisive. I envied that energy. I felt as drained as if a vampire had been sipping my blood. "You're right. I didn't mean to make it sound spontaneous. This thing has been festering for a long time."

"But why kill her? Why not just remove her from a position of power, where she can't do so much harm?"

"Because this wasn't done to prevent future harm, Thea. This was done to revenge past harm."

I roused myself. If she knew so much, why had I had to play Lone Ranger? "How do you know? And if you already know what happened, why didn't you tell somebody? Were you planning to sit on it? To keep it to yourself and eventually go home from this conference congratulating yourself on all the progress that had been made, regardless of the evil that went with it?"

Suddenly Jonetta's face was fierce. "So you think that you were able to put your scenario together tonight because of all your brilliant insights, and that's okay, but that I must have been harboring mine secretly in my mind for a long time, so that's not okay?" Jonetta was angry. "What if I told you that just as the pieces fell together in your mind just moments ago, the same thing happened to me while you were talking?"

Three hundred pounds of angry Jonetta was a daunting sight, especially leaning in close and personal. I was breathless with anxiety and confusion. I wanted to whimper pitifully and throw up my arms to protect myself. "I didn't mean that. Look, Netta, why don't I just shut up and you tell the story and then we can yell at each other for a while?"

I've been in some strange spots in my life, and I've had some disturbing conversations, but this was one of the oddest. The air in this haunted room seemed to be charged with electricity. The dark fearsome corners were alive with anticipation. We were just two women sitting in a hotel room talking. But look what we were talking about. I'd said I knew who dunnit and laid out my theory. Now Jonetta was saying maybe she was the one who knew who dunnit, and was laying out a different theory. I didn't think stuff like this was supposed to happen in real life. But then, my real life was pretty bizarre and from all she'd said, it sounded like hers was, too.

"Okay," she said, with a decisive nod of her head. "You shut up and listen. I talk. Then we talk. Decide what to do next. I think our killers are Linda Janovich—we have Rory's confirmation on that—and Rob Greene."

"Rob Greene!"

"You said you were going to be quiet." The turban and ruffles trembled menacingly as she leaned forward.

"I will be," I whispered, pressing back into the cushions.

"Hey, girl." She laid a warm hand on my arm. "Take it easy. We're just two people talking, okay? You look scared."

"I am scared, Netta. Two people dead. Someone wanting me to be the third . . ."

She took my hand between hers. "I'm your friend," she said firmly.

"What scares you, Netta?"

"You really want to know?" I nodded. "Failure. Letting all those girls down. Tellin' them they've got a chance and then taking it away from them." She inclined her head, regal and splendid. "Yes, I could have killed her for what she did. But what kind of example would I be setting them?"

I left my hand in hers. It was like plugging into a wall socket. I could practically feel her energy flowing into me, like a transfusion. "So," I said, "what about Rob Greene?"

She pulled her hand back, settling into her storytelling mode again. I felt bereft, deprived of that infusion of energy. "I didn't tell you all of Rob's story. I said he patched things up with his wife. That's not entirely true. At the time that this happened, though neither Rob nor his wife recognized what was going on, Rob's wife was suffering from a severe postpartum depression. It was their first baby. They were both busy professionals, and they didn't pay enough attention to what was happening. Marilee thought her exhaustion and dark periods and mood swings were all normal results of too little sleep and high stress. She didn't seek help. And Rob was so busy just trying to get through the days and nights, he didn't notice either."

She leaned forward, her earrings jingling, and looked me square in the eyes. "After Martina's mean little practical joke, Marilee Greene got off the phone, wrote a note, and took every pill in the medicine cabinet. The baby-sitter found her the next morning in a coma. She's gradually recovering but there was a lot of damage. She'll never be entirely right again. You can imagine how Rob felt about Martina."

Rob Greene. Pleasant, cynical, wisecracking Rob. How could I have not known that he was carrying such a festering hatred? How could Martina have not known? Perhaps she had known and hadn't cared, and that had been even more galling for him.

"But why would he try to kill me? I didn't even know the story."

Jonetta shrugged. "When you asked me to come up here, you said you wanted to go over things, see if you could figure that out. You still want to do that?"

I shrugged. I didn't feel the fuzziness I'd felt when Jonetta first arrived. Her story had gotten me too stirred up. But I did feel physically exhausted. These days I seemed to have either the spirit or the flesh but never the two did meet. Oh, well. We might as well see this through, whatever that meant.

"Sure," I said. "Sure. Let's do that. Ever since Rory said I knew too much, I've been obsessing about what she meant. I thought she was talking about the phone call to Jeff. But even if she wasn't, I'm still confused. Where does she fit into all this? What did she know that got her killed?"

Jonetta shook her shiny turbaned head. "I'm not sure. I think that Rory gave either Rob or Linda the key to Martina's room. I know she had one on Friday."

"And on Saturday we had to get security to let us in," I said. "No wonder she was so anxious to get into the room. But I'm sure that Rory thought Jeff had done the killing. That explains her hysteria and her silence. She loved him. She was helping him. And . . . what if Jeff was here? What does that do to your story? Why was he here? And why would she give Rob or Linda the key? I mean, what makes you think she did?"

"Something she said when we were waiting for the ambulance. She said she gave away the key. That she had given it to the wrong person. It was a mistake and she was sorry. You know she'd been drinking, too. If someone knocked on her door when she was half-asleep—"

"But that suggests there was a plan, that she'd planned to give someone the key. And you didn't tell this to the police?"

Jonetta sighed. "Maybe I should have, Thea. You know how I feel about the police . . . and then, this all has happened so fast . . . it's hard to know what might have made a difference. I think we need a pot of coffee and some sandwiches, if we're going to do this much longer. This brain of mine needs to be fed at regular intervals or it doesn't work at all."

What was a little more room service? I was already supporting half of the island's economy. A little more wouldn't hurt. I picked up the phone and ordered food. Lots of food. Enough for a small army. Undoubtedly, by the time it arrived, at least one more hungry person would have come knocking on my door. Wasn't it about time to feed Bernstein and Nihilani again?

"What makes you think Rob Greene is involved? I mean, for Jeff Pullman I've got the phone forwarding and his involvement with Rory and the fake name and the plans for a plane ticket in and out. What have you got?" I sounded like a little kid playing a stupid game of one-upsmanship.

She shifted her bulk around and put her feet up on the couch, propping them on the arm. "Looks fancy enough but this furniture's not very comfortable," she grumbled. "I don't think they make most of this stuff for humans to sit on. Mostly it's for show. There ought to be some kind of a law that furniture must be proved to be suitable for human use."

As a fellow tall person, or sister tall person, I should say, I had to agree. I thought the world was made for short people. My short partner, Suzanne, thought the world was made for tall people. Maybe, like with airbags in cars, everything was made for the guy who was about five feet nine or so and weighted about a hundred and sixty pounds. Maybe furniture should be sized like clothes and come in petites, regulars, and talls. Maybe, now that I was giving up the consulting business and the detective business and going into something safer and predictable, I would open Three Bears Furniture with something for momma bear, poppa bear, and baby bear. The thought was very appealing.

"Why Rob Greene?" I repeated.

"Three things," she said. "First, he was very agitated at dinner tonight. Not at all like himself. Second, I overheard him in a tête-à-tête with Linda Janovich late at night after the luau. I was on my way to a moonlight stroll; they were sitting on a bench overlooking the beach. Linda said, 'I'm not at all sorry about what happened. She had to be stopped and now she's been stopped.' He said, 'I know it's wrong, but someone had to do it. I've never hated anyone so much.' And then she said, 'The cops think it was Thea,' and they both laughed. Finally . . ." She paused for dramatic effect. It worked. I leaned forward to catch the words. "Finally, I was sitting on the Molokini boat, trying out my nice new binoculars, watching one of the divers come aboard and he did the most peculiar thing. He had a knife in his hand and appeared to 'accidentally' cut himself as he was climbing aboard. And guess who it was?"

"You tell me," I said.

"Rob Greene."

"Are you sure it was Rob?" I demanded.

"I couldn't swear it on a stack of Bibles, but that's who it looked like."

But Rob Greene had told me he was going to spend the afternoon sitting on the beach. At a distance, through binoculars, a man in a wet suit? It made me wonder. But she did seem awfully certain. "Did you tell this to the police?"

"No, but I will. I just hadn't put it all together until the end of dinner, when Jolene said you had stared at her Band-Aids in a really queer way earlier, and Zannah said she'd heard that you'd scratched your attacker on the wrist and that was probably why. Jolene got quite huffy at the idea of you suspecting her."

"But what about Billy?" I asked.

"Billy?" she said, puzzled.

"You remember at breakfast when he handed out those clippings about the lingerie killer?" She nodded, still puzzled, leaning forward attentively. "The details of the crime were a secret, Netta. Not in the papers. So how did he know? He says he hated Martina. . . ."

Her shoulders twitched impatiently. "Billy's just a kid. Besides, he wasn't here when—"

"Billy the kid was in Rory's bathroom on Saturday when I went to talk to her. That's why she didn't want to talk to me."

"So, he got the details from Rory—" she began.

"But whoever did this knew about the lingerie killer long before that. That was the model for the crime. And if Rory was involved with Billy, why would she be stealing money for Jeff?"

Jonetta threw her hands up in the air. "How the hell do I know? I just think Rob Greene had the best reason."

I rubbed my head, which was beginning to ache. Unfair, since it had been the one part of my body that *didn't* hurt. "Let's not fight about this. We've got a real mess of stuff here, Jonetta. What are we going to do with it?"

She took a deep breath and let it out slowly. "What any right-thinking citizen would do, I suppose. Call the cops." Jonetta tried not to hate, but she sure hated cops.

The phone rang again. Assuming it was Bobby, I picked it up, and said, "So, what have you got for me this time?"

"That you, Kozak?" a muffled male voice asked.

"What? You must have the wrong—"

"I don't think so. Here's someone who wants to speak with you."

There was a silence. I could hear a child crying and then a different voice on the line, small and scared and no more than a whisper. "Thea? It's the spy."

CHAPTER 30

"LAURA? I THOUGHT you were going to bed. What's going on?" I was annoyed with her and even more annoyed with her parents for allowing her—no, helping her—to call so late.

"I'm sorry. . . ." She was crying so hard I could barely hear what she was saying. "I need help," she said. I signaled for Jonetta to go into the other room and pick up the phone. "After a while I didn't feel so tired anymore. I got restless. We're supposed to go home tomorrow and I wanted to go exploring one more time."

"Yes," I said, "so what's the matter? Why did you call me? What kind of help do you need? It's very late."

"Because . . . because . . ." The sobbing got louder. "They say they'll kill me if you don't come. Kill me tonight and make me disappear and no one will ever know what happened. . . ." A brace of expletives rushed through my brain. *Here we go again,* I thought. Set yourself up once in life as a fixer and you'll never know a moment's peace again. Befriend anyone and they'll try to haul you into danger. I was developing an extremely skewed, pessimistic world view, wasn't I? Thea the grouch. Irritation was swept away in an adrenaline rush. This was a child in danger. A child. I had no time for dithering.

"Who are they, Laura?" I tried to keep my voice calm and level.

"The man who came out of the elevator . . . the one with the fancy shoes . . . and the woman who looks like you from the back. I don't know their names. Please, Thea . . ."

That was all Laura got to say. Someone snatched the phone away from her. Another voice, a woman's voice this time, came on the line. "She's a good little messenger, isn't she? You heard what she said. Meet us in twenty minutes at the end of the parking lot closest to town. Come alone or your little spying buddy has had her last adventure."

"Linda, this is silly," I said. "People already know too much. We know you killed Rory. It's too late to try and protect yourself with silly theatrics."

"Then I don't have anything to lose, do I?" she said. "Come alone. And bring Rory's laptop with you. Twenty minutes. 'Bye." There was a click and I was left listening to a buzzing line.

Jonetta came out of the bedroom, looking grim, and sat back down on the couch. "What a mess," she said. "I don't understand what they hope to gain by this, do you?" She clasped her hands to her head. "I just don't understand, unless we still haven't got it right, and there's someone else involved, someone we haven't thought of, who believes by doing this that he, or she, can eliminate potential witnesses." She lowered her hands and raised her head. "So what are we going to do? Call the cops, or go perform heroic acts ourselves?"

"I don't know about you, Netta, but I've sworn off heroic acts. I've gotten myself beaten up, stabbed, and shot enough for one lifetime, and that's all we get on this planet. I'm staying right here. Especially since tonight Dr. Pryzinski announced to Andre that I'm pregnant."

"You're what, child? Pregnant? How does he know?"

"Evidently, he can tell just by looking."

"Bull tweetie," she said. "He just wants you to be pregnant because you look so female and fertile. Those gentle, avuncular men always want us to be pregnant. They've got some hard-wired idea of how women ought to be and they go around casting it on us like a spell. 'Course, if we aren't pregnant, they know what to do about it, don't they?"

I shrugged. "That's what he said. Andre has already picked out names."

"Guy works fast, doesn't he? Meanwhile, little momma, we got us a crisis on our hands."

For all my bravado declaration that I was staying right here where I was safe, I didn't see how I could leave Laura in their clutches and not try to do something. She was a child; I was an adult, and I had wittingly, deliberately, involved her in this mess, both by handing her over to the police and by encouraging her spying. A more responsible adult might have done neither of those things. But now, by doing them, I had acquired an obligation to Laura that couldn't be fulfilled by sitting here while I called the police. She knew so little it was stupid of them to have grabbed her in the first place. But I didn't think they had taken Laura because they wanted Laura; they'd taken Laura because they wanted me. Because they were sure that I would come. Because they counted on my reputation as a professional rescuer. They might have over-estimated my skills as a detective, and what I knew, but they hadn't overestimated my sense of obligation.

If I didn't show up, what was going to happen? They'd still have to get rid of Laura. She'd seen them all now, and Laura, al-ready known to the police, was not the type to be intimidated into silence. Even if they could scare her that much, perhaps by threat-ening her family, would they rely on it? I doubted it.

What was I going to do? A smart operator doesn't go into a sit-uation like this without a plan. I didn't have a plan. I only had a goal. My goal was to find a way to keep Laura alive long enough to either let her escape—she was smart and small and quick on her feet—or stall them until the police or hotel security could arrive and effect a rescue. As a professional writer of plans, I knew that goals and objectives were worthless without a set of specific steps to take to achieve them. But writing a good plan takes weeks or months. I had ten minutes.

"What are you going to do?" Jonetta demanded.

"I was thinking about watching a movie."

"With that little child in danger?"

"Here's my plan, okay?" I said. It was crazy, but it just might work. "You go in my place. You're the bravest woman I know, Netta. You go, you take them the laptop, and make them let Laura go. They all like you. They aren't going to hurt you. Look, we can call the police first, so they'll be waiting. It's a lot less risky than if I go, because if I go, they'll be planning to kill me and Laura."

"And you think they won't kill me if I go instead?"

"No. Because I think they want two things—they want Rory's laptop, and they want me. If you go and take them the laptop . . . get them to agree to let Laura go . . . and then say that I'll be happy to trade myself for you . . . doesn't that achieve their goals? They get what they want and Laura is safe."

The look she gave me said better than words that she'd always thought me smart and now I was being unspeakably dumb. "That's no kind of a plan. What if they kill *me?* I can't take a chance like this. Let's just call the cops."

I checked my watch. We were almost out of time. I picked up the laptop and handed it to her. "Here you go. I'll follow you at a safe distance and as soon as they let Laura go, I'll come forward and take your place."

"Girl," she said, "you are out of your mind. I've got far too many children depending on me already. We'll call the police, and—"

"They'll never get here in time, Netta. We've only got a few minutes."

"If it's you they want, they'll wait."

"You go, Netta." It was beginning to sound like a good plan to me.

She shook her head. "It's crazy for either of us to even think of going. These people are killers. Let's call the cops." She reached for the phone.

"Wait," I said. "What about this? You come with me. We'll go together. . . ."

She shook her head. "No way. No way either of us should go."

"I've got to go."

"Oh, use your head."

"Laura's just a child. I have to go!"

She sighed in exasperation. "Who died and made you God?"

"Avenging angel," I said. "My sister, Carrie. Come with me, Netta. They won't hurt you."

"Bull tweetie, girl. How is the world helped by going out and getting yourself killed? You ain't no superheroine, you know. Little as I like 'em, times like this are what we've got cops for."

I was the one who had asked her up here to help me, so we were supposed to be working as a team, but deep down, even though I can be a good team player, I'm a lone cowgirl. I need to do my thinking by myself. I had to have a few minutes alone. Someone, something, had sucked all the air out of the room. Suddenly I was smothering, suffocating, and claustrophobic. Just as, earlier, the room had been filled with Rory's voice, now the silence echoed with Laura's small, scared voice.

"I'm just going to dash into the bathroom, Netta, and then let's put our heads together and think this one through."

I went into the bathroom, closed the door, and sat down on the toilet to think. Not very clearly, either. Thoughts buzzed around like a cloud of hornets. None of this made much sense. Not my scenario, not her scenario, not what was happening now. Even if they eliminated me and Laura and the laptop, there was still Jonetta, and the phone messages. And Bobby, back home, who would know enough to call the cops if anything happened to me. Or would he? What if I met them and they managed to kill me and Laura? Could they offer a reasonable explanation for my death? One that people would accept? Could any death of an interested party at this point be anything but suspicious? I didn't think so, but though this was amateur hour, so far, the amateurs had done a pretty good job. Still, there was Jonetta. And the messages. The bad guys didn't know that Jonetta and I had had this talk. Unless the plot had yet more surprises to yield, and Jonetta was one of them?

Over and above everything else, my most immediate thought was that Laura was a child. Whatever we adults might be up to, with our plots and schemes and tortured relationships, Laura was an innocent kid who had fallen into the midst of things. I, who of all people ought to have known better, had encouraged her to get involved, and highlighted her in the eyes of the bad guys by my presence. The strong voice of my conscience told me I had to get her out of this. An equally strong voice reminded me that I had more reasons than ever not to get involved. To stay behind my locked door and be very, very careful.

What was the old expression? Just because you're paranoid doesn't mean they aren't out to get you? Yeah. That was it. Earlier tonight I had vowed not to trust anyone. But I'd spilled everything to Jonetta. I trusted her. I loved her. I needed her backing me up. And yet. And yet. And yet. It wasn't Netta. It was circumstances. With so much unknown and unpredictable, I felt an edge of uncertainty, an urge to be secretive, unusually cautious. My feelings ricocheted. If I could trust anyone, it was Jonetta. But could I trust anyone?

I flushed the toilet, just to make it look like I was still engaged in appropriate bathroom business, and turned on the water. While it ran, I picked up the phone. One of the beauties of a suite is the phone in the bathroom—important people are assumed to want never to be far from their phones. Regardless of what I decided to do, I was going to leave a trail behind me. As I fumbled Bernstein's card out of my pocket, I realized that the phone was being used. I heard buttons being punched in, and then my messages were announced and Rory began to speak.

I opened the door and stuck my head out. "Netta . . . oh, sorry. I didn't know you were on the phone. . . ."

She turned, suddenly, guiltily, I thought. "I was just going to check on that room service," she said. "Seems like they've been an awful long time." She looked pointedly at her watch. "And speaking of time . . ."

Checking on room service? At a time like this? And anyway, that's not what she'd been doing. Not long ago, I had been chilled by fear, then stunned by lethargy. Now I could feel sweat trickling down my back, hear my heart pounding. Like a jet on the runway, revving its engines before take off, I was gearing up.

"Right," I said. "I'll be out in a minute." I closed the door and picked up the phone again. This time there was a dial tone. I called

Bernstein's beeper, and then called the number for the police station. When the dispatcher answered, I said, "Is this call being recorded?"

"Yes, ma'am," he said. "How may I help you?"

"I don't have time to tell you," I said. "It's an emergency. This is related to the hotel murder and the murder at the hospital tonight. I just want to talk to the tape." Sometimes in life you get lucky. He didn't interrupt or ask questions, he just let me talk. I told the tape, as rapidly and briefly as I could, who I was, why I was calling, everything Jonetta and I had discussed and what was going on. Then I said to the dispatcher, "Please get this to Detectives Bernstein and Nihilani as soon as possible. And can someone call the hotel and have them preserve my message tape?"

As I spoke, I was pulling on my running shorts under my sundress and pulling a tank top out of my bag. Clearing the decks for action, so to speak. One cannot move fast in a long, billowy sundress.

"Will do," he said. He sounded as eager to get off the line as I was.

Then, because even the Lone Ranger usually had Tonto, I called security and asked for Raoul, Alyce Edgerton's handsome friend. Better the devil you know than the devil you don't. Once again I got lucky. I explained as quickly as I could who I was and why I was calling, and then I asked if he could arrange to follow me unobtrusively when I left the hotel. He seemed delighted to oblige.

I couldn't reasonably stay in the bathroom any longer. The clock was running. As if she'd read my mind, Jonetta pounded on the door. "Thea, are you all right? We've got to do something."

I opened the door and went out. I felt rather like a prisoner marching to her execution.

"Now can we call the police?" she said.

"You call them. I've got to go. I wish you'd come with me, Netta. I'd feel a whole lot safer."

"The only way to be safe is to stay right here."

But Laura's voice was screaming in my head. "Except for Laura. She's not safe." I picked up the laptop.

"So you're determined to go?" she asked.

I nodded.

Jonetta sighed. "Just stay cool and use your head. I'll call the police."

It didn't sound like much of a plan. "Give me a few minutes and then follow me, Netta. The end of the parking lot closest to town. That's what they said. Will you at least do that?" I couldn't tell whether she nodded or not. I thought she did. I tucked the laptop under my arm and walked out. Stood outside leaning against the wall. Counted to ten. Let myself back in. Jonetta was on the phone but when she saw me, she replaced the receiver without saying anything. I pointed ruefully at my bare feet. "Forgot my shoes," I said. I quickly put on running shoes and socks, very elegant with my new sundress, and left again.

My heart was pounding, a rich, strong throbbing that reassured me that I was alive even if I didn't know for how long. Was there another heartbeat within me? Was I putting little Mason or Claudine at risk? Risking one child to rescue another? I really was going to have to get out of this business. This was no job for a mother. Far too risky. When I told casual acquaintances that I was a consultant, I could see the bored glaze steal over their faces. What if they knew the truth—that I had the world's most dangerous job? How many of them walked out to meet a gang of killers, with only a can of Mace in one pocket and an alarm in the other?

I left the laptop with the concierge with instructions to give it to no one but myself or the Maui police, amazed at my ability to sound calm and lucid when my insides were flipping about like a barrel of eels. I'd promised Bernstein I'd wait for his people, and give it only to them. But what could I do? I already knew the rooms weren't safe and I couldn't take it with me. Feeling his curious stare against my unprotected back, I opened the door and stepped out into the soft tropical night. As soon as I was in relative darkness, I stripped off the sundress, rolled it into a ball, and stuck it under a bush. Then, with the roar of my heart matching the external cacophony of the insects, I strode off down the parking lot.

CHAPTER *31*

THE PARKING LOT represented the triumph of atmosphere over practicality. Despite the fact that it was supposed to serve as a place for guests to park their cars and thus, presumably, to enable those guests to find the cars again at a later date, it was lighted with low, dim lights that mostly illuminated the dense surrounding shrubbery with small pools of green and orange light. Useful if you are less than two feet tall and can see in the dark. Not so good for a weary almost six-footer whose legs were rubbery. I was so scared that my teeth were chattering. Halfway down the long parking lot, I stumbled over an irregularity in the tar and twisted my ankle, knocking heavily into a parked car.

Like something from a bad movie, the car erupted into speech, commanding me to back away from the vehicle, followed by an assortment of whoops and bells and whistles. If I had ever hoped that my approach might be silent and subtle, that hope died here. I staggered away from the noise, hurried across the space between the parking aisles, and crouched between two cars until the clamor died down. No one came rushing to see what the problem was. The night remained still and empty. I stepped cautiously out and began walking again, squinting against the darkness to see where the lot ended. A faint mist hung in the air. Everything had a soft, amorphous quality. I seemed to be walking through a place from one of my dreams, an endless landscape. I could walk forever through that unpeopled, roaring night and never arrive.

I heard the distant crunch of tires and the soft purring of an engine. As I turned to see where it was, there was a sudden roar, the squeal of tires and a blinding glare as headlights came on and the car raced straight at me. I sprinted for the closer row of parked cars, hurling myself up onto a hood as the car rushed past, so close I felt the side of it thump against my flying foot. I didn't wait to see if they'd come back. I rolled off the hood, ran, crouching, in front of the cars, along the edge of the shrubs until I was several cars away. Then I crawled under a car and lay there, panting, trying to smother my breath with my hands. Trembling. Waiting. Nursing a savage fury.

A tank top and running shorts were great for moving swiftly and lithely through the darkness. They were not so good for lying on the ground under a car. I was acutely aware of the bumps in the tar and the gravel beneath me, of the new bruises I was getting on top of the old. I was also aware of how my five months in Detective Lemieux's fitness camp were paying off. A well-tuned body is like a quality watch—it takes a licking and it keeps on ticking. I shifted around so I could pat my pockets to be sure I hadn't lost my Mace or my alarm. Nope. They were still with me. I'd have preferred an Uzi at this point, but I'm sure that if I'd had one there'd be as much danger that I'd shoot myself as that I'd shoot one of them. Andre keeps offering to teach me to use a gun; so far, I've resisted.

A friend of mine, who scuba dives, liked to talk about the woman on one of her dives who had a knife strapped to her ankle. "Not my thing," she'd said, "but I suppose it makes sense. You never know what you might get tangled up in and when you're going to need it. And boy did it look cool." As my vision of myself changed, as I was forced to confront myself as a woman who needed to learn to defend herself, the image of a strong, tough woman with a knife strapped to her ankle became more appealing. Like my friend said, you never know what you're going to get tangled up in. I could have used it right now. I would have used it now.

I heard a car go by again, very slowly this time, and the mur-

mur of voices. I stayed put and waited. Eventually both faded away. I was alone in the loud night and woefully late for my rendezvous with killers. Just thinking about it spooked me. Finally I crawled out from beneath the car, dusted the gravel and sand off, and headed down the parking lot again.

I reached the end of the lot without incident but there was no one there. I walked slowly along the row of cars parked there, checking each one. All the cars were empty. I did find one with a warm hood suggesting it had recently been driven but there was no one inside and no one nearby. I tried the doors. It was locked.

Limping a little to favor my tender ankle, I began the long walk back through the lot, staying close to the parked cars this time, primed to dive for cover if necessary. My neck ached from the constant swiveling of my head, a neck already bruised and sore from that earlier pair of homicidal hands. A breeze had come up, raising goose bumps on my bare arms and legs. Against the backdrop of insect noise, there was now the occasional startling rasp of a stiff leaf being propelled across the rough, tarred surface. Each time one moved, I jumped.

As I walked, I wondered. Had they lured me out here just so they could run me down? They wouldn't have gotten me out just so they could get in my room again; I didn't have anything they wanted except the laptop, and I was supposed to have brought that with me. And meanwhile, what was happening to Laura? Where on earth had they taken her? Was she all right? I had so many questions and no answers.

Ahead of me, a dark shape stepped out from between two cars, blocking my path. I handled it like the soul of tact and cunning that I am. I put both hands over my mouth and screamed.

The figure jumped back, startled. "Please, Ms. Kozak. Don't scream. It's me. Raoul."

"Raoul? Where have you been? I thought you were watching my back."

"I have been all the time right behind you."

"Even when someone tried to run me down?"

"I don't understand," he said. "You came through the lobby in your peach-colored dress and nodded at me. I followed you out the ocean side of the hotel, around the hotel to this parking lot . . . then I lost you for a few minutes and now I've found you again."

So much for having someone watching my back. Raoul hadn't been there after all. Who knew who he'd been following. And no Jonetta, either, I noticed. There had been no one there. In an act of belated caution, I grabbed his arm and pulled him down between two cars. "I didn't nod at you," I whispered. "That wasn't me you were following."

"Then who was I—"

I heard footsteps across the lot. I pulled him farther back into the shadows. "Someone else," I whispered. "Probably Linda Janovich. She looks a little like me from the back, I've been told. Do you hear those footsteps?"

We held our breath and listened. Now it sounded like more than one person. Then a voice, very clear and distinct. "Thea Kozak? I know you're there. Just stand up slowly and come out from between those cars."

I stood up, very slowly, motioning for Raoul to stay put. Maybe, if I was lucky, they hadn't seen him. On the other hand, today didn't feel like a very lucky day. I stepped out into the driving aisle and waited. The cool wind brushed my arms and legs, my almost bare arms and legs, and sent little shivers down them. I felt like a horse walking to the starting gate. Jumping out of my skin.

"Very good. Now turn around and head toward the end of the parking lot again."

How the heck could he see so well, when I couldn't see anything? Maybe he had a night scope. You could buy them for a song these days. Suzanne's stepson wanted one for his birthday and he'd piled up a stack of catalogues with the appropriate pages marked. Thanks to the miracle of mail order, the whole world could be equipped like a squad of Navy SEALs. I closed my eyes and opened them again. Looked around. There he was. Quite close now. "Where is Laura?" I asked. "Is she all right?"

"For the moment," he said, "your pesky little friend is just fine. Whether it stays that way is up to you."

"My, aren't we melodramatic tonight?" I said. "You know this is stupid, don't you? I didn't know anything and I was going to fly out of here tomorrow, permanently out of your hair. Instead, you had to come after me and get in my face and threaten to harm a child. Not the best way to work at getting away with crime, is it, Jeff?" We were walking now with him slightly behind me, back the way I'd just come. Although the night seemed to call for whispers, I made no effort to lower my voice.

"Shut up," he said. His voice was almost a whisper. "You talk too much. You've always talked too much." He stopped, suddenly, grabbed my shoulders, and whirled me around to face him, giving me a couple of rough shakes for good measure. "Where's the laptop? Didn't we tell you to bring it?"

I bit back the retort that jumped to my lips and said, in a careful, calm voice completely at odds with the way I felt, "When Laura is safely back in the hotel, then you get the computer." I have a wonderful advantage over most people. When I get mad, really, seriously mad, it doesn't cloud my judgment or bathe me in a wild red cloud. I get colder and calmer and fiercer. I bring all the stubbornness my mother never could train out of me to bear on the matter—in this case, keeping the bad guys from winning. I knew this was a bad guy. Even in the dim light, I'd seen the bandages on his wrist.

"Bitch," he growled, shaking me fiercely with the hands that still lay on my shoulders, that lay much too close to my throat. "I told you—"

Suddenly I brought my arms up inside his, up and out, breaking his hold, and stepped back. "What the hell—" His voice shook with fear and uncertainty, as well as rage. These bozos didn't have a plan either, I thought. They were playing this by ear, too.

"Where's Laura?" I demanded.

"You'll know soon enough," he said, "now get moving!"

"You sound like a B movie, you know."

"Get moving!" His shove was supposed to send me careening down the parking lot. On TV, it would have. On TV, I also would have been whimpering and making other helpless female in distress noises. I was in distress all right, but not yet helpless. I took one step backward, stopped, and stood my ground.

There was a growing edge of hysteria in his anger. I wanted to keep pushing him and taunting him to make him lose control. In some ways, an uncontrolled bad guy without a plan was scarier but in other ways, it gave me an advantage, an edge, because, for all the awful reality of the moment, I had been here before, and he hadn't. Like I'd told Bernstein and Nihilani, I'd played with the pros. Not that that meant I was going to win. Jeff had already almost won the first round, but this time he was shaken. He'd tried to drown me, he'd tried to run me down with a car, and I was still standing.

"I'm taking you to that damned kid," he muttered in a voice nearly strangled by fury. "Now get moving!"

I wasn't going to walk with my back to him, though. Not when he was like this. I'd made that mistake once with this man. I dropped back so that I was walking beside him. So that he had to keep turning his head to watch me. He had something on a strap hanging from his shoulder. Maybe it was his night scope.

"I want you walking in front of me," he ordered. "Now!"

"Been there," I said. "Done that. Remember?"

He came to a halt again. "What the fuck is with you?"

It was stupid and dangerous, but I took a perverse pleasure in defying him. "The fuck with me is named Jeff Pullman," I said. "Wife killer. Seducer and killer of poor, trusting Rory Altschuler. She thought she was helping you to do something good, to set things right, and you used her and discarded her like she mattered no more than a tissue. You tried to drown me and now you're threatening a little girl. A little eleven-year-old girl. Younger than your own daughter. There's nothing wrong with me, Jeff. And there's everything wrong with you. You've been a lobbyist for so long, having your views and beliefs shaped by whomever will pay you the most, that you've lost sight of the possibility that there are some absolutes in this world."

Even from four feet away, I could feel his rage swell. With my infrared eyes I could see it billowing around him like a crimson cloud. He had to think of himself as the one who had been wronged. The victim of a bad marriage who was only trying to make things in his world right again, to get rid of his drunken sot of a wife and send his daughter back to the school she loved.

"Laura Mitchell is only a child," I repeated. "What, in your warped philosophy, justifies hurting an innocent child to protect your own sorry ass?"

"Shut up," he said. "Shut up. Keep moving and don't talk. You don't understand anything."

"I think I understand. But I don't think you do. Laura is a nice, bright, interesting little girl that nobody pays much attention to. She likes to read and she's interested in people and she likes to eat great big gooey ice cream sundaes. What are you going to do with her, Jeff? What's your plan? Are you going to strangle her like you did Martina? Close your big clumsy hands around that skinny little neck and squeeze until those innocent blue eyes pop out? Squeeze until she's limp as a rag doll and then throw her away? She has an awfully thin neck. It shouldn't be much of a job for a big man like you. I suppose once you've disposed of one or two inconvenient human beings, it gets easier, doesn't it, even though, as a father, you may feel a slight twinge at killing a child?"

I wasn't supposed to hear the footsteps sneaking up behind me. I wasn't supposed to notice the way his head jerked up, the way his eyes flickered as he watched the approach. I was supposed to be a dumb and cooperative victim, like his, like their others, had been. Twice today he had caught me off guard. This time he wouldn't be so lucky. I could hear as the person coming up behind me dug in her toes for the final leap. Quick as a wink I stepped sideways, turned, and stuck out my foot.

Linda Janovich, caught in midair, tripped over it and went sprawling. As Pullman rushed toward me, I brought out the Mace-and-pepper spray and gave him a couple blasts right in the face. At the same time, I hit the alarm and it began to shatter the night with its shrieks. Unlike a car alarm, this one would continue until someone turned it off.

Pullman was down on his knees, pawing at his face but Linda was up and coming at me. I had counted on them both being unarmed, since carrying guns is very difficult, particularly for the amateur crook. But I hadn't thought about knives. Or rather, I'd only thought about knives in the Scuba Woman fantasy. But the knife that she was carrying was very real and she was waving it in my direction like she meant business. Where the hell was Raoul? It sure was hard to get good help these days.

I bent down and snatched the strap off Jeff's shoulder, pulling the thing free. Whatever was in the case was nice and heavy. As she lunged, I swung. Point to me. The knife barely pricked my shoulder but the case made nice solid contact with the side of her head. I jumped back and swung again as she dove for my knees. I was aiming for her face but she dove low and I got a rather ineffectual hit off the back of her head before she knocked me off my feet and we both went down.

I had no false pride about the odds here. I was not Wonderwoman. There were two of them and they'd already killed twice. I'd had rather a debilitating day. I had never been on the high school wrestling team. I *had* been up close and personal with knife-wielding vermin. The rules of engagement were therefore very simple. I intended to walk away from here with my skin relatively intact. I didn't care whether Linda and Jeff walked away or were carried. At this point, I didn't even care if someone had to pick up their pieces and carry them off in baskets.

I grabbed the hand that had the knife, shouted for Raoul, and slammed my forehead into her face as hard as I could. The responding crunch was more satisfying than Maui potato chips. I pulled my head back and slammed again, following it up by jamming the fingers of my free hand into the base of her throat.

She made an ugly gurgling sound and dropped the knife, rolling off me and curling up into a gagging, whimpering ball, screaming that I'd ruined her face. She actually said, "How could you?" She killed people; under extreme duress I broke noses. I didn't see that there was any comparison. I certainly didn't feel any remorse.

I turned to see whether I had to deal with Jeff but by this time, the shy and reticent Raoul had finally materialized and seemed to have him subdued and was on his radio, calling for other security people to back him up. I stared at the knife, and at Linda and Jeff, and my hand reached toward it, trembling with desire, before I willed it back down to my side.

We still had to find Laura. "Look in his pockets and see if you can find any car keys," I said.

Linda was struggling to get up. She'd gotten as far as her knees and was swaying there on all fours, shaking her head like a confused bull. "Stay down," I ordered. As she continued to struggle to her feet, I yielded to a base impulse. I abandoned the moral high ground. I didn't warn her again and I didn't ask her nicely to behave. I was not the cops. I didn't have to give fair warning. I kicked her. A good, solid blow to the ribs, hard enough to jar my knee and hip and to promise days of limping from bruised toes. And damn, it felt good! She went down and stayed down.

I kicked the knife farther away from her hand. Raoul stooped to grab it. "Don't," I said. "You don't want to mess up the fingerprints. Let the police take care of it."

Jonetta came rushing up out of the darkness. "Damn it all, Thea," she said, "you didn't tell me there were two parking lots. I've been wandering all over hell and gone trying to find you. If it hadn't been for that alarm, I'd still be over there bumping around in the gloom."

I stood up and turned my back on all of them. I no longer knew who were the good guys and who were the bad guys. Away in the distance, where the hotel's own grand entrance drive met the main road, I could see the blinking emergency lights of the arriving constabulary. Behind me, keys jingled. "Here you go," Raoul said. I turned and took them from his hand and headed back toward the end of the parking lot. I wanted to find that car with the warm hood. I was still looking for Laura.

Jonetta came panting along behind me, jingling as she walked. "What is the matter with you, girl? You mad at me? It's not my fault that I was wrong."

Maybe it wasn't. And maybe it wasn't her fault that she'd gotten lost. But right now I had no response to that. My mother's oft-repeated instructions were that if you can't say something nice, don't say anything. For once, I was following her advice. I doubted if she would have been proud of me, though. For one thing, she's constantly admonishing me to stay out of trouble. For another, she'd be mortified to know she had a daughter who was a down-and-dirty street fighter. She would rather have me punctured by knives than smashing people's noses and crushing their windpipes. Or maybe not. Maybe I was wrong. I got this toughness from somewhere.

I couldn't remember which car it was. I had been under rather a lot of stress just then. I made my way down the row, feeling the engines, until I came to a warm one. I tried the key. Opened the doors. Looked in the backseat and the front seat. No Laura. I went around to the back and stuck the key in the trunk lock. All the while, Jonetta followed me, talking at me, demanding to know what was wrong and why I wasn't answering her. Before I opened the trunk, I put my finger to my lips and she fell blissfully silent.

The lid popped up, the light came on, and there was Laura, curled up on her side, terrifyingly still. She was encased in yards of duct tape like a badly wrapped package. I closed my eyes and leaned against the car for support, pressing back the ugly images that crowded into my mind. Another car. Another trunk. Another body. Just please God let her be alive.

CHAPTER 32

I TOOK A deep breath, opened my eyes, and leaned down into the trunk. Carefully, I slipped my arms under Laura's body and lifted her out. She was warm. Limp but warm, and she was breathing. I sat down on the ground behind the car, cradling her in my lap, and gently loosened the tape across her mouth, slipping a finger underneath to work it free of her lips. I knew only too well how easily torn-off duct tape can take a piece of the lip with it. Then I ripped it off. She moaned and moved in my arms but her eyes didn't open.

Jonetta was talking again but I didn't pay any attention. I was in a small universe that only had room for me and this child, this sweet, brave, mistreated child. The red marks on her arms and legs told a story of struggle. It made me regret not getting a few more licks at Jeff and Linda while I'd had the chance. By the time I'd freed her hands and feet, we were surrounded by police and security guards, people who jostled us and shouted questions at me as if I'd suddenly been rendered deaf.

Ignoring them, I folded my body protectively over Laura, trying to shield her from the eyes of this noisy, intrusive crowd. I heard a loud voice demanding quiet, demanding that everyone move back and then Kane Nihilani shouldered his way through the pack and squatted down beside me. "How is she?" he asked. "How are you?"

"She should have a doctor," I said. "I'm fine." He glanced heavenward but being a man of few words, said nothing.

Laura shifted restlessly in my arms and opened her eyes. "Thea . . ." she mumbled.

"Hi, little spy. How you doin'?"

She blinked her eyes and nestled closer to my body. "Ugh," she said.

Nihilani touched my shoulder gently, then pulled his hand back and stared at the blood on his fingers. "We've got EMTs right over here." He held out his arms to take Laura but I shook my head.

"I think she'd better stay with me. Everyone else here is a stranger."

He put a hand under my elbow and helped me up. "We're not strangers." Bernstein had materialized beside him.

"No. But you're big and scary and she's small and scared."

"Yeah?" Bernstein said, "well, you're big and scary, too." It was the nicest thing he'd ever said to me.

They fell in on either side of me, like an honor guard, protecting me as we made our way through the crowd toward the flashing red lights of an ambulance. The EMTs were working on Linda Janovich's battered face. One of them, a reedy blond man spattered with blood, turned as we approached. "Got another patient for you," Bernstein said.

"Be with you in a minute," he said.

"How about right now," I suggested. "That woman is the reason this child is in a battered, unconscious state."

"Yeah, well someone did a pretty good job on this woman, too," he said.

"Thanks," I said. Despite my full arms and abbreviated costume, I sketched a little curtsey. "The credit is all mine. And she was the one with the knife."

Linda snatched the scissors he was holding out of his hand and came at me, screeching like a banshee. Bernstein and Nihilani both dove for her as I turned away to protect the child I was holding. I felt something sharp dig into my arm as they seized her and pulled her back. "Everything would have been fine if it hadn't been for you," she screamed. "Nobody else cared what happened to Martina. If your partner, Suzanne, had come instead of you—"

I turned to face her. Everything was garish in the bright lights around us, headlights and red lights and blue lights. The whole world was awash with swirling lights, surreal, psychedelic, as though we'd stepped through time into another dimension, from the soft, damp, quiet darkness into this bright, noisy glare. A limp, trusting child lay curled against my chest. A pair of bright, shiny scissors was imbedded in my arm. I stood tall and bloody, fierce and angry, bruised and inutterably weary. I had heard this all before. I had been here before. Everything would have been fine.

"Whose idea was it, Linda? Yours or Jeff's?"

"Mine," she said, defiantly, her voice thick and stifled by the broken nose. "Jeff's like a parakeet. Attracted by bright, shiny things. Preferably bright, shiny dollars. That's how Martina got him. That's how Martina lost him. And if it hadn't been for you, getting her all stirred up about right and wrong, Rory would have been paid off, Jeff and I would have been rich, and Martina would have been another unfortunate victim of the lingerie killer."

"Who else was in on it?" That was the one thing I really wanted to know.

"That is for me to know and for you to always wonder about." She turned her back on me and sat down heavily on the stretcher they'd gotten out.

My knees were about to give way. I wanted to march over, toss her off the stretcher, and lie down on it myself. No. I wanted to lay Laura gently down and then kick Linda Janovich all over the parking lot the way, in moments of extreme pique, I sometimes kicked a stuffed cat around my bedroom at home.

The medic was staring, mesmerized, at the scissors in my arm. "You want your scissors back?" I said. "Go ahead. Come and get 'em." I was feeling mean. Mad at him for putting Linda's needs ahead of Laura's. For attending to the bad guy and making an innocent child wait. For having his priorities all screwed up.

I looked down. Laura's eyes were open. She was watching me closely. "You're so cool!" she whispered. I bent down and kissed her forehead.

The ground was breaking up around me. Hopping and jumping and buckling and writhing. Either we were having an earthquake or old iron-will Kozak was losing it. It was the scissors, I thought, slicing through my resolve, cutting my ties with reality. I didn't want to let Laura go but I also didn't want to drop her. I shoved her into Nihilani's arms as I sagged heavily against Bernstein. "Take her," I said. "Please. Take care of her."

The sight of scissors sticking out of me was making me sick. I grabbed them, pulled out the imbedded blade, and tossed them to the staring medic. My arm hurt like hell. The world was standing still again but I still felt shaky. "Lenny. I'd like to sit down somewhere. Please." He led me over to a cruiser, opened the door, eased me down on the seat. I buried my head in my hands. He went to the trunk, got a blanket, and wrapped it around me. Then he left me alone. I huddled with my eyes closed. Against my eyelids, car trunks flew open and revealed curled-up bodies. Again and again and again.

People came and whispered in my ear. People from the past. Telling me that it wasn't their fault. Telling me they just had to do it. Telling me I didn't understand, explaining why they'd killed, how helpless they were, how they'd been driven to it. I got up, clutching my blanket around me, and went to where someone was still working on Linda's face. "Don't try to delude yourself. It was your fault," I said. "You didn't have to do it. No one made you be a killer. We have a choice in this life whether to be good or evil. You chose evil. Now you've got to own that. You've got to live with that."

The EMT glared at me. "Do you mind?" he said. "I'm trying to treat an injured patient here."

"Yes. I mind. I mind that this woman conspired to take two lives and tried to take two more, one of them mine, one that helpless child. I mind that very much. I hope, during the years you're going to spend in prison, Linda, assuming you get prison and that Hawaii doesn't have the death penalty, that what you've done comes back time after time to haunt you. I hope it preys on your mind and gnaws at your guts. I hope that you see your victims every time you close your eyes. I hope, when you think about your son and daughter being deprived of their parents, that you also think about the others who lost people they cared about, like Rory's parents. I hope you ache. I hope you hurt. I hope you suffer long and hard."

Now I saw that a second ambulance had pulled up behind the first. I wandered over, trailing my blanket like a cape. It was absurd, huddling in a blanket on a warm night, but I still needed it. I found Laura on a stretcher with Bernstein and a friendly-looking EMT bending over her. She looked so small and scared but her eyes were open and she seemed to be more alert. "Thea . . ." She stretched out a hand toward me. "Why do you have blood all over your face? Are you hurt?"

I sat down beside her and took her hand, looking over at Bernstein. "Do I have blood all over my face?" He nodded.

"No, Laura, I'm not hurt." Much as I'd relished getting in my whacks against Linda, I was a little embarrassed explaining this to a child. "I had a fight with Linda. The tall woman with the dark hair."

"The one who put me in the trunk."

"Yes. That one. She came after me with a knife so I broke her nose."

The EMT finished whatever she was doing. "We're going to take her to the hospital now. Did you want to ride along?"

"I really think you ought to take her mother."

Laura clung to my hand. "I'd rather have you."

"You're not her mother?" the woman said, surprised.

I shook my head. I'd never been mistaken for a mother before I met Laura. It was a funny feeling. "No, Laura, I have to stay here and talk with the detectives. We'll get your mom down here and—"

"Do I have to go to the hospital? Why can't I just go upstairs and take a bath and go to bed now?"

I looked at Bernstein. He looked at the EMT. She shrugged. "Just as a precaution. In a case like this, where a child has been unconscious—"

"What if we got a nurse to stay with her?" I was thinking about Marie Pryzinski.

The EMT shrugged again. "It's up to her parents, really. Where are her parents, anyway? Shouldn't they be here?" She looked at Bernstein.

He called a uniformed officer over and instructed him to go find Laura's mother.

"Thea, you said you weren't hurt," Laura said. She was staring at our joined hands where a thin stream of blood from the scissors stab was coursing over the interlaced fingers.

"I'm fine, kiddo. I just need a couple Band-Aids."

The EMT rolled her eyes, came around, and started mopping up blood. She told me that the cut on my shoulder and the one on my arm ought to be stitched and asked when my most recent tetanus shot was.

"I hate stitches. Just stick 'em together with some butterfly Band-Aids. I'll be fine. I heal fast. And my last tetanus shot was . . ." I tried to remember. "Let's see . . . I got stabbed in December . . . maybe it was then. I don't know. It's current, though, I assure you." She rolled her eyes again. I knew I was a medic's nightmare. But I was being very good. Promise not to send me to a hospital and my mood instantly improves.

She was getting ready to stick on some bandages when someone behind me said, "You really ought to get those stitched."

Ed Pryzinski. I'd forgotten to call him back. "Oh, Ed . . . I'm so sorry . . . I—"

He waved away my explanation, looking around us angrily. "Looks like you've been busy." What a range of emotions. I'd gone from heroic to exhausted to chastened. I couldn't meet his eyes. "I'm very good at stitches," he offered, and I was childishly grateful that he wasn't yelling at me. He went away to consult the EMT about supplies, then came back and went to work. "You won't feel a thing."

Bernstein pulled out his notebook and looked down at Laura. "You ready to talk to me?"

She looked at me. "You'll stay?" she asked.

"If you want."

She looked from Bernstein to Pryzinski. "And will you both promise not to yell at Thea? She's very brave." Having secured their promises, she was ready. "I thought I was tired but I couldn't sleep, so I went back down to the lobby one more time and that man—the one Thea and I had seen in the bar—came up to me and said that Thea wanted me to meet her outside. So I went out and there was a tall woman with long dark hair but when I walked up to her, it wasn't Thea and then they grabbed me and put me in the car and drove somewhere and they parked and that's when they made me make the call. . . ."

"What call?"

"To Thea. Telling her she had to come and meet them and bring the computer or else they'd hurt me. Thea asked me who they were and I told her. That's when they got mad at me and she hit me and told me to shut up. And she grabbed the phone away from him and—"

Her eyes filled with tears. "I wanted to tell Thea not to come but I didn't get a chance . . . and then they started trying to tie me up with that tape and I kept fighting them and I was getting all scratched and bruised and then she hit me and I knocked my head against the car. When I woke up, I was someplace all dark and my face was wrapped with tape and I couldn't breathe and I was afraid that maybe I was dead . . . or going to be dead . . . and maybe they'd buried me or something. But I couldn't call for help or anything. I tried to get loose. I kicked and struggled and all I ended up doing was banging my head on something and then . . . ."

Ed Pryzinski laid a last strip of tape on my arm and patted my other shoulder gently. "You're all set," he murmured. "I'm going back to bed. And I promise not to tell your mother"— there was a significant pause—"or anyone else, what you've been up to. This time. But remember, Thea, babies need their mothers." He gave me a gentle hug and disappeared into the night.

"Excuse me! Just what the hell is going on here?" The polka-dot lady was standing there, glaring down at me. Tonight it was a lavender dress with tiny white dots. "Do you mind? This *is* my daughter. . . ." She looked at me like I was something the cat had dragged in.

I pulled the blanket back around me, struggled up, and shuffled a few feet away so she could sit down next to Laura, hovering there like a bedraggled crow, my blanket flapping in the wind. I felt like something the cat had dragged in and then played with for hours. Battered and depleted.

"Now then, Laura Mitchell, what kind of trouble have you gotten yourself into this time?"

"I got kidnapped and I almost got murdered," Laura said.

"The stories you tell," her mother said. "Detective, can you tell me what's going on?"

"She got kidnapped and she almost got murdered," he said. There were times when I really did like Detective Bernstein.

A small figure I hadn't noticed had sidled up beside her and was bending over the stretcher. Laura smiled up at her brother. " 'Lo, nerd," she said.

Geoffrey Mitchell smiled. He had Laura's fair skin, though with blonder hair, and already he showed the promise of the man he was becoming. There was something protective and reassuring in the way he looked at Laura. 'Lo, freak. Mind if I join you?" He sat down on the stretcher without waiting for an answer. "Boy, when you have to write that stupid essay about what you did on your summer vacation, you'll actually have something to write about, won't you?"

Okay, so their mother was useless, but at least the kids supported each other. I'd overstayed my welcome and I'd pretty much exhausted the capacity of my body to function. I pulled the blanket tighter and started shuffling off toward the hotel, away from the lights and the commotion, away from the bad guys and the bad gals.

Halfway there, Nihilani emerged from the darkness. "Mind if I come up with you and take your statement?"

"Not at all. Mind if I lean on your arm?"

I limped through the lobby on the strong arm of the law, stopping on my way to retrieve the laptop. Upstairs, I collapsed on my couch and he brought a washcloth and cleaned the blood off my face. I put my head down and closed my eyes. Limp. Defenseless.

I couldn't have moved again to save my life. Postadrenaline exhaustion.

"Wouldn't you be more comfortable in the bed?" he asked.

"The bedroom's haunted."

He grunted and then I heard him get up, cross the room, and take a look for himself. He came back with a weary sigh. "I see what you mean," he agreed. He spread another blanket over me and tucked it in, nice and cozy. I had the sudden, unexpected vision of great stolid Nihilani tucking in small children very gently. I heard a pen click as he lowered himself into a chair. "Okay," he said. "So why do you think they were after you?"

I told him how I'd questioned Rory about the phones. I told him how Linda Janovich had overheard my conversation with the Elliot sisters, when they told me they were sure they'd seen Jeff Pullman at the hotel on Friday night, when he was supposed to be at home in Washington. I told them about the stuff on Rory's computer and how I'd sent messages back to her correspondents. I told him how Laura was sure she'd seen Jeff on her floor around the time Martina was killed. "Even before I'd figured out what I knew, they'd figured out what they thought I knew. That's the downside, I suppose, of having a reputation for being a detective. They thought I was here because someone was suspicious, when the real reason I'm here is because my partner got sick."

"I see you've got your bags packed. Leaving tomorrow?"

"First light," I said. "Bernstein told me to get out of town. I wish I'd listened to him. Maybe Rory would still be . . ."

He shook his head. "That didn't have anything to do with you. They had to get rid of her. She knew too much and she was too unstable."

"At least little Laura would have been safe."

"Hard to make a call about that, either," he said. "That little girl saw an awful lot."

"That little girl is a treasure. I'd like to spank her mother, though."

"Me, too."

"Detective . . ."

"Yes?"

"There's still something that's puzzling me. About everyone else." I told him how everyone had a reason for wanting Martina dead. I told him about Jonetta and her strange behavior. About the tale she'd spun around Rob Greene. About how I'd found her listening to my messages again and then she'd lied and said she was calling room service. About her promise to follow me and how she hadn't. Why would she do all that?"

He lifted his broad shoulders and spread his hands. "Beats me. I guess I'll have to ask her."

"Will you tell me what she says? Please? Just this once, don't let it be a one-way street?"

"Just this once."

"And I suppose you've talked with Billy Berryman?" That time I only got one of Nihilani's grunts.

He got up, pulled his chair over, and took my hand. His was so warm, while I was shaking like a leaf. "For all the trouble we've given one another, it's been a pleasure doing business with you, Thea Kozak. I'm sorry we gave you such a hard time. And I'm sorry your visit to Maui was such a bummer. It really is a beautiful place. Come back sometime when you're not on business. Maybe on your honeymoon? I'd kind of like to meet this guy Lemieux. He's a brave man."

While I was still wondering what he meant by that, he dropped my hand and stood up. "Guess I'd better go interview bad guys." He hesitated, cleared his throat, and said, "Alleged bad guys. Maybe you ought to walk me to the door, so you can lock up afterwards?"

I pushed back my blanket and got to my feet. It wasn't easy. Lying down and letting my body relax had only given it a chance to realize how battered and broken it was. I felt like I'd been whacked from head to toe with baseball bats. I followed him to the door, depressed to see that I was shuffling like a grandma again, and waited to do the locks.

"You take care of yourself," he said, patting me on my unwounded shoulder.

"That advice comes a little too late. Say good-bye to Lenny for me." I shut the door behind him and locked it. I should have been happy. Laura was safe and the killers had been caught. But there was that lingering doubt in my mind about Jonetta. I still didn't know what to think. And for once I was too tired to march forth and gather the answers myself. I called and asked for a 4:30 A.M. wake-up call, took two Advil, curled up on my couch, and waited for sleep. Just another busy night in paradise.

CHAPTER 33

I WAS JUST drifting off when there was a knock on my door. I ignored it. The knocking got louder. Hell and damn. After all I'd been through, couldn't they leave me alone? I raised myself up on an elbow and yelled, "Go away. I'm sleeping."

The knocking stopped. I closed my eyes and lowered myself slowly back down, reaching for the blanket to pull it up. "Thea!" It was Jonetta's voice. "Let me in. We need to talk."

Wasn't this how everything had begun, with someone knocking on my door? "Go away!" I yelled again. I pulled the blanket over my head.

"If you don't let me in, I'll call security and tell them I'm afraid something has happened to you."

I'd heard that one before, too. I got up, ever so slowly, and made my way, crablike, to the door. I peered through the spyhole. Jonetta stared right at me, her brilliant turban askew, her face just inches from mine. "I'm giving you one minute," she said, "and then I'm calling for help."

I undid the locks, opened the door, and stood back to let her in. She swept past me, majestic, elegant. Behind her came Zannah, Rob Greene, Shannon, and Jolene. It looked, to my bleary eyes, as if we were about to have a board meeting.

I curled back up on my couch. I couldn't stand on ceremony,

no matter who came visiting. I couldn't even sit. I was too weary. I plucked at the blanket, but it was Jolene who pulled it up and tucked me in. "Jonetta was upset," she said. "She thinks you believe she was involved in Martina's death. She asked us to come with her to talk to you. So we can finally get all the stuff out on the table that we should have had out all along."

"Your timing sucks," I said.

She inclined her head in a schoolmarmish way. "We know that. We also know you're leaving tomorrow. We talk now or—"

"Forever hold your peace," I suggested.

"First of all," Zannah said, "we want you to know how grateful we are for everything you've done."

"You mean getting jumped, drowned, and stabbed on behalf of the organization, or do you mean getting the room arrangements straightened out and giving some necessary speeches?"

"She means both," Jonetta said. "Now, girl, we know that you have had an awful day, and you know that we wouldn't bother you like this if it wasn't important—"

I started to interrupt, but she put a finger to her lips and hushed me. "Before you spout off, just give me a chance. Just sit still long enough to hear what we've come to say. Then you can throw us out and go home and if it's what you want, you never have to see any of us again."

"Fat chance, Netta. We're all in the same business. You all going to quit if I ask you to?"

"Don't be such a brat," she said.

"Hey! I've just—"

"We all know what you've just been through. What, you think you're the first person in the history of the world to have a hard day?"

I closed my eyes and wished I could close my ears.

"We all care about you, Thea. We all admire you. We all think you're the bravest, toughest kid on our block, and we all want to be like you when we grow up," Jonetta said, "but sometimes even the tough kids get things wrong. Now, you think that because I wasn't as brave as you, because I wasn't willing to take that long walk in the dark to meet the bad guys, that I must have been one of them—"

"Oh, Netta, it's not that, I just—"

"You gonna let me finish or am I going to have to sit on you?" That was a fate worse than death. "Let you talk," I said.

"You heard me listening to that message, didn't you?" I nodded. "And because I was embarrassed, I told you a lie . . . which was stupid, because you then took that lie and decided that I was listening to that message because I was going to delete it, or some such thing, right?"

I felt like the interrogation victim in the movies, the one they shine the bright light on and then question for hours. "Right," I said sullenly.

"And you thought that I was trying to talk you out of going out there tonight because I didn't want those other guys, my accomplices, caught, right?"

"I did wonder. . . ."

"Well, I don't blame you for thinking any of those things. I was muddled and I was a coward and I wasn't a stand-up gal and I'm not particularly proud of that, Thea. Even us tough gals sometimes got feet of clay. But I couldn't let you go back to Boston believing that I was one of them. That any of us were involved in what happened to Martina." There was a chorus of affirmation from the group. "Now, you have heard everyone's stories, so you know we all had reasons to want her off the board. We all had reasons to dislike her . . . to hate her . . . intensely. But Thea, all that we are guilty of here is stupidity. Stupidity, blindness, and a failure to communicate."

She made a small sound, almost like a chuckle. I opened my eyes. She was smiling. "It's like you told that policeman. Nihilani. The stolid, sullen one with the gunmetal eyes. We have disagreements on this board, but we work them out by talking. We work them out like mature adults should. We don't solve our problems by killing each other—"

"At least," Jolene interrupted, "that's how we're supposed to work."

"And if we had been working that way," Shannon added, "this whole mess might not have happened. Jeff and Linda really took advantage of the situation, knowing that no one was likely to be forthcoming, because each of us had such strong resentments. They figured we wouldn't notice them because we'd be so busy wondering about each other. Each of us had . . . well . . . a motive."

"Especially me," Rob Greene said. "But she might not have spun so far out of control—Martina, I mean—if we hadn't all been so busy nursing our own private grudges that we forgot to work together as a board."

I struggled to a sitting position. Rob, who must have had a nice mother because he had wonderful manners, rushed to help me. "Look, we don't have to deal with all this tonight. When we get home, we can have a meeting, and . . ." I wanted to be civil. They were all being so nice, but I was almost too tired for speech. At this rate, someone was going to have to fold me and pack me and carry me to my plane.

"Poor Thea," Jolene said. "We didn't come here to be tiresome. We know what you've been through. We just came to assure you that we weren't involved . . . to have each of us, individually, assure you to your face . . . that . . . well, you know . . . what we've all said . . . and to ask you to forgive Jonetta and to stop acting like she carries the plague."

I looked over at Jonetta. A moment ago she had been on the verge of chuckling, but now she just looked terribly sad. "I think of you," she said, "as a wise and thoughtful co-worker. But I also think of you . . ." Her voice dropped into a lower register, one that was richer and more vibrant, a speech-giving voice. "I also think of you as a sister. As my beloved little sister, the one I'm so proud of when she does well, the one I admire, the one who always seems to be able to do things a little better than I can, and I'm not even jealous because I want her to succeed. So tonight, when my little sister wanted to go out and do something that I considered stupid and dangerous . . . I tried to stop you. I tried to slow you down and muddle things up to keep you from going. Listening to those messages again was a last-ditch effort to see if I could figure things out, find something to clarify this business. Maybe something to stop you. And what do I get?"

There was a long, long pause. "I get what I deserve. I get your suspicions and your doubts, because I didn't just come right out and speak what was on my mind. My momma used to say that a person should never go to bed mad. That it was better to get things off your chest and out in the open right away, and not give them time to fester. Doubt and uncertainty breed faster than mosquitoes, and they can itch at you and worry you worse than a mosquito bite. So . . ." She spread her arms wide. "Either slap this mosquito or give her a hug. Because I can't go to sleep until this thing is settled."

I held out my arms and Jonetta gathered me in. Gently, tenderly, the way you might hug a small child or a fragile old aunt. I thought I heard a collective sigh from the others. Then they all filed out, leaving me alone. There wasn't much time left for sleeping, but when I pulled up my blanket, I fell instantly into a sleep too deep for dreams.

CHAPTER 34

WHEN I GOT down to the lobby to check out, limping and aching and barely able to drag my suitcase behind me, I found Bernstein slumped in a chair, sound asleep, recognizable even from a distance by that distinct pile-of-laundry look he had. Despite being physically tattered and worn, I was feeling reasonably benevolent toward the human race, so I figured, since he was there, that I'd do the polite thing and say good-bye, even though it meant waking him up. After I'd dealt with the paperwork, and before I summoned a taxi, I stood a few feet from him and softly called his name. He came awake instantly and unfolded himself and rose to his feet as stiffly as Frankenstein's monster.

"What's the matter, Lenny? Don't you guys have homes?"

He shrugged wearily. Even his suit looked tired. "I don't remember," he said. "I think I have a home."

I held out a hand. "I wanted to say good-bye. I'm off to the airport."

He took the hand and bowed over it. "Leonard Bernstein," he said, "Maui Police and Taxi Service. I'm here to take you to the airport."

"You don't have to do that."

His exhausted face lifted in a smile. "How else can I be sure you'll leave?" He dropped my hand, picked up my suitcase, and headed for the door.

So it was that, like the president or a prisoner in transport, I had a police escort at both ends of the trip. Andre met me at Logan when I emerged, stiff as a board and overdosed on bad sleep, from one of those flying cattle cars they try to palm off on us as human transportation. One thing I know for sure, people my size should always fly first class. In fact, from L.A. back to Boston, I had upgraded to first class. It was a tragic waste, really. There they were, trying desperately to ply me with liquor, which I couldn't drink, food, for which I had no desire, and free movies when I couldn't keep my eyes open. Though I'm usually a fanatic about details, about the whys and wherefores, this time there were lots of things I still didn't understand and I didn't feel like trying. Maybe someday I'd ask the Midnight Twins to explain. All I wanted to do was rest. Rest and let my mind float. And finish my book. The wonderful, moving book that made me marvel at how well some people can write. That made me smile and cry.

I could tell he'd been in touch with his Hawaiian brethren by the careful way he hugged me without squishing my tender arm and shoulder. I could tell he'd missed me by the kiss he gave me. Some women go a lifetime never having a kiss like that. I'm sure. I'd gone several days and that was enough. But he gathered me in and I felt safe and loved and terribly happy to be home. He carried my suitcase and opened the car door and handed me in very carefully. Then he went around, got in on his side, and fished around under the seat.

"I got you something," he said, handing me a white plastic bag with big red CVS letters on it. CVS was our local chain of drugstores.

"Is this what I think it is?"

"You bet," he said. "Nothing is too good for my girl."

I left the bag lying in my lap and leaned back in the seat, closing my eyes. "You've been in touch with the boys from the beach?"

"Certainly. They had to call and apologize for sending you home in damaged condition. I said I usually got you back in much worse shape and it was okay as long as you were still good for basic things like—"

"Andre, you didn't. Tell me you didn't say that."

He reached over and put a hand on my thigh, running it up my leg underneath my skirt until it was snug against my body. "I wouldn't do something like that. I respect your privacy," he said.

"Seriously," I said, grabbing the hand before he could distract me completely. "Did they have any more news for me?"

"You think the Maui Police Department needs to report its every move to some nosy amateur detective from Massachusetts?"

"I meant, are they going to be able to make a case? If those two walked, after all they've done—"

"Nihilani seems pretty confident. You know how it is. They've still got a lot of work to do. He says you might have to go back and testify. But if you do, I'm going along."

"Fine with me." I moved the hand to his thigh. "I hear it can be a fun place."

"Maybe on our honey—" he began, but I wasn't listening. "I sure never expected the conference to turn out like it did...."

"I should hope not."

"I mean, I didn't expect to have so little time to concentrate on the important things. You know, that whole conference was supposed to be about educating girls, and yet I didn't think about anything except seating arrangements, room assignments, and looking over my shoulder for most of the conference. Flying home I was thinking that maybe I . . . we . . . we should resign from the board, let things get a fresh start, but we've all put so much work into learning about how to educate girls."

His hand reached over and settled on my abdomen. "Speaking of girls," he said, "how's little Claudine doing?"

"I think she and Ollie are fighting about what program they want to watch when they get home."

"Oh, domestic bliss," he said. "What are we going to do if you really are—" He broke off, jammed a hand on the horn, and slammed on the brakes as a car full of teenagers in a rust-blistered wreck suddenly pulled out in front of us. As if they'd rehearsed it, they all gave us the collective finger and disappeared in a cloud of dirty black exhaust.

"Hey, tough guy," I teased, "you gonna let those punks get away with that?"

"You bet," he said. "I'm in a hurry to get home. Besides, I'm carrying precious cargo."

We rode on in silence. It was nearly midnight. The roads were clear and we made good time. Despite all my sleep on the plane, I longed to take off the clothes I'd worn for so many hours, put on a clean, fresh nightgown, and climb into my own bed, at home, where there were no ghosts to haunt the dark corners and where I knew, with Andre by my side, that I could sleep without bad dreams.

I squeezed his thigh. "I've missed you so much."

"So you aren't thinking of replacing me with one of those attentive Maui cops?"

"Since that fateful night when we sat in Carrie's apartment and called each other names, Lemieux, it's been you and only you."

"Isn't there a song that goes like that? Old rock and roll? Something like 'There'll never be anyone else but you, for me. Never ever be, just couldn't be, anyone else but you. . . .' " He trailed off.

"Sorry," I said. "I'm much too young for old rock and roll. I'm too young for a lot of things. Too young to be a mother . . . I can't even take care of myself."

"You're getting better at it," he said. "Bernstein said you were incredible. He said when you went stalking down that parking lot, carrying the injured little girl and you wouldn't let anyone else touch her because she was too scared. . . . He said you looked about ten feet tall and ready to slay dragons. And he says you beat the crap out of one of the perps. He says you took on two of them at once, when one of them had a knife. . . ."

"I thought I was remarkably restrained."

He pulled the car into the breakdown lane and braked to a stop. Then he unfastened his seat belt, got out, came around to my side, and opened the door. "Aren't you even going to look in the bag?" he asked, pointing to my lap.

I reached into the white plastic bag and pulled out a pregnancy-test kit. He seemed so pleased with himself I had to laugh. "It's the best that money can buy," he said. "Go ahead . . . take a look at it."

"I don't need to look at it. I'm sure the directions are right on the outside of the box."

"Go on," he said.

I looked up at him curiously. At those shining brown eyes. The sexy arched eyebrows. At his firm jaw and perpetual five o'clock shadow. I reached up and touched his face. "Can't we hurry home? I can't wait much longer."

"Just as soon as you open the box."

"All right. But if something jumps out and hits me in the face, I'm going to be very angry at you." I opened the box and peered inside. There were no medicine droppers or test tubes or any of the paraphernalia I was expecting. Just a small black velvet box. I reached in and took it out. A little out of breath. Nervous. My hands were shaking.

"Okay," he said. "Now stop. . . ." He dropped to his knees, right there on the tar and the gravel, oblivious to the occasional cars whizzing past. He took my hand. "Thea," he said. I wasn't the only one who was shaking and nervous and a little bit out of breath. "Will you marry me?"

"You don't even want to wait and see if this thing turns pink or blue?"

He took the box from my hand and opened it. Took out a ring that twinkled like Venus, pulled my left hand toward him, very gently, and slipped the ring on my finger. "I don't care whether it's red or purple or sky blue pink. If you aren't pregnant now, think of the fun I'll have trying again. And again. And again. Will you?"

I reached up and locked my hands behind his head, pulling his lips down to meet mine. "Yes. Sure. Of course. Why not?" There was another old rock and roll song, I thought. Sealed with a kiss. The long, slow, breathtaking kiss I'd dreamed of ever since he'd promised it to me on the phone. Sometime later, he got back in the car and we drove home. Tomorrow we would get up and see whether we'd won first prize—marriage and happily ever after, or the grand prize, marriage, happily ever after, and a bonus baby.

The world outside was still full of evil, selfish people, and good generous ones. The bad ones would return to intrude on our lives. The good ones would touch us and nurture our spirits. But that was for another day. Tonight, we were inside our own charmed circle. Tonight, everything seemed perfect just the way it was.